Francesca *and* The Mermaid

Francesca *and* The Mermaid

Beryl Kingston

buried
river
press

ISBN 978-1-910208-07-6

Buried River Press
Clerkenwell House
Clerkenwell Green
London EC1R 0HT

www.halebooks.com

Buried River Press is an imprint of Robert Hale Ltd

2 4 6 8 10 9 7 5 3 1

Typeset in Palatino
Printed in Great Britain by Clays Limited, St Ives plc

AVE ATQUE VALE

Dearest of men, most loved and loving son
My quick and sunshine child who led
Sisters and cousins into rowdy fun
Through gob-smacked park and trampled garden bed.

You taught with teasing skill for learning's sake
Leading your scholars in Pied Piper style
To swim like dolphins in your steady wake
Cheerfully taking on that extra mile.

Forever questing and your own strong man
You took your pupils from the stress of school
To bold New York and tempting Amsterdam
A legend there and here, a Prince of Cool.

How we will live without you I don't know.
No smiling eyes, no arm to lean upon.
Our sun is set, we shiver into snow,
The very earth is darker now you're gone.

CHAPTER 1

I T WAS A shimmering summer day when Francesca saw the mermaid. It was swimming in the sea immediately below her, where she sat on the cliff top obediently guarding the coats and trying not to listen to Jeffrey because he was showing off to the guide. At first glance she thought it was a great fish struggling through a tangle of feathery seaweed. She could see a strong tail threshing white foam in all directions and the iridescence of scales, flashing red-bronze and blue-silver just under the curve of the wave. But then, just as she was wondering what sort of fish it might be, it rolled over and she saw a rounded and very human belly streaming water and two strong, pearl-white, sinuous arms moving in the trough of the wave. And she realized that the feathery weed was long hair darkened and tangled by water. And she knew that she was watching a mermaid.

She should have been surprised or shocked or even afraid, but she wasn't. She accepted the knowledge with a curious sense of calm, as if it had been vouchsafed to her, and watched, almost idly, as the creature rolled over again to disclose a compact little face with round golden eyes, a straight, straight nose and a thin mouth, dark-lipped and faintly smiling. And then she saw that clutched between the white buds of its bosom, placid and befurred as a child's toy, was a baby seal. For a long bewitched second, Francesca and the mermaid looked into one another's eyes. It's as if she knows what I'm thinking, Francesca mused, as if she's reading my mind. And the thought made her shiver because nobody had known what she was thinking, not for years, not since Bertie had gone to Australia and she'd moved in with Jeffrey.

She could hear his voice booming back at her across the clear air of the island, that pompous bray of his sounding even more objectionable in the open air than it did in town. 'The rock formation here is quite exceptional. As I was telling Professor Cairns only the other day. . . .'

I wish he wouldn't talk like that, she thought, gazing down at the mermaid. But then she checked the thought, because it was disloyal. And she couldn't change him. Not in any way. She knew that.

The mermaid lay in the wave and allowed it to rock
. her as though she were in a hammock, looking back at Francesca with her lovely golden eyes. Then she lifted the seal and let it slip between her arms and glide back into the wave. It plunged under the green water, became a sleek grey shadow and was gone. And in the second of its going, the mermaid disappeared too, back into the great wide freedom of that blue-green ocean as if she had never been.

On the rocks out in the bay, shags sat like long-necked statues, the gold of their gapes glinting in the sunshine. Two had their wings hung out to dry like bats. Further out to sea, a family of seals lay on yet another rock, basking in the noonday warmth, their fur dried to the softest palest brown. Occasionally one turned lazily to scratch its ear with its flipper, but apart from that they were still and content.

Wild creatures have such freedom, Francesca thought, admiring them. They mate as they please, breed for a season and then just move on. It's only human beings who chain themselves. But that was disloyal too. She wasn't chained to Jeffrey. She stayed with him voluntarily because he was vulnerable and unhappy and because he needed her so much. Even so, she couldn't help wishing she could change places with the mermaid just for a day and swim off into the Atlantic without a care in the world.

The climbers were returning. She could hear the sound of their voices and the tramp and scuff of their walking boots. Presently they appeared on the brow of the hill, awkward in their shorts and t-shirts, their backpacks like humps, their movements ungainly under a sky full of the graceful white wings of the skuas and herring gulls and the busy, bumblebee flight of the puffins.

Jeffrey was leading them. Naturally. 'All right?' he asked, as he approached. And he gave her the full charm of his public smile.

She answered him without stopping to think how foolish she would sound. 'I've just seen a mermaid,' she said. Her cheeks were still flushed with the wonder of it and her short crop of fair hair bushed about her face.

His expression changed at once. 'Try not to be a fool,' he said, quietly and angrily. 'If you must fantasize, keep it to yourself.'

The others were catching up with him and there was no time to say anything else, so he warned her again with a glare, his eyebrows hardened into a black line between his black hair and the fury of his nearly black eyes.

She winced into herself. It's almost as if he hates me, she thought. But of course he didn't. She knew that. He depended on her too much. She was the only one who knew how to support his weaknesses. It was just his rough way. He could be very harsh when he felt threatened. Nevertheless she decided not to walk with him just yet and waited until the group had collected their coats before she stood up and brushed down her skirt and set off to follow them.

'What did it look like?' a voice said behind her.

It was the scruffy old lady she'd seen at lunch, the one with the untidy hair and the extraordinary clothes. Miss Potts, wasn't it? 'Your mermaid,' she prompted.

'It was my imagination,' Francesca said quickly, ashamed that she'd been overheard being foolish. 'I probably didn't see anything.'

Miss Potts had caught her up. She had a trailing length of bramble stuck to her skirt and was carrying a bunch of wild flowers, thrifts and pink sea campions and the little white blossoms of the starry saxifrage. 'We see what we see,' she said, 'and there's always a reason for it. So tell me, what was it like?'

So, partly because she was still stinging from Jeffrey's rebuke and partly because Miss Potts was old and friendly and there was something about her that made confidences possible, Francesca told her.

'Quite delightful!' Miss Potts said when the tale was told. 'There will be a reason for it, you mark my words.'

'Come along!' Jeffrey called. 'We don't want to miss the zodiacs.'

The little bouncy rubber dinghies were waiting for them at the jetty and they all piled aboard, putting on their life jackets and sitting on the rim of the dinghy the way they'd been shown. The cruise ship lay at anchor in the bay, looking very smart in her blue and white trim.

'I'm going for a swim before dinner,' Miss Potts said, as the zodiac's outboard motor buzzed them away from the jetty. 'Why don't you join me?'

Francesca had spent the first six evenings of the cruise sitting in the bar listening to Jeffrey as he held forth about rock formations and the various geological surveys he'd undertaken for various prestigious customers. He'd explained to her, earnestly, before they set out, that this would be the most important part of the cruise. 'You never know who might be listening,' he'd said. 'If I play my cards right I could land another commission. That wouldn't be bad would it? Business and holiday all in one fell swoop.'

Now, remembering the grace of the mermaid's white arms, she suddenly felt she'd had enough of fell swoops. 'Yes,' she said. 'I'd like that. I haven't been swimming for ages.'

It was warm in the ship's pool and the motion of the ship rocked them gently as they swam, in exactly the same way as the swell of the sea had rocked the mermaid. Miss Potts progressed sedately with her head tipped back so as to keep her mouth clear of the chlorine. 'I'm not a good swimmer,' she said, 'but I do like being in the water.'

'So do I,' Francesca realized. 'It makes me feel so free.'

'Like your mermaid,' Miss Potts said. 'I wonder if you'll see her again tomorrow.'

'I doubt it,' Francesca laughed. 'We shall be miles away in Shapinsay. She'd have a job to follow us there, the rate we'll be travelling.'

But Shapinsay had a surprise for her.

It was another bright day and the sea was blessedly

calm, so they managed the trip to shore with barely a bounce. It was a steep climb to the castle but once they were there, the view was spectacular and their tour of the gardens was taken at just the right pace so that they could stop and admire whenever they wished. The young laird, who owned the castle and the village and most of the island, squired them round and answered their questions and finally invited them all in to the castle for coffee and cakes. They followed him to the entrance with happy anticipation.

It turned out to be an impressive gateway with an impressive coat of arms carved into the arch: a shield with four elaborate quarters, flanked on either side by a pair of sea otters, fierce-faced and pert-whiskered, standing on their hind legs with their front paws supporting the shield. Naturally everybody stopped to admire it. Even Jeffrey.

'Do tell me,' one lady asked. 'Why do you have sea otters on your coat of arms? Is there some significance?'

'I'm not sure about significance,' the laird smiled. 'There's a rather charming story about it though. I'll tell it to you if you like.'

'Yes,' they said. 'Please do. We'd love it.' What nicer way to spend a summer's morning than to stand in the sunshine and listen to a story?

'Well,' he said, taking up a stance on the cobbles. 'It seems that when my great-great-great – however many greats – grandfather was considering his first coat of arms, he needed a bit of peace and quiet to get his thoughts in order, so he came up here and stood just where you're standing now and looked over the bay, where your ship is anchored. And you can believe this or not as you wish, but apparently, just as he was giving up hope of ever finding anything suitable, a mermaid appeared with a sea otter in her arms and held it out to him. He took it as a sign.' He laughed. 'As one would. Commissioned a local stonemason that very afternoon to do the work. The otters have been here ever since, as you see.'

Francesca could feel the hair rising on the nape of her neck and turning she saw that Miss Potts was grinning at her in a really devilish way.

'Amazing!' the old lady said, as they all trooped into the castle. 'Exactly like your mermaid. Didn't I tell you there would be a reason for it?'

'It's a coincidence,' Francesca said quickly. 'That's all.' It had to be, didn't it? 'Something in the air up here. A trick of light. It makes you see things.'

Miss Potts gave her another grin. 'Or see things in a different way,' she said.

It was certainly doing that, Francesca thought wryly. It wasn't showing Jeffrey in a good light at all. As the days passed she was noticing more and more things about him that she didn't like; how he bullied his partners at bridge, analyzing their game after every hand and explaining how they ought to have played; how he dominated the talk at the dinner table, showing off about his wonderful relationship with Professor Cairns, when she knew they'd only worked together for six weeks and had parted acrimoniously.

She took to spending more and more time with old Miss Potts. They swam together every evening while he was playing bridge, explored islands and gardens every day while he was discussing rock formations, even met at breakfast while he was finishing his sleep.

By the twelfth evening they felt like old friends. Francesca had discovered that Miss Pott's Christian name was Agnes, 'although for God's sake don't let

13

anyone else know!' They'd told one another about their jobs – 'Very boring office work.' 'Me too! Did it for years,' – and their families – 'Aren't they complicated!' 'Aren't they just!' – so it was no surprise to either of them that they began to talk about love and marriage.

'Why did you marry your Jeffrey?' Agnes asked, as they swam together one evening.

'We're not actually married,' Francesca confessed.

'Well why are you living with him then?'

'He's a good man,' Francesca said, feeling defensive.

'I'm sure. But that doesn't answer my question.'

'I think it's because he was so unhappy,' Frances said. 'His wife had left him, you see, and his daughters – he's got two daughters, teenagers – well they were being horrible to him. They said they never wanted to see him again, and he wasn't very well, and he'd just lost his job. Well not exactly lost his job. He was between jobs.' Actually he *had* lost that job. He'd been fired. He'd shown her the letter. She'd forgotten all about it until now.

'So you were sorry for him,' Agnes said.

It was true. But she couldn't admit it. It would have made him sound like a wimp. 'He needed me,' she temporized. That was true. 'He still does actually. He may seem strong but he's really quite vulnerable.'

'The trouble with making decisions,' Agnes said, 'is that you have to live with the consequences for such a long time. I made the wrong decision when I was young.'

Francesca looked a question at her.

'I turned down the man I should have married because my mother was ill, or said she was ill, and I thought it was my duty to look after her. He told me I had to choose between them and I chose her. I thought she needed me. We're so stupid when we're young. She didn't of course. A nurse would have done. Or anyone

14

who would listen to her. She wasn't ill. She was just a nasty selfish old woman. The trouble was I didn't see it at the time.'

'Oh Agnes! I am sorry.'

'Serves me right,' the old lady said brusquely. 'I should have had more sense, paid more attention to my own needs instead of kow-towing to her all the time.'

'Yes,' Francesca agreed. 'I think you should.'

'So,' Agnes said. 'What do *you* need, my dear?'

Francesca suddenly remembered the mermaid, turning languidly into the wave and smiling at her with those great golden eyes. Freedom, she thought, and almost said so. But she didn't of course because that would have been disloyal. 'I need to go and get ready or I shall be late for dinner,' she said.

So they ate their penultimate dinner aboard and woke to their last day ashore. And Jeffrey announced that there'd been a change of plan.

'We're not going to the gardens this afternoon,' he said, when she returned to the cabin after breakfast. 'I need to visit the Gladstone Museum. There are some geological specimens there that are quite first rate, apparently. Henderson was telling me about them last night. Said I shouldn't miss them. Actually made a point of it. So I thought to myself, there could be a commission in this. He knows I'm in the market, so to speak, and he's very influential. You don't mind do you?'

She did mind. She minded very much. But she didn't say so because that wouldn't have been kind when he was so eager.

So when the rest of the party set off in their coaches for the final garden of the tour, she and Jeffrey headed off for the museum. It was excruciatingly boring, just case after case of rock samples in a great empty hall with windows so high she couldn't see out of them and nothing else to look at except the floor and the ceiling. The air smelt of dust and furniture polish, the silence hissed; every footfall was as loud as an express train. And Jeffrey didn't talk to her because he was too busy making notes.

By the time he'd seen all he wanted to, her mouth was dry with boredom.

'Have we time for a quick cup of tea?' she hoped.

He looked at his watch. 'Not if we're going to catch the zodiacs.'

'It's not far,' she urged. 'Only down to the jetty.'

'The jetty?' he mocked. 'That potty little place! Don't be stupid woman. They'll pick us up at the harbour.'

For once in her life, Francesca stood up to him. 'No,' she said. 'They told us they'd pick us up at the jetty. The coaches are going to park alongside. There was a space marked for them.'

'But we're not in a coach, are we,' He said heavily. 'We're on our own. They'll pick *us* up at the harbour. Trust me.'

So that's where she followed him, although she knew he was wrong.

They waited. And waited. It had obviously been a glorious afternoon, so Francesca sat on the grass hillock beside the harbour wall and enjoyed what was left of it. The sea glittered with sunlight, the sky was richly blue and heaped with bright white rolling clouds, shadowed in the same smoke-blue as the distant hills. But the expected dinghy didn't arrive, no matter how many cigarettes Jeffrey smoked nor how loudly he complained. After half an hour, she stood up and strolled to the edge of the hillock to look out into the bay and see if there was any sign of it.

There was a line of zodiacs bouncing back to the ship from the jetty, full of cheerful holidaymakers, but not a single one heading in the direction of the harbour.

Feeling justified and angry, she went straight back to tell Jeffrey.

He was very cross. 'But what's the matter with them? Have they forgotten us, the fools?'

'We're in the wrong place,' she said. 'I *did* tell you.'

He was agitated now and beginning to shout. 'Oh for God's sake! What are we going to do? They can't leave us behind. They've got our passports. What are we going to do?'

'I don't know about you,' she said, 'but I'm going to find the harbour master and get him to send a message, shore to ship.'

Which she did. And was surprised by how quick and efficient he was. The call was made within five minutes and with a lot of sympathy. Unfortunately the zodiac took half an hour to make the journey from ship to harbour and considerably more to struggle back again, for by then they were travelling against the tide and there was a heavy swell running. Dinner was nearly over by the time they arrived on board and everybody in the dining hall had heard of their adventure. They were teased and given mocking cheers all the way to their seats.

'Oh dear, oh dear,' Mrs Henderson laughed as they settled at the table. 'What happened to *you* then?'

'In the wrong place,' Jeffrey admitted, smiling his public smile. 'All my Franny's fault. She would have it we were to wait at the harbour. I told her she was wrong but you know how women are.'

The injustice of it was so crushing that Francesca could feel the heat rising into her cheeks. But she didn't correct him. She never corrected him. She just gave him her self-deprecating smile and let him run on.

'Women are all the same,' he was saying to Mr Henderson. 'Bless 'em. Illogical. That's about the size if it. But, like I always say, what would we do without 'em, eh.'

The scales were falling from Francesca's eyes, tumbling into the periphery of her vision, red-bronze and blue-silver, dazzling and revealing. How dare he do this to me? she thought. How dare he? It's disloyal. And that discovery brought another even more powerful. I don't love him, she thought, watching that public smile. I don't even like him. It was a terrible thing to have to admit but it was true.

'One more evening,' Mrs Henderson said to her, smiling across the table, 'and then I suppose we shall have to pack. Or do you think we shall be too illogical to manage it?'

'Oh no,' Francesca said. 'I think I shall pack very logically.'

So the last morning dawned, cool and quiet with a white mist rising from the sea. Francesca woke at first light and got up at once, leaving Jeffrey in his usual sleep. She was washed, dressed, packed and breakfasted before he stirred.

'Right,' she said, as he opened his eyes and scrabbled for his travelling clock, 'I'm off.'

He was puzzled and looked it. 'What do you mean off? What are you talking about?'

'I'm going. We disembark at seven thirty.'

He looked round the untidy cabin, scowling with displeasure. 'But we can't go yet. You haven't packed.'

'Yes I have,' she said, picking up her case. 'You're the

one who hasn't packed. You've got twenty-five minutes to do it. Like I told you, I'm off.'

He couldn't believe his ears. 'You're not going without me. We're going to Plymouth.'

'Yes,' she said. 'That's exactly what I'm doing. I'm going without you. I'm not going to Plymouth. I'm going off on my own.'

'Oh come on Franny,' he said, switching on the charm. 'This isn't funny. You make it sound as if you're leaving me.'

'That's right,' she said, surprised by how cool she was being. 'I'm leaving you.'

Now he was horrified. 'You can't.'

She wanted to laugh. 'I can. I am.'

'But you can't.'

'Why not?'

'I need you.'

'Do you?' she wondered.

'Of course I do,' he said, the old impatience returning to his face. 'I'm the sort of man who needs a wife.'

'But I'm not your wife, in case you've forgotten.'

He dismissed that. 'Wife, lover, it's the same thing. I need a woman to love me. Some don't. But I do. You know that. We've always said so.'

'No Jeffrey,' she said. 'You've always said so. You. Not me. I never said anything. And actually you don't need a lover or a wife, you need an echo chamber. And someone to pack your things and tidy up after you and take the blame when you make mistakes.'

'Look,' he tried, 'you're tired. You'll see things differently once we're back home. You don't really mean this. I mean, think of all I've done for you. Think of the car and the new kitchen.'

She opened the cabin door and pushed her case

through. 'Goodbye,' she said.

He sat up in the bunk, tried to smooth his hair, smiled and then thought better of it, struggled with disbelief, began to despair. 'I don't understand you, Francesca,' he said. 'You're hurting me and you never hurt me. Why are you doing this?'

In the wonderful clear vision of her new-washed sight, Francesca could see the mermaid, swimming luxuriously in blue-green water, her tangle of hair dark as seaweed fronds about the pearl-white of her long lithe body. 'For fun,' she said.

CHAPTER 2

THE MIST WAS still breathing up from the sea when
Francesca left the ship. The quayside was so heavily
swathed in it, that it looked like the set of a horror movie.
It sparked her imagination most powerfully. Intrepid
heroine steps boldly into the future, she thought, and
walked intrepidly off to find herself a taxi to Southampton
station. There was lot to be done and the sooner she
got on with it the better because Jeffrey would only be
in Plymouth for three days and she had no intention of
leaving any of her stuff in the flat. It occurred to her that
she'd have to leave Randall and Tongs too. She couldn't
go on working there now, even if she wanted to, which
she didn't. The office was only round the corner from the
flat, which meant that Jeffrey could find her whenever he
wanted if he decided to hunt her down, as he probably
would. He didn't like having his plans thwarted. Very
well then, she'd hand in her notice the minute she got
back and she wouldn't give them a forwarding address.

Then she'd have to find herself a bed for a couple of
nights while she looked for a new job and somewhere to
rent or buy. That could be a bit of a problem. She couldn't
go to her mother's because she'd never approved of
Jeffrey and she'd be bound to gloat now that they'd split

up; nor to her sister's because she was far too superior to take in a stray; and although there had been a time when she'd had quite a circle of friends, she'd seen so little of them since she took up with Jeffrey that she could hardly go to any of them *now* begging for a bed. It would have to be a cheap hotel or a B&B. Funds were too low for anything better. But it didn't matter what it was really. It would only be for a few nights until she got a new job. The great thing was that she was free of Jeffrey. She could go where she wanted, eat what she wanted, sleep when she wanted, say what she wanted, without considering anyone except herself. The sense of freedom was so exhilarating it was making her feel quite drunk. And she'd made it happen. She and the mermaid.

The train to London wasn't due for nearly twenty minutes but the platform was filling up as more and more passengers from the cruise ship trailed into the station, bent sideways by the weight of their luggage or pulling it bumpily along behind them. Most of them looked weary, as if they'd left their cheerful sea-going selves behind on the ship.

'Always a sad moment, the end of a holiday,' a familiar voice said, and there was Miss Potts, striding towards her, wrapped in a flowing dust coat with a crumpled red and blue scarf loosely knotted about her neck and dragging a very dilapidated case behind her. She looked as dishevelled as ever but, unlike the others, she was smiling like sunshine.

'Actually,' Francesca told her happily, 'it's not really an end for me, it's more of a beginning'

'Ah!' Agnes Potts said, looking round and understanding at once. 'No Jeffrey, is that it?'

'I've left him,' Francesca said. 'He's history. Can you imagine it, Agnes? I've left him. After all these years.

I've walked away.'

'Well good for you, me dear,' Agnes said. 'High time you got that sorted out. Welcome back to the world. What will you do now?'

'I've been standing here thinking it out,' Francesca said and outlined her plans. 'I shall have to find somewhere else to live, and as far away from Beckenham as I can get it otherwise he'll come after me and there'll be scenes. And a job of some kind, just to keep me in chocolate until I can work out what I really want to do. Not in an office. And somewhere to stay for a couple of nights until I can find something to rent.'

Agnes stood her case upright and perched on it precariously. 'In that case, me dear,' she said. 'Why don't you come and stay with me?'

It was such an unexpected, generous offer that Francesca was taken aback by it. 'Do you mean it?' she said.

'I never make an offer I don't mean,' Agnes said in her trenchant way. 'I should warn you though, it's very untidy – I'm not much of a one for housework – and it's right out in the sticks in the middle of darkest Sussex. But if you can stand a bit of mess and muddle, you're more than welcome.'

'Well if you're sure,' Francesca said. 'Yes, I'd like that very much. Just till I find somewhere to rent or buy or whatever.'

'Good!' Agnes said. 'That's settled then. It can get lonely in a big house on your own, especially after a cruise. I like a bit of company. And now look, here's our train coming bang on time. And if that's not a good omen I don't know what is. And no sign of Jeffrey. We've beaten him to it.'

'He'll be half way to Plymouth by now,' Francesca told

her. 'He's got a business meeting there. Very important according to him. He was bragging about it all through the cruise.'

Agnes gave her a shrewd look. 'Good!' she said again. 'Then we've got him right out of our hair and we don't need to bother with him again. I'm not going to London – I get off at Barnham and catch the Brighton train – so we'll swap phone numbers and addresses as soon as we've found our seats.'

Which they did. And as they rattled through the Southampton suburbs and passed the marina and the mist-covered sea, Francesca told her friend what a wonderful moment it had been when she told Jeffrey she was leaving him. 'I felt as if I was floating on air. You should have seen his face.'

'I don't know how you stood him for as long as you did,' Agnes said. 'If he'd been my husband I'd have emptied a bucket of cold water on him long since.'

Francesca grinned, imagining it. 'I'll bet you would too,' she said. 'He'd have gone ape.'

'Then he'd have had another bucket load and serve him right. I can't stand me-me-me men, especially when they think they're God's gift.'

'You'd've needed a bucket handy though,' Francesca pointed out, 'if you were going to catch him in mid rant. And one already full of water.'

'If I didn't have a bucket handy I would've hit him with something else,' Agnes said. 'All sorts of things would do. It doesn't have to be water to pull 'em up short. Broom. Poker. There's always something hefty to hand. I've got a horse shoe in the kitchen.'

'Why doesn't that surprise me?'

'Or I could use the garden rake if he was out in the garden.'

'Or the lawn mower,' Francesca said, extending the fantasy. 'You could do real damage with a lawn mower. You could drive it at him.' Oh she really didn't like him at all. How dreadful.

'That's an idea,' Agnes said wickedly. 'Whack him with the lawn mower, stick him in the wheelbarrow when he's flattened and tip him on the compost heap.'

The conversation was out of hand. 'What about a concrete mixer?' Francesca suggested, grinning.

'Sounds good. Or a fork lift truck?'

'Double decker bus?'

'Rear end of an elephant?' Agnes said. 'That'ud squash the bounce out of him.'

Francesca was giggling at the images they were conjuring up. She could just imagine Jeffrey being sat on by an elephant. And serve him right. 'We are being wicked,' she said.

'Fun isn't it,' Agnes said, looking wicked.

It was. 'I haven't laughed like this for ages,' Francesca said.

'Cleansing stuff, laughter,' Agnes told her. 'Good for the soul. Do you think they serve coffee on this train? I've got a terrible thirst. All that wine last night.'

They had coffee and relived the best bits of their cruise, sitting companionably together, side by side. It seemed no time at all before the train was pulling in at Barnham and Agnes was hauling her battered luggage towards the door.

'Ring as soon as you know when you're coming,' she said, pushing the straying hair out of her eyes and smiling. 'I'll make the bed up ready for you.'

'I'll be with you as soon as I can,' Francesca promised.

Beckenham seemed smaller than it had been when

she left it. And darker. But Randall and Tongs hadn't changed by so much as a paper clip. When she walked in, the two girls in the office were drinking grey coffee and filling envelopes in their usual desultory way. They said the boss was out with a client and they didn't know when he'd be back, so she sat at her old desk and typed him a letter of resignation, explaining that she'd been called away to look after a very sick relation, who lived in deepest Sussex, and that therefore she couldn't return to his employ after her holiday but she would be in touch in a few days time. Then she folded it into one of his envelopes and left it in his in-tray. It couldn't have been simpler. She still had three days' holiday to go and she could sort out the forms and the formality later. Then she went home to sort out the flat.

It was stale and dusty and reeked of old socks. And sure enough, when she followed the stink trail, she found a really obnoxious pair festering in the bathroom. She binned them at once and opened all the windows. Then she put her holiday clothes in the washing machine, found a stack of cardboard boxes in the cupboard under the eaves, and started to sort through her belongings. She was still sorting at midnight because she was enjoying herself so much. It was so cleansing. So right. So wickedly satisfying. And it gave her a prodigious appetite. At ten o'clock, she took half an hour off for a Chinese take away and ate it as if she hadn't fed for weeks. By mid day tomorrow, she thought, looking at the clearance she'd made, I shall be finished here for good and all and down in Sussex with Agnes. But she had reckoned without the corner cupboard.

The next morning she overslept. It was nearly eleven o'clock before she'd finished all her packing and there was still the corner cupboard to check. She stood in the depleted kitchen looking at it, debating whether it was even worth opening. It was an awkward cupboard and very difficult to get at, so it had become a place for pushing unwanted objects out of the way, things they weren't using but might need again at some time or another. Jeffrey called it the rubbish dump.

I'll make a cup of coffee, she decided and then I'll just take a look. She was nothing if not thorough. So sustained by coffee she opened the cupboard door as wide as it would go and shone her torch on the contents, old shoes, a squashed panama hat, the turkey dish, a box full of old CDs, his squash racquet. She was just thinking he'd never use *that* again, when she saw something else among the rubbish that made her heart miss a beat. It looked like her easel. It *was* her easel. Ohmigod! My old easel. She eased it out of the cupboard very gently and there, all carefully wrapped in old tea towels and tied with Christmas ribbon, were her paints and brushes and sketchpads, exactly where she'd hidden them all those years ago on that awful afternoon when he'd told her she had no talent and sneered that she was wasting her time. She stood in the kitchen with her bundle of brushes in her hand, aching with regret for having been such a fool as to have believed him and with sadness for all the years she'd wasted not painting because she *had* believed him. And over and above those rather shaming thoughts and reducing them to insignificance, was a roaring, yearning, riotous desire to paint again. And she knew that what she wanted to do was to paint the mermaid.

She was still in the living room, brush in hand and working happily, when the one o'clock news began. The sudden blare of sound from the TV made her jump. She'd drawn three passable sketches, but none of them

27

were good enough. The mermaid's sinuous beauty was still beyond her grasp and, although watercolour was the perfect medium for the translucence of sea water, she hadn't found the colours to match those iridescent scales. Even so, she'd drawn enough to know that she hadn't lost her skill. It was something she could work at, take her time over, think about, return to, the way she'd done at Art School. Eventually she might capture her vision. It was possible. Anything was possible now she was free of his disapproval. She cleaned her brushes, folded her easel and packed all her precious long-lost equipment in the last cardboard box. Then she carried it out to the car, squashed it into the last remaining space on top of the pile on the back seat, phoned Agnes to tell her she was on her way and set off for Sussex. The sun shone on her all the way.

Agnes had drawn a rough sketch map for her on the back of an old envelope, showing the country roads she had to follow with large black arrows to point the way. But even without it, Francesca knew she would find the house with ease. It was as if she was swimming home, driving effortlessly through the burgeoning, shushing waves of foliage that overhung the road, past hedges where finches flew swift and sudden as a shoal of fish, and where the reminder of the mermaid's shimmering scales flashed and shone in the sunlit windscreen. She was so caught up in the happiness of her imagination that she drove past the entrance to Agnes' house and had to back along the narrow lane before she could inch into the driveway.

Agnes was working in the garden, which looked as large as a park. She had an ancient straw hat on her head and a loaded trug over her arm and, when she heard the car, she straightened her back and waved her trowel.

'There you are me dear,' she called. 'I'm just gathering our supper.'

Francesca sat in her car and gazed at the house in awe. 'This is some place,' she said. It was a considerable understatement for it was quite the most extraordinary house she'd ever seen. It had originally been a solid, brick-built, late Victorian house, with a gabled porch, stone mullions and a wooden balcony on the first floor. Now it was so entwined with climbing plants that it rose out of the garden as if it had grown there. A horse chestnut loomed protectively beside it, wisteria curtained the porch with heavy clusters of lilac flowers, the walls were festooned with scarlet roses and fronds of honeysuckle and the balcony was so full of pots and plants it was like a hanging garden.

Agnes shook the earth from a large cos lettuce and walked over to the car. 'I like it,' she said. 'Leave the luggage for the moment. We can deal with all that when we've eaten.'

But Francesca couldn't wait to show her the mermaid. 'I'll just bring this,' she said and picked up the box.

'You paint?' Agnes said, looking at the legs of the easel. It was only just a question.

Francesca gave her a rueful grin. 'I used to.'

'And now you've started again,' Agnes understood, leading her round the side of the house.

'I've been trying to paint the mermaid.'

'Naturally,' Agnes said, passing a dozen planters full of herbs and walking through the open kitchen door. She set the trug on the kitchen table and held out her hand. 'Well show me then,' she said.

They sat on Agnes's well worn kitchen chairs facing one another across the table and Francesca handed her folder over, wondering what her friend would say about it. Then, because she was feeling anxious, she diverted herself by looking round the room. It was terrible untidy. There was a heap of crumpled washing mounded on top of the washing machine, piles of old newspapers stacked on the floor, a battered horse-shoe nailed to the wall. The sink was crammed full of unwashed mugs and plates, and the whole place was heavy with the scent of flowers. They were filling every available receptacle – cut glass vases, china pots, empty milk bottles and jam jars – and they stood on every available surface – the dresser, the draining board, the top of the fridge, even on two old chairs. After a while, as Agnes went on quietly examining the sketches, the scent of so many blossoms began to make Francesca's head reel. Please say something, she thought, watching her host, even if it's only 'they're not very good.'

What she said was completely unexpected. 'He squashed you right down, didn't he.'

'Well, yes he did,' Francesca admitted. 'But how do you. . . ?

'The sketches,' Agnes said, answering the question before it was completed. 'This is the first one, right?' And when Francesca nodded. 'And this is the second? And this the third. They get steadily more confident as you work. The brushwork in the first one is tentative, the next one is better, the third better still. Once you're back in your stride you're going to paint something superb. You're half way there already.'

To be praised so fulsomely was so pleasurable and unexpected that it brought tears to Francesca's eyes. 'I haven't captured her yet,' she said.

'You will,' Agnes told her. 'Tomorrow morning, when we've had our breakfast, and if the weather holds, we'll find a nice warm spot in the garden where the light's just right and you can get to work. Now we must prepare the supper. There's a cold roast chicken in the fridge and it won't take a minute to toss this salad.'

They had supper, they talked until midnight, when they finally remembered that they'd left Francesca's luggage in the car and decided that most of it could stay where it was until morning. 'Nobody nicks anything round here. It's too quiet.'

In the morning, after Francesca had insisted on washing all the dirty dishes and had scrubbed the draining board until it shone while Agnes removed the dead and dying flowers to the compost heap and replaced them with fresh ones, instead of dealing with the luggage, they went out into the sunshine and chose 'the best spot' for Francesca's easel. And Agnes wandered off towards the orchard to see how the apples were coming along and left her to it.

It was soothing to be in that vast, rambling garden with birds singing and chirruping all around her and the sun warm on the nape of her neck, and being soothed made it possible for her to see what had to be done to her portrait of the mermaid. It was the shape of that tail that was wrong. It was too stiff. It didn't flow. It should be more watery, more like a wave, more fluid. She took a sketch-pad and a pencil and began to draw, using long sweeping strokes, first for the lazily threshing tail and then for the long tangled fronds of the hair. She was so absorbed in what she was trying to do that she didn't hear the stranger's approach until he was standing beside her. Then she turned her head and looked straight at him. He was staring at her sketch-pad.

'Interesting design,' he said, still looking at it.

'It's a mermaid,' she told him and picked up the best of her first painted sketches to show him.

He took it from her and considered it for a long time.

'And now you are adding the movement you need,' he said. 'I like your palette. Tawny eyes are a lovely touch. Just right.'

For a second she almost told him that was the colour they were. Then she checked herself. He looked far too solid and sensible to believe that anyone had actually seen a mermaid. Too solid, too sensible, too middle class and middle aged and ordinary, in his buff chinos and his old fashioned check shirt, brown hair greying at the temples, large long-fingered hands holding her sketch. A bank manager, I'll bet. Or a teacher. Something dependable anyway. And dull.

'Blue-greens and tawny gold,' he said, 'with touches of bronze to set off the gold. Have you thought of giving her bronze hair?'

She hadn't but, now that he'd said it, she could see how possible it was. Dark bronze hair with gold highlights. Maybe he taught art.

'Henry, me dear!' Agnes was striding towards them through the long grass, calling as she came. 'How nice to see you. You never told me you were coming this morning. You could have had breakfast with us if you'd let me know.'

He handed the sketch back to Francesca and walked off at once to great his old friend, taking her hands in his and stooping to kiss her, first on one cheek and then on the other. 'Good cruise?' he asked. 'You look well.'

'Have lunch with us and we'll tell you all about it,' she said. 'Won't we Francesca?'

'Can't be done,' he said. 'Sorry about that. I've got a meeting in half an hour. I just popped by to invite you to supper on Friday. You and your friend here, of course. I've got a few people coming in. 7.30?'

'We'll bring some wine,' Agnes told him. And

watched as he walked across her shaggy lawn towards his car.

A Merc, Francesca thought, as it made a quiet turning in the drive. And very nice too. So he's not a teacher.

'I never introduced you,' Agnes said, as the car drove away. 'Never mind. I'll do it on Friday. What do you fancy for lunch?'

'Whatever you like,' Francesca said and then hesitated, saying finally, 'Do you want me to help you with it? Only I'd like to stay here for a bit longer, if that's all right. Your friend Henry's given me an idea.'

'In that case you must work on it,' Agnes said. 'I'll blow a whistle when it's ready.'

But Francesca had stopped listening to her. The mermaid was growing in her mind, as if she was ripening in the sun, bronze hair flowing and scaly tail curving and threshing. She couldn't wait to paint what she saw. When the whistle blew, the mermaid's lissom body was complete – golden eyes, slim arms, pearly skin and all – and her tail was very nearly right, and she was still hard at work, painting the long twisting curves of her bronze hair. 'Coming!' she called and went on painting.

'It's a pasta,' Agnes called back, 'and it won't wait. I'm bringing it out into the garden.'

They ate the pasta in the shade of the cherry tree and drank rather a lot of Chianti to wash it down.

'I don't know about you, but I needed that,' Agnes said, when their plates were clean.

'Me too,' Francesca told her. 'It was delicious.'

'Now what shall we do?' Agnes said. 'I suppose you want to get back to your mermaid.'

'Well, actually,' Francesca said, making a grimace, 'I think I ought to unpack my luggage first, if that's all right. I can't leave it in the boot for ever.'

'I don't see why not,' Agnes said. 'There's nobody here to mind what you do.'

'Some of it might spoil.'

Agnes put her head on one side and grinned at her. 'What sort of things have you got? It sounds like the crown jewels.'

'Bedding,' Francesca told her seriously, 'crockery, glasses, a telly, CDs, books, towels, clothes and shoes, of course.'

'Most of that can go in the garage,' Agnes said. 'It'll be safe there. Come on.' And she strode off across the garden.

The garage was as dilapidated as the rest of the house and it was packed with junk, spades and forks with broken handles, cracked flowerpots stacked one inside the other, a water butt with a hole in it, piles of earth-brown newspaper and ancient seed catalogues, several old raincoats and a selection of broken-down boots, bundles of raspberry canes, old stained paint-pots, jam jars full of stubby paint brushes, a lawn mower, a rusty scythe and what looked like the tattered remains of a garden tent.

'Heavens!' Francesca said, staring at it. 'Will there be room? I mean I've got rather a lot of stuff.'

'Room?' Agnes said in her trenchant way. 'Course there'll be room. Plenty of room. We'll just shift a few things around. You'll see.' And she picked up the tent and threw it across the water butt. Within two seconds the musty air was full of fluttering paper, tossed boots, tumbling brushes. It was so ridiculous and so uninhibited it made Francesca giggle. But it was also effective. Within twenty seconds there was a clearance big enough to take the first of Francesca's packing cases, within twenty minutes the car had been unpacked and all her belongings except her clothes were heaped in a neat pile in the middle of the muddle. She and Agnes were grey with dust and sticky with cobwebs but the job was done.

'Right,' Agnes said, cleaning her hands on her skirt. 'That's that. Now we can go back to the garden.'

Which they did, she drifting off to sleep on the hammock and Francesca, after washing her face and hands and carrying her suitcases up to her bedroom, returning to her mermaid. There was only the last of that long weed bronze hair to paint now and she was itching to finish it.

She worked steadily for the rest of the afternoon, pleased with what she was doing, feeling rewarded. It was well and away the happiest day she'd spent for years. And there was still a party to come.

Jeffrey Walmesly drove home from Plymouth that evening feeling tired and irritable. The conference hadn't gone at all well. In fact, if he'd been a man who let things get him down – which of course he wasn't, not by any manner of means – he'd have said it was a complete waste of time. The trouble was that the chairman of the firm he'd set his sights on had been a doddering old fool with no imagination, one of the old school, who thought he knew better than anybody else, because he was the boss, dyed-in-the-wool stubborn and as thick as his stupid concrete. It didn't matter what arguments he'd used to try and persuade him – and he tried every single one in his repertoire – he just hadn't seemed to understand how valuable it would have been to his ridiculous firm to be able to produce concrete in a variety of colours. Kept saying, 'No, no, we're fine as we are.' Damned stupid man. Sheer lack of intelligence, that's what it was. And now he'd wasted all that time and far too much of his diminishing cash and all to no purpose. It was enough to make him spit.

Never mind, he tried to comfort himself, I'll soon be home and then I'll have a good stiff brandy and tell old Fran how awful it was and she'll cook up something tasty for me and massage my neck and make me feel better. She might be a bit empty headed but if there was one thing she was really good at, it was wifely comfort. Niggling away in the back of his mind was the memory of that last stinging exchange of theirs and her voice saying 'I'm leaving you', but he knew she hadn't meant it. She wouldn't really leave him. Not after all this time and all the good things he bought for her. That kitchen cost an arm and a leg. Anyway she couldn't do it because she'd never be able to manage without him. They both knew that. She'd been upset, that's all it was. Time of the month probably. Women did all sorts of peculiar things then. They couldn't help it poor darlings. All those hormones rattling around in their systems. It was enough to drive anyone doolally. Oh no, she'd be there waiting for him, right enough.

It was a nasty surprise to open the door of the flat and call her name and get no answer. Oh for heavens sake! he thought, as he walked into his empty living room, what's she playing at? Where's she gone? She couldn't be out shopping. Not at this time of night. Could she? There was an easy way to find the answer. All he had to do was to go and see if she'd taken her shopping bags. But to his growing apprehension, the kitchen was even emptier than the living room and it wasn't just shopping bags that were missing. There was no sign of the saucepans or the cups and saucers. In fact there was no china or glass in the cupboards at all. He walked into the bedroom feeling distinctly uneasy and opened the wardrobe gingerly. Her rails and shelves were mockingly empty. All her clothes were gone, shoes, skirts, jumpers, coats, the lot. There wasn't a trace of her left. Now thoroughly alarmed, he made a full check all over the flat, looking in the bathroom – no towels, no bathmat; in the airing cupboard – no sheets or pillow cases; in the kitchen to check the fridge – not so much as a crumb; and finally back to the living room, where there were no cushions on the sofa and, horror of horrors, no telly. He didn't understand it. Wouldn't understand it. She must have gone mad. And just when he was looking forward to a good meal too.

The take-away was insipid and he had to drink his beer from the can, because she'd taken all the glasses, and he hated doing that. It was so vulgar. He sat among the debris of his meal in the silence of his denuded living room with no telly to look at, swilling beer and brooding. She can't have gone far, he thought. I mean to say, where could she go? She hasn't got any friends – except for me. And she'd never have gone to her mother's because she's such an old bat. And what's she going to live on? She hasn't got any savings. She can't just drift about with no money.

But at that point the answer to his problem switched on like a floodlight. If he wanted to find her, the place to look was Randall and Tongs. I'll go there first thing tomorrow morning and tell her she can come home. I won't read the riot act or tell her off or anything like that. I'll just be my magnanimous self, promise her a meal out or a night on the town or something. She'll be eating out of my hand in no time. She's probably been really miserable without me, living in some pokey room somewhere with nothing in her life except filing letters and answering the phone. Poor girl. It serves her right but you have to feel sorry for her. Yes, that's what I'll do. I'll soon have her back.

CHAPTER 3

ALTHOUGH FRANCESCA HAD pictured him in a bank manager's respectable house in the leafy suburbs of Lewes, Henry Prendergast actually lived in a converted oast house and as far out in the isolation of the countryside as Agnes Potts. It was sumptuously appointed, worth about three quarters of a million pounds – as he was well aware because he kept a close eye on the value of his assets – and it stood in a garden almost as big as Agnes's although considerably better groomed. It was the perfect setting for a party.

When Francesca drove her elderly Fiat into the drive that Friday evening, and parked it among the brand new Mercs and Volvos and Jaguars, she was impressed and surprised. If he was a bank manager, he was a very well-heeled one.

And extremely hospitable, welcoming them on the doorstep and smiling them into an elegant hall. 'We're all in the kitchen,' he said, taking Francesca by the elbow and leading the way. 'Come and be introduced.'

The room was full of people, all taking at once and most of them holding glasses. 'You all know Aggie don't you and this is her friend Francesca, who is an artist.' Glasses were raised in greeting. 'Hi there Aggie! Hi there Francesca!'

He walked her into the crowd, introducing people as he went, 'This is Liam, my accountant, and this is Yvette, my PA, and this is Molly, who does virtually everything'.

Molly was short and bubbly and everything about her was beautifully rounded. Her hair was a richness of auburn curls and her arms and shoulders could have been painted by Rubens. 'So *he* says,' she observed, laughing at Henry as she shook Francesca's hand. 'Little does he know!'

Henry grinned at her and went on with his introductions. 'This is John. This is Connie. And Babs and Reggie who are my nearest neighbours. Have some champagne. Nothing like champagne to start a party.'

'Half a mile up the lane,' Babs explained, as Francesca took a champagne flute from the proffered tray and Henry drifted away to talk to Agnes, 'which counts for "near" out here. So you're an artist.'

'Well . . .' Francesca said in her self deprecatory way. 'I wouldn't go so far as to say that. I paint a bit.'

'If Henry says you're an artist, then that's what you are,' Reggie said. 'He knows one when he sees one. You can take my word for it. Stout feller our Henry.'

'Well . . .' Francesca said again and sipped the champagne to cover her confusion. Was she really an artist? Had the mermaid given her status as well as freedom? What would Agnes say about *that*? And she looked around to see where her friend had got to. There were so many people milling about it took a few seconds.

She was on the other side of the room, talking to Henry and laughing at something he'd just said. She waved her glass at Francesca and mouthed 'OK?' And as she smiled back and waved her own glass, Francesca thought how very OK it was and how different her life had become since she'd left Jeffrey.

They dined on a patio beside a well-manicured lawn at beautifully set tables under green sunshades and were waited on at the serving tables by a team of slender young men in discreet uniforms. To Francesca's now decidedly dazzled eyes it all seemed a bit surreal.

'It's like a film set,' she said to Agnes, as their plates were being filled. 'I keep expecting Brad Pitt and Angelina Jolie to appear.'

'He likes to do things in style,' Agnes told her. 'Try the asparagus.'

She tried the asparagus and the smoked salmon and caviar, and when the meal had become positively sybaritic, she ate three sweets and enjoyed every one of them.

'This is the life!' she said to Agnes, leaning back in her chair.

Agnes grinned. 'Told you!' she said.

It was past two in the morning before they finally drove home and by then Francesca was dizzy with champagne and well-being. 'Does he often give parties?' she asked Agnes as she turned the Fiat into the untidy drive.

'Whenever the fit takes him,' Agnes said, easing out of the car. 'He's a hospitable man. I tell you what though, he keeps you up all hours! I shall need a good lie-in tomorrow morning.'

'You and me both,' Francesca said.

But in fact she was awake at seven as usual and, because it was another beautiful sunny day, she got up, made herself a pot of tea and some toast in Agnes's cluttered kitchen and went out into the garden to paint, not the mermaid this time – she'd finally stopped work on that on Thursday afternoon, having decided that she'd done all she could with it for the moment – but the mass of roses and honeysuckle that curled and entwined in intricate patterns across the front of the house. She'd started it just before they left for the party and it was pulling her powerfully. She worked as if she was mesmerized, her brush swooping across the paper with a quick controlled fluency that she'd never felt before, her imagination racing as the painting took shape. In the freedom and ease of the garden, and the growing strength of this new lifestyle, she was creating her own patterns from what she saw instead of painting slavishly from the life and the process was intoxicating. By the time Agnes finally came trailing out to join her, coffee cup in hand, the outline had been sketched and the first detailed section painted, its three artfully balanced crimson roses all voluptuous curves against the delicacy of the honeysuckle, with its tiny yellow trumpets and blue-shadowed white petals smooth as scrolls of sugar icing. It just needed a touch of alizarin on the rose thorns and the tips of the trumpets to pull it together and it would be almost right.

'I like that,' Agnes said, bending towards the easel.

Francesca sat back in her chair and considered. 'Yes,' she said. 'I think I do too. And I never thought I'd say that about anything I've painted.'

'Progress,' Agnes approved. 'What did I tell you?' She settled herself at the table and put down her coffee cup. 'Do you want to paint all day,' she asked, 'or are you game for a trip to town? I need to go into Lewes to replenish my stocks. I need fresh fish and meat and it's the Saturday market today.'

It was a chance to repay her hospitality. 'I'll drive you there if you like.'

'That would be handsome,' Agnes said.

'It's not all altruism,' Francesca told her. 'I ought to

start looking for a job and that would be a good place for it, wouldn't you say.'

'I'd say you don't have to start job hunting yet,' Agnes told her. 'I'd say go on painting for a bit longer while you're enjoying it. But I don't suppose you'll take any notice of that.'

'The thing is,' Francesca said, cleaning her brushes, 'I can't go on sponging on you forever. I'll feel guilty if I don't start paying my way. I must at least put out some feelers.'

'Just so long as you take your time over it and don't go rushing into something that won't suit you,' Agnes said. 'That wouldn't do at all. Let's have a bit of brunch, shall we? I don't know about you, but I'm starving. Could you face a fry up?'

They faced it together with a large pot of coffee and warm croissants to follow and they were idly throwing the crumbs to the birds that were waiting for titbits, when someone called them from the drive. 'Aggie! Francesca! Where are you?' and Henry strode round the corner of the house and came squinting towards them, shielding his eyes against the sun.

'I've been beating your door down for an hour and a half,' he told Agnes, sitting in the nearest chair. 'I was beginning to think you'd emigrated. Or dropped exhausted after the rigours of the evening. And here you are out in the sun, making pigs of yourselves.'

'In other words you'd like some croissants,' Agnes said.

He gave her a grin. 'Believe it or not, Agnes Potts, I'm not on the scrounge this time,' he said.

She teased him. 'No?'

'No,' he said. 'I've come to see the mermaid. If it's finished that is and if Francesca will let me look at it.'

'I wouldn't say it's quite finished,' Francesca said but as he was looking at her hopefully, she gentled it from her folder, explaining, 'but then nothing I ever do is what I'd call finished. There it is, for what it's worth.' And she passed it across the garden table into his hand.

He examined it for several seconds, thoughtfully. Then he looked at her and smiled. 'I'd like to buy it,' he said.

It was such a surprise, she responded without thinking, her eyes wide. 'Good God! Really?'

'Well that's refreshing,' he said. 'Most of my artists say *How much*?'

'How many artists have you got?' Francesca asked. The conversation was becoming as surreal as his party had been.

'Three,' he told her. 'More or less.'

By this time she was so gobsmacked she didn't know what to say. She stared across the table at him, trying to make sense of what she was hearing – and failing. She knew it was rude to stare but really she couldn't help it. It was like being in the middle of a dream. To sit here in this rustling garden with the scent of roses making her dizzy and house martins darting in and out of her line of vision giving their high-pitched piping calls and clouds heaped and riotous above her head and to hear that he actually wanted to buy her painting had been amazing enough without being told he had a stable of artists. She'd never heard of anyone buying up artists before. Her mind was spinning so much she was feeling quite seasick. If he really did 'have' three artists, what he was doing with them? Perhaps he was a collector or ran an art gallery or something.

'I've set her a puzzle,' he said to Agnes with obvious satisfaction.

'You're a bad lot,' Agnes rebuked him affectionately. 'Don't tease her.'

He stood up and handed the painting back to Francesca. 'I tell you what we'll do,' he said. 'You don't have to make up your mind at once. You'll need a day or two to think it over. That's quite understood. So, let's put first things first. Before we go any further, you'd better see what I want to do with it. I'll call for you at half past eight on Monday morning and take you on a tour.' And he bent to kiss Agnes on the cheek, and strode away from them, oddly stiff-backed. As the car turned out of the drive, Francesca was still struggling to think what to say.

'Lewes,' Agnes said. 'We'll leave the dishes.'

Francesca sat where she was, too stunned to move. 'What did he mean by a tour?' she asked. 'A tour of what?'

'Oh I couldn't possibly tell you that,' Agnes said wickedly. 'He wants it to be a surprise.'

'How do you know that?'

'Body cues,' Agnes said. 'I've known him a long time. Used to work for him. He's a great one for surprises. That's why he throws parties because you're never quite sure what will happen at a party. He likes the uncertainty.'

It had seemed a very well organized party to Francesca, a controlled party – if that wasn't too strong a word. She hadn't seen any uncertainty about it at all. But she didn't argue. After all, Agnes *had* known him a long time. That was obvious. And yet that stiff spine was a body cue too and one that seemed more like anxiety than a man who was teasing. It was all rather baffling but perhaps that was because so many unexpected things had happened in such a short time and, what with the

45

sunshine and the roses and the house martins and the joy of painting, she was finding it hard to digest them all. Freedom rather comes at you.

'Come and see what you think of Lewes,' Agnes said, laughing at her bemused expression. 'You can work things out later.'

So Francesca left her puzzles in the garden and they drove to Lewes.

Jeffrey slept late that morning, and woke with his brain muddied by poor food, too much beer and a complicated nightmare. It took him half an hour to get out of bed and then there wasn't any coffee. Not that it would have done him any good if there had been when there were no cups to drink it from. The sooner he got Fran to see sense and come home, the better. He showered miserably, dressed in his one clean shirt and his new jeans – at least he could put on some style – bought himself coffee and croissants at Starbucks and, suitably sustained, strolled into Randall and Tongs ready to forgive his runaway lover. There was nobody there but that idiot girl, Tasha or whatever she was called, the one with the green fingernails.

'Ah,' he said, giving her his best smile. 'Fran not in?'

She didn't look up from her computer. 'She's gone,' she said.

'Gone?' he echoed, feeling very put down. 'What do you mean gone?'

'Gone,' she repeated. 'Handed in her notice. Did you want her for something?'

'You mean she's got another job?'

'No idea,' the girl shrugged, typing on. 'Like I said, she's gone. Handed in her notice and went.'

He was baffled but persisted. She couldn't just have

gone. People don't walk out of their jobs. Not in a recession. They stay where they are. 'You mean to another branch,' he prompted.

Tasha examined her nails. 'Don't think so,' she said.

'Think about it,' he advised. 'You must know where she is. She would have told you. I mean, she wouldn't just have walked out, now would she. She must have been going somewhere.'

That provoked a response although not a very satisfactory one. 'She did say something, now I come to think about it. In her letter. I remember Mr Randall said to file it.' She looked up from the keyboard at last, and gazed into the corner of the room, trawling her memory. 'She was going to nurse some relation in Sussex. Old or something. Very ill. Or that's what she said.'

Ah! Now we're getting somewhere. There was a letter so she'll have left an address. 'Whereabouts in Sussex?'

'Don't ask me. I've told you all I know.'

'But you saw the letter.'

'I don't read letters,' she told him sternly. 'I file them.'

'Maybe I could see it then.'

'What?'

'The letter,' he said with heavy patience. The time it takes to get through to these idiot children. Don't they teach them anything in school?

Her eyebrows arched in disbelief. 'Oh no,' she said. 'Letters are private. We can't divulge letters. Not to anyone. They're ever so strict about it. If you want to know any more you'll have to ask Mr Randall.'

He couldn't do that. Randall was altogether too acute and too capable of putting two and two together.

She was typing again, frowning at the keyboard. 'Was there anything else?' she said.

He felt dismissed and angry. 'No, no,' he said, as

casually as he could. 'It's not important.' But he was fuming as he walked out of the shop, angry with Tasha and her asinine green nails for not telling him what he wanted to know, which she could easily have done if she'd wanted to, cross with himself for not being able to make her do as she was told and absolutely furious with Fran because this was all her fault, silly self-willed woman. How dare she walk off and not tell him where she was going! It was – he scrabbled around in his mind for a suitable word and couldn't find one – thoughtless was too mild, stupid wouldn't do, although it *was* stupid, and childish wasn't right either. But for God's sake, how could he find her if he didn't know her new address. She *must* have left an address. Going to look after a relation in Sussex was too vague to be any good at all. He'd never heard of any relations, in Sussex or anywhere else. He'd always assumed she didn't have any.

He checked his appearance in the nearest shop window and sighed heavily. There was nothing for it, he'd have to go traipsing over to that terrible boutique in Streatham and ask that awful old harridan of a mother of hers. He didn't want to in the least because she'd always been hostile but if her fool of a daughter really had gone haring off to look after a relation, she was the only one who would know where she was. He'd have to be very careful how he approached her or she'd clam up and make a point of not telling him anything. She was such a dreadful woman it was hard to know the best way to handle her. Then he'd have to find a job of some kind, to tide him over until he'd set up his next deal, because his bank balance was downright unhealthy. It was all very trying. And unnecessary. And all Fran's fault. Well I hope she's thoroughly miserable, he thought, wherever she is. It serves her right.

*

Francesca was actually ridiculously happy. The sun was shining, the sky was a gorgeous blue and she was charmed with Lewes. After years growing steadily more jaded among the long Victorian streets of Beckenham with their identical houses, it was a revelation to her to walk along a short High Street in which every building was markedly different from the ones on either side of it and to look east to the edge of the town and see a green hillside rising before her. The first shop she saw when she and Agnes left the Westgate car park was so extraordinary it silenced her in mid sentence and she only just stopped herself from saying 'Wow!' It was labelled the Fifteenth Century Bookshop but a label was unnecessary for its antiquity was plain for every passer-by to see. The oak beams that striped its sagging frontage were faded to the colour of cafe latte, the windows were wonderfully out of alignment, squinting like drunks, and the lintel so low she had to duck her head to enter, even though she was a mere five-foot-five. And once inside she was into stunned delight, for the place was so full of books it would have taken a month to look at them all.

'I should think they've got a copy of every book that's ever been written,' she said to Agnes, touching a rather grand edition of *David Copperfield*.

Agnes laughed at her. 'If you're going to look through the shop, we shall never get our meat,' she said. 'You can always come back another time. It won't go away. It's been here since the fifteenth century.'

So they left it, Francesca grudgingly, Agnes briskly, and walked uphill to the western edge of the town for their shopping, past the elaborately fronted rectitude of the Victorian Grammar School and a hotel called

Shelley's, until they came to a family butcher where Agnes bought liver and bacon, a sirloin of beef, a free-range chicken and a side of salmon. 'We'll have some of that poached for our dinner tonight.' Then on to a green-grocer's for oranges and lemons and a pineapple 'to add to our soft fruit'. And then they were off again, heading for the Saturday market which turned out to be right at the other end of town.

Francesca didn't mind how far they went or how long it took them to get there. There were things to see at every pace of the way: a house where the great Tom Paine had lived, opposite a church dedicated to St Michael, whose image flew on the wall of the twelfth-century tower, bold as brass and green with verdigris, and a bit further along the road, to her happy amaze-ment, the entrance to a castle.

'I feel as if I'm walking about in a fairy story,' she said to Agnes, standing at the gate and looking in. 'Fancy having a castle in the middle of a high street. I've never seen anything like that before.'

'You saw a mermaid as I recall,' Agnes said. 'I'd have said a castle was small beer compared to that. Come on or everything'll be gone before we get there.'

'I wonder whether there's a dragon,' Francesca said, still gazing through the gate. 'That would be something to paint.'

'Stick around,' Agnes told her, 'and I'll take you in and show you the whole thing. But not today. Today is the Saturday market and Saturday markets get crowded.'

So they walked on down the hill, past the impressive white frontage of the County Courthouse, two splendid Georgian houses and lots of intriguing alleys, which were narrow and cobbled and lead precipitately down-hill towards the open country.

I wouldn't mind living here, Francesca thought, and wondered whether she'd have time to look in at a few estate agents and see what was on offer. But the afternoon was skimming them away. By the time they'd bought all Agnes wanted at the market – which was every bit as crowded as she'd predicted – there was only just enough time for Francesca to walk down to the station area and visit the job centre.

'Give me the keys and I'll wait for you in the car,' Agnes said. 'Just in case. We don't want a parking ticket. Turn left at the bottom of Station Road and then left again. You can't miss it. It's one of those awful modern buildings like a concrete box with windows.'

Which it was and it looked decidedly off-putting after the elegance of the Georgian houses in the High Street. But there was a job to be found, so Francesca reminded herself that she was being intrepid now, straightened her spine and walked in.

The interior was much more promising, large, open-plan and warmed by strong colours, the walls painted scarlet, orange, green and yellow like an infant school and with plenty of computers standing ready to enlighten the job seekers. The only problem was that although there were quite a few vacancies, they were for van drivers and delivery drivers, carers, cleaners and caterers, and none of them were jobs that Francesca really felt she wanted to do. If push came to shove, she might have to take one of them if nothing better offered and, before she saw the mermaid and acquired a taste for freedom, she would probably have chosen one and tried to make the best of it, but now she knew she couldn't face the idea of being a carer or a kitchen hand. I'll wait until I know what sort of price I'm going to get for the mermaid, she decided, that might keep me going for a week or two. Then I'll see.

'Very sensible,' Agnes said, as they drove home. 'There's no rush. Sit in the sun and paint till something turns up, that's my advice.'

But there was no painting in the garden that Sunday for the weather changed overnight and when they woke it was pelting with rain.

'It's coming down stair rods,' Agnes said, looking out of the kitchen window at it. 'Which is good for the garden but not exactly the best thing for alfresco painting. I shall stay indoors and make cakes. What will you do? '

'Actually,' Francesca said, 'I'd rather like to sketch you - if you don't mind. I've never tried my hand at a portrait.'

'I'm flattered,' Agnes said and looked it. 'Just as long as you don't expect me to stand still.'

'It'll only be sketches to start with,' Francesca told her. 'I'd like to see if I can catch you.'

Agnes laughed at that. 'You make me sound like a mouse,' she said, pulling a mixing bowl out of the cupboard. 'Can we have a bit of music or will that put you off? I usually have a bit of music when I'm baking.'

They had Classic FM which they both enjoyed and for more than an hour they worked companionably together, while the rain pattered against the window and the roses were tossed about until they drooped and dripped and lost their petals. Francesca surprised herself by how easy it was to sketch her new friend. Her hands were wonderful to draw even though they were on the move all the time, creaming the butter and sugar together, beating eggs, sieving the flour into the bowl, pushing her hair out of her eyes. There was such strength in them now that Fran was looking at them closely. After a while, when she'd drawn Agnes' hands several times and made a swift pencil sketch of her head, she remembered how she'd stood on that cliff on the day she saw the mermaid, with a bunch of wild flowers in her hand and brambles and burrs sticking to her skirt and the wind blowing her grey hair, and she knew she would like to do a full scale portrait of her just like that, burrs and brambles and all, and began a full length study there and then, while the thought was in her head.

Neither of them paused in their work until the cakes and pastries were in the Aga and the outline of the portrait had been completed. Then Agnes made a pot of coffee and sat down at the kitchen table to see what Francesca had done.

'Heavens above,' she said, considering the portrait. 'Do I really look like that?'

'You do to me,' Francesca told her, 'although it might not be the way you see yourself. We all have our own ideas about how we look. I found that out at my first life class.'

'I like those hands,' Agnes said. 'They look. . . .' And she considered for a while before deciding, 'I suppose competent is the word I'm after.'

'Yes,' Francesca said, looking at the models as they poured the coffee, 'that's exactly what they are.' And she hazarded a compliment, for she felt she knew Agnes well enough by that time to be pretty sure she would accept it. 'Competent and caring. I've never been so well looked after in all my life.'

They smiled at one another like old friends. 'I'm very glad to hear it,' Agnes said. 'We all need looking after now and then. And you more than most.'

Francesca sipped her coffee and looked out of the window. 'I do believe the rain's clearing,' she said.

And it was.

'I wonder what it will be like tomorrow morning,' Francesca said fishing for an explanation. 'When I get taken on my tour, I mean.'

Agnes' smile became a wicked grin. 'You'll have to wait and see,' she said.

'So it would appear,' Francesca said.

'Surprises can be fun,' Agnes told her.

CHAPTER 4

HENRY PRENDERGAST ACTUALLY gave some thought to what he was going to wear that Monday morning. It was a rare thing for him to do. He usually chose his clothes by simply skimming a hand along the rows of waiting garments until he came to a shirt and trousers he hadn't worn for some time and then pulling them out to do duty for the day. All his clothes were good quality and they were always returned by the laundry spotlessly clean and well pressed so it really didn't matter what he chose. Not now that Candida was dead.

When she was alive, he'd dressed to please her, or to earn her praise, which amounted to the same thing, for whatever pleased her she'd praised in that easy loving way of hers, inclining her elegant head towards him and smiling into his eyes. Dear God but he *did* miss her. Even now, after five empty years, the thought of her could make his body yearn with grief. He stood before the opened wardrobe door looking at himself in the long mirror where they'd so often stood side by side to admire one another in the halcyon days before she was taken ill, and he ached with the need to see her again, just once, just for five minutes. That was all he wanted. Just five minutes. It was all foolishness. He knew that, just as he knew he never *could* see her again. Never ever. His life with her was over and done with. But he grieved for her nevertheless. He couldn't help it.

He stood bleakly before the long, neat rails full of useless, expensive clothes and frowned at himself in the implacable mirror. There were things to be done. He must choose what he was going to wear, close the door on that awful empty reflection and get on with the day. The blue check shirt perhaps. But maybe checks wouldn't look business-like. A crisp white would be better. With grey trousers and his grey-blue Pringle sweater. He remember that that was what he'd worn the last time he'd had a difficult buyer to persuade and it had worked well then. Not that he was expecting Aggie's artist friend to be difficult. She seemed an amiable sort of girl. A bit shy but not difficult. But there were things about her that made him feel he should treat her carefully and it was as well to be on the safe side as far as possible.

For a start, although she hadn't made it explicit, he'd understood from her guarded body cues that she wasn't particularly keen on selling her picture of the mermaid and the more he thought about that picture, the more he wanted to buy it. He'd had the strongest reaction to it the moment he saw it. A gut reaction, of course, but none the less valuable for that because he was sure it was right. This unusual beautiful image could be just the thing to restore the firm's failing fortune. And with Candida gone, the firm was the most important thing in his life. But I mustn't rush her, he told himself, as he buttoned his white shirt. She's gentle and vulnerable and that wouldn't do at all.

When Jeffrey Walmesly set off for his tedious drive to Streatham he was in such a bad mood he didn't stop to think how he should be dressed. It wasn't until he was inching past the Streatham Home for Incurables that it dawned on him that he should have put on some style for a visit to a boutique and by that time it was too late for him to do anything about it. He sat in the long traffic jam, drumming his fingers on the steering wheel and scowling. Being constantly thwarted was making him irritable. He was beginning to feel that all the people he came into contact with were deliberately going out of their way to make things difficult for him. He was still simmering with resentment at the way that stupid green-nailed girl had treated him. And now he'd got to try and charm the truth out of that grisly old bat in the boutique without letting her know that Fran had walked out on him. Life was very unfair.

The grisly old bat was stroking the gowns on one of her gilded racks when he walked in. She was so totally artificial that the sight of her made him wince. Artificial women always set his teeth on edge and this one was worse than most. She was wearing a powder blue trouser suit that emphasized how impossibly thin she was, her hair looked exactly like candy floss above her raddled face and she had far too many diamond rings on those bony fingers. Downright ostentatious and he wouldn't mind betting half of them were glass. Turn on the charm, he reminded himself. You're going to need every ounce you can summon up if you're going to outwit this one. And he advanced towards her, smiling his practised smile.

She turned towards the sound of his entry wearing her own professional face, complete with smarmy smile. Then she saw who it was and changed her expression.

'Oh,' she said. 'It's you. I hope you're not going to stay long. I'm expecting some important customers this morning.'

'I was just passing by,' he said, 'and I thought, being in the area, I really ought to pop in and tell you how sorry I was to hear about your relation.' And he gave her the benefit of his sympathetic smile. 'Being so ill and all that.'

She looked surprised, her painted eyebrows rising into the candy floss. Then she scowled. 'What are you talking about?' she said, turning back to the gowns. 'What relation? I haven't got any relations. Unless you count Francesca.'

'The one who's so ill,' he explained. 'In Sussex.'

'You don't listen do you,' she said, not looking at him. 'I haven't got any relations. None at all. Not here. Not in Sussex. Not anywhere.'

He tried to make a joke of it. 'You must have had a mother and father. We all have a pair of those. Or did you spring fully armed from. . . .' Oh shit where was it? He'd forgotten the story. 'Some Greek god or something?'

'They've been dead long since,' she said. 'And good riddance to them.' Then she gave him a sly look. 'I'd have thought Francesca would have told you that.'

'No, no,' he tried to murmur, hoping she wouldn't notice the implication. 'We don't discuss our relations. We've got better things to talk about.' And when she gave him a scathing look, he pushed on, trying to keep his voice light. 'Anyway, I've only just heard about it and I thought it being your relation, and me being in the area, so to speak, I'd just pop in and see how . . .' was it a he or a she? This was getting worse and worse, 'um, they were.'

She was as sharp as a razor. 'You haven't talked to Francesca about it, have you?' she said. 'I'd have thought she'd have been the first person you'd have asked. Or aren't you on speaking terms? Is that what it is?'

'No, of course it's not,' he said crossly. 'Of course we are.'

'Then you should have asked her before you came barging in here.'

'Well, I like that,' he said, now thoroughly riled. 'I didn't barge in. I never barge in. Never. Anywhere. I went out of my way to commiserate with you. That's what I did. Out of the kindness of my heart. And you just . . .' He was spluttering but really this was too much. 'You just cast aspersions.'

She gave him a really evil grin. 'You don't know where she is, do you?' she said.

He answered her sharply. 'Of course I know where she is. Don't be ridiculous. She's at work.'

'Um!' she said. 'Could you just step a bit further away from that rail? I've got some very expensive gowns on that one and you're making me nervous.'

Damn the gowns, he thought. There's more at stake here than a line of expensive tat and he was just opening his mouth to say something really cutting to her when another grisly old gargoyle strode into the shop and the bat leapt forward arms outstretched to greet her. He left – quickly. There was nothing else he could do.

And then, to add insult to injury some moron had given him a ticket. 'Oh for Christ's sake!' he said glaring at the fucking thing. First that stupid girl and then the grisly old bat and now this. It was too much. Well that's it, he thought as he got into the car. I'm not wasting any more time on that stupid Fran. She can go to hell in a handcart for all I care, stupid silly woman. I've got a life to lead. And he put his hand on the gear lever expecting to slip into gear in his usual quietly competent way and managed to grind the bloody things. Wouldn't you know it?

That stupid Fran was checking her appearance in the wardrobe mirror and feeling quite pleased with what she saw. She'd decided to wear her best pair of jeans and her favourite shirt for her mystery tour and had flung her cream jacket over her shoulders as a last minute addition. It was the only one she'd unpacked so it would have to do. She knew she really ought to get around to sorting out her tumble of belongings and putting everything away, if only to make her bedroom look more homely, but there'd been so much going on in her life she hadn't had the time for it. I'll do it tomorrow, she promised herself, as Henry's Merc purred into the drive. Now, with her folder under her arm, she was the intrepid traveller again, off to adventure and mystery.

It was a luxurious ride. Henry drove smoothly, just as she'd expected, there was very little traffic on the narrow roads and the CD he was playing was something rhythmic and gentle that she'd never heard before. She would have liked to have asked him what it was, but thought better of it in case he was one of those men who didn't like to talk while they were driving. So she simply sat beside him and listened to the music and watched the rural world go by and didn't speak.

Her quietness gave Henry pause. On balance he would have preferred it if she'd made conversation. That way he might have found out more about her which would have made it easier to negotiate with her. But she was obviously a private person – or shy. Either way, once they'd started their journey in silence, he couldn't break in on her reverie. It didn't matter. In another twenty minutes they would be at the workshop and there would be plenty to talk about then.

Past the roundabout, left at the trading estate and there it was. Prendergast Pottery, its well-designed sign clean and elegant above the entrance. It gave him the usual, familiar kick just to see it. He parked the car in his designated space and glanced at his passenger to see what impression it was having on her.

She looked him, clear-eyed in the morning sunshine. 'A pottery,' she said. 'You want to put my mermaid on the side of one of your pots, is that it?'

Her face was showing so little expression he couldn't tell whether she was pleased or annoyed by the idea. 'Among other things,' he told her, rather ambiguously and swung his long legs out of the car onto the gravel. 'Let me show you.' Then he walked round the car and opened the passenger door for her, giving her a little bow as she eased out of the car, partly to reassure her and partly to soothe himself. Having reached this point, he was actually feeling nervous but he certainly wasn't going to let her see *that*.

They walked into the building side by side and even despite her misgivings Francesca was impressed by it. When she'd seen the word 'Pottery' over the door, she'd expected a dusty hut with one or two potters hunched over their wheels, the way she'd seen them in documentaries, probably wearing aprons spattered with clay, with a few pots on a shelf behind them and the odd kiln here and there. What she found was a factory and a kiln that ran the full length of the shop. She saw at once that moulded utensils were being put into it at one end and being taken out of it, newly baked, at the other. There were men and women in green aprons stacking cream coloured cups and plates in long rows on wooden racks. 'Among other things' is about right, she thought. There were jugs, plates, teapots, vegetable dishes, vases of every size in bright swirling colours, even a huge soup tureen with a green turtle as a cover.

'What do you think of it?' Henry asked, feeling more hopeful now that he'd watched her surprise.

'Extraordinary,' Francesca told him, still watching as the work went on. She caught sight of Molly, checking the cups and plates, and the two of them waved to one another. 'Where do you sell all this stuff?'

'Department stores mostly,' Henry said. 'And shops that specialize in fine china. Your mermaid could be seen all over the British Isles, if you let me have her. Come and see the sort of things I hope to do with her.'

They progressed through the shed and Francesca noticed that he was greeted by all his workers 'morning Mr Prendergast' and that he seemed to know all their names and had something to say to each one of them. 'Morning Joe. How's the baby?' 'Morning young Sarah. Was it a good party?' They like him, she thought, and he likes them. He's a good boss. Then they walked through a door at the end of the shed and were in the relative peace of a computer room. There was a young man sitting in front of a screen full of shifting patterns.

Henry introduced him as 'the whizz-kid of computer enhancement' and said his name was Paul and the young man looked up from the screen and smiled.

'This is Francesca,' Henry said to him. 'She's an artist. If I can persuade her, I hope she'll agree to be one of *our* artists. Perhaps you'd like to show her the sort of thing you do.'

'Geometric designs at the moment,' Paul said, pressing keys, 'like this one for a vase. It's mostly squares and oblongs – d'you see? – but they work better with rounded sides to fit the shape of the vase, which is there in outline – d'you see? Now like that it doesn't fit, but if I change the line here and here, it does.' He rotated the design on the screen so that she could see the vase in three dimensions.

The easy way he manipulated the shapes made her

worry. What if they wanted to change the shape of her mermaid? She couldn't bear that. Not now she'd finally caught the creature as she was, she didn't want anyone to change her.

'Francesca has designed a superb mermaid,' Henry said. 'The colours are spectacular. I think we should show her what it would look like were we to use it. On a dinner plate perhaps.' And he turned to Francesca and added. 'Would you be happy to let Paul see it?'

She hesitated, loath to agree because it was *her* mermaid and she didn't want anyone to mess about with it, but in the end she took her painting from the folder and handed it to the young man.

His reaction was immediate and gratifying. 'Wow!' he said. 'Now that's something. Really something! What gorgeous colours! Love the golden eyes. And those scales. Wow! A dinner plate did you say, Mr Prendergast?'

The picture was carefully positioned in a scanner, a white dinner plate appeared on the screen and was enlarged until it filled the entire space and seconds later the mermaid was swimming in the middle of it, the blue-green of the sea flowing right to the edges of the plate. And watching Francesca's face, Henry knew that a deal could be done.

'What do you think?' Paul said.

Henry signalled approval with his eyes but said nothing. It was Francesca who answered him. 'I think she looks good,' she said, trying not to be too grudging. 'Providing you don't alter her.'

'I think it might be an idea to trim the sea back a tad,' Henry said, looking at the screen. 'I think there's too much of it. But of course, it's your painting and if you don't approve we wouldn't do it. But in my opinion, for what it's worth, I really think your mermaid would have more impact if we trimmed it back. We wouldn't reduce it by much because the colours are such a perfect foil for those scales. Just sufficient to give her more prominence. Shall we show you?'

She said yes even though she couldn't see that anything in her picture needed any alteration at all and watched with misgiving while the greeny-blue waves retreated towards the centre of the plate and were then extended in several different directions and pulled back again into slightly different positions. It looked like a tide that had been filmed over twenty-four hours and was being played at ten times its normal speed. At first she was fascinated and appalled but after they'd shifted the position of the mermaid and changed the waves around her more than six or seven times, she began to get used to the idea that what they were trying to do was to set her painting in the best possible position to do justice to the mermaid's sinuous curves. And then a curious excitement took over and she began to suggest other variations.

'Coffee break,' Henry said at last. 'And doughnuts.'

So they left the mermaid with her long tail echoing the curve of the plate exactly as she'd suggested, and she and Henry went off to his office for refreshment and negotiation.

'I'm not going to rush you,' he promised when the coffee and doughnuts had been carried in and set carefully on the desk before him. 'When we first talked about it, I got the feeling you were – shall we say – not too keen on selling this painting to anyone. Right?'

She nodded as he poured the coffee.

'So my first question,' he said handing her a full cup and suggesting sugar and cream by looking a query at her, 'has to be – are you still of the same mind?'

She helped herself to cream and sugar and drank her

coffee while she thought about it. He was quite right, of course. She hadn't wanted to part with her painting at all. Now, having seen it on the dinner plate, she wasn't quite so sure.

'Perhaps it would help if I were to tell you what I would like to use it for. . . ?'

She looked at him steadily over the rim of her cup.

'What I have in mind is to produce a mermaid dinner service,' he told her. 'It would be very high quality, naturally, because it would be costly to produce given the number of colours involved, but I think it would be well worth the outlay. We would aim at the higher end of the market which is where the money is – or perhaps I should say where the money still is – and advertise in all the quality magazines, that sort of thing. Like I told you, if we can pull it off, your mermaid will appear in all the best shops in the British Isles.' She was looking interested but still hesitating so he decided the time had come to talk money. 'I would offer you £5,000 for the copyright to the design and a position as a permanent member of my staff to do the painting. Naturally. I wouldn't let an image as splendid as this one be handled by anyone else.' And as she still seemed to be hesitating, he added, 'It's a generous offer.'

It was so generous it had taken her breath away. £5,000 was a fortune, maybe even enough to put down a deposit on a flat and give her a place of her own. But even so, the mermaid was hers, and precious, and she wasn't sure she wanted to spend her time painting it over and over again on a succession of dinner plates. Not now she was moving on to portraits. 'I do appreciate what you're offering me,' she said. 'I wouldn't want you to think I don't, but. . . .'

'But?'

What could she say without making him think she was disparaging him or belittling his offer? She didn't want to be rude or ungracious. Before she left Jeffrey she would have given him what he wanted without offering any resistance. Now she couldn't do it, or at least she couldn't do it yet, and she had to say so. Freedom may be a wonderful thing, she thought, but it's difficult to handle. Finally she temporized. 'I'd like to talk it over with Agnes,' she said.

It was a disappointment but he swallowed it. 'Of course,' he said. 'Talk it over with anyone you like. You must take your time. It's a big decision. Now is there anything else you'd like me to show you while you're here?'

He took her to every workshop and showed her the entire production process from start to finish, to the room where huge sacks of raw clay were stored, to rooms where cups and plates and saucers were being moulded and another where what he called biscuit-ware 'that's clay after the first firing' was being painted by his artists and glazed ready to be fired again, to the dispatch rooms where dinner services and tea services were being encased in bubble wrap for protection and packed into cardboard boxes marked by the company logo, then back to the computer room so that she could collect her painting and finally to the canteen, where Molly and Paul were having lunch with their friends and stopped eating to wave to her. After that the tour was over and he had to face the fact that, although he'd waited patiently for her to change her mind and give him the decision he wanted, she wasn't going to do it. So he escorted her out to the car and drove her home.

It was another silent journey because they were entirely caught up in their own thoughts; he determined to keep his impatience and disappointment under control and to remain his usual calm and gentlemanly self, she torn between her long ingrained obligation to please other people and this new undeniable desire to keep her painting and find a job she really wanted to do.

After she'd got out of the car in Agnes' overgrown drive and he'd waved and driven away, she felt rather ashamed of herself. He'd made her the most generous offer she'd ever had in her life and he hadn't pushed for an answer and she ought to have said yes there and then. But the moment was past and besides she *did* want to talk it over with Agnes and she hadn't actually made a decision. I'll tell her all about it, she thought as she drifted towards the kitchen door and if she says yes, I'll do it.

She said yes as soon as the story was finished. 'It's a wonderful offer. It could be the making of you. You'd be a fool not to take it.'

Francesca was still doubtful. 'All of it?'

'Why not?'

'Well I can see selling him the painting – that *was* a good offer, I mean nobody's ever offered me anything for one of my paintings before, let alone five grand – but I'm not so sure about taking the job.'

Agnes looked at her in her shrewd way, 'Why not?'

'It might be boring, painting the same thing day in day out.'

'Or it could be fun. You can't tell. He might commission other paintings. There are all sorts of possibilities.'

That could be true, Francesca thought. On the other hand. . . .

'It's your life,' Agnes said. 'You're free to live it any way you choose. I'd take it if it was me, but it's entirely up to you when it comes down to it.'

The decision was made, suddenly, the way she'd decided to leave Jeffrey. 'I'll ring him.' She felt as if she was jumping into a very cold swimming pool and the shock of it was taking her breath away, but it *was* the right decision. 'I expect you've got his number haven't you.'

By the time they went to bed that night, the mermaid was sold, she'd agreed that she would be one of Henry's artists and that she would start work on Monday, she'd written to Randall & Tongs to ask for her P45 and her life had taken a heart-pounding turn in yet another direction. Tomorrow, she promised herself as she settled her head on the pillow, I'll have a nice, quiet, ordinary, domestic day and tidy up this bedroom.

It didn't turn out in quite the way she'd planned, which wasn't for lack of effort on her part but for a reason she hadn't foreseen.

CHAPTER 5

A S SOON AS they'd finished breakfast the next morning, Agnes picked up her gardening hat from the table, rummaged among the cups on the dresser until she found her trowel and ambled off to the vegetable patch. Francesca stayed behind in the kitchen and washed the dishes, feeling virtuous and helpful, and when everything was cleared to her satisfaction, she went upstairs to begin her unpacking, deciding as she climbed that she would start with her clothes, because if she left them in her suitcases any longer they'd be so creased she'd have to iron them all over again.

It didn't take much time to empty the cases and hide them under the bed the way she'd done in her cabin. Then it was simply a matter of finding somewhere to store the various things that were now lying all over the duvet. There was a sizeable chest of drawers in one corner of the room and a long fitted wardrobe against the wall opposite the window so there was plenty of space. She opened the top drawer of the chest expecting it to be empty and thinking in a vague sort of way that that was where she would store her underwear. What she revealed gave her a shock. It was full of discarded clothes – felted jerseys, badly creased blouses, crumpled pants, laddered tights, petticoats that looked like museum pieces, frayed scarves, even a pair of battered old slippers – all tangled up together in such a tight mass that it took a considerable effort to shut the drawer again. Heavens! she thought. What a collection! I'll bet she hasn't used any of that for years. I'd chuck it all away if it was me. Maybe I ought to offer to sort it out for her. But just for the moment she had to concentrate on the job in hand and get her own clothes stored away. She opened the second drawer, ready to begin.

It was the second shock of the morning. It was as full of tangled clothes as the first one had been and so were the third drawer and the fourth. She stood looking down at the muddle she'd revealed, feeling baffled by so much rubbish. Then she struggled all three drawers shut and turned her attention to the wardrobe. There were bound to be drawers or shelves in there that she could use. It ran the length of one wall and looked big enough to take everything she possessed. But it was a vain hope, as she discovered as soon as she opened the doors. The wardrobe was piled with old clothes too, not hanging up on the rails but lying in a pungent mound on the floor – coats, jackets, dresses of all kinds, skirts, trousers, more down-at-heel shoes. What an extraordinary thing! Doesn't she ever throw anything away?

She pulled a couple of dresses from the pile, thinking she might be able to hang them up and make a bit of room in the wardrobe that way, and then she realized why they'd been kept. They both had expensive designer labels, one Worth, the other Christian Dior. To see such beautiful, classy clothes flung on a pile as if they were rubbish gave her another palpable shock. She remembered that Agnes had warned her that she lived in a bit of a tip but she'd never imagined the tip would turn out

70

to be like this. She was flooded with pity for her friend. Poor Agnes, she thought, this is what comes of having to look after this great house on her own. It's too much for her. I must pull my weight a bit more. Right then, the first thing I'll do is to sort out all these lovely clothes for her and hang them up. There are plenty of hangers on the rails.

She was hard at work when Agnes called up to her that lunch was ready. The pile was considerably diminished by that time and the carpet was covered with gowns and coats and dresses all neatly laid out and waiting for hangers. I'll just do three more, she thought, and then I'll go down. Three more was too many. She was smoothing out some of the creases in a blue velvet coat and thinking how gorgeous it was, when she became aware that there was somebody in the room, breathing heavily, and she looked up to see Agnes standing in the doorway with the oddest expression on her face.

They looked at one another for several seconds, then Agnes said, 'What are you doing?' in a voice that was so tight with suppressed emotion that it threw Francesca into a panic. She didn't stop to think, couldn't stop to think. She just plunged straight into a garbled explanation, talking too quickly and waving her hands. 'These were all sort of lying in a heap in the wardrobe,' she said, 'sort of just lying there and I thought I'd try and . . . well sort of hang them up. I mean, they're too beautiful to be left on the floor. That blue velvet's. . . .' But she knew she was saying the wrong things because Agnes was growing more and more angry with every word, her throat reddening and her jaw set.

'I'll thank you to leave my things where they are,' she said coldly. 'I like them where they are. Don't touch them.'

Francesca was frozen by the ice of her anger. 'I was only trying to help,' she began, 'I thought . . .'

'Well don't,' Agnes said. 'I don't like my things being moved. I like to know where they are. Just don't touch them.' And she turned and walked out, her spine rigid.

Francesca was so upset she didn't know what to do or say. She hadn't meant to make Agnes cross. That was the last thing she'd wanted to do. She'd been trying to help, that was all. She stood in the middle of the room biting her lip, looking at the tangle of clothes, struggling to think of some way to put things right and feeling utterly miserable. It was dreadful to find herself in the middle of a quarrel with Agnes when she'd been such a good friend to her. But how could she have possibly known that wasn't the thing to do? It had seemed really helpful while she was doing it. Oh dear, oh dear. Eventually she left all the clothes where they were and crept down the stairs making as little noise as she could and feeling like a naughty child.

There was no one in the kitchen and no sound of movement from anywhere in the house. But, standing among the dust motes that were lazily swirling in that quiet empty hall, it occurred to her that, since she'd arrived in this house, she'd only ever been in the kitchen and there were three other rooms downstairs that she'd never entered. Maybe Agnes was behind one of those closed doors. Maybe she should go and look. Or would that be the wrong thing too? Indecision was paralyzing her but she couldn't go on standing there, wanting to say sorry and make amends and doing nothing about it. This is cowardly, she told herself. I'm really fond of Agnes. I wouldn't have deliberately upset her for the world. On the other hand if she *was* in one of the rooms she might be hiding in there to get over being so upset and if I go barging in I might make her feel worse and that would be awful. But I can't let this go on. I must do something. Eventually she decided she would open the nearest door and just peep in. If Agnes *was* there and still cross or upset, she'd back out quietly and hope she hadn't been noticed. She took a deep breath, gathered up her courage and eased the door open as quietly as she could.

The shock of what she found there was so profound it took her breath away. The room was full of rubbish. It had obviously been a dining room once for there was a classy looking table and eight elegant chairs in the centre of it and an equally classy dresser against the wall facing the window but every single surface was covered with junk. The table was stacked with tatty old books and piles of newspapers and magazines, all of them faded and dog-eared and browning, and littered among them there was a collection of chipped cups and broken vases, old flower pots and crumpled packets of seeds, a watering can with a hole gaping in its side and more broken pencils and discarded pens than she could count. There were coats and mackintoshes slung over the backs of the chairs and files and folders heaped on every seat. And all over the carpet and leaning against the walls, there were dozens of old cardboard boxes stacked on top of one another. Some of them had fallen to pieces and were spilling old shoes and socks, bits of half-finished knitting and what looked like used polishing rags. There were piles of ancient gramophone records still in their tea-coloured wrappers on the dresser and in one corner of the room an old water butt full of broken umbrellas and walking sticks. It was just like the garage only worse because this should have been a living room not a rubbish dump. Outside the window the honeysuckle was clean and fresh and breathing of summer but inside the room there was nothing but dirt and dust and ancient decay.

Ye Gods! Francesca thought, gazing at it. I thought all those clothes were bad enough but this is appalling. She'll get mice. If she hasn't got them already. Doesn't she ever throw anything away? Some of this stuff must be years old. Decades even. She picked up the nearest newspaper and checked the date. It was over twelve years old. Twelve years! She ought to hire a skip, she thought, and get rid of it all. I would if it was me. But then she thought of Agnes's angry face and the way she'd said 'I like to know where my things are' and she remembered a programme she'd seen on TV years ago about an old man who never threw anything away and lived in a house so full of junk he could barely get in the door. There was only one room where he could move around and that was full of rubbish too. The commentator had said it was some sort of compulsion, she remembered, but she'd thought he was just a filthy old man and needed sorting out. And now here she was, dithering in a room full of rubbish that belonged to a woman she admired, a woman who'd been kind to her, and all her certainties were being muddied and muddled away and she didn't know what to do.

She drifted out of the room, feeling she ought to try and find poor Agnes, even though she didn't have the faintest idea what she could say to her when she did, and she opened the next door vaguely, her mind in such indecision she hardly knew what she was doing. She was standing in another filthy room, this time a library. The walls were lined with bookshelves, once white, now tea brown and all of them jammed with elderly books, and there was a rather handsome desk set beside the window. But every other space was full of decaying cardboard boxes, filthy soft toys oozing kapok, bulging plastic bags and boxes full of old socks, rags, folders, boots, newspapers, rubbish, rubbish, rubbish, everywhere she looked. This is terrible, she thought, and went to inspect the third room, knowing even before her she'd turned the handle that it would every bit as bad – as it was.

Now there was nowhere else to look except the kitchen and she knew that Agnes wasn't there. She crept into the room, noticing the pile of crumpled washing, the heaps of rubbish on the dresser, all those flowers in their crazy containers. The signs had all been there, right from the beginning only she hadn't seen them. Oh dear, oh dear, what *could* she do? The kitchen door was ajar, so she stepped out into the lovely clean sunshine. There was nowhere else she could go.

Agnes was sitting on the hammock, wearing her battered straw hat and with her head bent over a book.

Now what shall I do? Francesca thought. I shall have to apologize, that's obvious, but what shall I say? She didn't want to upset Agnes again. She'd upset her enough already and if this *was* a compulsion she needed careful handling. She walked towards the hammock as she was thinking, trying to find the words she needed and failing. She still hadn't done it when Agnes looked up.

'Ah, there you are, me dear,' she said, in her usual voice. 'Sorry about all that.'

Francesca was limp with relief at being spoken to kindly when she wasn't expecting it. She sat on the rough grass at Agnes' feet and tried to begin her own apology, stammering because she felt so bad about what had happened. 'No really,' she said. 'It was my fault. I shouldn't have been . . . I mean I was out of order. . . .'

'I can't bear to have anything changed you see,' Agnes said. She looked sad now rather than cross. 'I can't throw things away. It isn't possible. I *did* warn you.'

'Yes,' Francesca said. 'You did. I wasn't paying attention. I mean, I didn't know it was so important to you.'

'I did try,' Agnes went on, staring into the middle distance. 'When I was younger. Valiant efforts I made. Even got as far as putting things in the dustbin but then I got up in the middle of the night and took them all out again. Couldn't part with 'em, you see. That was the trouble. It set me in a panic, thinking I'd never see them again.'

Francesca didn't say anything. There didn't seem to be anything she could say.

'It's change you see,' Agnes said. 'I find any change very painful. Very, very painful. Terrifying really, if I'm truthful. I want my life to go on as it's always been, here in this house, not changing anything or disturbing anything, just leaving things as they are. I know it's peculiar but that's how I am.'

Francesca sat on the long grass with her arms round her knees and tried to make sense of what she'd been told. It was hard to believe that anyone could be so afraid of change that they would be prepared to live in squalor rather than alter anything or throw anything away but, now that she'd seen the evidence, she had to accept it. It *was* a compulsion. The man on that TV programme had been right. She looked at Agnes with a new-found sympathy and her friend's face was so full of pain she felt she had to say something to reassure her.

'I won't change anything, Agnes,' she promised. 'I didn't know it would hurt you. I wouldn't hurt you for the world.'

'No,' Agnes said. 'I do know that.'

Then neither of them knew what to say next. There was a robin trilling in the cherry tree above their heads, the feathers at its throat fluttering with effort, and when Fran looked up at it, almost idly, she saw that the leaves around it were highlighted with a white so bright it was dazzling and wondered how she could translate such an amazing whiteness into paint. Touches of blue in the green perhaps. And then she felt ashamed of herself for letting her mind wander and looked back at Agnes and smiled at her.

The smile was lost. Agnes sat on bleakly, gazing into that impenetrable middle distance again. 'I've been like it ever since I was quite a little thing,' she said. 'I've never understood it but that's how it's been. My mother used to give my clothes to her sister for my cousins to wear – she called it 'passing them on' – and she was always throwing my toys away. Even when I thought I'd hidden them. It cut me to ribbons every time. They were such a loss. It was no use saying anything to her. She never listened to anything anyone said. Ever. She just went crashing on, going her own way. Got her own way usually too. Had to have it. Wouldn't let anyone argue with her. My father had a terrible time of it, poor man.' She gave Francesca a rueful smile. 'Amateur psychologist, that's me,' she said. 'I've probably got it all wrong but there you are. I think her ruthlessness made me the sort of person I am. And it got worse when my father died. She was terrifying then. Anyway, that's my excuse. Things are part of my life now, part of me. It would be like cutting off an arm to throw them away. Especially those gowns. My father bought them for me.'

'Yes,' Francesca said. She still didn't really understand it but she felt she had to agree. Poor Agnes, she thought, it *is* a compulsion. She can't help it. But she knew in that moment that she would have to move on and find a flat for herself, because dear though Agnes was, she couldn't live in such an impossible mess, not now she knew how bad it was and that she couldn't clean it up. It wasn't in her nature to live in a muddle. She was too fond of order. She liked to be clean.

'You know when we first talked about me coming here,' she said tentatively. And then stopped.

Agnes gave her a shrewd look. 'You're going to tell me you want to move on,' she said.

Francesca's cheeks were hot with the shame of being so transparent. 'Well not straight away,' she tried. 'But . . . well . . . maybe I ought to start thinking about it. I mean, I never intended to stay here for very long. It was only till I found my feet, sort of thing.'

'And you'd like to go looking for them, is that it?' Agnes said. And when Francesca looked puzzled, she grinned. 'You want to find your feet.'

'Well either my feet or a flat,' Francesca said, trying to join in the joke. 'Or both.'

'Quite right,' Agnes said cheerfully. 'This was only ever pro tem. We both knew you wouldn't be staying here for ever.' It was almost as if she was relieved by what they were saying.

'I don't want to rush anything,' Francesca said, feeling embarrassed to be even talking about moving. 'I wouldn't want you to think that. It's just, maybe I ought to start looking for somewhere. See what's on the market sort of thing.'

'Hereabouts?'

'Maybe in Lewes.'

'A good place to start,' Agnes approved. 'There are lots of very pretty houses in Lewes.'

'Only if you don't mind,' Francesca said. 'I mean, I wouldn't want you to feel I was deserting you or anything.' Then she blushed even more hotly because she knew she *would* be deserting her and she knew that Agnes knew it too. 'I mean, if I could be useful here I would. . . .' Oh God! Worse and worse. Now she sounded as if she was criticizing the state of the house. As she was. Oh God! Oh God! What could she say to put things right? Quick! Quick! Think of something. 'I mean . . . what I mean to say is. . . .'

Agnes was laughing at her. 'My dear gel,' she said. 'Don't take it to heart so much. If it's the right time for you to start house hunting, then that's what you should do. *Carpe diem* as my old classics mistress used to say. If I were you I'd go down to Lewes and start looking. Don't make that face. You might not find anything suitable for ages and, even if you strike lucky straight away, it'll be weeks before you can move and you'll come and visit, won't you?'

'Of course,' Francesca said, feeling relieved that her friend was taking it so well. 'There are still lots of things in your garden I want to paint. And besides I should miss your cooking.'

'Right. That's settled then,' Agnes said, closing her book. 'I'll go and make some sandwiches for our lunch. I did make omelettes but they won't be up to much by this time.'

It was as if the row hadn't happened, as if they'd both been asleep and dreamed it. Agnes made a plateful of sandwiches and a jug of lemonade and they sat in the garden and enjoyed them. After that Francesca carried her easel out to her favourite place and spent the afternoon painting the chestnut tree and a pair of bullfinches while Agnes gardened. And that evening they cooked a roast and prepared the vegetables between them and ate a cheerful meal together and drank a lot of wine.

Francesca lived with their uneasy truce for two more days. She put the dresses back in the wardrobe and went back to living out of suitcases, she painted every afternoon, cooked every evening and neither she nor Agnes said a word about the row they'd so very nearly had. But on Thursday morning she decided the time really had come for her to start house hunting.

'If you don't mind,' she said to Agnes as they sat together over their lunch, 'I think I'll pop into Lewes this afternoon and just sort of see if there are any flats on offer.' And as Agnes simply nodded, she went on in a lighter vein, feeling worried in case she'd said the wrong thing and treacherous, in case she shouldn't have been saying anything at all. 'I need some more paints and canvases and I'd like to see if I can find a dragon in that castle. I'll sketch him if I can catch him. Is there anything you'd like me to buy while I'm there?'

'I'll write a list,' Agnes said, calmly. 'We're running short of pasta and flour for a start and I could do with a pineapple. If I had a pineapple and some flour, I could make a pineapple upside-down cake.' And she grinned. 'Give me a few minutes.' And she got up from the table and began to open cupboards.

The list was written, they kissed one another goodbye and Francesca drove away, smiling brightly but still feeling treacherous and concerned.

Luckily the road to Lewes was soothingly empty, apart from one lone tractor gently rocking between the hedgerows and as Francesca purred along, her concern was gradually eased away by sunshine and solitude. She was surprised to realize that she could recover from a quarrel so quickly. A mere two weeks ago she would have turned herself inside out to avoid giving offence to anyone but, of course, that was when she was living with Jeffrey and she had to be constantly on the alert. It was different now she was living with Agnes Potts. *She* was old and sensible and, even though she wasn't as tough as she'd seemed at first, she certainly wouldn't take offence at anything anyone said or did as long as they'd done it in good faith. That was obvious from how rapidly she'd recovered from being cross. It was a novel experience to be living with someone who took upsets so gently.

By the time she reached the Westgate car park, she was quite herself again and headed off for the nearest estate agents to start flat hunting, feeling she was doing the best she could in the circumstances.

It was a bit of a disappointment. She tried all five agents in the High Street asking for flats to rent but there was very little on offer and what there was turned out to be extremely expensive, from £500 a month to well over a thousand. But she thanked the various men and women who'd entered her 'particulars' on their computers and went off clutching a sheaf of papers to study later, telling them she would have to do 'a spot of advanced maths' to see what she could afford and promising to get back to them if she found anything that was possible.

Then she went shopping and, having found an excellent supplier in the Station Road, she bought paints and canvas and everything else she needed and took it back to the car: that done, she tackled Agnes's shopping list and took all those purchases back to the car too. Then, as there was still plenty of time on her ticket, she strolled back along the High Street and treated herself to a Mars bar and a ticket to the castle. It looked a quiet, peaceful sort of place and a few minutes there would give her a chance to mull over the particulars she'd been given and think about them. But she'd barely put the papers down on the seat beside her and taken one bite from her Mars bar when she was diverted by the chirruping arrival of a group of small school children, all very excited and very eye-catching, the girls in green dresses and the boys in grey trousers and green t-shirts. They had three teachers with them and were clustering around them asking questions. 'Sir! Sir!' 'Miss! Are we going up the tower?' Their bright faces and moving bodies were too much of a temptation to Francesca Jones, artist. She took her sketch-pad and pencil from her handbag and began to draw them at once, quickly, as they went haring off to run up the zig-zagging steps to the keep. There were so many of them and they were all worth a sketch, here two little girls walking soberly together hand in hand, one with very dark hair and the other very fair; here a boy with wrinkled socks, all by himself, leaning against the railing looking dreamy; there a flock skimming up the steps, their bodies bent forward with eagerness, tousled heads beautifully rounded, mouths open and talking, hands gripping notebooks as yellow as daffodils, ponytails flicking, legs at splendid angles. They were a joy to draw.

She was so busy sketching she didn't notice that there was somebody sitting beside her. She'd heard someone sighing rather heavily but took no notice. What was sighing compared to a small boy painstakingly doing up his shoelaces. It wasn't until she stopped drawing to stretch her neck that she realized that she had company and that it was male and rather fat. As she turned to look at him, he put his head in his hands and sighed like a horse blowing.

Her sympathy was engaged at once, instinctively.

82

'Are you all right?' she said.

He lifted his head wearily. 'Oh yes,' he said and his voice sounded bitter. 'I'm fine. Just fine. Been made redundant, that's all.'

She commiserated vaguely, glad that was all it was. 'Oh dear! That's horrid.'

'I'll live,' he told her. 'It's all par for the course. The boss had it in for me. That was the trouble.'

Having stretched her neck, Francesca went back to her sketchpad, eager to catch the last of her models before they all disappeared into the keep. There was a little boy lying on his stomach at the top of the third flight of steps, writing in his yellow notebook. She could see the careful movement of his pencil from where she sat and he was concentrating so hard his tongue was sticking out of his mouth. Irresistible.

The young man was still complaining. 'Made my life a total non-stop misery. Total, non-stop. That's the truth of it. Between you and me, I've had a hell of a time. I'm actually quite glad to be out of it. Course, I should've seen it coming. Only I always see the best in people. Well you do, don't you.'

She said 'Um,' as he seemed to expect an answer but she was too busy drawing the child's lovely floppy cowlick to pay attention.

He went on talking anyway. 'I'm a fool to myself,' he said. 'I know that. A fool to myself. I *always* think the best, you see, always. That's the way I am. You can't help the way you are, can you. I think the best of people and then they treat me like shit, because they think they can. They think I'm weak, that's the trouble. They can't see the difference between being weak and being kind. And there *is* a difference. An enormous difference. Only they can't see it.'

The child was getting up, scrambling after his friends. There was a blur of green-clad movement, a final chirrup of voices and they were gone. But the sketchpad was full of drawings and some of them were all right. I'll flesh them out when I get back to Agnes', Francesca thought, while I can still remember the colours.

The young man was looking at her earnestly. 'You don't think so do you?' he said. 'If you don't mind me asking.'

It troubled her to realize that she didn't know what he was talking about. 'Sorry?' she said.

'You don't think I look weak, do you.'

It was such a direct appeal she had to answer it. 'No,' she said, briefly and untruthfully.

'And you would know, wouldn't you,' he pressed on, 'being an artist. You *are* an artist aren't you. All those drawings.'

'Yes,' she said, feeling happy with the description. 'I am.' And she thought what a rewarding thing it was to be able to say.

'Life's a bitch,' the young man told her miserably.

After so much successful sketching, she was so easy with happiness she felt she had to correct him. 'Well it can be. But not always. Things do change.'

'I wish,' he said dismally.

She checked her watch. 'Come and have a cup of tea,' she said, the old urge to be helpful dragging at her. 'Things always look better after a cuppa. I've got half an hour on my ticket. We've just got time.'

He was sighing again.

'Come on,' she said. 'My treat.'

He actually managed to smile at her. 'You're a star,' he said. 'And I don't even know your name.'

They exchanged names – his was Kenneth but he

said his friends called him Brad – and they had tea in the nearest café, while he told her again what a hard time he'd been having and she watched his face. He really was a most unprepossessing man and much too fat, with podgy fingers and a round fleshy face with very fat cheeks and the beginning of a double chin. His hair was quite nice, thick and dark, and he had straight white teeth, but his mouth was turned down more often than it was turned up and that made him look petulant. But he *had* had a hard time of it. That was obvious. And he *was* grateful to her for listening to him and taking him to tea. He said as much as they were parting adding, 'I couldn't have your phone number could I? I'd like to take you to tea next time.'

The idea of any further contact with him made her shudder. 'You don't have to do that,' she told him. 'Like I said, it was my treat.'

'But I'd like to,' he said.

She dithered, wondering how she could put him off without hurting his feelings. Eventually she said, 'I don't have my phone with me. Sorry about that.'

He wasn't deterred. 'I don't want your phone,' he said. 'Only the number.'

'Oh I never remember numbers,' she said, speaking as if it were a joke. 'I'm not mathematical at all.'

He shrugged his fat shoulders. 'Oh well,' he said. 'Can't be helped, I suppose. Anyway, I'll see you around.'

She felt mean to have lied to him but, really, she didn't want to spend any more time with him. Their tea party had been quite enough. He'd made her feel quite depressed. It was her own fault. She knew that. She shouldn't have felt sorry for him. Feeling sorry for people was always her undoing. It was high time she learnt not to do it. Then she too shrugged her shoulders, walked to

the car park and set off for her drive back to Agnes'. It
had been an eventful afternoon.

CHAPTER 6

AGNES WAS LYING in her hammock fast asleep with her hat tilted over her face, compost smearing her hands and the trowel on her lap. She woke up when Francesca walked towards her, took the hat from her face and looked up brightly. 'Ah there you are!' she said. 'Did you find your dragon?'

Francesca had forgotten all about dragons. 'I didn't actually look for one,' she said. 'I found a lot of children though. There were kids all over the place. I think it was a day for school visits. Anyway I did a few sketches. I had to be quick because they were all rushing about, so they're rather rough but I think I've caught enough to be able to work on them.'

'It's always the day for school visits,' Agnes told her. 'The castle's a popular place. Come and sit next to me and let me see them.'

They sat side by side on the grubby hammock, swinging gently, and Agnes wiped her hands on her skirt and considered every sketch, nodding and saying, 'Yes, I like that one.' 'And that.' 'And that.' When she'd examined them all, she went on looking at the last page and asked, just a little too casually. 'And what else did you do while you were there? Did you find any flats?'

'Well I took the details of anything that was going,' Francesca said, fishing them out of her bag. 'Let's put it that way. I'm not sure whether any of them would do and they're hideously expensive.' And as Agnes was looking at her expectantly, she handed the bundle over.

Agnes flicked through them. 'I see what you mean. Did you look at any of them?'

'No. I got waylaid by the children.'

'There's one here that might do,' Agnes said. 'A studio flat down by the river. Hillman Court. Somewhere to paint, maybe?'

Francesca laughed. 'It depends what they mean by studio and what sort of light it gets.'

'Worth a look?' Agnes asked.

Francesca's mobile was jingling in her bag. 'Sorry about this,' she said, retrieving it and lifting it to her ear. It was Henry.

'Where are you?' he said. 'I've been ringing Aggie for nearly half an hour.'

'Out in the garden,' she told him.

'Ah, that accounts. Party on Friday, tell her, to celebrate the arrival of my new artist.'

Given how unsure she felt about this job, Francesca didn't know what to say. But when the pause had gone on rather too long, she contrived, 'I *am* spoilt!'

'And so you should be,' he said. 'See you there. Usual time.'

She put the phone back in her bag thinking what a warm voice he had. He makes you feel as if he's wrapping you up and caring for you, she thought, even when you haven't really done anything to deserve it. Then she passed on his news to Agnes.

'Oh good!' Agnes said. 'We'll take him some raspberries and add them to the feast. I wonder who we shall meet this time.'

Francesca was wondering what she ought to wear if the party really was in her honour. The blue and white dress maybe. She'd put it on top of the pile on the bed and it was on the top of the pile on the carpet now so at least she knew where it was. She'd have to find her iron and her ironing board and freshen it up. And her blue and gold flip-flops. Or her gold sandals. Would they do? And a pretty bag, if I can remember where I packed them. Then another thought struck her.

'If I'm going to start work on Monday,' she said. 'I suppose I ought to go and look at that studio flat while I've still got time to do it.'

'Very sensible,' Agnes said and smiled at her. 'Let's go tomorrow.'

Francesca was touched to think that Agnes wanted to come with her but she didn't comment. Their very nearly quarrel was too recent for searching conversations.

So they went to Lewes the next morning and inspected the four flats that Francesca thought she could afford. The first was small and dark and smelled of drains, the second was above a shop and there was nowhere to park, the third was grubby and run down and had the most unpleasant cooker Francesca had ever seen. The fourth was the studio flat which they'd saved till last because they thought it was the most promising one. It was on the eastern edge of town down by the river and the approach to it along a narrow road full of parked cars, wasn't encouraging. But when they reached the flats themselves and found the one that was up for rent, it was a revelation.

It was newly painted and wonderfully clean, and, although the bedroom and bathroom were a bit small, the kitchen was excellent, fully and newly equipped with cooker, fridge freezer, washing machine and even a small dishwasher, and the living room was exactly what Francesca wanted. It was a very good size, overlooked the river and was lit by a long tall window and, as she saw at once, it would be perfect for painting. There was even a little balcony leading out of it, just big enough for two. She opened the door and she and Agnes stepped out into the sunshine.

It was quiet and peaceful out there and the view was spectacular. Two floors below them the river flowed gently toward the sea, its shifting shadows nut-brown and weed green, with occasional, ephemeral highlights of pale sky blue. It was a delight to her eye and so was the wooded field that flanked the opposite bank and the high chalk cliff that dazzled in the eastern distance. She'd been impressed by the flat but this view made up her mind.

'I could live here,' she said, looking back into the living room and watching as sunlight reflected from the river made rippling patterns on the cream walls. 'It's got pretty well everything I want. I really like that kitchen. I could move into it tomorrow. And it would be perfect for painting. I could paint in there or out here on the balcony. What do you think Agnes?'

'If that's how you feel about it,' Agnes said, 'I think you should take it, me dear.'

So they went back to the estate agents and Francesca spent the next hour filling in forms, paying her deposit, which was three months rent in advance and made a sizeable hole in her mermaid money, and then providing the names and addresses of what seemed like an interminable list of people, her previous employer, her bank managers, previous and present, someone who would be able to vouch for her character. 'That'll be me,' Agnes said and gave her address at once.

'Now we just need the name of your present employer,' the estate agent said, smiling encouragement. 'Do you work in Lewes?'

'She's the principal artist at Prendergast Potteries,' Agnes said, grinning at Francesca.

The estate agent was impressed and showed it. 'Mr Prendergast is very well thought of hereabouts,' she said as she wrote the details on her form. Then, because she was a kindly woman and could sense how much her new client wanted to take possession, she added that with Mr Prendergast to support her it shouldn't be too long before she could move in.

'Can you give me some idea how long it might be?' Francesca asked, trying not to sound too eager because that wouldn't have been kind to Agnes.

'All depends on how quickly your referees get back to us,' the agent said. 'The flat's ready for occupation now, as you saw. It's just a matter of dotting the 'i's'. Probably about a month. Two at the outside. Certainly no more.'

As they left the office and strolled along the familiar, friendly High Street, Francesca began to think aloud. 'I shall need to buy some furniture,' she said, 'and curtains and rugs and that sort of thing. It's just as well I sold the mermaid. I'd never have been able to do all this if I hadn't.'

'Good old mermaid,' Agnes said. 'Let's have a spot of lunch and then we'll go shopping.'

Her easy, uncomplaining friendship was so touching that Francesca was gripped with conscience pangs all over again. 'You *are* good to me,' she said 'I mean, I'm moving out, sort of leaving you and . . .'

'Don't start all that again,' Agnes said, sternly. 'You are *not* leaving me. You're setting up home on your own.

You'll come and see me, won't you.'

'Of course. Often. I've still got your portrait to paint now I've got the canvas and everything.'

'Well there you are then. Let's have a sandwich and then we'll go to Shoreham and get cracking on this furniture of yours. I like shopping. And I know just the place for it.'

It was a huge shopping complex with all the major department stores within easy reach of one another and autumn sales in every furniture department.

'That's a bit of luck,' Francesca said.

Agnes laughed at her. 'They have sales all the year round,' she said. 'I haven't seen a sofa at its "full" price for years. Come on. What d'you fancy?'

By the end of the afternoon Francesca was foot-sore and desperate for tea but she'd bought all the basic furnishings for the flat and left instructions that it was all to be held until she knew her completion date.

'Won't we have some tales to tell our Henry on Friday,' Agnes said as they drove home. 'It'll be quite a party.'

It was and it began with a positive explosion of champagne and a chorus of congratulations 'to our new artist and her mermaid!' So much champagne and so many congratulations that Francesca grew pink with pleasure and embarrassment and, as more and more people flocked around her to tell her how glad they were she was part of the firm, she began to look around for someone to come and rescue her. Agnes was on the other side of the room talking to Henry and, although she caught sight of Molly through the crush and tried to send her an eye message for help, Molly just waved her champagne flute and mouthed, 'Congrats!' and stayed where she was. And there were three more people bearing down on her, champagne in hand.

'Rescue me!' a voice said in her ear.

For a bewildered second she thought it was someone reading her mind but then she turned her head and saw the fat young man from the castle. Brad who was christened Kenneth. Oh for heaven's sake! How did he get here? 'Hello!' she said and she knew her voice was cold.

He didn't seem to notice. 'You don't know how glad I am to see you,' he said, taking her by the arm and turning her away from the advancing hordes. 'Friendly face sort of thing. I don't know a soul here. Not a single soul! I was beginning to think I'd have to hide behind the curtain.'

'You must know Henry,' she said to him. Not a single soul seemed a bit over the top. 'I mean he must have invited you.'

'No, I don't,' he said, edging her towards the French windows. 'Wouldn't know him from Adam.'

She didn't know much about Henry herself except that he was kindly and generous and a good boss but she didn't think he was the sort of person who kept open house. 'Then how did you get here?' she asked, stepping out of the room into the garden. It was cool and a great deal quieter out there.

'He invited my aunt and *she* brought me,' he explained. 'I didn't know it was going to be a big affair or I wouldn't have come. I mean I don't know a single soul. And look at them all.'

'They're very nice people,' she told him. 'They don't bite.'

And as if to prove her point, Babs and Reggie drifted out through the French windows to kiss her and congratulate her.

93

'My dear,' Babs said, tossing the trailing end of her chiffon scarf over her shoulder, 'I'm so happy for you.'

'Didn't I say you were an artist?' Reggie said, leaning forward to kiss her.

'Actually,' Babs said, correcting him but making eyes at him at the same time, 'Henry said she was an artist and you agreed with him.'

'Amounts to the same thing,' Reggie said affably. 'You *are* an artist and now you've got a job with the firm and the mermaid's going to save its fortune or so they've been telling me. Henry's cock a whoop.' Then he noticed Brad. 'You haven't got any champagne young feller,' he said. 'Must put that right. Hang on a tick.' And he ambled back into the room again.

Francesca was digesting what he'd just said. Was the firm in trouble? Was that what he meant? Or was it just the sort of extravagant talk you get at parties? It hadn't looked as though it was in trouble. But there wasn't time to think it through. She had to introduce the two people he'd left standing on either side of her as they were both obviously expecting it. 'This is Brad, Babs,' she said. 'He's come with his aunt. Brad this is Babs, Henry's nearest neighbour.'

'Half a mile up the road,' Babs said, shaking his hand, 'which passes for near hereabouts. Who's your aunt? Do we know her?'

'Tall woman,' Brad said. 'In a fluffy sort of white blouse thingy. Long face. Looks like a poodle.'

While Francesca was thinking what an unkind description it was, Babs was peering into the room. 'I can't see anyone in a fluffy blouse,' she said. 'Not that I can see very much. They're all on the move. Are they coming out for supper, do you think? Yes. Yes. That's what it is. They're coming out for supper.'

Which they were and, naturally enough, the first person through the French window was Henry, leading the way, with Agnes beside him.

'Ah there you are!' he said beaming at Francesca. 'I wondered where you'd got to. Come on. Can't have supper without the guest of honour.'

'No, quite right,' Babs said, nodding at him. 'I should think not.' She gave Francesca a little push towards her new boss.

'Guest of honour?' Brad said, but Francesca was already walking away from him following Agnes and Henry to the serving table. If he was going to say unkind things about his aunt, let him make his own introductions.

The food was every bit as good as last time, the wine as copious and the conversation at Henry's table as lively. This time it was about the current spate of trashy television and was very funny but, despite the humour, Francesca's mind kept drifting off to other things. Was the firm really in trouble? Did they really expect her mermaid to rescue it? Was that why Henry had taken her on? He *had* said it would sell. All over Great Britain, he'd said. If that was what he was hoping for, it was a putting a heavy responsibility on her shoulders. What if it *didn't* sell? There was no accounting for taste. Or worse, what if she couldn't paint it over and over again? It wouldn't be the same as painting it for the first time and she might do it badly. Eventually, she lost track of the conversation altogether and found herself sitting mute and puzzled and feeling horribly uncomfortable as everybody round the table looked at her, obviously waiting for an answer to something they'd just said.

'Sorry,' she said, trying not to blush. 'I missed that one.'

'She's in a world of her own,' Henry said in his avuncular way. And changed the subject. 'Who's for a sweet?'

As they all strolled off towards the serving table, he put his arm round Francesca's shoulders. 'Don't worry,' he said.

'I'm not,' she said, trying to sound convincing and failing. 'I mean. . . .' She couldn't admit to worrying because that would mean asking him if the firm really *was* in trouble and this wasn't the time or the place for that sort of conversation. 'It's just I'm not used to being a guest of honour.'

'First time nerves,' he said. 'You'll get used to it. Wait till your mermaid goes on sale. Now then what do you fancy? The profiteroles look good.'

'Oh!' a voice squealed beside them. 'Profiteroles. I just *love* them.'

Francesca turned her head, glad of an opportunity to talk to someone else and found that she was standing beside a woman who looked like a poodle. She had very pale blonde hair arranged in a bun on the top of her head, small brown eyes and false eyelashes, a long broad nose in a very long pale face, and she was wearing white slacks and a white blouse made of some fluffy material that looked so much like curly fur that Francesca was almost tempted to pat it. Then she had such an overwhelming need to giggle that she had to turn her head and concentrate on the sweets on order to control herself.

'Do you know one another?' Henry asked, ever the attentive host.

'I know who *you* are,' the poodle said, looking at Francesca. 'You're Francesca Jones, aren't you, the *artist*. I'm Clara. God-awful name, but that's parents for you.'

Francesca said 'Pleased to meet you,' but kept her eyes on the food.

Clara didn't seem to notice. She was giving her attention to Henry, batting her false eyelashes at him and nodding her head so that her pompom trembled. 'I never thanked you, my dear,' she said, 'for letting me bring that *awful* nephew of mine. I *do* appreciate it. If I'd left him at home it would have been a *tip* when I got back. He's got *absolutely* no sense of propriety. I never *knew* such a boy. He's just been kicked out of another job. Did I tell you that? No surprise to me. He's absolutely bone idle. Never done an honest day's work in his *life*. And so *greedy*. You'd never believe. It's like having a *locust* in the house. Oh you've got a trifle too! I couldn't have both could I?'

'Feel free,' Henry said and grinned at Francesca while the lady was piling her plate.

And Francesca, having put a modest helping of trifle on her own plate, feeling abstemious and sensible, looked across the table straight into the self-justified grin of the young man called Kenneth/Brad. 'See what I mean?' he mouthed at her. Maybe I misjudged him, she thought. If he doesn't like his aunt very much, maybe he's got reason. She certainly doesn't like him. And she *is* like a poodle.

The party improved considerably after that, sweetened by trifle and trifling talk. As she walked about the gardens with Henry and Agnes after the meal, talking to people who greeted her like old friends, Francesca became philosophical. It was no good worrying about whether the firm was in trouble or whether she would be any good at her new job. She'd find that out on Monday. And in a few weeks time she would be moving into her flat and putting her new furniture in place and unpacking all her things again. Much better to concentrate on that. Packing and unpacking she *could* do. She'd done enough of it, God knows, when she was living with Jeffrey.

It was very late by the time the party finally came to an end and she and Agnes walked rather unsteadily to their car, giggling and holding on to one another's arms. There was a shadowy figure leaning against the bonnet, silhouetted by moonlight, fat legs sticking out before him.

Agnes squinted at him. 'Who's that?' she said.

'It's only me, Miss Potts,' the young man said and stood up to smile at Francesca. 'Come to offer my services to this lovely lady. I hear you're moving house.'

Francesca was surprised and not pleased. 'How do you know that?'

'My spies are everywhere,' he said. 'Nothing escapes my net. Thing is, I was wondering if you'd like a helping hand. Fetch and carry. That sort of thing.'

Francesca didn't want his help at all. 'I've got rather a lot of stuff,' she said, hoping it would put him off.

It didn't. 'Say no more,' he told her. 'I'm just the man you need. What time shall I arrive?'

'We don't have a moving date yet,' Agnes told him sternly. 'You're being a bit previous, young man.'

'I'll be there,' he said to Francesca.

'You'll have to watch that one,' Agnes warned, watching him as he went swaggering off along the drive. 'He's too cocky by half.'

'Don't worry,' Francesca said, as she slid into the car. 'He might be cocky now but you should hear him when he whinges. Then it's all *"Pity me! Pity me! I'm a poor diddums. Nobody loves me."* And I've heard all that before with Jeffrey. I shan't get caught twice. I'll let him carry the packing cases but that's as far as it'll go.'

'I'm very glad to hear it,' Agnes said, as she eased into the passenger seat and tucked her skirt in after her. 'You've got far too much talent to waste your life with some idle great lump of a man.' She waited until Francesca had edged her car through the drive and out into the lane and then she said, 'I wonder what happened to the other one.'

'No idea,' Francesca said. 'Like I told you, he's history.'

'I must say I'd have liked to have seen his face when he got home to an empty flat,' Agnes said. 'I'd have enjoyed that.'

She would have enjoyed the sight of his face at that moment.

He was sitting on the sofa in his empty flat surrounded by the smelly debris of a take-away Chinese, checking his Barclaycard statement. When he'd opened the letter that morning and seen the total, he'd dismissed it with a snort of disbelief. He couldn't possibly have got into so much debt. He wasn't extravagant. They must have made a mistake. But now he was reading it carefully, checking it item by item and what he was discovering was making him scowl like a gargoyle. In the present state of his finances, he was going to have a job to find the minimum payment, never mind shifting any of the debt. It was astronomical. And over half of it had been run up entertaining fucking useless clients, which had been a fucking waste of money. If only some fool would take an order for his coloured concrete. There must be someone somewhere with a bit of fucking imagination.

But even as he raged and scowled at the figures and bit his pen, he knew his concrete was a failure and that nobody would take it. There was nothing for it. He would have to find another line and find it PDQ. As if he hadn't got enough to do. If he had someone to look after him and cook him decent meals it would be easier. But thanks to that useless Fran, he was on his own and had to do every mortal thing for himself. He was sick to death of making his own tea, and getting into a crumpled bed, and the washing up was endless and so was washing clothes and ironing the damned things but he could hardly go to a board meeting in a dirty shirt. It was all so unnecessary. It could all have been avoided if she'd shown some fucking sense. She didn't have to go walking off like that. They could have patched things up if she'd made the effort and then he wouldn't be in such debt. It would serve her right if he found someone else.

'Life is so fucking unfair,' he said to the curtains. 'First Nancy and the girls treating me like shit and now Fran buggering off and leaving me all on my own. It's enough to make you weep.' He didn't know when he'd felt so sorry for himself. 'There's no justice,' he told the curtains. 'No justice in the world.'

But the curtains were dry-eyed.

'Now I shall have to go and get some crummy job to pay the bills,' he told them miserably. 'Stacking shelves in fucking Tesco I expect and I'm a cut above stacking fucking shelves. There's no justice at all.'

CHAPTER 7

THE MERMAID WAS swimming strongly, plunging through the rolling waves, her pale body gleaming like pearl against the swelling walls of green water, her long tail threshing and showering spray. It was all Francesca could do to keep her in sight, leave alone catch up with her although she was straining every sinew, her arms and legs dragging with fatigue. 'Don't go!' she called. 'Please don't go!' But the mermaid shook her tangled hair and swam on.

It was so important to keep her in sight. More important than anything else but that great fishy tail was moving with such speed and strength it was more and more impossible to do it. Oh make an effort! Try harder!

She sensed a shadow behind her and turned her head, feeling afraid, and saw that it was Jeffrey, sitting in a motor boat and glaring at her, those awful eyebrows a solid line of disapproval. 'Stupid fool!' he shouted. 'You'll never make it. Face it. You're not good enough. Don't even try!'

She shrieked back at him, still swimming with all the strength she had left. 'Go away! Go right away. I hate you!' But then she saw that the mermaid had put on speed and she called out again. 'I didn't mean you!

Mermaid, dear, I didn't mean you! Please don't go! Oh please, please don't go!'

The water was looming over her head. She was sinking, losing the power to swim, struggling for breath. And Jeffrey was sneering at her. 'Oh please! Please!'

She woke with a palpable start and for a few seconds she lay quite still trying to work out where she was. Heavy rain was rattling against the bedroom window and beyond the streaming panes the roses and honeysuckles were dripping and dishevelled. And she knew that it was Monday morning and that she was due to start work at Prendergast Potteries. And she was full of anxiety.

Agnes was stirring the porridge when she drooped down to breakfast. 'What's up?' she said as she dished up.

'Bad dreams,' Francesca told her and shivered as the residue swam in her memory.

'Just as well I made porridge then,' Agnes said and she put a steaming dish of it on the table. 'Get that inside you and you'll feel a hundred per cent better. Guaranteed. Says so on the box!'

Francesca picked up her spoon and shivered again.

'Oh dear!' Agnes said, filling her own dish. 'It *was* a bad dream. Tell you what, eat your porridge and tell me all about it and I'll analyze it for you.'

'Analyze it?'

'Best way to knock a bad dream on the head,' Agnes said cheerfully.

So Francesca did as she was told and by the time she'd drunk her tea and finished the porridge and the story she was grinning. 'Yes,' she said, putting down her spoon, 'I see what you mean.'

Agnes grinned back at her. 'Told you,' she said. 'So

what are you really worried about? It's something to do with our mermaid, that's clear, but what is it exactly?'

'It's painting her on china,' Francesca confessed. 'I've never painted on china before and I'm not sure I can do it. I mean I wouldn't like to let them all down.'

'You won't let them all down,' Agnes said, refilling their mugs.

'Yes but I might, mightn't I? And I shan't know until I've tried and failed. . . .'

'Or not.'

'Or not,' Francesca agreed, looking at her empty dish. 'Either way it'll be too late by the time I find out.'

'True,' Agnes said, putting the teapot back in its stand. 'I suppose it's no good me telling you that you won't fail.' And when Francesca grimaced. 'No, obviously not. So all right, I'll tell you something else instead. Henry wouldn't have given you the job if he hadn't been sure you could do it and he's employed dozens of artists, so he should know. He's got an instinct for picking talent. Never failed him. Fact, I've never seen him make a bad judgement in all the years I've known him.'

Francesca looked across the table at her friend's honest, loving expression, at those capable hands curved around the warmth of the teapot, at the reassuring ease of her eccentric blue skirt and her old-fashioned blouse with its pearl buttons and all those neat Edwardian pleats, and she yearned to be persuaded of the truth of what she was saying.

'Well yes,' she said.' You could be right. It's just . . .'

'You've still got that wretched Jeffrey on your back,' Agnes said in her trenchant way. 'High time you shook him off. Or have I got to fetch the lawn mower to him?'

'You'd have a job. He was in a boat.'

'Don't make difficulties,' Agnes said grinning at her.

'Anything's possible in a dream.'

'Or on a train,' Francesca said, remembering. 'We ended up with an elephant.'

'Exactly. Let's have some toast shall we?'

How easily she comforts, Francesca thought, as Agnes cut two slices from the loaf, and how sensible she is. And she began to think she might be able to paint the mermaid after all. Maybe I'll ask Molly if she can get someone to show me how it's done.

Molly was waiting for her in the lobby, standing by the entrance and gazing out into the rain. 'What weather,' she said. 'Glad you've got a brolly. You'd have been drowned else. It's chucking it down. There's stands for them over there.' And when Francesca had given her umbrella a shake and tucked it inside the nearest stand, she said, 'All set?' and led the way through the workshop to the artists' work-benches where she produced a mop cap and an overall and gave them to her newest recruit.

'First day takes a bit of getting used to,' she said in her cheerful way. 'Always too much to learn on a first day. Not to worry. There's no rush. We'll give you a hand. Now that's your first plate, all ready for you. And there's your paints and your stencil.'

'Stencil?' Francesca said looking at it.

'You fix it right across the plate, like this,' Molly explained, 'and then you dust it with charcoal, like this, and when you take it off again, like this, there's the outline of your mermaid and all you've got to do is paint her. Simples!'

'So that's how it's done,' Francesca said, perching herself on her stool.

'That's how part of it's done,' Molly said. 'That way the images are all the same size and in the same position and we get a matching set. Good luck. Give me a shout if there's anything else you need.' And she walked briskly off to the other end of the shed.

Left on her own at her unfamiliar work station, with the three other artists on either side of her all disconcertingly hard at work, Francesca chose her first brush and, after staring at the naked plate for several minutes, gathered her courage, arranged her original painting on the desk, took a deep breath and started to paint. It was easier than she expected although when she sat back and looked at the picture she'd created, she wasn't happy with it. The eyes weren't right and neither were the scales.

She was scowling at it when she became aware that she was surrounded by people and looked round to see who they were. All three of the artists, Molly, six people she didn't know and Paul, who was grinning at her.

'Now that's something,' he said. 'Mr P'll love it.'

'It's not quite right,' Francesca said, self-deprecating as always. 'I don't like the eyes and the scales are. . . . I mean, what I'm saying is, it needs work. I'm not happy with it. I'd rather Hen – um – Mr P didn't see it yet awhile. Not as it is.'

'I can't see anything wrong with it myself,' Paul said. 'I think it's stunning.'

There was a murmur of agreement.

'So do I,' Molly said. 'And you needn't worry about Mr P. He'll love it. Anyway he's with Mr Norris this morning, putting the world to rights, so he won't be seeing anything except balance sheets. Time for coffee, I think.'

*

Mr P was arguing with his accountant. It didn't look like an argument, for he was speaking gently and looked like his usual relaxed self, sitting back in his chair with his tie loosened, his hands behind his head and coffee on the

105

desk in front of him, but it was serious for all that and Liam Norris knew it.

'I wouldn't be much of an accountant if I didn't point out the risks,' he said.

'Of course,' Henry said, equably. 'That's your job. You point out the risks. I take them. That's mine.'

Liam smiled at that. 'I still say I'd be happier if we could halve the outlay,' he said, rubbing the side of his face, which was a telling sign of how anxious he was. 'We have to bear this recession in mind. Sales could be slow and publicity on this scale will be costly.'

'I'm offering them "Magic on your table",' Henry said, quoting from the advertisement he'd designed. 'They won't be able to resist.'

'We can't second guess the market,' Liam said, rubbing his face again. 'Especially in a recession.'

'Trust me,' Henry said. 'It'll be the best dinner service we've ever produced. They'll buy it in scores.'

'Well I hope you're right,' Liam said, but his voice was doubtful.

'Actually,' Henry said honestly, for he *was* taking a huge risk, 'so do I.'

Liam accepted that his advice wasn't going to be taken, sensible though it was. 'When will you have a full service ready for the photographer?' he asked.

'As soon as Francesca can finish it,' Henry told him.

'Week?' Liam asked. 'Fortnight?'

'As soon as,' Henry said. 'We mustn't rush the girl. She's an artist.'

*

The artist took fifteen days of concentrated effort until her first dinner service was completed to her satisfaction and ready for the photographer and by then she was completely exhausted. But it was a rewarding moment to

106

see it all laid out on a table set with a new white cloth, with a vase of white flowers beside it, and to watch as her new friends and workmates gathered round to see the first shot being taken and applauded when it was. Even *she* was proud of what she'd achieved for it did look good, now that the plates were gold rimmed and bright under the lights. And the vegetable dishes were splendid. She'd made a really good job of *them*. All in all it was a happy way to spend the last moments of her first fortnight at work.

'Superb,' Henry said, standing beside her with his hand on her shoulder.

'I hope it sells,' she said, still looking at it.

'Like hot cakes,' he told her. 'Wait till you see the advertisement. It'll keep us in work for months. Take my advice and have a good rest this weekend. You'll be hard at it again on Monday.'

'I'm moving into my flat this weekend,' she said.

'In that case,' he said, 'cancel my advice. But try not to work too hard.'

'I'll do my best,' she said. But she was thinking what bad timing it was for she could actually have done with a rest after such a lot of work, a chance to get up late and sit out in Agnes' garden while there was still sunshine to sit in, maybe even paint something for fun. On the other hand she *did* want to move into her flat and what Agnes called 'the small van' was ordered to take her things and was coming 'first thing'.

It arrived before she and Agnes had finished breakfast and, two minutes after the removal men had started to fill it, a strange car turned in at the drive, its wing mirror brushing the laurel. They watched as it stopped behind the van. And Brad/Kenneth swung his chubby legs out of the driver's seat and stood before them on the drive.

'Come to offer my services, fair lady,' he said. 'Morning Miss Potts.'

'How did you know it was today?' Francesca asked. She was quite cross to see him. She'd got enough to do for one day without having to listen to him whining about how hard his life was.

'I have my spies,' he said. 'I'm odd job boy for Chazza here.' And he grinned at the driver. 'Isn't that right, Chaz.'

'Only for the day, mind,' Chaz said. 'And only if you pull your weight.'

'You know me,' Brad said, following him into the house.

'I gather you didn't know he was coming,' Agnes said, frowning at his back.

'No,' Francesca said, feeling annoyed. 'I didn't.'

'Well he'd better be useful,' Agnes said, sternly. 'Work him hard. That's my advice. And don't let him think he's moving in with you.'

Francesca made a grimace. 'Oh per-lease!' she said.

'Watch him, that's all,' Agnes said, walking back to the kitchen. 'There's altogether too much of that young man.'

But in fact he worked very hard that day, carrying in boxes and cases, and when the van was gone, shifting the new furniture about, making tea, hanging curtains, even popping out for a take-away late in the evening, saying 'You stay here and put your feet up. Leave it to me. I know where the best places are.'

Of course, she didn't put her feet up. There was still the bed to make, which she could hardly have done while he was around, and then there were more clothes to unpack and the knives and forks to find and the mirror to hang in a suitable place in the living room.

When she finally sat down at her new dining table with her familiar plates set out before her, she felt tired, but so pleased with herself that fatigue didn't matter. A home of my own, she thought, looking round at it. All of my own. I can eat what I like and listen to music when I like and paint when I like and go to bed when I like and there'll never be anyone to stop me. I couldn't have more freedom if I really *were* the mermaid. I hope he hurries up with that food. I'm starving.

It was another half an hour before Brad got back and when she lifted the take-away cartons from their plastic bag, they were barely lukewarm. 'Sorry about that,' he said airily, when she frowned. 'Met up with some mates and they would talk. You know how it is. We can pop 'em in the microwave though, sort of hot 'em up. Won't take a minute. No problem.'

'I haven't got a microwave,' Francesca told him, rather crossly. 'Just sit down and let me dish up. I'm starving.'

'Sorry about that Boss,' he said, 'but they *would* talk. I *did* get us some beer.'

She was peeling off the lids and didn't look at him. 'Sit down and eat it,' she ordered, 'before it's stone cold. We've wasted enough time as it is.'

She was quite startled when he flung himself on his knees at her feet and spread out his arms towards her dramatically. 'Have pity on your devoted slave, most beautiful lady!' he begged. 'I would go to the darkest corners of the earth for you. Have pity!'

It was so ridiculous she didn't know whether to be cross or laugh at him. 'Get up do!' she said. 'This food'll congeal if we muck about any longer.'

But he grabbed her hand and held on to it which made her cross. 'I am your devoted slave,' he said. 'Your word is my command.'

She was very cross by now but she held on to her self-control. 'Well I'm eating mine,' she told him. 'If you want to play silly buggers that's up to you. I'm hungry.'

He got up and dusted down his trousers. 'Silly buggers!' he said to the mirror in tones of feigned outrage. 'I declare my undying love and she calls it silly buggers!'

'I'll dish yours up, shall I?' she said mildly.

'You know your trouble,' he said as he sat down at the table. 'Your trouble is you've got no romance in your soul.'

'Romance is greatly overrated,' she told him. 'I'd rather have a warm meal.'

'Oh well,' he said, sighing extravagantly. 'Back to the real world. D'you want some of this beer?' And he smiled at her.

The smile made her feel a bit ashamed of herself. She was treating him unkindly and he *had* been a help to her even if he *was* fat. 'Eat your meal and I'll make some coffee when we've finished.' she said.

'You're a star!' he said, opening the first can and handing it across the table to her.

They sat over the coffee until past midnight, even though she was aching for sleep. She should have seen the danger signs as she poured the first mug and handed it across the table to him. He was sitting just a little too comfortably in his chair, gazing at her just a little too earnestly and reminding her of someone she didn't like. But she was too tired to force her mind to work out who it was.

'You don't know how good it is to have a friend like you,' he said.

'We've hardly known one another long enough to be friends,' she said, hoping to put him off.

He wasn't put off in the least. 'But it's not time that counts, is it?' he said earnestly. 'It's how we treat one another. I set a lot of store by how people treat me. It's what comes of being treated so badly when I was young. And you'd never believe how badly treated I was.'

She sipped her coffee, closed her eyes with sheer fatigue and then opened them again and said 'No' because he seemed to be expecting her to say something.

'I had a terrible time of it,' he said, leaning forward towards her. 'You'd never believe the half. Looking back on it and between you and me, I think they were going out of their way to put me down and make me miserable, though for the life of me I can't see why they should. I mean when you think about it, what's the point of making a child miserable? They said they were toughening me up. Cold baths in the middle of winter. And I mean cold. Icy. I ask you. Was that kind? It makes me shiver to remember.' He gave an elaborate shiver. 'Out for a run every single rotten day of my life. Never mind if it was raining – or snowing even – off I had to go. It's a wonder I didn't get pneumonia. And if I didn't do it I got a clip round the ear. And then there was the porridge. Porridge for breakfast every morning. Every single rotten morning. Usually lumpy. They said it was healthy. It was to make me grow big and strong. All that sort of bosh. Mind you I did grow big and I'm very strong. Well you've seen that today, haven't you? Yes. You could hardly be off seeing. But it sure as hell wasn't the porridge.'

His voice droned on and after a while Francesca closed her eyes and stopped listening. It was altogether too much effort. From time to time she forced her eyes open again and looked at him to show that she was still awake, and then a few words penetrated her fatigue. 'Nag, nag, nag all the time. I used to feel I couldn't do a thing right. Fact, to tell you the truth, I was glad when they took themselves off to rotten Australia. They said I could go with them or stay with my aunt. So I stayed with my aunt. That was a fool's trick and no mistake because she's worse. Well you saw that at the party. She puts me down all the time. Never has a good word to say for me. I'm lazy, I'm bone idle, I turn the house into a tip, I deserve everything that's coming to me . . .' But once she'd closed her eyes again, he was just a wasp buzzing in a corner. If only he'd drink up his coffee and go home.

She woke with a start and for a few bewildered seconds she couldn't think where she was or why she'd been asleep sitting up in her chair. Then she realized that someone was crying, in great gulping sobs, and she looked across the room towards the sound and saw that Brad had his head in his hands and was weeping with abandon, his shoulders heaving. And before her reason could wake and rescue her, her overactive sense of pity kicked in and she leant towards him to try to comfort him.

'Don't cry,' she said.

She knew it was a mistake as soon as the words were out of her mouth. He looked up at her with such a tragic face, it was painful to see it, and made a grab at her hand as if he was drowning and needed to be pulled ashore.

'You don't know what it means to me to have a friend like you,' he said, earnestly. 'All these years I've been so unhappy. You'd never believe how unhappy I've been.' He stopped and gulped, choking back tears. 'And now I've found you. You're like a beacon in my life. I don't know how to thank you.'

What could she possibly say? She was trapped in her pity for him. 'It's very late,' she said, glancing at her clock. 'Past midnight. I think we ought to call it a day.

You'll feel better in the morning.'

'I can come back, though, can't I?' he said. 'I can see you again in the morning. Please say I can see you again in the morning.'

She was too tired to resist the pressure he was putting on her, and she didn't have the heart to tell him she'd rather be on her own, not after all the sad things he'd been telling her about and the way he'd cried. 'I suppose so,' she said and she sounded as weary as she felt.

He didn't seem to notice her fatigue. 'I'll see you then,' he said and walked to the door. At last.

I shall sleep for a week, she thought, as she finally crumpled into bed. She was wrong. She was awake at half past four.

The room was full of light, washed and refreshed by the delicate pale gold of early morning. The window sill glistened as if it was wet, the creamy walls were patterned with the shifting, smoke-blue shadows of leaves and branches and, beyond the window, birds were singing in a chorus of complicated, full-throated trebles. The combination of movement, sound and colour was so unexpected and delicious that for a few seconds she lay where she was and enjoyed it. Then she realized that she was watching a sunrise and got up and walked into the living room and out onto the balcony to see more of it. It was a revelation. For now she was receiving the full impact of the sumptuous colour in the skies, long swathes of orange, scarlet, lemon yellow and pale, pale green interlacing and drifting as she watched while above them the lighter blue of day eased into the darker tones of night. In the rising light, trees took colour and changed shape but the river was white as polished silver and the two swans sailing downstream in their imperturbable way were gilded like golden toys. She had a paintbrush in her hand almost before she realized what she was doing. Oh, quick, quick, she urged herself. Catch it before it fades.

She had no idea how long she painted. Time enough to make two passable sketches, to catch the colour of the swans and at least part of that amazing sky. Someone came knocking at the door but she ignored them. She wasn't even interested enough to wonder who it was, for by that time there were skeins of colour in the river too. It was all too good to miss. It wasn't until the knocking began again that she bestirred herself to answer and then she wandered to the door with her paintbrush still in her hand.

It was Brad with croissants, peaches and an enormous bar of chocolate. 'Breakfast,' he said, 'because I'll bet you haven't had any.'

He was right. She'd quite forgotten about eating and seeing the croissants made her aware that she was hungry. So they carried her occasional table out onto the terrace and breakfasted in style and sunshine. It was easy to forgive him for interrupting her when he'd provided a feast to start the day and anyway the sunrise was over.

When the last crumb had been eaten, she cleared the cups and plates and washed them up, wondering how she could get rid of him. There was still a lot to do and she wanted to get on with it in her own way and her own time. But he seemed to be impervious to any sort of hint.

'Right,' he said, rolling up his sleeves. 'I'll start on those shelves, shall I?'

'I can manage,' she told him.

But she was wasting her breath. 'Not to worry,' he said, smiling a superior smile. 'I'll have it done for you in a jiffy. You watch.'

So as she couldn't see how to stop him, she let him

put up the shelves, while she cleaned her brushes and hoped that he'd go home when he'd done it. But no, when all the shelves had been tested and pronounced 'secure', he unpacked the rest of her kitchen ware, without asking her or telling her, and then took the cardboard boxes out to the salvage bin, as if he were the man of the house, and when the flat was cleared to his satisfaction, he fixed her portable radio and the TV remote. Fran grew crosser by the minute. He was trying to be helpful, she had to admit that, but he was cutting into her precious independence. She could have fixed the shelves herself – and the remote and the radio.

She was tidying her clothes in the bedroom, more to get away from him than because it needed doing, when someone rang the doorbell. This time she was glad to think she'd got company and she left the rest of her jumpers unfolded and went off to see who it was. But he was already calling 'Don't worry! I'll get it!' and opening the door as if he was in residence.

'Miss Potts!' he said. 'How nice to see you.'

Agnes gave him a look that would have withered an oak and strode past him into the flat. 'Me dear,' she said to Francesca, 'I've come to take you to lunch. Leave what you're doing. It'll be there when you get back.' It was like the cavalry arriving.

'I'll just get my bag,' Francesca said, gratefully. 'Won't be a minute.'

Agnes was turning her formidable attention on Brad. 'You'd better be getting back, hadn't you,' she said. 'Your aunt's been asking for you.'

She took his breath away. 'My aunt?' he said, looking bewildered.

'Your aunt,' she told him firmly. 'You know the one. Your aunt Clara. The one you live with.' And she opened

115

the door for him. 'Look sharp. You don't want to keep her waiting.'

He went out obediently – what else could he do? – just as Francesca was walking back into the room with her bag and a jersey.

'How did you do that?' she said to Agnes. 'I thought I'd never get rid of him.'

'You're too soft,' Agnes said, watching to make sure he was getting into his car. 'Right. He's gone. Come on. I've got a sirloin cooking.'

CHAPTER 8

Henry's eye-catching advertisement for Prendergast Potteries' new dinner service appeared at the most appropriate time. It came out in all the classy magazines in the week after the first ten sets had been completed and were ready for dispatch. Copies were pinned on the staff notice board at mid morning break and instantly gathered a crowd. There was much happy admiration for how splendid they looked.

'Wow!' Sarah said, her blue eyes wide. 'They're well good. They must have cost an arm and a leg. At least.'

They laughed at her happily. 'And quite right too,' Molly told her. 'Good advertising brings in the business. The doom an' gloom boys won't be so quick to write us off now.'

It was a chance for Francesca to ask her worrying question. 'Have they been?' she said.

'There's always gossip,' Molly told her, 'especially when there's a recession. It gets more dog-eat-dog then. But this should do the trick. If I'm any judge we shall be working our socks off in the next few weeks.' Then, having reminded herself of what they should be doing, she got them back to business. 'Time for work, everybody. Chop chop. Break's over.'

Francesca returned to her latest copy of the mermaid, thinking hard. Then it was true. They *had* been in trouble and they *were* hoping the mermaid would pull their fortunes round. It wasn't a surprise because she'd expected it since the party, but even so it was quite a responsibility and she wasn't at all sure how she felt about that. She was pleased to think that her image could have so much power – or so much potential power – but it worried her too, in case the advertisement didn't pull in the orders they wanted and needed. Not that there was anything she could do about it if it didn't. But oh, she thought, picking up her brush, imagine if it does. I do so hope it'll work for us. Mr P deserves it to work. We all deserve it, come to that. And as she painted the first sweeping stroke, she wondered when the orders would start coming in and how they would cope if there really were a lot of them. Just as well I've learnt to paint at speed, she thought. It had taken her nearly two days before she'd fined down her original to the smallest number of brush strokes that were absolutely necessary for a copy and, although it had grieved her to see her painting reduced to a design, she'd grown so accustomed to it as she'd painted it day after day that now she barely noticed the change. Go girl, she said to the mermaid. Make it work for us.

The advertisement was pinned on the cork wall behind Henry's desk like a talisman. It was the brightest thing in the room, its expensive sheen catching the sun and the attention, and when he'd first put it up it had filled him with such hope and optimism he'd grown warm just looking at it. But, as the days passed and became a week and then two and there were no orders, he grew more and more pessimistic, although he did his best not to show it.

His work force waited for news with greater patience because they had less knowledge of the market and simply went on stacking up new sets in the store room, singing and chatting as they worked. Only Francesca, Molly and Liam Norris were concerned and they kept their opinions to themselves, Molly and Liam because they were determined not to be negative, Francesca because there was too much going on in her life to give her time to brood and worry about sales.

For a start, Brad was pestering her so much she was beginning to think she would have to say something to him about it. She'd been looking forward to the freedom of having a home of her own and he was wrecking it. The trouble was he seemed to think that because he'd helped her to move in he had the right to call whenever he felt like it and he usually felt like it at just the wrong time of the evening, when she was cooking her dinner and, what was worse, he always arrived with a present of some tatty flowers or a small box of chocolates. Which was all very well but it meant she felt bound to ask him in, because he was trying to be kind even if his timing was bad, and once he was over the doorstep, he said such complimentary things about her cooking that she felt compelled to invite him to stay to dinner which meant she had to halve her own meal. She didn't know how to deter him without being unkind. She'd tried hints but he didn't seem to hear them or he was ignoring them, the way Jeffrey always did when she said something he didn't want to hear. She was beginning to think she'd have to tell him he wasn't welcome, straight out, and that seemed harsh when he was so pathetically grateful for her attention and he'd had so many awful things to put up with when he was a child. But it couldn't go on because it was getting in the way of her new life. She

119

didn't feel she could settle down to the next picture when he was sitting in her armchair talking.

But even with all his interruptions to contend with, her painting was getting stronger and more competent by the day. The portrait of Agnes Potts was almost finished and she was really rather pleased by it. She'd caught her almost exactly as she remembered her, standing on the cliff-top with the wind tangling her hair and bellying her skirt into a rounded sail and wild flowers tumbling from the bunch she was carrying and trailing back along the path. It was a bold, strong composition which was fitting for such a bold, strong woman and yet she'd managed to catch the compassion and kindness in her face. When she took it to Agnes' house for the last minute touches on a mild Saturday morning, she felt she'd really achieved something.

'Yes,' Agnes said, looking at it intently. 'Not half bad.' And that was praise indeed.

'I'll frame it for you,' Francesca said as she cleaned her brushes.

'Thank you me dear,' Agnes said, still looking at the portrait. 'That would be kind. I shall hang it in the hall.' Then she turned away from the picture and gave Francesca one of her searching looks. 'Who are you going to paint next?'

'I'd rather like to tackle Henry,' Francesca told her. She'd been thinking about it for several weeks and the more she thought, the more tempting the idea became.

Agnes was intrigued. 'Why?' she asked, filling the kettle.

'He'd be a challenge,' Francesca told her. 'He's got two faces. A private one that you see at his parties, warm and relaxed and sort of twinkly – if that doesn't sound sloppy – it probably does but you know what I mean – and a public one we see at work. That one's stiff and formal. Almost stern. He's been wearing it a lot recently.'

Agnes understood the situation at once. 'No orders yet, is that it?' she said, settling the kettle on the Aga.

"Fraid not.'

'They'll come, me dear, 'Agnes soothed. 'Give 'em time.'

'It's beginning to be a bit of a worry though.'

'But it's not *your* worry,' Agnes said firmly. 'It's Henry's. Let him carry it. He's got broad shoulders.'

'And good hands,' Francesca said, 'I've done a few sketches of them.'

'Can I see them?' Agnes said, opening the biscuit tin.

She examined them as they drank their tea and was impressed. 'It's extraordinary how much hands can reveal someone's character,' she said. 'Is that why you always draw them first?'

'Do I?'

'That's how you started *my* portrait.'

'Yes,' Francesca admitted, sipping her tea. 'I suppose I did. So yes, I suppose I do. It's not just the hands though. I mean, it's the way they're used. The way they move. Yours are always busy. They look competent, dependable.'

'You said that when you were drawing them.'

'Yes, I did.'

'And what do you see in Henry's hands?'

Francesca was looking at two of her sketches and answered without thinking. 'Tenderness,' she said and was then horrified to find herself blushing and added a few more acceptable attributes at once, stammering a little, 'and strength, of course, confidence, dependability. They're like yours in a way, worker's hands. I don't like idle hands. They look so flabby.' And an image of Brad's

121

hands suddenly filled her mind, fat-fingered and white, lifting a forkful of her food to his mouth.

'You're right about the tenderness,' Agnes said. 'I can remember thinking that whenever I saw him with Candida. They were lovely together. It was a joy to see them. He was so gentle with her, poor woman.' She sighed. 'Cancer is a monstrous illness.'

Francesca hesitated before she spoke again. 'I know it's not my business,' she said, 'but was she ill long?'

'Three years,' Agnes told her, 'and he nursed her every second of the way.'

'Than that's the sadness you see in his face sometimes.'

'He was lost when she died,' Agnes said. 'Absolutely, totally lost. It was terrible to see. And the house was so quiet. Like a museum. I think that's why he started giving parties.'

'To fill the house.'

'To fill the house,' Agnes agreed.

'You make me want to paint him more than ever,' Francesca said, finishing her tea. 'Do you think he'd sit for me?'

'You could ask him,' Agnes said. 'There's no harm in trying. D'you want another cup?'

I could, Francesca thought. There wouldn't be any harm just asking. Of course, she had to remember that he was the boss and she might be overstepping the mark. It might not be the sort of thing an employee was supposed to do. But she *would* like to paint his portrait.

Agnes was adding more water to the teapot and looked up to see her protégée lost in thought. 'Don't worry,' she said. 'The orders'll come. They're just taking a bit longer than you all expected. That ad's much too good to be ignored. They'll start noticing it sooner or later.

Especially if he runs it for a few more weeks. As I'm sure he will.'

'We can't stop now, Liam,' Henry said, keeping his patience with an effort. 'We *must* keep up the pressure. We'll give it two more weeks. Then we'll reconsider.'

'We've been running it for a month,' Liam pointed out, 'and the costs are beginning to look prohibitive.'

The two men were arguing through their usual Monday meeting and although the proceedings seemed calm they were both in a state of controlled agitation. Liam had just presented an expense sheet that was, as he put it, 'somewhat alarming' and Henry, who'd been growing more and more alarmed as the weeks passed, was now in his most determined and recalcitrant mood.

'Two more weeks,' he said doggedly. 'If there are still no takers after that, *then* we'll reconsider. I can't stop now. There's too much riding on it.'

'Perhaps we should cut back production a tad,' Liam tried. 'We're seriously in the red.'

'That would spread alarm,' Henry told him, 'which I don't want. Not at this stage.'

'Well then at least slow it down a bit, 'Liam suggested. 'They're working flat out. The stock's building up.'

'No,' Henry decided. 'We'll leave things as they are for another week. Someone's bound to pick up on it sooner or later and then we shall need all that stock and more. Was there anything else we should consider?'

Privately, Liam thought his boss was making a mistake but he didn't comment. The decision had been made and had to be accepted. It was Henry's money and Henry's firm. But it made him feel cross just the same. 'No,' he said. 'We've done all we can for now.' Then he gathered up his files, gave Henry a nod and left the room.

He met Francesca on his way back to his office and managed to summon up a smile for her. Poor girl. It wasn't her fault that the dinner service wasn't attracting custom. And she had such a dear little face. All that fuzzy hair and her way of turning her head sideways and looking apprehensive when she asked a question.

'Is he busy?' she asked, inclining that head towards Henry's door.

'We've just finished,' he said, opening his own door. 'Worth a try.' He watched as she gave her timid knock and, on an unexpected impulse, wished her good luck as he left her.

Henry was sitting behind his desk in his shirt sleeves, scowling at the balance sheet, as if he could force it to improve by glaring at it. It was the first time Francesca had seen him without a jacket or one of his now familiar jerseys and the sight made her pause. Then she noticed that the October sunshine was casting a bright white halo all round his head and shoulders and that took her aback too. It made him look distant and formidable like a painting of some ancient patriarch, especially as there was so much tension and anger in his face. This isn't the time to bother him with requests, she thought, and she turned and put her hand on the doorknob, ready to escape.

The abrupt movement alerted him and he looked up, gathered his thoughts with an effort, and told her to come in. 'What can I do for you?' he said and tried to smile at her. But the smile was strained and he knew it even as it was on his face and was annoyed because he ought to have had his feelings under better control. Then he realized that that he'd alarmed her and that annoyed him too.

'It's nothing,' she said, apologetically, backing towards

the door. 'I mean, it's not important. It'll keep.'

The self-effacing expression on her face made him feel ashamed and he redoubled his efforts and smiled at her again, this time more easily. 'Come in and tell me about it,' he said, trying to be reassuring. 'Is it work?'

'Oh no,' she told him, sitting, rather reluctantly, in the chair opposite his desk. 'Nothing like that. Like I said, it's not important. It'll keep.'

'Now you're making me curious,' he said. 'What is it?'

She hesitated, still feeling that this wasn't the time, while he watched her and tried to look as encouraging as he could. In the end she plucked up her courage and said, 'It's just I've got a favour to ask you. Not a big one. Just something I've been thinking about. Well, wondering about really. It's been in my mind for quite a long time so it'll keep a bit longer. I mean, it's nothing important. Nothing to do with work. I could come back later.'

She's so unsure of herself, he thought, and that saddened him. It seemed wrong that she should be vulnerable and insecure when she had such talent. 'I won't bite,' he said, smiling at her. 'You're quite safe.'

It was the smile she was used to and it reassured her. But only a little. She still wasn't sure. To give herself a pause she looked away from his face and up at the wall behind his head. And there was her mermaid glowing in the warming sunlight, her lovely, free, confident mermaid, ready to swim off into the adventure of the ocean. And she remembered the moment in a clarity of sunshine and how she'd felt, aching for the same freedom, the right to live her own life, the right to be herself.

'Well,' she said. 'I've been wondering if you would let me paint your portrait. I've done Agnes' and it's come out really well. We're both quite pleased with it. She said it "wasn't half bad". Anyway what I mean is, it's sort of given me the taste for it. It wouldn't take long. Maybe a couple of sittings. When you're not too busy. I mean, you could choose the time. I could fit it in whenever you wanted. I know how busy you are. I could do some of the preliminary sketches while you were at work.' Then she stopped because his face had changed and this time really alarmingly. He'd drawn in his breath and pulled back from her almost as though she'd hit him. Oh God, she thought, what have I said?

'Look,' he said. 'I'm sorry but you've asked me for the one thing I can't give you. I don't have my picture taken, ever, not in photographs, or snaps, or pictures or anything.' Then he realized that she was looking shocked and felt he ought to try to explain. 'I can't bear it,' he said. 'Ask for anything else and I'll give it to you like a shot but not that.'

I've hit a nerve, she thought. I've been clumsy somehow. I shouldn't have asked him. I knew I shouldn't. She was washed with shame and didn't know what to say after such a bad mistake. 'It's all right,' she stammered, 'I mean, it's not important. I shouldn't have asked you. It wasn't. . . . I mean I ought to have known. . . . It was really. . . .' And she scrambled to her feet. 'Must get on or Molly'll be after me.' And fled.

As the door closed behind her, he realized that he was trembling. 'God damn it!' he said, taking his anger out on the empty room. 'Why don't those bloody fools wake up to what a bargain we're offering. It's the best ad we've ever produced. Why don't they bloody look at it?'

In a dentist's waiting room in Beckenham, Jeffrey Walmesly was looking at the ad with considerable interest. He'd been flicking through the quality magazines trying to keep his mind occupied before he had to face the dreaded chair. Not that he was nervous or cowardly or anything like that – perish the thought – but it was sensible to think of other things in a place like a dentist's. The bright colours and unusual pattern took his attention most strongly. Now there's a firm that's going places, he thought. I wonder who provides their clay. I might do some business there. A new improved clay that doesn't craze and holds its colour. He wasn't at all sure such a thing could be produced but what of that. It was the presentation that counted and he was a whizz-kid at presentation. I could buy the clay at trade prices, doctor it a bit and charge a good mark-up. I could make a killing.

The waiting room was empty except for an old man who seemed to be asleep and a woman with a toddler who was climbing over the chairs and taking all her attention. He picked up the magazine and pulled the page out as quickly and quietly as he could. The woman was alerted by the sound and looked up at him but the deed was already done. He gave her his most charming smile as he folded the page in quarters and tucked it into his pocket. This could be just the answer, he thought. All it needs is a bit of skilful salesmanship and I've got that in bucket-loads. In fact the more he thought about it, the more possible it seemed. I could make a fortune. That'll show that stupid Fran.

'Mr Walmesly,' the receptionist called in her sing-song voice. 'Surgery four.'

Fran was sitting at her work station feeling terrible. It was always the same when she'd upset someone. She was sick with guilt and remorse, wishing the words unsaid, afraid she'd done more damage than she could put right, hearing her mother's scathing voice. *'You want to mind what you're doing you stupid, clumsy girl! I don't know what I*

ever did to deserve such a great lummox. You're useless. D'you
hear me? Useless. You'll never amount to a row of beans.' Even
the memory of the words could cast her down. They'd
been said so often and so bitingly and they'd cut her to
shreds every time. And whenever she upset someone she
proved them true. First with Agnes and now with Henry.
She really should have been more sensible. She stared at
the plate with her paint brush useless in her hand and
was too miserable to move. 'You let me down that time,'
she said to the mermaid.

Molly materialized beside her, her round face crin-
kled with concern. 'You all right, kid?'

Before she came to work in Prendergast Potteries,
Francesca would have kept her misery to herself. Now
she looked up at Molly's sympathetic face and confessed.
'I've just made an awful mistake,' she said, putting her
brush down. 'Awful.'

'I can't see any mistakes,' Molly said, looking at the
plate. 'Looks perfect to me.'

'Not the plate,' Francesca said, actually smiling at the
misunderstanding. 'I've upset Mr P,' and she told Molly,
briefly but truthfully what she'd done.

'Ah!' Molly said. 'That's still going on. I thought he'd
got over it.' And when Francesca looked a question at
her, she explained. 'After Candida died, he was in such
a state he could barely talk to people. Couldn't bear to be
photographed or give interviews or anything. Liam had
to do it for him. He sort of went into hibernation.'

'Ah!' Francesca understood. 'And now I've come
bouncing in asking him to sit for a portrait. No wonder
he was upset.'

'He'll get over it,' Molly reassured, patting her arm.
'Don't take it to heart. He's got over much worse than
that.'

'But it makes me feel dreadful,' Francesca said. 'I wouldn't have hurt him for the world.'

'I tell you what we'll do,' Molly said, solving the problem since that was part of her job. 'We'll get him a special tea this afternoon and you can take it in to him and tell him you're sorry and put everything right. How would that be?'

'I don't think a tea would work,' Francesca said doubtfully. 'It was more serious than that.'

'Well we'll try it. He enjoys his tea. If it doesn't work, no harm done.'

Francesca sighed. 'This is what comes of fancying myself as a portrait painter,' she said. 'It was such fun painting Agnes. I'd never painted a portrait before and it came out really well. I was really quite pleased with it. But you see how it is. It's made me conceited. I've got too big for my boots. I should stick to plates.'

'I don't see why you should,' Molly said stoutly. 'You're an artist. Artists can do anything.'

'I wish!' Francesca said. Talking about her predicament was making her feel despondent. 'No, whichever way you look at it, I've made a right pig's ear of this. And now I've lost my model and upset him into the bargain. I should stick to plates and vegetable dishes.' And even though she was trying not to, she sighed.

Molly patted her arm again. 'If you're looking for a model,' she said, 'I'll sit for you any time.'

The offer was such a surprise it gave Francesca quite a lift. 'Really?' she said.

'You bet,' Molly said. 'I'd be honoured. I've never had my portrait painted.'

Sunlight washed into the workshop, leeching colour from the walls and turning everything in it a pale misty blue, potters' aprons, slip-wear, long shelves, moving feet, tiled floor, even the air around them. The long kiln, which she'd always thought of as solid, was pale grey with long mist blue highlights. It was the perfect back-drop for a study of Molly's sturdy figure, with those sun-browned arms and busy hands, that round face smiling, all those thick chestnut curls escaping from her cap, as if there were too much life in them to be constrained.

'I might take you up on that,' Francesca said.

'Do,' Molly grinned. 'Like I said. I'd be honoured.' And she went off to supervise the stacking.

Francesca picked up her paintbrush again and turned her attention to the blank plate on her turntable. And the mermaid flicked her iridescent tail, flickered her golden eyes and swam into the freedom of the sea.

From time to time during the rest of the morning, when she stopped painting to stretch her back and her neck, Francesca thought of Molly's portrait, collecting details for the background while the sunshine was still misting the room; here two women stacking vegetable dishes; there a row of cups, glinting; there one of the men pushing a loaded trolley, its horizontal lines echoing the long pale flanks of the kiln. By the time Molly came to collect her for lunch, the shape of the portrait was clear in her mind and she'd made her first quick sketches for it.

Molly was too preoccupied to notice it. 'Come on,' she said, 'and then we can order Henry's cakes while we're getting our lunch. Half a dozen fancies. What d'you reckon?'

But when they reached the serving counter, the cook shook her head. 'He won't be eating none a' my fancies today,' she said, looking aggrieved. 'I can tell you that fer certain sure. Nor the hotpot neither an' I made that special. Gone up to London he has. Took a dinner service, so Liam said, and then off like a flash. He'll have to have 'em tomorrer.'

Molly took her tray and eased through the crush until she found the table where Liam was sitting. 'Well come on, then,' she said to him. 'Spill the beans. Has Mr P really gone rushing off?'

Liam had a mouth full of hot pot so he just nodded.

'Where to?' Molly asked, settling at the table. 'That's not like him.'

'I don't know any more than you do,' Liam told her, mildly. 'He just came out of his office and said he was going and went.'

'He's up to something,' Molly said, darkly. 'Mark my words. It's not like our Mr P to rush off *anywhere*.'

It does seem out of character, Francesca thought. I hope it wasn't me upsetting him. She didn't say anything because that would have made her feel even more guilty than she already did, but the thought kept her quiet all through lunch and niggled in her head all afternoon, no matter how hard she tried to push it away. It was so easy to upset people, even though you didn't mean to. And he'd been so kind to her and was such a gentle man, she wouldn't have upset him for the world. She was quite glad when her working day was over and she could drive home to her nice quiet flat and be alone with her thoughts. I'll have an easy supper, she promised herself, beans on toast or something, and then I'll sketch out Molly's portrait, while the ideas are fresh.

Brad was crouched on the doorstep with his back against her front door and the most disagreeable expression etched on his face. 'You're late,' he said accusingly.

The sight of him, sitting on the step as if he had every right to be there, tipped her into tetchiness. 'Long day,' she said. 'Shift yourself. I can't reach the keyhole with

131

you all over the place.'

'Don't be like that,' he wheedled, gazing up at her earnestly. 'I've had the most terrible time today. Terrible. My aunt's thrown me out of house and home. Right out. Threw my clothes all over the lane. I've had to put them in my boot. I mean, how cruel can you get? There are times when I despair of human nature. I truly do.'

She looked at him with distaste, wishing he'd shut up and go away. 'Get up,' she said. 'I want to open the door.'

He didn't seem to notice her expression. 'I knew it would be all right once you got home,' he said, as she walked into the hall. 'You're such a star.' And before she could tell him not to, he followed her in.

'Now look,' she said, 'I've had a long day too and I'm really tired. I haven't got the energy to look after someone else.'

He was unabashed. 'Just as well I'm here then,' he said, walking into the kitchen. 'My turn to look after you. Let's have some tea, shall we. And then I'll rustle us up some supper. Unless you want a take-away. You've only got to say.'

She couldn't say anything. She just stood in her kitchen watching him fill *her* kettle and reach up for the jar containing *her* tea bags and plump himself in *her* chair with one of *her* mugs in his fat hand and she couldn't think of a thing to say although her thoughts beat in her head like birds in a net. How could anyone be so thick-skinned? She'd stopped short of telling him outright, but hadn't she made it clear she didn't want him here? She thought she had. So why couldn't he see it? And how could she get rid of him now, if his aunt had thrown him out and he was going to cook her supper?

She took the mug he offered her and sat down with a sigh. This was worse than living with Jeffrey.

'Now,' he said, 'what do you fancy for dinner?

'Peace and quiet,' she said.

'You just sit there then,' he told her in his lordly way, 'and I'll be cook.'

There didn't seem to be any way she could stop him short of physically throwing him out. He cooked what he called 'a good old fry-up' using every frying pan she possessed, ate it hungrily and seemingly unaware that she was eating very little of it and left the kitchen in such a shambles it made her feel weak just to look at it.

'We'll do the washing-up later,' he said. 'What's on telly?'

This is awful, she thought, as the television shouted and fired guns and she washed up and cleaned her kitchen. He's settling in for the night. How on earth am I going to get rid of him? But the longer she struggled to find an answer, the more she couldn't do it.

'You look all in,' he said, when she finally drooped into the living room. 'I'd have an early night if I was you. I can make up my own bed.'

'I think you ought to be going,' she said. 'Don't you.'

'Nowhere to go to, old thing,' he said. 'Like I told you, I've been thrown out. You don't mind if I stay the night, do you?'

A direct appeal made her dither. 'Well . . .' she said. 'I suppose . . .'

'That's sorted then,' he said. 'You're a star!'

She went to bed feeling as if she'd just run a marathon. And couldn't sleep. The hours crawled by, half past one, twenty to three, ten past four. I must just make sure he goes in the morning, she told herself, sternly at six o'clock. I can't put up with this.

CHAPTER 9

Henry Prendergast drove to London that morning in such a furious temper he found it quite cleansing. He'd been holding it in check all through those long, waiting weeks but Francesca's impossible request had pushed him beyond restraint. Then and oddly, when it broke, instead of making him feel ashamed of himself, as he usually did when he lost his temper, it filled him with a reckless, unstoppable energy. It was like riding a surf wave. He knew at once that he had to go to London and offer his new dinner service to a few prestigious clients in person instead of waiting for them to notice his advertisements and then sending his salesmen to display the goods in the usual gentlemanly way. And the first person he would contact would be old Johnny Makins. A good bloke, old Johnny. They'd done a lot of business in the early days. Truth-straight-out sort of man. Called a spade a spade. If anyone was going to see what a seller this service could be, Johnny would be the one. And if he couldn't take an order for it he'd know someone else who might. He dialled his number at once and fixed a meeting. By the time he walked into the restaurant they'd chosen, he was warm, happy, ridiculously confident and quite sure that he'd made the right decision.

They spent the first half hour of their reunion sharing trade gossip and enjoying one another's company just as they used to do. Johnny was much the same as he'd been in the old days, rather heavier perhaps, and a bit more thin on top, but the wit and the cynicism were undiminished. As they ate their starters, they had fun tearing various politicians apart for brown-nosing Rupert Murdoch; as they enjoyed their steaks, the spate of quizzes and 'talent' shows on television were analyzed, shredded and dismissed as 'bread and circuses'; but eventually, when his second plate was clean, Henry's impatience bubbled over and he simply couldn't wait any longer to show his old friend what he'd brought for him to see. He picked up his briefcase, carefully unpacked his precious dinner plate and laid it on the table. And then, before he could even look up to ask Johnny Makins what he thought of it, the waiter reappeared at his elbow and gave him an instant and gratifying answer.

'Oh wowie!' he said. 'That is ver' pretty plate, sir. If you don' mind for me sayin' so. I never see a plate with mermaid on. If you don' mind for me sayin' so.'

Henry grinned at him. 'I don't mind you saying so at all,' he said. 'I think it's pretty good too.'

Johnny picked up the plate and examined it while the waiter cleared the table and laid the menu in front of them again, this time rather reverently. 'Full dinner service of course,' he said. 'Who's taken it?'

'As of this moment, nobody at all,' Henry admitted.

'Which is why you're showing it to me.'

'Got it in one.'

'I'd order it like the proverbial if it was up to me,' Johnny said. 'But everything has to be run past a committee these days. What sort of ads have you taken out?'

Henry pulled four magazines from his briefcase and

passed them across the table, where they were studied knowledgeably and the various dates noted.

'It's strong,' Johnny said. 'Very strong. Quirky. Good colours. Eye catching. You've got a top-rate artist, that's for sure. If you want my opinion, and I suppose that *is* what you want, I'd say this is just the sort of thing our benighted super-rich would lap up. I'd like to see the full service.'

'It's in my boot.'

Johnny had his mobile in his hand. 'In that case,' he said, 'we'll strike while the proverbial is hot.' Then he spoke into the phone. 'Steven. Makins here. Yup. Got something that might interest us.'

There was a long pause while Henry gazed round the restaurant and tried to look unconcerned. Two young men in expensive and almost identical suits strutted in, yah-yahing, and were led to the table in the window; his waiter grinned at him as if they were conspirators, glasses gleamed against the starched white of the tablecloths, gilded chairs looked like stage props, the wine waiter descended on the new arrivals, gliding across the carpet as if he was dancing. It was all a bit unreal. Oh come on Johnny!

Finally his old friend spoke again. 'The mythological figures was a winner though,' he said and it sounded as though he was wheedling. 'Sold like the proverbial. You've got to admit that.' Another pause, then he said, 'Similar but better. It's a mermaid. Very classy. Yep! A mermaid.'

Then there was a very long pause indeed while Johnny nodded as if the invisible Steven could see him and Henry tried to control his impatience. But eventually the phone was put down and Johnny grinned at him across the table. 'He'll give us ten minutes at half past four,' he said. 'Get your skates on.'

They collected the full service and skated to their prestigious destination in a taxi. By that time Henry was in a state of such racing excitement he could barely breathe. The walk to the committee room pushing his precious packing case on his portable trolley calmed him a little but when he opened the door and saw that a full committee was sitting round the central table, he felt as if he was on a high diving board waiting for the order to jump and his throat was so full he was reduced to mumbling as they shook hands.

'Well then, let the dogs see the rabbit,' the chairman said, when he and Johnny were comfortably seated

They lifted the case from its trolley, unpacked it as rapidly as they could and set the service out all over the table so that the committee members could get a good look at it. The given ten minutes passed and passed again and they were still handing plates and dishes to one another and talking and considering. Henry watched their body cues and tried to listen to what they were saying and anguished. He had never found patience more difficult in the whole of his life. Eventually after twenty-two minutes, the decision was made.

They would take four services, sale or return, at the usual discount plus the one on the table, which they would use for display. Henry was so relieved he wanted to cheer and punch the air.

He was purring all the way back to Lewes. Hadn't he always known the mermaid was a winner? Right from the moment he first saw her. The very first moment. And now here she was selling at last and selling in the best possible place what's more. Where Harrods led, the rest would follow. It was too late to tell anybody, because the pottery would be closed by the time he could get there but that was a minor disappointment. He would drive in early in the morning and pin a notice on the board so that everyone could see the good news as soon as they arrived. And they would have a celebration at coffee time. He couldn't wait.

Once he was back at home, loneliness dampened his euphoria somewhat. He wandered aimlessly in and out of the empty kitchen and the even emptier living room, wishing there were someone he could phone. For a few minutes he wondered whether to ring Francesca but decided against it because even though he knew she'd be pleased to hear that her mermaid was selling at last, it wasn't the done thing for a boss to ring his employees in the evening. They had lives of their own and bosses shouldn't impinge. Agnes was a possibility but she had a disconcerting habit of telling you things too bluntly and she might think he was showing off and give him a wigging. In the end he poured himself a double whisky and settled down in front of one of Johnny Makin's castigated TV shows and didn't watch it. Triumph would have to wait till the morning.

Francesca overslept the next morning and got up in a panicked rush to find that Brad was still sprawled all over the settee and snoring. He was even more unattractive asleep than he was awake.

'Get up!' she said, as she passed him. 'I'm late.'

He grunted.

'Up!' she repeated. 'Get up!'

He didn't open his eyes. He just groaned and grumbled. 'Do I have to?'

'Yes,' she told him firmly. 'You do. I'm off to shower and I want you up and dressed before I come back. You've got ten minutes.'

He was still sprawled all over the settee when she looked in on her way to the kitchen, clean, clothed and feeling disgruntled. 'I shall be off in half an hour,' she said 'and if you're not dressed I shall put you out in the street as you are. Get up.'

He opened his eyes and squinted up at her. 'You're the most hard-hearted woman I ever met,' he grumbled. 'It wouldn't hurt you to let me stay here. Orphan of the storm and all that. Oh come on Fran! Be a sport.'

'Get up,' she said, unsportingly, and went to put the kettle on. 'I mean it. I'll throw you out.'

But he was more artful than she expected. As she prepared her breakfast she heard him blundering about and nodded her head with satisfaction to think she'd got him to move, but by the time she'd cleared the work top and put her mug and plate in the dishwasher, he was in the shower where she couldn't reach him and singing so noisily she couldn't make herself heard above the racket.

There was no time to wait for him to finish. If she didn't leave that minute she'd be late for work. She frowned with fury all the way to the pottery. Damned boy, she thought, as the green miles gentled past her window, lolling about on my new settee and getting in the way of everything and eating all my food and turning my nice new kitchen into a tip. And he snores! He's got about as much sensitivity as a slug. This whole thing is ridiculous. He's got no right to take over my home. No right at all. But even while she was ranting she was aware that the real source of the problem was her own inability to get rid of him. But how could she do that when he didn't take a blind bit of notice of anything she said? She could hardly frogmarch him out. He was too heavy. He'd simply shake her off. And then what would she do? It was like having a tapeworm in her innards.

She was still seething when she strode into the workshop but then everything changed. The long hall was fizzing with excitement and nobody was working. They were all crowded round the notice board, talking in loud excited voices. She caught sight of Sarah, jumping up and down in the middle of the throng and, not far away from her, the cook clapping her hands and smiling at her friends, and Liam thumping Molly on the back and grinning all over his face. And standing in the middle of the melee was Mr P, all over smiles and looking so happy she knew at once that the mermaid had begun to sell.

'Here she is!' he called. 'Here's our Francesca. The girl of the hour.'

Faces turned towards her, their eyes beaming like searchlights and the little crowd parted and made a way for her so that she could walk up to the notice-board where Henry was standing. She felt like royalty.

'I gather it's started to sell,' she said to him, trying to stay calm.

He waved his hand at the notice and they all waited while she read it. Then the racket erupted again. 'Isn't it good?' 'Great eh?' 'Five sets to Harrods.' 'How about that!'

'I'll bet you're chuffed,' Molly said, giving her a hug. And Henry caught her by both hands, bent his head and kissed her on both cheeks, as his workers cheered and applauded.

It would have been hard to say which of them was the most surprised, she because it had been a long time since anyone had kissed her, even on the cheek, he because he'd acted on impulse for the first time since Candida died, and that was now so out of character it took his breath away. He recovered himself quickly, of course, told them there would be cakes for them all at coffee time 'as a little celebration', smiled at them when they applauded again, sent a rapid eye message to Molly that they should all get back to work, and retreated to his office.

But his surprise went with him and kept him puzzling and inactive at his desk until an incoming phone call gave him something else to think about. It was from a buyer wanting to order three sets of 'your mermaid dinner set'. He dealt with it calmly but his hands were shaking. They were selling at last. Just as he'd always known they would.

Francesca worked doggedly that morning. She was afraid that excitement would make her hands unsteady so she concentrated hard to make sure it didn't. If this dinner service was really going to sell, and everyone here seemed to think it would shift like the hot cakes Henry had promised, she had to put in her best work on every piece. After a while the rewarding movements calmed her and the calm gave her a space in which to think. There was a lot to be thought about. Not just the first sale but everybody it was affecting. Agnes and Henry and all the people round her here who were beaming at her every time she raised her head. And specially Agnes. Dear Agnes, she thought. She'll be so pleased when she hears the news. I'll call in and see her on my way home from work. Henry's probably told her already but I'd like to see her anyway. I wonder whether he'll throw one of his parties. I'll bet he does. He's so predictable. But at that point her thoughts went into a spin because he hadn't been a bit predictable when he kissed her. That had been really unexpected. Totally unexpected. To be kissed by the boss. She couldn't imagine any of the other bosses she'd worked for doing anything even half as graceful. It had been a lovely moment. She had to admit it. It had made her feel so good, so valued, so special. If that wasn't too strong a word to use. Even the memory of it was making her glow.

When they all began to troop down to the canteen for their promised cake, she realized that she hadn't thought about Brad since she set foot in the workshop. All this has put him in his place, she thought, as she linked arms with Molly. I could have strangled him when I was driving here. Now he's just an irritating nuisance and I haven't got time for him. She knew in a vague corner of her happy mind that she would have to deal with him sooner or later but it could wait. This was a day to enjoy.

The coffee break was a celebration. The cakes were carried in to applause and whistles, Henry walked from table to table chatting, coffee mugs were raised in Francesca's direction as if they were champagne flutes. They only needed paper hats and it would have been a party. And sure enough when he reached the table where she was sitting with Molly and Liam, there were invitations for all of them to a celebratory supper that Friday.

'It's too cold for a garden party,' Henry said, 'so it'll have to be indoors. Seven-thirty for eight. Is that all right?'

'You spoil us,' Molly laughed at him.

'You're worth spoiling,' he said. 'I've had three more orders since I put that notice up.'

'That,' Molly said, grinning at him, 'is the icing on the cake.'

'Everything's happening so quickly,' Francesca said as she and Molly left the canteen together. 'I can't take it in. I mean, five orders yesterday and another three this morning. I feel as if I'm dreaming.'

'And this is only the beginning,' Molly said. 'What did I tell you? I knew we'd be rushed off our feet once it got started. Don't you go rushing though. Your work's too good to spoil by skimping. It's quality they'll be looking for.'

'Don't worry,' Francesca told her. 'I shan't skimp anything. That's not my style. I want it to be as good as I can make it. But what a day this is!'

'And it's not finished yet,' Molly said happily as they parted.

Which was true enough, although not in the way either of them could have imagined at that moment. In the middle of the afternoon, when the daylight was beginning to fade, Francesca's mobile started to trill. It was the first time she'd had a call while she was at work and it rather alarmed her. As she said, 'Hello?' she was wondering who it could be and why they were ringing.

It was Agnes. 'Me dear,' she said and her voice sounded faint and far away.

'Agnes,' Francesca said. 'What is it? Is something up?'

'I've had a little *contra temps*, me dear,' the faint voice said. 'Not too well at the moment.'

Alarm fluttered in Francesca's throat. 'Where are you?'

Agnes didn't answer for several seconds but Francesca could hear her panting. Then she said, 'In the garden.' And her voice sounded so fragile that Francesca was seriously alarmed. She's either ill or hurt, she thought, and the thought propelled her into action.

'I'm on my way,' she said. 'I'll be with you as soon as I can.'

She put down her brush, ran to Henry's office, knocked much too loudly and walked in as soon as she heard his voice. He was sitting at his desk dictating letters to Yvette.

'Agnes is ill,' she said. 'She's just rung me. Can I go and see. . . .'

143

Yvette turned in her seat, looking shocked, and Henry was instantly on his feet. 'Of course,' he said. 'Do you know what it is?'

'She couldn't tell me. Sounded bad.'

'Take my mobile number,' he said, writing it on his notepad and handing it to her. 'Let me know as soon as you know yourself.'

She nodded, took the note, and ran again. Out to the car, out to the road, determined and afraid, imagining all sorts of terrible possibilities, each one worse than the last, trying to stay sensible, heart and car racing together. Oh Agnes, dear loving, untidy Agnes, please don't be too ill.

The garden was lush with autumn colour and looked like an oil painting. 'Agnes!' she called, running past the vegetable patch. 'Agnes! Where are you? Agnes!' Past the cherry tree, the soft fruits, the grubby hammock, the meadow crazed with wild flowers, into the shadows of the orchard, pushing intolerable branches aside as she ran. And there she was, lying on the ground under one of the apple trees, ominously still, with a ladder fallen beside her and a basket spilling newly picked apples a few yards away. Oh God! She must have fallen out of the tree.

She was on her knees beside her friend in seconds, examining her quickly, alarmed by the tracery of dark blood criss-crossing her face, checking quickly to see where it was coming from. She didn't find any deep gashes but Agnes was cold and obviously in shock and from the awkward angle of her right leg it looked as though she must have either broken her leg or her hip. Now what shall I do? Get her warm or call an ambulance?

'Me dear,' Agnes said, in that alarmingly faint voice, opening swimmy eyes and struggling to focus them. 'So stupid.'

'You're all right,' Francesca said, leaning forward to kiss her cheek. 'I'm here. Don't worry. I'm just going to phone for an ambulance and get you a blanket or something. I'll be right back.' Now that she knew she was going to take action, she was in complete control of herself and the situation.

She dialled 999 as she walked to the house, and gave the details calmly. Then she went upstairs and pulled Agnes's duvet off her bed and carried it back to the garden.

'They're on their way,' she said as she wrapped her now-shivering friend in the warmth of her bedding.

'I'll get up in a minute,' Agnes said, thickly. 'Bit of a shock, that's all.'

'Yes,' Francesca said, agreeing with her. And she took her friend's cold hand and chafed it. 'They'll soon be here.'

They were remarkably quick and wonderfully, reassuringly, gently efficient, both of them bulky in their fluorescent jackets, and sure-footed as cats. They explained what they were going to do before they did it, inserted a cannula into the back of Agnes's hand and gave her a morphine injection 'to deal with that pain', and held her hand until it started to take effect. Then they managed to get her to tell them exactly where she hurt even though her first faint answer had been 'all over' and when they'd finally lifted her onto their stretcher-bed and strapped her in very gently, making sure that every-thing was secure, they pushed it over the rough grass of the orchard as smoothly as they could, telling her every few feet that she would 'soon be there'. And Francesca, needing to feel useful, righted the ladder and stood it against the tree, gathered the fallen apples into the basket, picked up the duvet and carried the whole lot into the kitchen. When she got back to the garden the paramedics were pushing the stretcher into the ambulance.

'Hop aboard,' the taller one said to her, when the stretcher was in its place. 'We're ready for the off.'

So she retrieved her bag from the orchard and climbed aboard. It was an impressively smooth ride and while his partner drove, the tall paramedic was busy with Agnes taking her temperature and her blood pressure and checking on any medication she might be taking, smiling at her when she said, 'I don't take drugs.'

'That makes a nice change,' he said. 'Most people take all sorts of things. I usually get a list as long as my arm.'

Then he asked a question that took a bit of thought. 'Can you tell me your date of birth?'

'January,' she said at last. '14th.'

'And the year?'

'Um ... 1941, I think. Yes. Second year of the war. 1941.'

'Thank you,' he said. 'That's good. How's the pain now?'

'Easier,' Agnes said and closed her eyes.

She's over seventy, Francesca thought, looking down at her. She should never have been climbing trees. But then that was Agnes all over wasn't it. Oh poor Agnes.

The drive continued and seemed to be going on for rather a long time. Francesca had a vague idea that the hospital in Lewes was at the west end of the town and was worried by the time it was taking to get there, especially as Agnes was so pale. Eventually she decided to ask where they were going.

'Brighton,' the paramedic said. 'The Royal Sussex. They don't set broken bones in the Victoria Hospital.' And seeing her anxiety, he reassured her. 'It won't take long. We're nearly there. They know we're coming.'

She looked at his compassionate face and was comforted, thinking what wonderful people paramedics were, impressed by the way they coped and how calm they were. So she held Agnes' hand and waited more patiently and presently she felt the ambulance driving up a short incline and knew that they'd arrived. It wasn't long before the doors were opened and Agnes was wheeled into A&E and all four of them were swallowed up by the life and pace of the hospital and time became expandable and relative.

Agnes and Francesca waited in their curtained cubicle while the paramedics went to book them in; a nurse arrived, smiled at Agnes and asked all the same questions as the paramedic had done, which irritated her; then a doctor came through the curtains with another nurse following him and said he'd like to check her over and was that all right, which annoyed her even more.

'Why else am I here?' she said, truculently.

'Exactly so,' the doctor agreed smoothly. 'So let's have a look at you, shall we.' He was examining the cuts and bruises on her face as he spoke and taking a close look at her eyes. 'Do you have any pain?'

'Not as much as I did when it happened,' Agnes said.

'Whereabouts?'

Agnes turned her head to one side on the pillow and began to groan as if talking about the pain made it worse.

Francesca grew alarmed. She'd never seen Agnes truculent before nor heard her groan. She leant forward until her mouth was on a level with Agnes's ear. 'Can you tell them where it hurts?' she said, speaking as gently as she could.

'I've told them,' Agnes said without opening her eyes. 'I keep telling them.'

Francesca prompted her, looking at the doctor. 'It's your right leg, isn't it?'

'I've told them.'

The doctor nodded at Francesca and the nurse eased Agnes's shoe off her foot very gently and looked at her stocking, which was torn and blood-stained. 'We'll have to cut your stocking off,' she said to Agnes.

Agnes didn't open her eyes. 'Cut it off then,' she said,

The stocking was cut away, the doctor took a cursory look at the grazes that were now revealed and then examined the leg. 'I'm going to send you for an X-ray,' he said to Agnes. 'Then we'll get that leg set and plastered. You might need a few stitches on your face and your head. You've got one or two slight cuts there. Nothing terrible. All right?'

'No, it's not,' Agnes said and groaned again.

'We'll give you something for the pain presently,' the doctor promised, writing on his clipboard. But Agnes wasn't listening to him.

'We shall keep her in overnight,' the doctor told Francesca. 'Delayed concussion is always a possibility after a fall. I don't think it's likely but it's better to be on the safe side. You can't go with her to X-ray of course but there's a waiting room along the corridor. It shouldn't take long.'

The waiting room was empty, which was a bit off-putting because she'd have liked a bit of company, but sitting there on her own she realized she'd been given the chance to ring Henry and tell him what was happening. It was high time she did and she *had* promised. But when she heard his familiar voice on the end of the line, she tumbled into a sort of panic. There was so much to tell him she hardly knew where to start. He listened patiently for several minutes while she tried to make sense of it all, stumbling and repeating herself, and feeling cross because her mind wasn't functioning at all well. Eventually, when she paused to take breath, he said. 'I think I ought to come and see her.'

'Now?'

'Yes. It must still be visiting time. Then you and she can tell me everything and I can ask you both questions. Phones aren't very good for this sort of thing. Thirty minutes? OK?'

He was with her in twenty-five and looking so competent and so much in charge she was limp with relief to see him. 'Oh,' she said. 'I *am* glad you're here. She's been in a lot of pain. I told you didn't I?'

'Yes, you did. Is she still in A&E?'

Her mind seemed to have stopped functioning completely and now it went into a whirl. She didn't know. She'd just wandered away from the place as they wheeled poor Agnes out of it. She hadn't thought to ask what was going to happen next. Or where Agnes was going or anything. Oh dear. 'They were taking her to have an X-ray when I left her,' she said. 'They sent me down here because I wasn't allowed go with her. Because of the radioactivity I suppose. She might be back there by now. But then they were going to set the bone, so they said. Oh dear, I don't know where she'll be.'

He looked at her puckered, anxious face and felt overpoweringly protective towards her. It was a familiar, almost forgotten emotion, which he hadn't experienced since Candida died. 'Don't worry,' he said. 'It's been a long day. We'll go down to A&E together and see if we can find out what's happening. There's bound to be someone there who could tell us.' And he took her by the arm and followed the signs.

She allowed him to lead her, suddenly aware that

she was very tired and perilously near tears. And there was Agnes, sitting up on her stretcher bed and looking more like herself again, even though she was wearing a voluminous hospital nightgown and had stitches on her cheek and a plastic bracelet round her wrist. She didn't seem to be in pain so they'd obviously given her more painkillers.

'So ridiculous,' she said, when she saw Francesca. 'All this fuss. They're going to keep me in overnight. I can't see the necessity. I'm feeling a lot better now. Hello Henry, me dear.'

Henry kissed her cheek. 'I hear you've been falling out of trees and breaking your legs,' he said.

'One tree. Singular,' she told him sternly. 'And one leg. Don't exaggerate.'

A nurse came cheerfully through the curtain. 'Are you ready to have this bone set then, Agnes?' she said.

Agnes growled. 'If I must.'

'That's the style,' the nurse said, accepting the growl as agreement. 'Then we can get you settled on the ward and make you more comfortable. Your friends will come in and see you in the morning.' She gave Francesca a card. 'There's the visiting hours,' she said, 'and that's the ward. Just follow the signs.'

A porter had arrived. Agnes' bed was being wheeled away. Henry and Francesca could see her hand waving and then she was through the swing doors and they were on their own in the empty cubicle. Francesca felt exhausted.

'I don't know about you,' Henry said, as they walked out of the hospital into the autumn darkness, 'but I could do with a meal.'

Francesca shivered. It was cold out there under such a black sky. 'Yes,' she said. 'So could I. I haven't had

150

anything to eat since lunch.'

'Nor me,' he said. 'I know a good place not far from here. Would you care to join me?'

'I'm not properly dressed,' she said, doubtfully. 'I mean, I'm in my work clothes.'

'They don't stand on ceremony,' he said. 'It's an eccentric sort of place. Very welcoming. French. I think you'd enjoy it. And don't worry about getting home. I'll drive you back.'

'Well in that case,' she said. 'Yes. I like to. Thank you very much.'

CHAPTER 10

THE SEX SEEKERS were out in South East London that night, prowling the pubs and clubs, sharp eyed, preened, perfumed and predatory. Some prowled in packs, urging one another on; others hunted alone, like a certain Mr Jeffrey Walmesly. He was thoroughly prepared, chin, chest and armpits carefully shaved, wearing skin-tight jeans, a Ralph Lauren chequered shirt, lashings of his favourite aftershave, his Gucci watch, a fake tan and all the bling he possessed. He'd examined his image in the wardrobe mirror with passing anxiety while he was making his final choice of clothing but all in all, when he'd finally decided what to wear, he thought he looked pretty cool. It was the right sort of image, perhaps a tad too suave but interesting and with a bit of mystery about it. Chicks liked a bit of mystery. Now all he had to do was to find the right chick. It had taken him three nights of trial and error before he'd discovered the most likely club but now he was dancing in a close-packed mass of wriggling bodies in the Cuddly Bunny, and he'd reached the point when he could start sizing up the talent. Lots of blondes, all skeletal and heavily made-up and very loud.

'Hi there, gorgeous,' he said to one particularly pretty one.

Her answer was a bit off-putting. 'Yeh, yeh!' she said and put her arms round the neck of a pimply youth who was gyrating beside her.

Not her, Jeffrey thought, walking awkwardly away from them through a forest of waving arms. Not to worry. There were plenty of others. Now that he'd finally made his mind up that Fran had got to be replaced, he could play the field. And he *had* made up his mind. It was no good waiting for her to see sense and come home. He'd given her plenty of time to come to her senses – far more then she deserved – and if she couldn't see what was good for her that was her hard luck. She'd regret it in the end. Women were all same. No logic that was their trouble. Needed a good man to guide them.

The volume of sound in the Cuddly Bunny was so loud it was making his belly shake. Why does this music have to thump so much? he thought as he scanned the talent. It's enough to turn you deaf. It's no wonder they all shout. And those flashing lights are murder on the eyes. He had to keep blinking and it was worrying him in case it made him look foolish. A beam of nice steady light was what he wanted. A beam of nice steady light to help him see what he was looking for. He blinked again and saw a possibility. Another blonde and with very nice tits. But very nice tits or no, she looked down her nose at him as if he were something nasty the cat had brought in. And the next girl wasn't much better. Nor the one after that. He was beginning to think he'd have to give up and choose another venue that wasn't quite so loud or so full of impossible lighting effects, when he noticed a girl standing all by herself under the exit sign. Pretty in an understated sort of way, brownish sort of hair, big eyes, quite nice legs, very skimpy shirt, and obviously on her own. That was better.

He sidled up and stood beside her. He even managed to wait until she looked round at him. 'Crowded isn't it,' he shouted above the din. 'Could you fancy a drink?'

She turned her head like a sleepwalker, looked away, and then looked at him again. It was rather sexy. 'Don't mind if I do,' she shouted back. 'Sex on the beach.'

He thought he'd misheard her. 'What?'

'It's a cocktail.'

'Ah yes,' he said, recovering. 'Of course.' And went to get it.

It looked pretty sickly to him but she took it, sipped it and seemed to enjoy it.

He tried the next line. 'D'you come here often?'

She didn't hear it. 'What?'

'D'you wanna dance?'

'Not really,' she said. And sighed.

He moved into suave and caring mode at once. 'Don't sigh, pretty lady!' he shouted at her. 'Tell your uncle Jeffrey what's up.'

'What?'

'Tell me what's up,' he shouted.

'People are foul,' she shouted back.

He gave a deprecating smile. 'Not all of us.'

'My flat mates are,' she said. 'You'd never believe the way they go on. Never believe it. Never. They won't let me say nothing. It's all what *they* want, *their* music, *their* programmes, every single fucking night, *their* programmes.' She was shouting in earnest now, her face distorted, and her eyes staring. 'I got rights too. They're not the only ones at uni. I got a career to think of an' all. I pay my share of their fucking mortgage. More than my share. It's not right now is it.' Then she burped and put one rather fat white hand over her mouth. ''Scuse 'ee!'

154

Useful facts slotted themselves into his mind, one after the other, neat and slick as cards sliding into a cash dispenser. She was drunk and she paid a mortgage and she wanted out of her flat. 'Sounds tough,' he said, arranging his face into a suitably sympathetic expression. 'Tell you what. Why don't we go and have a bite to eat somewhere and you can tell me all about it.'

'What?'

'Bite to eat,' he said, miming lifting a fork to his mouth and munching.

She watched him in the bemused, lop-sided way that drunken girls so often assume, then she shrugged her shoulders so that her tits swung inside her skimpy t-shirt. 'Why not?' she said.

He put a hand under her elbow and escorted her out of the club, his expression all tender concern.

'I suppose we'd better introduce ourselves,' he said suavely. 'I'm Jeffrey.'

She looked at him lopsidedly. 'Bubbles,' she said.

'That's a pretty name,' he said, thinking how silly it was. But what did her name matter? Inside his head he was crowing. It was in the bag. It was a done deal. Give him a week or two and she'd be moving in. Then they'd see some changes. With her paying half the mortgage – and if she was shelling out towards a student flat she could certainly pay towards his mortgage – and cooking the meals and shopping and that sort of thing, he'd have time for business again. He'd get that china clay thing sorted out for a start. Visit the bloke with the Magic Mermaid pottery. I'll bet he'd be up for it. And actually she was quite pretty now he came to look at her. Or she would be if she wasn't sloshed. She'd do very well. That'ud show that damned fool Fran. She needn't think she can walk out on me and get away with it.

Francesca was actually walking into the restaurant that Henry had chosen and feeling decidedly hungry. It was an elegant place, black, white and gold and softly lit but it contained such a variety of people in such amazingly idiosyncratic clothes that she felt happily at home there. And the food was excellent. She chose melon and smoked salmon, a perfectly cooked steak and crepes suzette and enjoyed every mouthful. Henry ordered half a bottle of red wine, 'can't have any more as we're both driving,' and that was a revelation to her. She'd always avoided red wine because she thought it was too rough but this one slid down her throat like velvet. She felt better with every course she ate and when her last plate was clean, she leant back in her chair, smiled at Henry across the table and told him she felt like a different person.

'I hope you're not,' he said, smiling back. 'I shouldn't like to lose my premier artist.'

What a compliment, she thought. 'Oh that won't change,' she assured him. 'I shall always want to paint.'

'Glad to hear it. Ready for coffee?'

'Please. I think I need sobering up.'

'Well now,' he said when the coffee had been served and poured, 'we must give our minds to how Agnes is going to manage when they send her home. She'll never be able to get up and down those stairs with her leg in plaster. We shall have to move a bed downstairs for her. I presume she's got a downstairs loo?' Francesca nodded. 'With a wash basin?' And when Francesca nodded again. 'Right. So it'll just mean moving the bed. And some of her bedroom furniture, dressing table, chest of drawers, that sort of thing. We could do it between us. My gardeners would give us a hand.'

'Yes,' Francesca said but she spoke doubtfully,

wondering whether she ought to tell him something about Agnes's living arrangements.

He was too busy thinking and planning to notice her doubt. 'It'll mean shifting some of the furniture about downstairs to make room but that shouldn't be a problem.'

He was so full of enthusiasm, she felt she had to warn him. 'It could be.'

'Tricky stairs, is that it?'

'No, no nothing like that. The stairs are fine.'

He looked at her quizzically. 'Then what is it?'

'I'm not sure I should tell you,' she said, looking worried again. 'I mean, it could be private. She might not like it. I mean it might upset her.'

Henry watched her with growing affection. She looked so lost when she was worried and that crumpled expression brought Candida back to him most power-fully, especially now, when the table lamp was gilding her usually pale face. 'I would be the soul of discretion,' he tried to reassure her. 'Nothing you tell me would go beyond these four walls.'

'Yes, I know that,' she said. 'But I wouldn't want to upset her. I mean, I want to help her.'

'We both do,' he said, 'which is why we need to know what the problems are. Once we know that we can begin to solve them.'

She sighed. 'You make it sound simple.'

'I'm not saying that. It could be quite difficult but if we want to help her. . . .'

Francesca put out a tentative feeler. 'Have you ever been to her house?' she asked.

'No,' he said, a little surprised by the question. 'No. I haven't. I've been in the kitchen and the garden, of course, because that's where she is when I go calling but most of our socialising has been in my house. I don't think she's much of a one for entertaining. It's not big enough? Is that what you're saying?'

'No,' she said. 'It's plenty big enough. There are three rooms downstairs apart from the kitchen. It's just. . . . Well. . . . What I mean to say is, she doesn't like things being moved.'

He took that lightly. 'That's not a problem,' he said. 'We'll put everything back as we found it. I'll make a floor plan to show where everything should go.'

Oh dear, Francesca thought, he doesn't understand what I'm trying to tell him. 'I think you ought to look at the place before you start talking about floor plans,' she said.

'Good idea,' he said. 'And the sooner the better if we've got furniture to shift. Look here. I've got to drive you back to pick up your car. I'm assuming you left it there? Right. Why don't we take a look at things tonight? Then we could make plans. Although I don't suppose you've got a key to the house, have you?'

'No,' Francesca told him, 'I haven't, but the back door's never locked. She says you don't get burglars out in the sticks.'

'Fine,' he said. 'In that case, we'll go and take a look. See the lie of the land.'

I ought to tell him, Francesca worried, but she couldn't think how to do it without being disloyal to Agnes. It was very awkward. 'Be prepared for a few shocks,' she warned.

It was very dark in the empty country lanes and the hedges were grey as ghosts in the headlights. Halfway there, a dog fox ran across the road just ahead of them, its russet coat bold in the sudden light of their approach.

It looked at them briefly before it streaked into the hedge and the road seemed darker than ever after it had gone. Then they'd reached Agnes' house and were edging through the overgrown hedges that bulged over the drive. The house was so wrapped about by darkness they could barely make out its outline and the garden was sentinelled by black trees, where half-hidden stars flickered and swung like tiny candles. There was a faint smell of wood smoke in the air and the night was full of unfamiliar sounds, shuffles and creaks and a distant bird hooting. Francesca shivered despite herself and was glad when Henry put a hand under her elbow and led her towards the back door.

They switched on the light in the kitchen and went off rather gingerly to start their tour of inspection. Francesca led the way and stopped to tell Henry what each room had originally been before she opened the door on the chaos inside. It was perverse of her and she knew it but it pleased her to see how shocked he was.

'Poor Aggie!' he said, when he'd taken note of all three rooms and was back in the hall again. 'I didn't realize the housework had got on top of her like this. She must have been struggling for quite while. I can see what you meant about it being difficult to move the bed. You forget that your friends are getting old, that's the trouble. Poor old Aggie. I shall send my cleaners in to help her. She shouldn't be struggling with all this on her own.'

'I don't think that would be . . .' Francesca began. 'I mean, she might not . . .'

He wasn't listening. 'If we're going to bring her bed down here we shall have a helluva lot of clearing to do. I'll get my cleaners on to it. We'll do all three rooms while we're at it. We'll have to hire a skip for all the rubbish. There's far too much for the dustmen to take. If only she'd said I could have helped her earlier. I shall get on to it first thing.'

'If she'll let you do it,' Francesca managed to say. 'I don't think she will.'

'I take your point,' he said reasonably. 'She won't want us to know she can't manage. Don't worry. I'll do it tactfully. It's not her fault she's getting old, poor Aggie, but she'll have to face up to it sooner or later. She can't go on living in this mess. It's not hygienic. Anyway, given the situation she's in at the moment, she doesn't really have a choice. She can't struggle up and down stairs on crutches and we can't get her bed into any of these rooms unless we shift the junk. Don't worry. She'll come round to it. Think how much clearer and cleaner it'll be when it's done. She'll be grateful then.'

Francesca looked at him steadily. 'I keep trying to tell you, Henry. She won't want it to be done at all.'

'She hasn't got a choice.'

'So you keep saying. But she *thinks* she has and her choice is to keep things as they are and not change a thing.'

'Then we shall have to persuade her otherwise. We'll do it together first thing tomorrow morning. The sooner the better, don't you think. Of course, she'll have to stay with you until we've got this all sorted out. Is that OK?'

Francesca assured him that it was but privately she didn't think Agnes would take very kindly to that idea either.

'And of course all this clearing up could take quite a while. Three or four days probably. So we'll have to tell her that too.'

He's so sure about things, Francesca thought, watching him. That's why he's such a good boss. But he's wrong about this. If he goes barging into the hospital tomorrow telling her things she doesn't want to hear she's going to be terribly upset. I shall have to stop him, somehow.

'Look,' she said. 'I don't think it's a good idea for us both to visit tomorrow morning. I mean, it might seem a bit heavy handed.' And when he frowned and looked hurt she tried to modify her words. 'I'm not saying it would be, but it might seem like it to her. I mean she's had quite a shock. She could be feeling – um – tender about things. It might take quite a time to get her to think about anything and you know how slow they are in hospital. What I'm saying is, it might take all day and you ought to be at work with all these orders coming in.'

'I thought I would be a help to you,' he said, rather huffily. 'Being two-handed so to speak.'

She took a deep breath and spoke while her courage was high. 'I think it would come better from me on my own, if you don't mind me saying so.'

'Well if that's how you want to play it,' he said, still huffy. 'You'll let me know how you get on though, won't you. If we're going to get the place cleared I shall have to put things in motion as soon as I can. You've got my number.'

'Of course,' she promised. 'I'll ring as soon as I know anything.'

He looked at his watch to bring the conversation to an end, the way he did at work. 'It's late,' he said. 'I ought to let you go home or it'll be morning before you get to bed. We can't do anything more here.' And he raised his head and gazed round the half-lit hall, trying to remember which door led to the kitchen. And found himself face to face with Agnes' portrait.

It was an extremely uncomfortable moment, because it pushed the memory of his anger at him and did it so powerfully that it took root and grew before he could shake it away. He'd treated her much too roughly, poor Francesca, and there hadn't been any necessity for it. She hadn't known she was touching a nerve, poor girl. He remembered her face, gazing at him across the desk, looking stricken, and he stood quite still, staring at the painted face of his old friend and, for the first time in years, he felt ashamed of himself.

Francesca stood still too, watching his changing expressions and the way his spine had stiffened, and even though it was late and she was so tired she could barely keep her eyes open, she read his thoughts and knew he was remembering their awful conversation and regretting it. She was beginning to wonder whether she ought to say something to show him she didn't hold it against him and dithering because she was so exhausted by the effort she'd made in opposing him that she couldn't think of the right way to do it, when he turned his head to look at her and spoke again.

'It's very good,' he said. 'You've really caught her likeness.'

To be praised when she wasn't expecting it and after she'd taken such a stand against him, made her blush.

The blush eased him. 'You must be pleased with it,' he said.

'Well yes, I was,' she admitted, looking at the portrait. 'Was?'

'I think you're always pleased with something when you've just finished it,' she explained. 'You see all the faults later on.'

He smiled at her. 'There speaks a perfectionist,' he said. 'I think it's splendid. You've caught her character.'

That was such a fulsome compliment and so exactly what she wanted for this portrait of hers that she glowed with the pleasure of it. 'Well thank you,' she said. 'That was what I was trying to do.'

He was intrigued by her skill and touched by her obvious pleasure in his praise. 'Have you painted a lot of portraits?'

'This is the first,' she told him, looking at it. 'I did life classes at college, naturally. It was part of the course. But that was different. I mean, we weren't trying to reveal a character, we were trying to get the proportions right. It was bodies and limbs all sitting perfectly still, not faces.'

Talk of revealing character made him feel uncomfortable again. 'Come on,' he said. 'Time for home. You're asleep on your feet.' And he turned to walk through the kitchen, talking as he went. 'Now be careful how you drive. These roads are very dark at this time of night. We don't want an RTA on top of everything else.'

'I'll be fine,' she told him. But actually when they were out in the creaking darkness again she didn't feel quite so sure of herself. There was something spooky about all those noises that made the hair rise on the nape of her neck. She was quite glad to slide inside the security of her car.

As she settled behind the wheel, there was a loud screech somewhere alarmingly close by. The sound made her jump. 'It's only an owl,' Henry said. And watched her until she'd eased her car safely out of the drive. It had been quite a day.

Francesca drove home to Lewes extremely carefully and sensibly. It was dark and late and she was so tired her bones were aching. As she negotiated the black lanes, she thought longingly of the warm comfortable bed that was waiting for her and yearned to be back in the peaceful order of her flat. When she finally eased her key into the lock, she was limp with relief to be home. And the first thing she smelt as she stepped inside the hall was dirty socks. That damned Brad! she thought, irritably. He's still here. After everything I said this morning. And the morning's anger returned to flood her with energy and she stomped into the living room to sort him out. There was no doubt in her mind that she could do it, not after all the things that had happened that day.

He was sprawled across her nice, new sofa, looking as frowsty as he smelt. She took the duvet in both hands and skinned it off him. 'Get up, you lazy great lump!' she shouted at him. 'Time you were out of here. Get up!'

He was in his nasty cheesy socks and his unsavoury underwear which was grey and grimy and made his legs look flabby. 'Whazzat?' he said thickly. 'What's amarrer?' And he opened his eyes blearily and tried to focus them.

She was stripping the duvet of its dirty cover, thinking she'd have to open the window and give the place an airing. 'Get up,' she said. 'Put some clothes on. You look repellent.'

He was squinting at his watch. 'Do you know what time it is?' he said, sounding aggrieved.

'Time you were out of here.'

'It's ten past two.'

'Get your clothes on.'

'You're not throwing me out.'

She pulled the pillow from underneath his head. 'I'm throwing you out,' she said implacably. 'I threw you out this morning only you chose not to take any notice. Now it's comeuppance time.'

'You can't throw me out in the middle the night,' he said aghast. 'Oh come on Fran. Have a heart. I've got nowhere to go.'

'Tough,' she said. 'I need this bed for Agnes. She's

broken her leg.'

He didn't seem able to take it in but sat on the edge of the sofa blinking. 'What?'

'Agnes has broken her leg,' she explained with icy patience. 'She's in hospital and she's coming here tomorrow.'

'Oh!' he said. 'Poor old thing.' Then he tried wheedling. 'But she doesn't need a bed now, does she? Not right this minute. I mean to say, she's not here now is she? I could stay till morning.'

She was adamant and enjoying it. 'Get dressed,' she said. 'I'll give you five minutes and if you're not dressed by then I'll throw your clothes in the street and you after them.'

His mouth was a circle of horror. 'You wouldn't.'

'Five minutes,' she said.

He grumbled but got dressed and she watched him implacably until the deed was done. Then she walked to the front door and opened it. She didn't say anything, she simply insisted with her face. And a little to her surprise he shuffled out.

Once she'd shut the door on him she began to laugh. Then she opened the windows to the clean night air and pulled the horrible crumpled pillow case from the pillow. She didn't feel the slightest sympathy for him. Not even a twinge. It had been a triumph.

CHAPTER 11

'POPPYCOCK!' AGNES SAID fiercely. 'That's what it is. Absolute poppycock.' She was up and dressed and sitting in a hospital armchair with her plastered leg propped on a chair in front of her and she was extremely cross. 'It's no earthly good them keeping on.' She mimicked a silly little girl's voice. *'You must consider the stairs Miss Potts. We can't have you falling again can we.* Consider the stairs? Did you ever hear the like? I've been up and down those stairs every blessed day of my life. I know every inch of every single tread, they're *my* stairs, for crying out loud. And now some idiot child pops her stupid head round the curtain just when I'm sitting here ready to be discharged and tells me to *consider* them. They're treating me as if I'm half-witted and I won't have it. Do they really think I can't manage to get up my own stairs? I don't need a lecture about stairs. I'm not an invalid. It's only a broken leg. I've shown them I can use their horrid crutches.'

Francesca sat on the edge of the empty bed and tried to think how to comfort her. It was awful to see her so angry and distressed. 'I don't think they mean to be unkind,' she said. 'They're trying to help you.'

That didn't ease the situation at all. 'Help me!' Agnes

snorted. 'Well they're going the wrong way about it. And another thing. She said they can't discharge me until they're sure I can manage and they're going to send some nosy social worker to inspect the house. I don't need my house inspected. That's bullying. And insulting.'

She's frightened they'll throw things away, Francesca understood. 'Would you like me to go and talk to them?' she offered.

'You can try if you like,' Agnes said and shrugged her shoulders. 'You won't get any sense out of them though. I can tell you that for nothing. I've been trying since breakfast.'

Francesca slid off the bed, kissed her friend's hot cheek and went off to find a nurse, thinking hard all the way. She still hadn't found the right words when she arrived at the nursing station, where a woman who looked as though she might be the Sister was checking the drugs trolley. She looked up as Francesca approached, smiled and said she wouldn't be a minute so Francesca smiled back and went on thinking.

'It's about Miss Potts,' she said when the trolley had been wheeled away. 'I'm her friend Francesca.'

'Ah yes,' the Sister said. 'She gave your name as next of kin. How can I help you?'

'She wants to be discharged.'

The Sister made a grimace. 'So we gather,' she said. 'We've been trying to explain the situation to her. I don't think she understands we have to make sure she can cope when she gets home.'

It was time for a judicious not-quite truth. 'Actually,' Francesca said. 'I'm taking her home with me so she won't have to cope with anything. I live in a ground floor flat. There aren't any stairs to worry about and I can look after her. If she'll let me. She's very independent.'

The Sister smiled. 'Yes,' she said. 'We've noticed. But of course if she's going to stay with you that makes all the difference. I'll tell doctor there's been a change of plan. Just give me a few moments.'

'Well?' Agnes said as Francesca walked back towards her. 'What did they say?' She was scowling like a goblin. 'Don't tell me. Let me guess. They won't let me go home.'

'Actually,' Francesca said, enjoying her moment. 'They will. They're going to sign you off as soon as they can get in touch with the doctor. But be warned. Just don't argue with them. Right? I've had to tell a porky pie to get them to agree. Just listen to them and keep schtum, whatever they say, even if you think it's daft.'

Agnes was delighted. 'You bad girl,' she said. 'And I thought you were the soul of virtue. Don't worry. I'll lie through my teeth.'

But her discharge was quick and simple. She was given a card with the time of her follow-up appointment written on it, warned not to put any weight on her injured leg and eased into a wheelchair with her crutches across her knees. Then, when she'd been pushed to the side of Francesca's car and gentled into the passenger seat, they were off.

'About time too,' she said, closing her eyes as they took the Lewes road. 'I can't wait for a nice cup of tea from my own pot. I can't be doing with tea-bags.'

'I'll put the kettle on first thing,' Francesca promised. And did.

They sat in her untidy kitchen and drank several cups of tea and Agnes looked so relieved and happy it tugged Francesca's heart to watch her, knowing that sooner or later she would have to face the challenge of the stairs. But for the moment it was enough for her to be back in the house, holding her warm mug in both hands and admiring her garden through the window.

'What could you fancy for lunch? Francesca said, when Agnes finally looked her way. 'It's nearly one o'clock.'

'Is it too?' Agnes said. 'Um. Well I tell you what, I'll think about lunch when I've been upstairs. Come on. I've got something to prove.' And she slid her arms into her crutches and struggled to her feet.' Her face was so determined, Francesca simply followed her and tried not to show how worried she was.

'No problem,' Agnes said when she reached the foot of the stairs. 'I'll soon get the hang of it. You watch.' And she gave the lowest stair her fiercest scowl, swung up a crutch to give her support and stepped onto the stair with her good leg. 'There you are. Easy-peasy. Just a matter of taking it a step at a time.' And she hauled her plastered leg up to the step and stood in one-legged triumph on the bottom step.

'Take it gently,' Francesca urged but Agnes was already trying to swing her crutch onto the next step and was discovering how painful it was to be off balance and forced to put weight on her plastered leg. The pain of it was so excruciating she called out 'Aah! Aah!' and clung to the banister for support.

'Bloody hell fire!' she said when she'd caught her breath. 'That hurt.'

'Maybe you should . . .' Francesca began but Agnes turned her most determined face to glare down at her.

'I've started,' she said sternly, 'so I'll finish. I can't expect it to be easy.' She swung her crutch up to the next step for the second time with redoubled concentration, a lot of heavy breathing and no success at all. Again the lack of balance, again the awful pain. And this time it took her longer to recover. But her spine was set with the determination not to be beaten. She gritted her teeth and swung at the step again.

Her struggle went on for more than ten minutes and at the end of it she hadn't moved from the first step. Her face was streaked with perspiration, she was panting and very near tears. 'This bloody sodding leg,' she said and sank sideways onto the step, tears oozing from her eyes. 'I can't do this Francesca. There isn't room for me and this bloody crutch and all this bloody sodding plaster. The step's too small. How am I going to manage if I can't get upstairs? I shall have to sleep in a chair. And what will I do with my leg then? I'd like to cut the bloody thing off. And how am I going to get on with my work? That's all upstairs too.'

Francesca eased herself onto the stair beside her and held her while she ranted about her bloody sodding leg and her bloody sodding plaster and how she wished she'd never gone out to pick the bloody sodding apples until she'd sworn herself to a halt and was weeping and exhausted.

'You're right,' she soothed. 'It's not fair. Life's a bummer.'

Agnes wiped her eyes. 'What am I going to do?' she said.

'Well,' Francesca said slowly, stroking the damp strands of hair out of her friend's eyes and smiling at her. 'I'll tell you what I think. It's only what *I* think, mind. If you don't like the sound of it, you've only to say. I'm not telling you what you ought to do. I'm only saying it's a possibility.' Agnes gave her a lop-sided grin. So she went on, aware that she was taking a risk but feeling that the moment was right. 'I think you ought to come home with me and let me look after you for a little while.' And when Agnes scowled, she modified quickly. 'Just until you've got used to these crutches. Maybe this happened because you're trying to rush things. It could be, couldn't it?'

Agnes looked doubtful but admitted that she supposed so.

'Well then,' Francesca said. 'Let's give it a try, shall we? For a few days. To see how you go on. If it doesn't work or you don't like it, you can always come back.'

Agnes leant her head against the banisters and closed her eyes. 'I can't leave the house,' she said. 'Not now. There's too much to do. I ought to be here.'

'You left it to go on the cruise,' Francesca said reasonably.

'That was different,' Agnes said with her eyes still shut. 'There wasn't so much work to do then. It's different now. Bonfire'll be on us before we know it and I haven't sent out any information. They'll all be waiting for it and I haven't even addressed the envelopes.'

Francesca had no idea what Agnes was talking about but she tried to find an answer that would comfort her. 'You can address envelopes at the flat,' she said. 'I'll help you.'

'It's all upstairs,' Agnes said despairingly. 'I can't do a thing if I can't get at the folders.' She was beginning to weep again. 'And it's not just envelopes. There's a newsletter to write and all sorts of things.'

This would have to be tackled head on. 'Just tell me what I've got to look for,' Francesca said, 'and I'll go upstairs and get it for you.'

Agnes stopped crying and gave Francesca a long hard look. 'You're determined about this, aren't you?' she said.

'One of us has to be,' Francesca said lightly, 'or we shall sit on the stairs all afternoon. Now tell me what I'm looking for. Are they labelled these folders? Presumably they're in your bedroom. Right?'

'Down by the bed,' Agnes said. 'They're all labelled. I work on them most afternoons and evenings now. I've got my laptop and printer up there and the box full of paper and envelopes. Oh dear, I was going to get everything ready for Bonfire and now look where I am. I'm being such a nuisance.'

'No you're not,' Francesca said. 'I can be up and back in a second. You just stay there and get your breath back. I'll bring your night things down too, shall I? Now is there anything else you need? Apart from the folders and the laptop and the printer, I mean. We can come back tomorrow and pack properly.'

Having agreed to their arrangement, Agnes was recovering her humour. 'You're such a bully, Francesca Jones,' she said in mock complaint and grinned at her.

'That's me,' Francesca agreed happily and went upstairs.

Given how untidy Agnes was, she was rather surprised to discover that the folders were exactly where she'd said they would be, and in a neat pile. There were seven of them and the top four were boldly labelled 'Bonfire', 'Badgers', 'Soil Association', 'Big Pharma'. The bed wasn't made, but she didn't expect that, and there were discarded clothes and crumpled towels all over the place and a pile of bulging cardboard boxes in one corner but the laptop and the printer were side by side on the dressing table alongside the stationery box. She found the current pyjamas slung over a chair, a dressing gown hanging from a hook behind the door and a down-at-heel pair of slippers tossed askew beside the wardrobe so it didn't take her long to gather all she needed. Methodical as always, she made a careful pile of it, the folders and the box on top of the laptop, then the printer, then the nightclothes carefully folded and finally the slippers, one tucked inside the other. Within five minutes she was carrying the whole lot downstairs. Agnes was still sitting where she'd been left.

'I've been thinking,' she said. 'If I'm going to stay with you I must pay my way. That's got to be understood or I shan't come.'

'Naturally,' Francesca agreed. 'We'll go fifty-fifty. Now let's have you on your feet and we can get going.' She felt it was necessary to keep up the impetus before Agnes changed her mind. 'I don't know about you but I'm starving. I've got a quiche in the fridge and chips in the freezer and you can toss a salad can't you. How will that be? I've got your things. All I need now is a bag to put them in. I'll try the kitchen shall I?'

'And another thing,' Agnes said, worrying on. 'Where am I going to sleep? You've only got one bedroom and this damn leg takes up a hell of a lot of room.'

'We'll sort that out when we've had lunch,' Francesca promised, heading for the kitchen and the necessary plastic bag.

'And another thing,' Agnes said as she returned. 'What if. . . ?'

'Can you get up on your own, or do you want a hand?' Francesca said as she packed the bag.

Being challenged, Agnes made a great effort, hauled herself to her feet on the bottom step and eased down until she was standing on the hall carpet.

'Right,' Francesca approved, smiling at her. 'We're all set. I'll go ahead and get the car door open for you.'

Half an hour later they were in the flat, drinking a bottle of red wine and eating a happy lunch together. Francesca was inwardly purring at a job well done. It felt like a victory.

*

That was Henry's opinion of it too when Francesca arrived in his office later that afternoon to tell him how she'd got on. He ordered tea and cakes to celebrate and, while they were waiting for the tray to arrive, questioned her closely and happily. When she told him about the folders he laughed out loud.

'That's just typical of our Agnes,' he said. 'Always took her work very seriously. She was the best secretary I've ever had.'

'The thing she was most worried about was a bonfire,' Francesca told him, as the tray arrived.

He drank tea, smiling at her. 'She would be,' he said, as he put his cup down. 'That's Bonfire she's talking about. That's what we call Guy Fawkes' Day around here and it's the biggest event in the Lewes calendar. You wait till you see it. It's quite something. The bonfires are spectacular, built like ships and palaces and dragons and all sorts. It takes about a week to set them up and there are torch-lit parades and people dressing up and bands and fireworks. People come for miles to see it. The town's packed. It takes a lot of organization and she's the secretary of our group. Has been for years. We depend on her to keep us all informed. She'll have been working on that all afternoon if I'm any judge. You see if she hasn't. I'll ask you tomorrow.'

Now Agnes' concern made sense. 'I knew it couldn't be just an ordinary bonfire,' Francesca said.

'Nobody could call our Bonfire ordinary,' he told her happily. 'Like I said, it's spectacular. A legend.'

Above his head the mermaid smiled mysteriously. The tea was hot and strong, the cake delicious. Agnes was going to be looked after. Francesca sat back in her chair, feeling pleased with herself. All was right with the world. And then Henry put down his cup and changed

174

the subject and the tone.

'Now we must get that house of hers cleaned up,' he said. 'I know we've got six weeks but it's going to be a massive job so the sooner we get on with it the better. I shall start first thing tomorrow morning. Get a couple of skips organized and put my cleaners on to it.'

I can't let him do this, Francesca thought. It would cut her to pieces. But how could she stop him? He was the boss and she was one of his workers. Workers don't tell the boss what to do. She sat quietly in her chair watching him as panic tied knots in her chest.

'We'll get one of the downstairs rooms cleared first,' he was saying. 'We'll make a really thorough job of it, curtains, carpets, upholstery, cushions, everything, Then if she comes back for a visit during her six weeks, which she well might if I know anything about our Agnes, you'll have something good to show her.' He was smiling to think what a pleasant surprise it was going to be and how much it would cheer his old friend.

His enthusiasm beamed across the desk towards Francesca, the warmth of it paralyzing her. He was so determined and so sure he was right and he was planning this for all the best reasons. She sat very still thinking hard and finding no answers. What on earth could she say to persuade him? She couldn't think of a single thing.

'Well,' he said, smiling at her. 'What do you think? Have I left anything out?

Two direct questions had to be answered. 'No, no,' she said. 'You've thought of everything. It's just. . . .' And then she stopped.

He went on smiling at her, intrigued by her serious expression and the puckered forehead that showed she was worried. Her hesitancy reminded him of Candida, when she was hiding how she felt about that dreadful cancer because she didn't want to worry him. 'Just?' he prompted.

'Well, what I mean is. . . . The thing is, I'm not sure. . . . I mean I know how much you want to help her, I'm not saying that. Of course you do. You're fond of her. We both are. I mean we'd never do anything to hurt her, would we. It's just. . . . Not that it's my place to say it, I mean.' She glanced up at the mermaid for inspiration but the mermaid was looking enigmatical.

The disjointed ambiguity of what she was saying caught Henry's attention and held it. Why was she talking about Agnes being hurt? That didn't make sense. 'Spit it out,' he said. 'I shan't bite you whatever it is.' And he leant across the desk and patted her hand to encourage her.

'It's just . . .' Francesca said, looking down at the tea tray because looking at him was making her feel uncomfortable. 'I know you want to help her by cleaning her house and getting rid of the junk and everything and it *would* be a help, I'm not saying it wouldn't, but. . . . Well, it might not be what she wants.'

'No woman in her right mind could *want* to live in that sort of squalor,' he told her reasonably. 'She'll be relieved to get shot of it if I'm any judge.'

'I don't know how I'm going to explain this to you,' Fran said, forcing herself to look up at him, 'but actually she *does* want to live in it.' His expression was hard with disbelief and she realized that now she'd started she would have to give him reasons for what she was saying, even if it meant being disloyal to poor Ages. 'I tried to tidy her wardrobe while I was living there,' she said, 'and it upset her dreadfully. I mean there were all these lovely clothes lying in heaps on the bottom of the wardrobe and I thought I'd hang them up for her. I thought it would be a help. But it was absolutely the wrong thing to do. She was so upset. You'd never believe how upset she was. She said she didn't want anything touched. She couldn't bear it. She wants everything to stay as it is. I think it's a sort of obsession. A compulsion. Not being able to throw things away. Not wanting to accept change. Something like that.' Was she making herself clear? His face was puzzled so it was impossible to tell.

There was a long pause while she examined the tea tray until she felt she knew every line and colour and shadow of every cup and saucer and plate. Eventually he cleared his throat.

'So what you're saying is we shouldn't go ahead with this plan to clean the house.'

'I'm afraid so,' she admitted and because he looked stern, she rushed to modify it, her words tumbling over one another. 'I mean, we might be able to persuade her to do it, later, when she's got over the leg, back on her feet, I mean, well you know what I mean, and then we could help her, if she wanted us to, and I'm sure she would, but it ought to come from her in the first place. After all it *is* her house.'

'You're very fond of her,' he said, but his tone was too bland to interpret.

'She's been very good to me.'

At that, he smiled. 'I can't say I understand this,' he admitted, 'I really don't know enough about compulsions or obsessions or things like that, but if you think we'd be doing more harm than good, then obviously we don't go ahead with it. The aim is to make her life easier not compound her difficulties.'

She felt limp with relief. 'Thank you,' she said and smiled back at him for the first time since their difficult conversation began. Then her conscience stirred. She'd wasted enough of his time. 'I'd better be getting back to work,' she said.

'You had,' he agreed, beaming at her, 'or we shan't have enough mermaids to meet the demand.'

On which happy and positive note they parted.

After she'd gone Henry stood by the window, with one hand on the sill and looked out at the neat garden below him and frowned. The interview had made him feel decidedly uncomfortable. It was the first time he'd given way to anybody since Candida died and he was torn between feeling pleased by his tolerance and annoyed by the fact that he'd agreed to change his plans, when they were so obviously positive and helpful. He prided himself that he was a good judge of character but he'd underestimated Francesca Jones. There was iron underneath that diffident exterior. He'd known there was more to her than met the eye from the moment they'd met and that being an artist she saw things other people missed. You only had to look at her portrait of Agnes to see that. It was really very perceptive, but even so, she could be wrong this time.

There was a discreet knock at the door. Liam, he thought, and called to him to come in. There was work to be done.

Agnes had spent a productive afternoon in the flat. Having plugged in her laptop and printer and been surprised to discover that they worked as well in Francesca's living room as they had in her bedroom, she'd settled herself comfortably at the table and started work. By five o'clock she'd written the Bonfire newsletter, run off the requisite number of copies, addressed all the envelopes and was feeling very pleased with herself. Cup of tea, she thought, and put on her crutches to walk to the kitchen to make it.

She'd only hopped three steps when somebody rang the doorbell. It took quite an effort to turn round and hobble off to answer it, so she was none too pleased when she found Cora's unpleasant nephew, Kenneth or Brad or whatever he called himself, slummocking on the doorstep, looking sorry for himself. His hair was stiff with gel and sticking up like a lavatory brush, which made him look even more stupid than usual, and he was wearing the shoddiest T-shirt she'd ever seen.

'Yes?' she said, in her most disapproving voice.

He gave her his unctuous smile. 'Is Francesca there?'

'She's at work. Where do you imagine she'd be at this time of day? Some of us work.'

She was pleased to see that she was making him uncomfortable. He shifted his feet and tried another smile. 'Maybe I could come in and wait for her. I wouldn't be any bother.'

'No. You couldn't. I've got work to do too.'

'I wouldn't be any bother. Really.

She glared at him. 'What part of the word "No" do you have trouble understanding?'

He pressed on, beginning to look desperate. 'Only I haven't got anywhere to stay, you see. I thought maybe she'd let me sleep here for a few days. It wouldn't be for long. Just a few days. Till I find my feet sort of thing. To sort of tide me over. I've had such a terrible time of it. You'd never believe how unkind people are.'

Agnes could see there was a major whinge coming and cut it off at once. 'There's no room for you here, young man,' she said briskly. 'We've only got two beds. I'm in one and Francesca has the other.'

'I could sleep on the floor,' he said eagerly, putting one foot over the doorstep. 'I wouldn't mind.'

'You most certainly could not,' she said. 'Move your

foot. I'm going to close the door.'

'Oh come on Aggie,' he wheedled, 'be a sport. I haven't got anywhere else to go. You wouldn't turn me out on the streets would you?'

She gave him one of her stern looks. 'Miss Potts to you,' she said. 'Move your foot and I'll give you some advice.'

He moved his foot and looked plumply hopeful.

'Right,' she said. 'Do you know where Station Road is? Yes I can see you do. Very well, go there and follow it until you get to a building called the Job Centre. That's the place for you to go to.'

He shuffled his feet and looked sullen. 'There aren't any jobs going,' he told her. 'I've looked.'

'That,' she said sternly, 'I can't believe. There are always jobs going in that centre.'

'Not good jobs,' he objected. 'Not the sort of jobs anyone would want to do. Oh I know there *are* jobs but they're things like van drivers and cleaners and carers and trolley-walleys. I don't want to do any of *them*. I mean to say.'

'Beggars can't be choosers.' Agnes said. 'As you should have learnt by now. Well there it is. That's my advice to you. Get a job. Any sort of job. Get it and hold it down for long enough to earn the money to keep yourself and rent a room. Stop sponging off other people and learn to stand on your own feet. Now I'm off. Some of us have got work to do.' And she closed the door on him.

As she propped herself against the sink so that she could fill the kettle with her free right hand, she was grinning to herself. That's the way to deal with selfish young men, she thought. What a good job Francesca wasn't here. She'd have let him in.

CHAPTER 12

JEFFREY WAS SLOUCHED in his armchair in his horribly untidy living room biting his nails and feeling sorry for himself. It was nearly two in the morning and life with Bubbles wasn't working out. She was appallingly selfish. He found it hard to credit how selfish she was. She ate her way through everything in his cupboards and never offered to buy replacements: she stayed out clubbing until the small hours and never got up before eleven: she never did a hand's turn in the flat. There were dirty mugs and plates all over the room and the kitchen was a tip. She didn't cook, she never made the beds, and she took her washing home for her mother to do so it was no good expecting her to run his machine for him. And on the one horrible occasion when he'd made a few amorous advances to her she'd flicked him away as if he were a bluebottle or something, and said 'You've got to be joking!' in that unpleasant voice of hers and then stared at him in such a withering way he could feel himself shrinking away to nothing. If it hadn't been for the fact that she was going to pay half the mortgage and keep him solvent, he'd have parted company with her after the first week. As it was he'd hung on until the second payment was due and he was sitting up at that moment, waiting for her to come home so that he could remind her of her obligations when she did. It was no good trying to open a conversation about it when she finally got up in the morning because all she ever did then was grunt. He sighed and sloped off to make himself another cup of coffee. You need stamina in this game, he thought, looking at his watch. She'd better pay up and look cheerful, that's all.

Somebody was scrabbling a key in the lock. About time too. There was a lot of murmuring and giggling outside the door. They don't care if they wake people up, he thought, pouring hot water on his Nescafé. He was tempted to shout at her to come in and stop making a row but thought better of it. If he was going to talk to her about the mortgage it would be silly to put her in a bad mood. And eventually his patience paid off and the door was pushed open and two people came giggling through into the hall with their arms round each other.

'Hello,' Bubbles said. 'You're up late.' She waved a drunken hand at her partner and burped. 'This is Chris. Say hello Chris.'

'I've been waiting up for you,' Jeffrey said.

'You sound like my mum,' she said and giggled. 'This is Chris.'

'You told me.'

'Is there any coffee? You'd like a cup of coffee wouldn't you Chris.'

'I've just used the last spoonful,' Jeffrey said with great satisfaction and watched while Chris struggled to speak. God, they *were* drunk.

'I Brett,' Chris said thickly, as if he was introducing himself. 'Brett. Um.' Then he steadied himself and delivered his message in a single breath. 'Bretter ge' goin.'

'Quite right,' Jeffrey said, giving him the full benefit

of his blackest frown just to make sure he did. 'The door's behind you. You can find your way, can't you.'

'Don't be like that,' Bubbles said, scowling at him. 'He can have a cup of tea even if you *have* scoffed all the coffee.' But her partner was stumbling towards the door, muttering to himself, struggling to focus his eyes sufficiently to find the handle. When he'd blundered through it and was gone, she turned on Jeffrey, scowled at him again and began to scold. 'That wasn't very hospitable.'

'I had no intention of being hospitable,' he told her, drinking his coffee. 'I've got more important things to do.'

'Well you can do them,' she said, flouncing away from him. 'I'm off to bed.'

'Not yet you're not,' he said. 'We've got something to discuss.'

She gave him a quick glance, saw trouble and moved straight into her good little girl voice, pouting and posturing and flicking her fingers at him. 'Don't be like that, Jeffy Weffey. I'm only a little whittle Bubbles. You know that.' And when he didn't respond, she went on, 'Anyway I'm not fit for anything this time a' night. I'm sooo tired I'm ready to drop. It'll have to wait till morning. It can, can't it? Jeffrey? Oh come on Jeffy Weffey, don't be nasty to me.'

He was irritated by her silly voice and all that stupid finger flicking. It was artificial and unnecessary. For a drifting second he thought of Fran with an unexpected sense of affection. She'd had no business walking out on him like that but even at her worst *she* never put on a silly voice. 'The mortgage is due,' he said shortly, keeping his temper with an effort. 'And it's your turn to pay.'

She blinked at him and resumed her normal voice. 'What, now?'

'I'll have to show you who to make out the cheque to,'

he said, 'so the sooner the better.'

'Write it down for me and I'll do it tomorrow,' she said and giggled. 'Or today, I suppose I mean.'

'Do it now,' he said. 'You'll have forgotten all about it by the time you wake up. Get your cheque book.'

She made a moue, trying to tease him into a better humour. 'You're such an old bully.'

He was implacable. 'Get it.'

She staggered off towards her bedroom, burping. 'Fifty wasn't it?' she said.

'Fifty?'

'Pounds.'

He gave his barking laugh. She really was stupid. Fancy imagining you could get a mortgage on a place this size for fifty a month. 'Add another two hundred,' he said.

She stopped and turned, with difficulty. Her face was a study in horror. 'Two hundred and fifty pounds?' she said. 'I can't pay that. I'm at uni. I told you. I'm living on a loan.'

'We're all living on loans,' he said coldly.

'I paid fifty at the other place.'

'You agreed to pay the mortgage, every other month.'

'Not that amount.'

'That's how much it is. And before you make any more excuses, I might point out you've been living here rent free since you arrived.'

'I'm not making excuses,' she said. 'I'm stating a fact. Fifty is all I can afford. I'll pay that willingly but not a penny more. I can't. I haven't got it. And that's all there is to it.'

'Then extend your loan.'

'You've got to be joking,' she said scathingly. 'It's big enough as it is. Have you any idea what the fees are for uni? They run into thousands, every fucking year. Thousands. I shall be paying this lot off until I'm in my wheelchair.'

Temper was beginning to bubble in his chest. He knew he wasn't going to be able to control it for very much longer. 'That's your choice,' he said coldly. 'Nobody forced you to go to college.'

She mocked him. 'Oh come on! This is uni we're talking about. I bet you'd have gone if you'd had the chance.'

The implied insult pushed him over the edge. 'I'll have you know I did go,' he said untruthfully, 'and got a First what's more. There's nothing you can tell me about "uni" as you call it.'

She went on mocking. 'Well pardon me for living.'

The supercilious expression on her stupid face was more than he could bear. 'Now look here,' he said. 'You've got to get a few things clear in your head if you're going to go on living with me.'

'Living with you?' she sneered. 'Do me a favour. I wouldn't live with you if you were the last man alive.'

'Allow me to point out you're "living" in *my* flat,' he shouted. 'My flat. That's where you're "living" and you're "living" here rent free. Rent fucking free. And look at it. You've turned it into a pigsty.' He waved a furious hand at all the dirty coffee cups and the tumble of stupid magazines. 'This is all your rubbish. Yours. And you never clear any of it up. You treat me like a servant and you never pay a penny piece for anything. Well it's got to stop. You can just get your fucking cheque book and pay your share.' He was hot with anger. 'D'you hear me?'

'Oh I hear you,' she shouted, equally furious. 'I hear you good, don't you worry and if you think I'm going to go on living in your rotten flat after this you've got another think coming. I shall move out, first chance I get.'

'Good riddance,' he shouted back. But she'd already left the room and was banging her bedroom door shut. Fucking woman, he thought. I'll be better off without the likes of *her*. I'll show her. I sit up half the night waiting for her and she gives me a faceful of shit. She's vile. I'll be well rid of her.

Anger propelled him to action. He threw one of her filthy coffee cups at the wall so that it smashed to smithereens, scooped up all her stupid magazines and threw them in the bin so violently that half of them fell out again, and stamped off to bed making as much noise as he could, banging every door on the way. Fucking woman. I'll show her.

It wasn't until past ten o'clock the next morning that he woke to a sullen day and a throbbing headache to realize that he'd got to pay the fucking mortgage himself. Oh for fuck's sake! How was he going to manage that? He'd have to get another loan and that would be fucking difficult. The bank manager had gone all stern on him and said he was pushing his limit last time. He growled out to the kitchen and growled himself a cup of tea as somebody selfish had used up the last of the coffee and then growled off to the living room feeling monstrously sorry for himself, glancing at the doormat to see if there was any post but not really expecting any.

It was a happy surprise to see that he'd actually got a letter. What splendid timing. He'd sent out countless letters and application forms for a whole variety of jobs over the last few weeks and he'd never had an answer to any of them so he'd rather given up hope. And now here was a comfortably official looking envelope just when he needed it most. The letter inside wasn't the offer of a job – that would have been too much to expect – but it was the next best thing. It was an answer to a general letter of enquiry that he'd sent out last week to every firm he thought might have a post he could fill. This one was in the Midlands and the writer, whose signature was illegible, told him the company was looking for a qualified geologist to join the team and suggested that he might care to fill in the enclosed application form. At last, he thought, beaming at the letter. Someone with a bit of sense. He would do it at once, while he drank his tea. Or better still he'd go down to Starbucks and have a coffee and a croissant and fill it in there. That would be much more congenial. He checked to see that he had enough change and having established his solvency, showered and dressed and took the letter, his laptop and the form to his favourite coffee house. He would have to bend the truth a bit if he was going to tempt them but needs must when the devil drives.

It took him an hour and a half, three cups of coffee, considerable imagination and the frequent use of Google but at the end of it he'd produced something suitably tempting, filling in the form at just the right level of honesty and composing an accompanying letter that was quite simply a masterpiece. He'd stressed his great experience in the field; referred lightly and modestly to his three degrees, which was stretching the point a bit because he'd only just scraped a low O-level in Geography and had no geological qualifications at all but you have to embroider a bit if you're going to get noticed; gone into some detail about his invention of coloured concrete and what a boon that was to the building industry; mentioned half a dozen reputable geologists and said he was sure they would be happy to provide a reference for him. Three of them were people he knew about but had only met briefly, the others were names he'd found on Google. If this doesn't clinch the job, he thought happily, as he strolled back to the flat to print off the letter, I don't know what will.

The living room was in the same disgusting state as it had been when he left it but the door to the spare room was open and there was no sign of Bubbles, which was gratifying. His self-confidence was fully restored and he had the rest of the day to spend as he pleased. There's not a woman alive who can put *me* down, he thought, as he printed off his letter. It doesn't matter who she is.

It took Agnes and Francesca just over twenty-four hours to find a working pattern for their new life together in the flat. When Francesca got home from work on that first Friday there was a rabbit stew on the hob, an apple crumble in the oven ready for their supper and an opened bottle of red wine on the table.

'Tuck in,' Agnes said as she dished up.

'I am spoilt,' Francesca smiled at her. 'How did you get all this? Have you been out shopping?'

'No. Course not,' Agnes said. 'I'm not daft. I rang my nice butcher and told him he'd have to deliver things to me for a week or two and your nice neighbour on the next balcony along gave me the apples. We had quite a chat across the balconies.'

Francesca felt rather ashamed to think that she'd only ever nodded to her neighbours in all the weeks she'd been in the flats. Trust Agnes to make friends. 'I shall have to go and thank her,' she said.

'Eat your supper first or it'll get cold,' Agnes said, picking up her fork. 'How was work?'

'Manic,' Francesca told her. 'The Christmas orders are coming in. Henry's like a dog with two tails. This is good. I haven't had rabbit for ages. It's delicious.'

'Glad to hear it,' Agnes said. 'So you won't mind if I appoint myself chief cook and bottle washer while I'm staying here.'

'Chief cook sounds like a perfect arrangement,' Francesca told her happily. 'Especially if it means coming home to a meal like this. I'm not so sure about the bottle washer bit though.'

Agnes laughed. 'Well all right then. You can wash the bottles. That's a good division of labour.'

'You'll have to put up with me tidying the place up,' Francesca said.

'It's your place, me dear,' Agnes said. 'Just providing you can face me making your bedroom a bit untidy.'

This time it was Francesca's turn to grin. 'I expect that,' she said. 'It's not in your nature to put things away, now is it.'

Agnes was rueful but honest. ''Fraid not. But I make a mean crumble.'

'And a gorgeous rabbit stew.'

Agnes beamed. 'Want some more?'

'We'll go back to your house tomorrow,' Francesca said as Agnes emptied the serving dish, 'and get a change of clothes and anything else you need. After I've been to thank my neighbour. Must do that first. What's her name? Did you find out?'

'Sandra,' Agnes told her. 'And her little boy's called Tom. I'll make a list of what I need while you're out.'

The next morning they woke to an easy autumn day, cloud dappled skies reflected in the river and the railway land on the opposite bank lush with reddening foliage. Francesca stood on the balcony, teacup in hand, and luxuriated in the richness of the colour.

'I know,' Agnes said, hopping up behind her. 'You'd like to paint it. That's what you're thinking isn't it.'

'I'd like to do a series of paintings', Francesca said. 'In all weathers.'

'Well you can, now I'm here to feed you,' Agnes said. 'What's to stop you?'

A rowing boat passed below them, oars creaking. Its wash broke the gentle reflection of sky and cloud into shimmering patterns. It was a great temptation. 'Half an hour,' Francesca decided, 'and then I really must get on.'

She painted for nearly two hours, while Agnes cooked a cake, and she would have gone on longer if someone hadn't come knocking on their door. As it was she drifted to the door with the paintbrush still in her hand.

Her visitor was a small boy holding a bag of plums. 'Is Miss Potts there?' he asked. He had a lot of thick fair hair flopping over his forehead, large almond shaped hazel eyes and a very earnest expression and, for an odd, brief moment of *déjà vu*, she thought she'd seen him before. Then Agnes came swinging towards the door and greeted him by name.

'Hello Tom. What can we do for you?'

He held out the bag towards her, then saw that she was using crutches and couldn't take it and was blushingly embarrassed, biting his lip, uncertain what to do. And the bitten lip revealed who he was. The little boy in the castle, the one she'd sketched lying on his stomach, writing in his yellow notebook and concentrating so hard his tongue was sticking out. 'Mum thought you might like these,' he was explaining, giving the bag a little shake. 'My Nan bought them over for us and there are ever so ever so many, and she thought you might like some, 'cos you can't get to the shops. My Mum I mean not my Nan.'

'Well how kind,' Agnes said. 'Yes, we would, wouldn't we Francesca. We could make a plum pie. Tell her thank you very much. Would you like to come in? I've just made a chocolate cake. You could taste it for me and see if it's all right. Give the plums to Francesca.' And she led them off towards the kitchen, where the cake was on the rack cooling and the percolator was bubbling coffee.

'I'll just clean my brushes,' Francesca said, putting the plums on the worktop and heading for the living room.

'Francesca is an artist,' Agnes told the little boy. 'She's been painting the view from our balcony.'

He was impressed. 'A real artist?' he said and when she nodded, 'Wow!'

'You can come and see what I've done, if you like,' Francesca said.

He followed her into the living room, eyes shining. She was rather touched.

'There it is,' she said, starting on the brushes.

He looked at it in silence for a long time. Then he turned and gave her his slow smile. 'I like the little boat,' he said. 'Did you make it up?'

She smiled back. 'Oh no. It was a real boat. I paint from the life. Always have. In fact. . . .' And she paused because she knew that what she was going to say would have an impact and she didn't want to miss a second of it. 'Somewhere in that folder over there I've got a sketch of you.'

He was so surprised his mouth fell open. 'Really?' he said. 'Really truly?'

'Really truly,' she said, enjoying herself. 'You were in the castle on a school trip. I'll find it when I've cleaned up and you can look at it while you have your cake.'

It took her quite a while to sort through all the sketches in the folder but eventually she found his little portrait just as Agnes called to them from the kitchen that the coffee was ready. Then she waited until the three of them were sitting round the kitchen table and

Agnes had cut the cake and poured the coffee. Tom was impressively patient, eating his cake politely and sipping his coffee neatly although she could see from the surreptitious glances he was giving the folder that he was itching to see his picture. His behaviour didn't surprise her. She'd recognized something special in him the first moment she saw him. He'd been so quiet and so absorbed. 'There you are,' she said, taking the sketch from her folder and handing it across the table to him. 'That's you writing in your yellow notebook.'

He stared at it for a very long time without saying anything, then he looked up and gave her an absolutely rapturous smile. 'That's well good,' he said. 'I always write like that. My Mum'd love to see it. I couldn't take it home and show her, could I?'

'I don't see why not,' Francesca said. 'I'll put it in a folder for you. But tell her she'll have to give it back. I'd let her keep it only it's going to be part of a big picture I'm going to paint later.'

'There you are, you see,' Agnes grinning at Tom. 'You're going to be famous. Any more cake for anyone?'

Francesca found a new folder and put Tom's portrait inside it, well away from the new influx of chocolate. Then they all enjoyed a second slice and a second mug of coffee. And then Tom said he thought he ought to be getting home or his Mum'ud be wondering where he was. It had been an extraordinary visit.

'We'll have to look sharp with our lunch if we're going to my house this afternoon,' Agnes said.

'Have you made your list?'

'All done and dusted.'

'Then let's go now,' Francesca suggested, looking at her watch. 'We can have a sandwich or something when we get back. What do you think?'

It was peaceful driving between the long rustling hedges and the blushing, shushing trees. Once, a kestrel hovered above them, its eyes focused on the fields below, once the red fox streaked across the road ahead of them. It reminded Francesca of the first time she'd driven these lanes, full of hope and excitement. I knew my life would change, she thought, but I didn't realize how profound the change would be. 'I like Tom,' she said to Agnes.

'You'll like his mother too,' Agnes said. 'It's a good family. You only have to talk to them for half an hour to know that. A good family and very fond of their children. Which is why our Tom's such a dear little boy.'

That was an intriguing idea. 'Do you think families make you what you are then?'

'It's an old debate,' Agnes said. 'Been going on for donkey's years. Nature versus nurture. Or to put it another way, is it your inborn nature that makes you what you are or the way you're brought up? My money's on nurture. I think that's well and away the most influential. It can make or mar you.'

Francesca was intrigued. 'In every family?'

'When they're loving families, certainly,' Agnes said. 'I'm sure of it. You can see it happening. When they love you as you are and allow you to *be* as you are, you become as you are and it's the best you can be. You're happy in your skin. That's why Tom's such a charmer. He's happy in his skin. Of course, it works in quite a different way when their love is conditional. But that's because they're trying to turn you into something you're not. I'll give you a for-instance. My mother insisted on making me tidy everything up. I had to tidy my room every single blessed day. She used to say, "There's a place for everything and everything should be in its place."

And look at me now.'

Francesca bit her lip to stop herself from laughing. 'I take your point,' she said.

Agnes gave her a shrewd look. 'And yours put pressure on you too, didn't she?' she said. It was only just a question.

Francesca wasn't sure how to answer it. Not for the first time she was surprised by how easily a car could become a confessional. 'Well yes,' she said, 'I suppose she did.'

'I knew that as soon as I met you,' Agnes said.

Francesca felt compelled to say more, even though she'd never told anybody about her childhood and she wasn't at all sure that it was wise to do it then. But Agnes was smiling encouragement and the weight of her unspoken questions was heavy in the air between them so she had to say something. 'She didn't nag me to do things,' she said at last. 'I mean it wasn't anything like that. She didn't tell me to tidy my room or give me orders.'

'But it was pressure,' Agnes prompted, 'or you wouldn't have ended up with so little self-confidence. Until you saw the mermaid, you let that hideous Jeffrey trample all over you. It used to make me want to thump him.'

That made Francesca laugh and after that, carried along on the warmth of her laughter, she found it possible to make an admission of sorts. 'Well, yes,' she said. 'I suppose it was pressure. I don't think she meant to be unkind, though. It was just her way.' Then she stopped, feeling she really shouldn't be telling tales on her mother, even to Agnes.

'Um!' Agnes said. 'So what *did* she do? It must have been something. It's OK. I'm not judging her, I'm just interested.'

Francesca frowned and licked her lips. The confession had to come. She couldn't avoid it. And it *was* OK.

Whatever else you might think about Agnes Potts she wasn't judgemental. 'Oh,' she said, trying to make it sound light and unimportant, 'she just said I wasn't any good at anything. I think she wanted to spur me on.' My God, she thought, it still hurts me, even to remember it.

Again the shrewd look. 'And did it spur you on?'

'Well no. Quite the reverse really.'

Agnes looked another question at her.

'I believed her you see,' Francesca said. 'Well you do, don't you, when you're a child, I mean, and when it's your mother who's telling you. If she said I wasn't any good, then I wasn't.'

'Well you've proved her wrong now,' Agnes said. 'You're a superb artist and if that's not being "good" I don't know what is.'

'Well . . .' Francesca said. 'I suppose. . . .'

'Never mind "suppose,"' Agnes said trenchantly. 'Your work is good. Very, very good. And I'll tell you something else while I'm about it. You paint with affection. You like your models and it shows.'

Francesca could feel the blush spreading from her neck to her face.

'You've driven past the house,' Agnes said.

It was possible for Francesca to laugh at herself. 'Oh for heaven's sake,' she said. 'I did that the first time.'

'You're perfection,' Agnes said, as Francesca reversed. 'Tell you what, when we've got all the things we need, let's go down the pub and have a pie and a pint.'

'That,' Francesca teased her, 'is the most sensible thing you've said all morning.'

Jeffrey Walmesly had a pub lunch that Saturday too but he was in such a bad temper it gave him indigestion. That stupid Bubbles had got up early for once, just when he'd have preferred her to be out of the way, even if she did snore, and then she'd banged about the flat packing her things all the time he was trying to eat his breakfast which was very annoying and totally unnecessary. And just as he'd worked himself up to give her a piece of his mind, that moronic Chris had arrived and she'd gone giggling off with him.

'This is Chris,' she said, as they were going through the door. 'I told you that didn't I? I'm moving in with him, aren't I Chris my little honey woney? Thought you ought to know. See you around.'

And before he could think of anything to say to her, she'd flicked her fingers at him and gone. She hadn't paid a penny piece towards her keep or the mortgage or the gas bills or anything. She'd just gone swanning off and left him with all the debt. And the flat was a tip. And there wasn't any coffee. And her ghastly lipstick was all over all the mugs. And he hadn't got a job or even a hope of one. Life was just fucking unfair. It was enough to make a saint weep.

He could have wept in earnest if it hadn't been for the fact that the phone rang.

'Not now,' he said to it. 'Not now, you stupid thing. Can't you see I'm busy?' But then it occurred to him that it might be somebody ringing him with the offer of a job or an interview. They ought to. God knows, he'd sent out enough letters. He rearranged his expression, took a deep breath and picked the phone up in mid squawk. 'Jeffrey Walmesly,' he said and was pleased by how smooth his voice sounded.

'And about time too,' a woman's voice said crossly.

'Excuse me,' he said, being splendidly polite. 'To whom do I have the pleasure of speaking?'

'Come off it Jeffrey,' the voice said. 'Don't give yourself

airs. It's Mrs Jones. Francesca's mother.'

He was instantly deflated. 'Oh,' he said flatly.

The voice went on, now gratingly familiar. 'I've been trying to get in touch with my daughter for weeks. I've sent her two letters. Did you forward them?'

'Of course,' he lied.

'Well she hasn't answered. I suppose it's too much to hope she's at home with you.'

''Fraid not.'

'No. I didn't think she would be. If she knew what this is about she'd come home like a shot, I'm certain sure.'

There was such a sneering tone to her voice he was intrigued. 'Perhaps if you told me what it was about,' he suggested, 'I might be able to help you.'

'She's come into some money. Rather a lot of money.'

It was on the tip of his tongue to ask how much but he forbore. 'Ah,' he said, 'I see.'

'My fool brother-in-law's only gone and left her all his money,' Mrs Jones said. 'It should have come to me by rights but he was always an idiot. Congenital. Anyway the long and the short of it is the solicitor wants her address so that he can contact her.'

That put him on the spot so he said 'Ah' again.

'I assume you do know where she is.'

'Well not exactly.'

'What do you mean "not exactly"? Either you do or you don't.'

'She moves around a lot.'

'I thought you said she was looking after some old relation.'

'Well that's what she told me but you know what Fran's like. Anyway she moves around a lot. It's – um – not always possible to know where she is.'

'You're worse than bloody useless.'

He decided to change the subject to something a bit more congenial. 'Is it a lot of money?'

'Over twenty-four thousand,' she said bitterly. 'I'd call that quite a lot, wouldn't you?'

He'd call it a life-saver. An absolute, stone-bonker, once in a lifetime life-saver. He could pay off the mortgage, start a company, buy some decent clothes. He'd be made. 'I tell you what,' he said. 'They could put it in my bank account pro tem, if that would make things any easier.'

'Oh you'd like that wouldn't you,' she said and there was no mistaking the sneer this time. 'It won't wash Jeffrey. This is her money and she's the one who's going to get it. The only one. All I need is an address. Now can you get it for me or can't you?'

'No problem,' he said and tried to joke. 'I'll go and get my deerstalker.'

The joke was lost on her. 'Your what?'

He sighed. She was so thick. But he answered her politely. 'Never mind. Don't worry. I'll get it sorted.'

'Well see you do,' she warned. 'That's all.'

He was gritting his teeth as he put the phone down. It was all so fucking unfair. If Fran hadn't walked out on him they could be living the life of Riley. And now he didn't even know where she was. And what was worse he had no way of finding out. He couldn't put a message on Facebook. That would give the game away to the old bat. And he couldn't trawl round to Randall and Tongs. They wouldn't tell him anything and they'd laugh in his face. But what *could* he do? He had to find her. He just simply had to. I mean to say twenty-four grand. Oh why, oh why was everything so unfair?

CHAPTER 13

A GNES AND FRANCESCA came home from their visit to the house in high good humour. Agnes had spent almost her entire visit out in the garden inspecting her crops. Francesca had watched her go, feeling anxious in case she found it difficult to walk on the rough grass or was upset by what she found by but she came back looking resigned.

'The apples are still in pretty good nick,' she reported. 'I thought they'd be rotting by now. But they're not. It's frustrating seeing them still on the tree though and me with this stupid leg. I've half a mind to ask Henry if I could hire his gardener for a few hours just to get them in for me.'

Francesca answered her calmly, although her mind was racing with relief. 'Why don't you?'

'I'd pay him,' Agnes assured them both. 'I wouldn't want our Henry to be out of pocket.'

Francesca thought of all the money he'd been planning to spend on skips and cleaners and tried not to grin. ''Course' she said.

'There's no need to rush into it,' Agnes said. 'I'll think about it.' Then she closed the subject. 'Now then what about these clothes?'

Francesca pointed to the neat pile of underwear and cardigans on the table and the thick coat and skirts hanging in the doorway. 'All done,' she said. 'You only need to check them through.'

Agnes glanced at them and nodded. 'You're such a friend,' she said. 'I'm so glad you saw that mermaid.'

'Me too,' Francesca told her. And as things were going so well, she dared a suggestion. 'I've been wondering,' she began.

Agnes gave her an odd look, half smile, half question. It made Francesca's heart lurch. 'Go on,' she said.

'Well,' Francesca said. 'It's just that while we're here I was wondering whether it might be a good time to clear out the fridge. It's only a suggestion mind. Only if you want to. I know you can't do anything that requires standing – or climbing – but you could do this sitting down.' And when Agnes looked thoughtful and didn't say anything she went on, trying to sound casual and not urge her too strongly. 'There might be things in it that ought to be on the compost heap. I mean you forget how the days pass don't you? We could do that while the weather holds. I mean, you could tell me what's to go and what's to stay and we could sort it all out. We could take the good stuff back with us, couldn't we? I'm sure we could use it.' She was frightening herself by her daring. Oh come on, Agnes, she thought. Say something. Even if it's only no.

But Agnes surprised her. 'Yes,' she said, nodding again. 'Why not? We've got time for it if we're going to have that pub lunch. You'll have to do the donkey work mind.'

They cleared the fridge between them, Francesca being careful to check with her friend before she took anything out to the compost heap and Agnes sitting at the kitchen table packing the good stuff in her shopping basket. It took them over an hour but when they'd finished and Francesca had cleaned the fridge outside and in, they left it with its door ajar and went off to the pub feeling well pleased with themselves. It was a triumph of friendship and diplomacy and they both knew it.

It was a good lunch too. By the time they finally got back to the flat they were well fed, thoroughly at ease and happily contented. And to crown the day, Tom came knocking on their door, as soon as they'd put the food in the fridge, bringing his mum with him and his mum was so excited she was pink cheeked and shining eyed.

'I had to come and tell you,' she said to Francesca. 'That painting's just stunning. There's no other word for it. Stunning. Me and Kev love it. I mean it's him to a T. We've took great care of it.' She handed the folder over reverently, watching as Francesca put it on the table. 'Stunning.'

'Hello Sandra,' Agnes said. 'Your apples made a splendid crumble.'

'Glad to hear it,' Sandra said. 'I thought of you the minute the old love arrived with them. She always brings us more than we can eat. She thinks we'll fade away if she don't feed us.' Then she turned back to Francesca again. 'Tom says you're painting a big picture.'

'I'm hoping to,' Francesca said. 'It's at the complicated stage at the moment, all sketches, ideas, possibilities. You can see some of it if you like.'

Sandra didn't have to say how much she *would* like. Her face was glowing.

'Give me a minute to clear the table,' Francesca said, 'and then I can arrange the sketches to give you some idea what I've got in mind. Tom will be right in the centre because that's where he was when I first saw him.' She put his sketch in the middle of the table. 'The

still centre with all his friends running up the mound.'
It took a little while to put the sketches in position and
Sandra watched as if she was spellbound.

'It's going to be ever such a big picture,' she said. 'Oh
look Tom, there's your teacher. That's good of him too.
He's always got hordes of kids round him. We call him
Mr Magnet.'

It *is* going to be a big picture, Francesca thought. It'll
be the biggest I've ever painted. But oddly the thought
didn't daunt her. After such a successful morning she
felt equal to anything. And now that she was looking at
her sketches she could see where the movement of the
picture should be. It should flow like the mermaid's tail,
round Mr Magnet, over the mound, with clouds above
it to echo its movement and the tower and the green
mound as a solid focus to offset all that moving energy.

She blocked out the entire picture that afternoon. And
it *was* big but it worked or perhaps she ought to be more
realistic and say, it would work when it was painted.
From then on she worked on it every day while the light
held and Agnes fed her and watched her and didn't
say much. And that was all right too because there was
nothing to say while it was being painted. That would
come when it was completed.

But then when it was more than half done, Molly
asked when she was to come for her next sitting. 'I didn't
like to worry you with Agnes and her leg and everything,' she said, 'but I've got an afternoon to myself this
weekend and I wondered . . .'

Put like that Francesca could hardly refuse her. Not
that she wanted to because that painting was pulling her
most strongly too. So from then on she had two pictures
to finish, the easel was in perpetual use and the living
room was never free of canvasses. But it was peaceful

there with paint and conversation flowing and Agnes on hand with cups of coffee and admiration.

'This is such a good life,' she said to Agnes as they were eating their supper after a particularly fruitful afternoon.

'Long may it continue,' Agnes said. 'Shall we finish this treacle pudding? It'ud be a shame to waste it.'

Change, when it came was like a thunderclap.

Francesca had driven to the potteries that September morning, with the sun on her face and the painting in her mind, dreamily and rather slowly but when she walked into the workshop, she was so taken aback by the noise and passion she found there that for a few seconds all she could do was blink. The place was crackling. There was so much powerful excitement there it was as if someone had set light to the air. Nobody was at their work station, most people seemed to be running from one end of the room to the other and they were all talking at once.

'What on earth's going on?' she asked as Molly trotted up to join her, pink in the face and so out of breath she was panting. 'Have we got the day off?'

Molly grabbed hold of her hand. 'Come an' see,' she puffed and trotted them both off to the other end of the room.

Now Francesca could see that there was a crowd gathered there and that they were reading a notice. Some of them turned and saw her and stood aside to make way for her so that she could read it too. 'Wait till you see this,' they said, their faces shining. 'It's great.' And young Sarah said, 'You must look at it Miss Jones. It's well good,' and gave her a little push towards the notice board.

It was one of Henry's brief announcements with his

203

modest signature at the bottom. 'I thought you all ought to know this as soon as possible. I had a phone call last night from the *Sunday Times* to tell me that the paper intends to feature our mermaid dinner service in one of their pre-Christmas issues, which they are calling "Must-haves for Christmas". They will be here on Thursday and Friday this week to interview me and as many of you as they can and to take pictures. How's that for a feather in our caps?'

The others waited quietly while she read it, then they crowded round her again. 'Well?' they asked. 'What do you think of that? Is that good or what?'

She was overwhelmed. To have her mermaid featured in the *Sunday Times* was almost too good to be true. 'It's wonderful,' she said. 'I can't believe it. You'll have to pinch me or I shall think I'm dreaming.'

She was pinched at once, very tenderly. And from somewhere behind them, Henry's voice said, 'Now how did I guess you'd say that?' And there he was, striding towards them, having his hand shaken and his back slapped and beaming at Francesca all the time. 'Have you got a minute?' he asked her.

She followed him up to his office and they were clapped and cheered all the way. It was like something from a fairy tale. If a frog dressed as a footman had suddenly appeared to open the door for them she wouldn't have been the least surprised. They sat in his two armchairs and smiled at one another, savouring this amazing success.

'Now then,' he said, turning their attention to the second subject on his agenda, business-like as ever. 'I'm going to give a party on Friday and I'm going to ask the reporter and the photographers to come along. I'm sure they will. Parties are good copy. I thought they might like to see us having fun. But the thing is, I want to make sure that you and Aggie can come before I send out invitations. Will she be up for it, do you think?'

There was no doubt about the answer. 'I'm sure she will,' Francesca said. 'She'll love it. She's getting used to the plaster now. It's the fourth week. And she's a dab hand with her crutches. She goes like the clappers. You should see her.'

He laughed at that, his eyes smiling. 'In that case I shall send out the invitations by the next post,' he said.

Then there was a pause while she waited and he picked up a pen from his desk and twirled it between his fingers. Finally he said, just a little too casually, 'I suppose you haven't had a chance to talk to her about her house.'

The question made her catch her breath. He's not still going on about that, surely, she thought. But he was wearing his determined expression. Oh dear. 'Well no,' she said carefully. 'I mean I thought I'd give her a chance to get used to being on crutches, to get a bit stronger. I don't want to upset her.'

'No, no, I understand that,' he said reasonably, 'but she can't go on living in that mess. We shall have to do something about it sooner or later. Don't worry. She'll love it when we've done it, believe me.' And when she looked doubtful, 'I know you think it's some sort of compulsion and I daresay some cases are. But not this one. The evidence is against it. No one in their right mind could *want* to go on living with all that rubbish and I've known Agnes for years and I can tell you she's always been entirely in her right mind.'

I can't argue with him, Francesca thought. She knew she ought to but she couldn't. Not at that moment when he was on such a roll. 'Well,' she said. 'Possibly. But don't let's do it yet. Not just yet anyway. Not now.' And as he still looked determined, she added, 'You wouldn't want to upset her just before your party.'

That made him smile. He had to admire her skill at persuasion. It was a good point. 'We'll defer it,' he promised. 'Just for you because you're the star of the show. And now we'd better get on. Could you ask Molly to come up for a minute?'

She left him with an answering smile but on the way back to the workshop she was frowning. She really couldn't allow him to put pressure on Agnes. Not when she was recovering so well. And not when they were living together so happily. She hadn't eaten so much or so well since she'd moved and she'd got such a lot of painting done she was quite dizzy with the pleasure of it. The picture of the castle was almost finished and she'd painted two more studies of the river and Molly's portrait was looking really good. But that determination of his was a force of nature and it was in full flow. She knew she'd have a hard job to hold it in check and she knew she had to do it. If only he wasn't such a *good* man. It was galling to have to accept that all this was because he wanted to make life easier for Agnes and he couldn't see that it would upset her. *'She'll like it when we've done it'* was a real give-away. I shall put my mind to it while I'm painting the mermaid, she thought.

But she had so many visitors to her work station that morning it was hard to think about anything except the coming visit and the painting under her fingers. Just before their lunch break Molly arrived with an invitation to the party addressed to Francesca Jones and Agnes Potts.

'Won't we have some fun,' Molly said. 'I can't wait.'

That was Agnes's opinion too. 'We shall have to take

206

another trip back to the house,' she said. 'I shall need my pretty shoes and my shawl. What a lark to be in the *Sunday Times*. I should think Henry's like a dog with two tails.'

They went to the house as soon as Francesca got home the following evening and after a lot of rather muddled instructions, Francesca found the things Agnes needed and they packed them all in their shopping bag and Francesca struggled out to the car, with the bag in one hand and the pretty shoes in the other.

'I wonder how my poor apples are,' Agnes said, peering into the dusk.

'Bit too dark to see them,' Francesca said, arranging the bag on the back seat. 'We'll take a look next time.'

'They'll be rotting on the bough by now,' Agnes sighed. 'Bound to be. It's such a waste.'

The sigh gave Francesca an idea. 'Why don't you ask Henry to get his gardener to come in and crop them? You *were* thinking about it.'

Agnes eased into the car and gave it thought. 'Do you think he would?' she said as Francesca switched on the headlights and eased the car out of the drive.

'I'm sure he would,' Francesca said. 'He likes to help people. And he's got a very good gardener. I mean just think how good his garden looks. 'Course, he might not be able to get it done until after the party because he'll have to make sure Henry's garden's in good shape but I'm sure he'll come and do it after that.'

In fact it was done the very next day because Henry was delighted with the idea and rang to arrange it as soon as Francesca suggested it. And that evening, he appeared at the flat with a box of pears, a dish full of blackberries and a huge box of apples. 'John's been in your garden all afternoon,' he reported, 'and it's all done and dusted. He's picked all the apples and put the rotten ones on the compost heap. He says to tell you that you didn't lose many. And he thought you'd like these as well as they were ready for picking. If there's anything else you'd like him to do just say the word.'

It would have been hard to tell which of them was the more pleased, Henry because he'd helped his old friend, Agnes because the apples hadn't been left to rot or Francesca because she'd given them both what they wanted. 'If you could carry them into the kitchen,' she said to Henry, 'I'll find homes for them.'

Henry followed her happily but on the way he glanced into the living room and caught sight of her paintings.

'I see you've been busy,' he said to Francesca.

'You should see the painting of the Castle,' Agnes said, lolloping after him. 'For my money, that's a masterpiece.'

'May I?' Henry said to Francesca when he'd put the fruit down on her worktop.

She was anxious at once. 'It's not quite finished,' she warned.

He smiled at her. 'Neither was the mermaid, as I recall,' he said. 'And look where she is now.'

So she took him into the room, where the painting of the Castle was still on her easel, the three river sketches were standing against the wall and the table was covered with paintings and sketches of all kinds, including her picture of the workshop and Molly's half completed portrait. He examined them thoughtfully and for a long time, turning them towards the light. 'Who's the person in this one?' he asked, looking at the painting of the workshop. 'It's our workshop. Right?'

'It's Molly,' she told him and found her original

sketches. 'I thought she'd look good against pale blues and greys.'

'She will too,' he approved. 'She's a colourful character.'

'Yes,' she said seriously. 'She is. It was the first thing I noticed about her. Warmth and colour.'

'I can't wait to see the finished portrait,' Agnes said. 'I'm going to cook a meal for them while Francesca paints and she stands. It's almost finished now.'

She waited for Henry to answer her but he was completely absorbed in the pictures and sketches so she sat down to wait for him and Francesca stood between them and watched them both, wondering what he was thinking. It was hard to judge from his face.

Henry went on turning the sketches over, picking them up and looking at each one with great attention. She can put her hand to absolutely anything, he thought, turning from her artfully composed picture of roses and honeysuckle to her sketch of two little girls walking hand in hand and deep in conversation. There was a quality about her painting that was making him feel unaccountably vulnerable and he couldn't put a word to it although he was recognizing it most strongly. It was there in all the sketches she'd done of the children in the castle, touching, warming, and disturbing. Then he turned over the next picture and found himself looking at a small painting of a chaffinch feeding her chick and he knew what it was. He could see it clearly in the trusting open beak of the fledgling and the movement of its mother's head as she bent towards it. It was tenderness, the thing he'd loved so much in Candida. And now here was this hesitant girl who was so unsure of herself that she still didn't believe in the value of her work and there was so much tenderness in what she'd painted that he could feel the tears pricking in his nose at the impact of it.

She was looking at him with her anxious expression so he looked away from her pictures and answered her.

'This is a very impressive collection,' he said. 'There are so many and they're all different. I tell you what I think. I think you ought to hold an exhibition.'

Francesca was very surprised. It wasn't at all what she'd expected him to say. An exhibition was what a proper artist had. Not someone like her. But before she could open her mouth to tell him so, he was making plans.

'I'll organize it for you,' he said. 'There are one or two excellent rooms in Lewes. I'll put out a few feelers and see what I can come up with. After the party probably. Don't worry. I shan't rush you. You'll need to give it thought and it'll take a bit of time to get it right. Now I shall have to be getting back. The caterers are coming in half an hour.'

'Good heavens above,' Francesca said to Agnes when he was gone. 'Do you think he means it?'

'Wouldn't have said it if he hadn't. Oh no, he means it right enough.'

'But he's so busy.'

'He's always busy,' Agnes told her. 'Always was. From a very young man. He wore me out. Do we have any cream? I fancy blackberry and apple pie. And you need building up ready for tomorrow.'

'I wonder what it'll be like,' Francesca said as she started to peel the first apple.

'Hectic, if I'm any judge,' Agnes said, getting out the mixing bowl.

She was right. It was two days of happy chaos.

CHAPTER 14

THE REPORTER AND photographer didn't arrive at Prendergast Potteries until well past eleven o'clock and by then the general excitement had run its course, coffee break was over and everybody was back at work. It was a quiet entrance. In fact, the photographer had taken two shots of Francesca painting her mermaid before she looked up and saw what was happening. Then the two young women smiled at one another, one artist recognizing another, and the photographer said her name was Jane.

'And this is the famous mermaid,' she said. It was hardly a question.

'So they tell me,' Francesca said, feeling proud to be able to say something like that so lightly and easily.

'Could you stop work for a little while, maybe, so that I can get in close?'

The reporter joined them while Jane was concentrating on the plate. 'Jennifer,' she said introducing herself. 'And I know who you are. You're the girl who put magic on a plate.'

'That was what Mr Prendergast said,' Francesca told her.

'I know,' Jennifer smiled. 'It's his shout line. Can you

211

paint and talk at the same time? I'd like to interview you first.'

'I'll give it a go,' Francesca said and dipped her brush.

Jennifer drew up a chair and sat down. 'What made you chose a mermaid?' she asked.

The question gave Francesca's pause. She could hardly say, 'because I saw one,' although the answer sprang to her tongue at once. She painted the mermaid's flowing hair while she tried to find something diplomatic to say, glad of the diversion. 'I think it was the movement,' she said at last. 'The flow of that long tail and all this hair. My painting is often about movement.' Then she stopped because she thought it sounded pretentious.

But Jennifer took her seriously. 'Interesting,' she said. 'So I gather you're not just a pottery designer.'

'Oh no. The painting came first. I got into the business because Mr Prendergast bought the painting.' How long ago it all seemed now.

'So how would you describe yourself as a painter?'

That was another difficult question so she paused again.

Jennifer encouraged her. 'Portraits? Landscapes?'

'Both I suppose. I've painted two portraits and several riverscapes. I tend to paint what I see. Things that catch my eye. Oh dear, that's not very helpful is it. I don't really know, if I'm honest. You're the first person to ask me.'

'I won't be the last.'

The thought made Francesca feel as though she was important and she had to duck her head so that the reporter wouldn't see her blushes.

'I'll let you get on,' Jennifer said. 'I'm supposed to be interviewing Mr Prendergast first but you were irresistible. I'll get back to you later, if that's OK.'

Molly was heading towards them, all smiles. 'We've

got the presentation all ready for you,' she said.

Jennifer smiled back. 'We're on our way,' she said.

It was a carefully lit display of the full dinner service on its dazzling white cloth with a vase of white lilies to set it off and Jane was already at work on it. If they print a picture of it like that, Francesca thought, it'll sell in spades.

Henry was striding through the workshop beaming at everybody. He was wearing his familiar chinos and an equally familiar blue sweater and for a second Francesca wondered why he hadn't dressed in one of his impressive suits. After all he *was* the boss and they'd be bound to take his picture. But there was so much going on there was no time for speculation. Jane was taking pictures of the kiln being emptied, Jennifer was interviewing Henry and they were both laughing as if they'd known one another for years, the place was buzzing with excitement and importance, everything seemed to be playing at twice the speed. It was really rather fun.

Their two visitors had lunch with Henry in the canteen and continued work all afternoon. By the time they all packed up to go home Francesca felt she'd been at work non-stop for a week. And there was still another day and a party to go.

Agnes wanted a blow-by-blow account of what had happened and was pleased by everything she heard. 'Not that I'm surprised,' she said. 'Henry will have had it organized down to the last button. I'll bet the champagne will flow tomorrow evening.'

It began to flow the following morning because the two J's had decided they wanted to 'shoot a party.' Molly greeted them at the door and told them not to put on their overalls or their caps and aprons just yet and handed them a paper hat. Where on earth had she got *them?* They trouped into the workshop giggling and ready for anything and there was Henry standing beside a dinner table – where had that come from? – all elegantly laid out with flowers and table napkins and silver cutlery and set with their precious dinner service. He was pouring champagne into his familiar flutes and he handed each of them a glass as they approached and told them to gather round. Fourteen of them were allotted places at the table and told to raise their glasses and smile at one another, which was easy enough, especially for Francesca who was sitting next to Henry, and then a Christmas tree was carried in, fully decorated in red, gold and white and Jennifer told them all to gather round with their glasses. It took such a long time and there was so much movement and rearrangement and so much champagne had to be drunk to keep the glasses topped up, they were all stupid with laughter and the fun of it. At which time, cook arrived to say she was ready to dish up and how much longer they were going to be.

'Adjourn for lunch?' Henry asked his guests.

'We're going back to our B&B to send in our copy,' Jenny told him. 'Just in case there's anything we've missed or something else they've thought of that we ought to cover. We'll come back and do it this afternoon, if there is. Otherwise we'll see you at the party. Eight for eight-thirty, right?'

'We shan't get much work done this afternoon,' Molly giggled. 'Not after all this.' Her paper hat was over one eye and she looked decidedly and happily squiffy.

But she was wrong. They worked very well, a little more slowly than usual but with all their customary attention to detail. And at the end of the afternoon Henry came down to thank them and to say he'd see them all at the party. Francesca went home singing.

Jeffrey Walmesly had never felt less like singing in his life. 'No,' he shouted at the phone. 'I haven't. I do have to earn a living you know. I can't spend all my life trying to find your wretched daughter.'

'You don't know where she is,' her mother said tartly. 'That's the truth of it. She's walked out and left you and you don't know where she is. You were too much of a wimp to tell me. That's the truth of it. And now I've wasted all this time waiting for you to do the right thing and find her. You're a total waste of space.'

'I haven't got all evening to stand around talking to you Mrs Jones,' Jeffrey said as icily as he could. 'I've got work to do.' It was horribly true. He'd had to take a job stacking shelves at Tesco otherwise he wouldn't have had enough money to eat and they'd put him on the night shift. 'Some of us work.'

'We all work,' Mrs Jones said, 'only some of us do it more reputably than others and don't make so much of a song and dance about it. Ah well, if you can't find her we shall have to put an advertisement in the papers, which is very annoying, I'll have you know. Advertisements are expensive and it will come out of the inheritance. So what paper does she read?'

The question irritated him. How was he supposed to know? He'd never seen her reading anything. 'She doesn't read papers,' he said.

'Try not to be foolish,' the acid voice told him 'Everybody reads papers.'

'Not your daughter.'

'Oh for heaven's sake Jeffrey!' The voice said and he could hear her sighing. 'You're worse than useless. Think about it. I'm sure you'd remember if you tried. Concentrate your mind. Does she read the *Mail*? Or the

Telegraph? Or something else. Think.'

She was making him feel sullen. 'It's no good keeping on,' he said. 'I don't know and that's all there is to it.'

'I despair of you Jeffrey,' she said and hung up on him.

Fucking awful woman, Jeffrey thought. How dare she speak to me like that? I'm a grown man, not a child. Calling me names. 'Worse than useless.' 'Total waste of space.' It made him snort just to think of it. I'm a graduate, or I would have been if I'd had half a chance, I'm a skilled man, a person with a position, which is more than can be said for her and all her tarty friends. I should have told her so. That would've put her in *her* place. He was checking his pockets to make sure he had enough money for the bus. Fucking woman. Now she's made me late.

He walked to the bus stop, hunched with bad temper, glowering. The fucking bus had better come on time, he thought. Otherwise it's going to make me late. But ten minutes went by and there was no sign of it. This is all Fran's stupid fault, he thought. If she hadn't gone rushing off in that stupid way, none of this would have happened. Leaving me to pay the mortgage all on my own and taking all my belongings with her. Even the fucking telly. So selfish. Well I hope the old bat does find her. I need *my* share of that money. I've earned it when all's said and done, looking after her all those years. She needn't think she's going to hog it all to herself. Fair's fair.

The bus was crawling towards him. He gave it a hideous scowl. And about time too. It was going to be a fucking awful night. He could feel it in his bones.

'What do you think?' Francesca said to Agnes, pirouetting before her in her new dress. 'Will I do?' She'd chosen it for its autumnal colours and was trying not to be too pleased with it because that would be conceited.

'Gorgeous,' Agnes said. 'You need a necklace to finish it off. I've got just the thing at home. Garnets. We'll call off on the way and I'll tell you where to find it.'

Francesca was doubtful. Jewellery sounded a bit daunting and it might look like showing off. 'Have we got time?'

Agnes brushed her doubts aside. 'We'll make time. It'll be the perfect finishing touch. Don't worry. You won't have to go on a hunt. I keep my jewellery box in the airing cupboard under the sheets. Always have.'

'Oh Agnes! Only you!'

'Ready for the off?' Agnes said, giving her a hug. 'Don't look so worried. This is going to be a great occasion. I intend to enjoy every single minute of it.'

The box was exactly where she'd said it would be, neatly hidden under a pile of sheets and duvet covers. It was a bit dusty but she could clean it up when she got downstairs.

'Goes back years,' Agnes said, looking at it fondly while Francesca rubbed it down with a duster. 'My father bought it for me and most of the jewellery too. Bit by bit. Usually for my birthday. He was a lovely man. Right. It's clean enough now. Hand it over.'

It was handed over, opened and the contents emptied out onto the kitchen table in a tangled pile. There were some stunning pieces there. She could see two diamond rings for a start and several beautiful necklaces. The garnets were caught up with another piece with very pretty pink and green stones. 'Peridots and pink topaz,' Agnes said as she disentangled them. 'He bought that for my sixteenth. I used to wear it a lot when I was young.' She held up the garnets so that the stones dangled and

217

shone. 'Turn round and I'll fasten it for you. There are some earrings somewhere to match. Give me a tick and I'll find them. You might as well go the whole hog as you've got pierced ears. Right let me see you. Very pretty. Go and look at yourself in the hall mirror while I find the earrings.'

When Agnes was in this sort of mood you did as you were told so Francesca went off to look in the mirror and sure enough the garnets looked very fine and were a perfect match for her new dress. She was surprising herself by how well she looked in evening dress. And how natural it seemed to be wearing it.

'Got 'em,' Agnes called from the kitchen. 'Stay there and I'll bring them out to you.'

They were long drop earrings and the stones were exactly the same shape and colour as the ones in the necklace. 'Perfect,' Agnes said. 'You'll be the star of the show and quite right too.'

'I feel very spoilt,' Francesca said, smiling at her.

'If you can't be spoilt tonight, me dear, I don't know when you could be,' Agnes said. 'Come on. Mustn't be late. It's going to be a big do.'

She was right and it was obvious from the moment they arrived, for instead of simply turning in at the drive as they usually did, they found that there was a young man standing at the gate with a lantern waiting to direct them to a nearby field and another one in the field ushering the latest arrivals into a parking space. The next car through the gate was Reggie's impressive Daimler with Babs in the passenger seat, looking through the windscreen at them and waving wildly

'What sport!' she said, as she climbed out of the car. 'Imagine being in *The Times*. Henry's cock-a-hoop. I like your dress. Hello Agnes. How's the leg?'

218

'Hideous,' Agnes said, 'but I'm not going to let a stupid thing like a plaster keep me away from this.' She was looking round at the long row of cars. 'However many people has he invited?'

'You know Henry,' Babs said, flicking her customary scarf over her shoulder and making eyes at Reggie. 'Come on slowcoach or we shall go without you. Oh look! There's Clara. I hope she hasn't brought that awful nephew with her. He ate all the trifle last time.'

Guests were streaming toward the lights of the house, all talking at once. Francesca and Agnes followed more slowly because Agnes was being sensible and taking care as she picked her way across the grass in the darkness but once they were on the drive and she could walk more easily she swung into her stride and by the time she reached the drawing room where Henry was greeting his guests and his caterers were serving champagne she was back to full confidence and balanced on her crutches like a veteran so that she could lean forward and kiss him.

'You don't have to tell me how pleased you are with all this,' she said. 'It's written all over your face.'

He nodded and smiled, saying, 'Good isn't it.' And watching him, Francesca sipped her champagne and was struck by how handsome he was and how much younger he looked than he usually did. It was having his hair a bit scruffy probably and wearing that silky looking shirt and those classy trousers. The greeny blues of the shirt suited him. If I ever got to paint him, she thought, that's what I would ask him to wear. But then the next arrivals rushed at her and her thoughts were smothered by their excited greetings.

'Find me a seat before I get knocked off my feet,' Agnes said when there was pause in the onrush. 'I'm finding this a bit tricky.' So they went off to find a safe corner where she could watch the arrivals from a distance. But if she was hoping for a little peace and quiet she didn't get it. The next incoming stream swirled round their host and then headed off to find *them*. They were bubbling with excitement. 'The *Sunday Times*! Wow!' 'You'll be famous.' And in the middle of the crowd, dressed in an incredible party dress of pink and purple frills, with a huge pink bow in her frizzy hair was Clara.

'Isn't this wonderful!' she said, grabbing Francesca's arm. 'Next thing you know you'll be on telly.'

Francesca laughed and tried to withdraw her arm. 'I doubt that,' she said.

'Oh that's how these things start,' Clara said, clinging on hard 'I know. First the papers, then the telly. That's how it starts. And once you're on telly there'll be no *end* to it. You'll be a *celebrity*. You see if I'm not right. I shall tell all my friends I know you. They'll be *so* impressed. I shall say, did you see Francesca Jones on the telly last night? Well she's my *friend*.'

Francesca watched her empty avid face and tried to pull her arm away from those clutching fingers and thought how foolish she was.

'You're losing your bow,' Agnes said.

'What?'

'Your bow. It's coming loose.'

The fingers fluttered to Clara's mound of hair and pushed at the bow and Francesca was able to move away and turn her attention to someone else.

'How's that nephew of yours?' Agnes said, steering the conversation away from all that fawning admiration because she could see how uncomfortable it had made Francesca feel. Obtuse woman.

'No idea,' Clara said, fiddling with the bow. 'Some silly girl took him in for a little while. Lived in a flat down by the river. He was full of it, how pretty it was and how she was looking after him and what a good cook she was and how she was feeding him. I thought what a fool she was. But there's no telling these young girls. They're all the same. More fool her. Anyway he's a bit quiet about it these days so I suppose she got sick of him and slung him out.'

Francesca listened with surprise and shame to hear herself described in such a way. It was a jarring leap from being fawned over and told she was going to be a celebrity. 'It might interest you to know,' she said,' that the stupid girl you're talking about was me. I took him in because he told me he'd got nowhere else to go.'

Clara wasn't the least bit put out by the revelation. 'He would,' she sniffed. 'That's his usual stock in trade. Poor me. Pity me. Whinge, whinge, whinge. Used to wear me out. I used to say, "Get a job. Stand on your own two feet." I'm glad you threw him out. Serve him right.'

Francesca couldn't think how to answer that but she didn't have to bother because Molly was rushing across the room towards her, arms outstretched to hug her. 'I've drunk so much champagne today I shall be tiddly for weeks,' she giggled. 'The two J's have arrived. We're going in to supper. Mr P sent me to fetch you. You're to lead us in.'

In fact she led the supper parade into the dining room on Henry's arm, blushing with a mixture of undeniable pleasure and residual guilt at having to acknowledge that she was the star of the show and secretly delighted that she chosen such a grand dress to star in. It was a noisy supper and a great deal of wine was drunk and then as if that weren't enough, they finished it with more champagne ready for the toasts and a speech from their host.

It was, as his old friends told one another afterwards, the best speech they'd ever heard him make. He started conventionally enough by thanking all his guests for their company and telling the 'special guests who call themselves the two J's' how much they enjoyed having their lively company over the last two days. 'For most of the time,' he told them, 'life in a pottery is pretty humdrum. We enliven it with tea parties for time to time but the fact is that making pots and plates can some-times get a bit boring.' Appreciative laughter. 'However, for the last two days everything has been transformed. Our work has become something special, not because we were putting on an act for the camera or posing or being poseurs – or at least I hope we weren't.' That brought a laugh too. 'No. It was for two different reasons. The first one was because it was such an experience to see two other workers doing a very different job, the second was because it gave us a chance to see ourselves as others see us. For which, "two J's", we are happily grateful. Ladies and gentlemen, I give you the "two J's."'

The toast was drunk and the two J's were smiled at. Then they settled down to wait for the next part of the speech because they hadn't drunk a toast to Francesca and her mermaid yet and there was obviously more to come.

'And now,' he said, smiling round at them all, 'I've got a little bit of news for you all. Our artist is going to hold an exhibition of her work. I made the final arrange-ments this afternoon. It will be during the last full week of October, just before Bonfire, running from Friday to Friday in the Riverside Gallery. You are all invited to the opening on the first Friday, when, besides being a chance to see a lot more of Francesca's work, some of which will probably be for sale – we haven't discussed the finer details yet, have we Francesca – there will also be champagne and nibbles of various kinds. Ladies and gentlemen, I give you Francesca and her mermaid without whom this party wouldn't be happening.' He raised his glass and looked straight at his artist. 'To Francesca and her mermaid.'

Francesca was so surprised by the news that her mouth had fallen open and she'd forgotten to close it. He arranges things so quickly, she thought, trying to compose herself. She'd hardly had time to decide whether she wanted this or not. She supposed she did but even at that moment she wasn't sure. But it was done and there didn't seem to be anything else she could do except go along with it because he was so pleased about it; he was like a smiling sunshine. She gathered her wits together and turned from side to side raising her own glass at her friends to acknowledge their chorus of excited voices.

And then the banquet was over and although Agnes declared she'd eaten so much she didn't think she'd be able to stand up, they all went off giggling and cheer-ful to the living room which had been transformed into a ballroom in their absence, the carpet rolled up and carried away, a DJ with all his gear at one end of the room and chairs set in rather a haphazard way round all the sides of the room with small tables beside them in case, as Henry explained, they needed anything more to drink, which provoked laughter and cheers. And the music began and Henry and Francesca led the dance, which was an easy old-fashioned waltz, as their guests clapped and cheered. It was almost like a wedding party.

'Good?' Henry asked as other couples began to join

them on the floor. It was a happily rhetorical question and didn't require an answer but she gave him one anyway.

'Fabulous,' she said.

They were dancing so close together and were both so happy and pleased with themselves, he gave her a hug. This time he was answered with a radiant smile. It was the perfect start to the second half of their evening. After that they danced together so many times he lost count. He hadn't felt so happy in years, not since Candida died in fact. It was a triumphant occasion.

By the time Francesca and Agnes got back to the flat, it was past two in the morning and they were so tired that Francesca said she was asleep on her feet.

'Me too,' Agnes said. 'I don't know about you but I'm going to have a quick pee and give my teeth a miss for once and get to bed.' Which she did, snuggling under her duvet with such a contented sigh that Francesca heard it in the living room.

I shall never get to sleep after all this, Francesca thought, as she too slid into bed. Seconds later she was dead to the world.

They slept on until late the next morning and even then they were languid when they finally got up. They yawned into the kitchen in their dressing gowns and slippers, and made tea and toast in a leisurely way, dissecting all the events of their extraordinary evening as they worked. Francesca was still a bit stunned by Henry's announcement. But Agnes said it was 'first rate' and predicted a great success. 'With Henry backing you, the place'll be packed,' she predicted. 'He'll have the press there and everything. You see if I'm not right.'

'I'm not sure I want to sell my pictures though,'

Francesca said, frowning. 'I mean, they belong to me. I think I'd like to keep them.'

'Don't worry,' Agnes said pouring tea. 'He won't make you do anything you don't want to. He may go at things like a bull at a gate and he's brilliant at getting publicity but if you say you'd rather not sell that'll be your decision. Watch out! You're burning the toast.'

Francesca gave a shriek and rushed to the grill to rescue it but it was too late. 'Past tense,' she said. 'Oh look at it! It's burnt black.'

'Never mind,' Agnes said easily. 'You can always make more.'

And there was a knock at the door.

'Someone's called the fire brigade,' Agnes said, swinging off to answer it. But it was Henry, in his old chinos and his favourite sweater.

'Glad to see you're up,' he said. 'I've got some news for you.'

'I suppose you've come to breakfast,' Agnes said, standing aside to let him in.

He grinned at her. 'If there's any going. Or have you burnt it all?'

'We've got company,' Agnes called to Francesca. 'Put out another cup and saucer.'

'I'm watching the toast,' Francesca called and then blushed when she saw who'd arrived. 'Oh hello!' she said. 'I'm sorry I'm not dressed. I mean, if I'd known you were coming, I'd have. . . .'

He thought she looked very pretty in her blue dressing gown with the blush colouring her cheeks. 'Not to worry,' he said. 'I've come over much too early but I couldn't wait to tell you my news.'

Agnes was pouring the tea for him. 'Sit down and spit it out,' she said. 'We don't want you bursting a blood

225

vessel in our nice clean kitchen.'

'Toast?' Francesca asked. And when he nodded, she turned her back on him to watch it while it cooked. So she missed the mischievous expression on his face as he began his story.

'I've got you a commission for a double portrait,' he said. 'What do you think of that?'

She turned to face him. 'A commission?'

'Reggie and Babs,' he said, and this time she saw the mischief. 'Mad keen. They came over to speak to me just after you'd left. Wanted to know if you'd be up for it. I told them I thought you might be and promised to ask you. What do you think?'

Francesca had no doubt about it. 'I'd love to,' she said. 'They'd make good models. He's always so – well, solid, I suppose – and she's chiffon, gossamer, sort of floaty. They're the perfect foil for one another.' She was already beginning to see how it could be done.

Henry beamed at her. 'Well that's just as well,' he said, 'because I've negotiated your fee.'

He was expecting to impress her, but she was embarrassed. 'Oh I wouldn't want a fee,' she protested. 'I mean, I'd like to do it. I'd do it for free.'

'I'm sure you would,' he said, 'but you're an established artist now and established artists charge a fee. It's all right. You needn't worry. They're quite happy about it. They've agreed to it. Reggie said it was very reasonable.'

It was necessary to find out how much money he was talking about. 'How much did you ask for?' she said.

'Three thousand pounds,' he told her. 'Three thousand pounds but they've got to give you permission to display it in your exhibition. How would that be?' The mischief on his face was as bright as sunshine.

'Excellent!' Agnes said. 'Quite right.'

Francesca was shocked. There was no disguising it. 'I can't ask them for all that,' she said. 'I mean, it's much too much. It's . . .' then she was lost for the right word and hesitated, her blush deepening.

'Look,' he said seriously, feeling he had to explain himself. 'This is just the start. They're getting a bargain and they know it. By the time you've had your exhibition you'll be in such demand you'll be able to charge anything you like. It's a commercial world out there and you'll be valued according to the price you ask for your work. That's the way commerce works. You'll have to get used to that.'

She struggled to think of an answer. He was plainly right. That *was* the way the market worked but she didn't want to be part of a market. She simply wanted to paint. It was good to think that she could earn her living with her brush. She had to admit that. And she knew he'd done it because he wanted to help her. But even so. . . .

Watching her anxious expression, Henry realized that he'd been too quick and too clumsy and that he'd upset her. It was a difficult thing for him to have to admit because it wasn't what he'd intended at all but that anxious face of hers revealed more than she knew. Modesty, he thought. That's what it is. Modesty and lack of self-confidence. She really doesn't know how valuable she is. And he was caught up in a rush of protective pity for her and rushed to make amends.

'You don't have to make a decision yet awhile,' he said. 'There's no rush. Or compulsion, come to that. If you'd rather not take a fee that's up to you. It's your painting. But I can tell them you'd like to paint them, can't I? They were very keen.'

'Oh yes,' she said, hastening to reassure *him* because she could see he was upset. 'I'd love to paint them. Like I said. It would be a challenge.'

He took a deep relieved breath and realized that he could smell burning again, quite strongly. 'Your toast's in flames,' he said and when she rushed to the grill to attend to it he followed her. 'Tell you what,' he said. 'You sit down and drink your tea and I'll make the next lot. I make a mean toast.'

The awkwardness had passed. She sat down, sipped her tea and watched him as he made three rounds of perfect toast. And Agnes watched them both and pondered. And when the toast was cooked golden, they sat round the table and had breakfast together and were simply and effortlessly happy, as if there'd been no difference of opinion and no upset and no embarrassment.

He's so like Agnes, Francesca thought. He puts rows behind him just like she does. He doesn't hang on to bad emotions. After years spent with her mother, she was struck by how easy and admirable it was and how quickly he'd found a compromise they could both accept.

They talked about the party and the two J's and Agnes wondered when the article would be published, which Henry said he couldn't tell them. 'Yet. But I will as soon as I know anything.' And when Francesca went to fill the kettle to make a second pot of tea, they started to talk about their childhoods.

'I was thinking the other night how you used to squeeze through that hole in the fence and come in and play cards,' Agnes said. 'Do you remember?'

'Like yesterday,' Henry said, smiling at her. 'Beat your neighbour out of doors. You used to cheat so that I could win.'

'Did I?' Agnes asked and then answered her own question almost at once. 'Yes, I probably did. You were such a dear little boy and you did so want to win.'

'We used to live next door to one another when we were young,' Henry explained to Francesca. 'Just round the corner from here as it happens. She took me to my first Bonfire. Do you remember that?'

'You were horrid that night,' Agnes told him putting on her stern face. 'You threw fire crackers into the crowd.'

'You just said I was a dear little boy.'

'Not that night you weren't. You were a pain in the bum.'

'And you were bossy-big-sister.'

'Only because you needed it.'

They were speaking so easily and intimately together that Francesca felt she could ask, 'How old were you?'

'About ten I should think,' he said. 'Still at prep school anyway.'

'It was the year Ralph proposed and my mother decided to be ill,' Agnes said, making a grimace.

He leant across the table and patted her hand lovingly, without saying anything and she smiled at him with affection as if she really had been his bossy big sister and he really was her brother. And watching them, Francesca was warmed and touched by what she saw. This is what it's like to be part of a proper family, she thought, accepted and loved no matter what sort of person you are. If only my mermaid could give me that.

CHAPTER 15

LIFE WAS A bit flat at Prendergast Potteries in the week that followed the party. The weather was cold and damp and cheerless. There weren't so many orders coming in so there was a general air of restlessness and uncertainty about the place. Molly was fidgety with impatience for the *Sunday Times* to publish 'our article' so that trade would pick up, Liam worried over the sales figures, the cook was in a bad mood because she'd burnt one of her big saucepans. Francesca was the only person in the works who simply went on stolidly painting her plates and dishes and didn't seem to be worrying about anything, but that was because she was planning her double portrait. She'd decided not to think about the fee until the painting was done and now she was trying to solve the enjoyable problem of how to present these two very different people to show them to advantage. Having found the perfect settings for Agnes and Molly she couldn't be content until she'd thought of something equally suitable for Babs and Reggie.

Henry was his usual cheerful self and that was partly because he had more patience than his workforce, partly because he was busy putting the finishing touches to Francesca's exhibition but mostly because he was savouring a daydream, which was surprising him because it was most unlike him to dream about anything. But there it was. Ever since his happily domestic breakfast with Agnes and Francesca he'd been indulging the hope that meals together could become a regular treat. It had been such a long time since he felt as though he belonged to a family and, even though it had been a fleeting experience, it had affected him strongly. From time to time he told himself that he was being foolish but he couldn't get the idea out of his head even though he tried to remove it by keeping himself occupied. By the end of the week he'd arranged for one of the directors at the gallery to visit Francesca and assess her paintings, phoned all his friends on the local papers and enthused them for the Exhibition – 'an amazing talent,' he'd told them, 'as you'll see' – written the guest list for the exhibition and had begun to organize the catering. He came down into the workshop just before they all went home on Friday evening, feeling rather pleased with his efforts, and headed straight across to Francesca's workstation to ask her if she and Agnes would like to go out for a meal.

Francesca was cleaning her brushes but she looked up at him with such obvious pleasure at the idea that it made his heart leap. 'When?' she asked.

'Tonight?' he hoped.

'Well I would,' Francesca said, 'but I can't speak for Agnes. She's a bit touchy at the moment. She's getting sick of the plaster.'

'Ah!' he said, smiling at her. 'In that case I'll call round at half-past seven and we'll take it from there. How would that be?'

He's so kind, Francesca thought, and so generous. 'It would be lovely,' she said.

But Agnes had a different opinion. She was perched

on the kitchen stool peeling apples for a crumble when Francesca came in. 'I've got a leg of lamb in the oven,' she said, 'and the vegetables are all done. You don't really want to go dragging out to a restaurant do you? It's a miserable night.'

'I wouldn't mind either way,' Francesca said. 'It's just I think he wants to take us out.'

'He wants company,' Agnes said sagely, putting the apples on the gas. 'He's been lonely since he lost Candida. And then there's the party. Loneliness always seems worse when you've just thrown a big party.'

She could be right, Francesca thought. She found it hard to think of Henry being lonely when he was always surrounded by people, but once he got home and was all by himself, it was quite possible that he *could* feel lonely. *She*'d often felt very lonely in that flat when Jeffrey was out fixing up deals. 'He's coming at half-past seven,' she said. 'Let's have the table all set and ready for him and see what happens.'

What happened was another family meal and a very happy one. They talked of the two J's and what fun they'd been, tried to guess when they would hear about the publication date and Henry held his peace until Agnes was dishing up the crumble and then gave them his news.

'I've got the press coming to your exhibition,' he said to Francesca, trying to sound modest about it.

'Heavens!' Francesca said. She wasn't sure whether she really welcomed all the fuss he was making. What if nobody liked the pictures and it was a flop?

'I shall get to work on the TV people on Monday,' he told her. 'They ought to film it if the schedules aren't full. And there's a woman called Christine from the gallery who wants to come and see your pictures to give her some idea how they can be displayed. How's the double portrait coming along? Have you got any ideas for it? It would be an idea to put that on display too.'

'I've been thinking about it,' Francesca told him.

'And?' Henry said. And when she frowned, 'What's the problem?'

'I can't find the right setting,' she confessed. 'They're such strong personalities and so different from one another, that's the trouble. Well, no, it's not a trouble, not really, it could be a strength, if I could get it right. Ideally, you see, *he* ought to be sitting in an office and *she* ought to be strolling through a rose garden but I can't see how to get all that on one canvas without making it look contrived.'

'I know just the place,' he beamed at her. 'They've got a summer house in their garden. He does a lot of work there, when the weather's warm and there's a rose garden right near it. I'll give them a ring and fix a time when you can go over and see it. How would that be?'

'Could be just the thing,' she said and beamed at him, thinking how quick and decisive he was.

'I'll fix it for some time this weekend,' he promised. 'If you're going to get the picture done in time for the exhibition, the sooner the better, don't you think.'

'It would have to be Sunday,' she told him. 'Molly's coming for her last sitting tomorrow.'

'Sunday it is then,' he said. 'Then you can get straight on with it.'

'Yes,' she agreed, although doubtfully because she was beginning to feel pressurized. 'I don't want to rush it, the painting I mean. It'll be a big canvas so it'll take a while.'

'Tell you what,' he said. 'Why don't you take a week's sabbatical? On full pay of course. That would give you the time you need, wouldn't it.'

It would. There was no doubt about it and it was a generous offer. 'But what about the mermaid? What if you get a lot of orders?'

'Orders are slow at the moment,' he said. 'They'll pick up when the colour supplement comes out and you'll be back in time for that.'

'Are you going to eat that crumble?' Agnes said sternly. 'Or are you just going to sit there and let it get cold?'

He picked up his spoon obediently and ate a spoonful. 'She always was a bully,' he said to Francesca. 'I could use some cream on this, Aggie.'

'And you were always a glutton,' she said. 'Cream as well as custard! I never heard the like. It's in the fridge but you'll have to go and get it.'

He went, giving her a grin.

'He takes my breath away,' Francesca said, when he'd gone. 'He's so quick.'

'Always was,' Agnes said. 'Always will be. Good meal?'

'Lovely,' Francesca said.

Agnes purred. 'I might have a gammy leg but I'm still a dab hand with roast lamb and apple crumble,' she said.

'I'll put the coffee on,' Francesca said.

When the meal was over, Francesca cleared the table and she and Henry washed the dishes, then they went back into her all-purpose room, pushed the table against the wall and turned it into a sitting room again. As she sank back into the cushions on her sofa-bed, she thought what an easy cosy room it was, curtained against the dark and containing them all so warmly. And watching her, Henry was touched by her contentment and knew he was sharing it.

He stayed with his hosts until it was past eleven

o'clock and Agnes was yawning.

'I'm keeping you up,' he said to her.

'Yes. You are,' she said but she spoke so affectionately that he didn't even feel rebuked.

'I must go,' he said and stood up.

'We'll see you on Sunday for our trip to Reggie's,' she said to him.

'I'll fix it first thing,' he promised her and bent to kiss her, first on one cheek and then on the other.

So when he and Francesca reached the front door and said goodbye, it was only natural that he should kiss her in the same way. It moved him far more than he expected. To be standing so close to her in that tiny hall and actually kissing her, brief though the contact was, roused him powerfully. He wanted to put his arms round her and kiss her properly, to hold her face between his hands, to feel the warmth of her body, close and urged closer. I could love you, he thought, looking down at her trusting face under that tangle of frizzy hair and he wondered what on earth she would say if he spoke his thoughts. Instead, he said goodnight quite gruffly and left before he could make a fool of himself.

As he drove home he began to analyze what had happened. He hadn't felt like that since Candida died. Or if he had, it had been such a fleeting sensation he'd forgotten it. If he was honest, he'd been so sure he would never feel like that again he hadn't even let the hope of it enter his head. But now it was there and roaring at him. He'd stood in that hall with a vulnerable, talented, complicated woman and there'd only been one idea in his head. And now he didn't know whether to be ashamed of it or glad. It was extraordinary, ridiculous, breath taking, almost like falling in love. Oh for heaven's sake. He couldn't be falling in love, could he? Not at his age! But when he'd eased his car into the garage and opened the door to his empty house, he wasn't at all sure.

Molly arrived at Francesca's flat the next morning, spot on time, with an armful of chrysanthemums and her bright hair damp with rain.

'They're for you and Agnes,' she explained to Francesca. 'I thought they looked so pretty.'

'Thank you, me dear,' Agnes said, taking them from her. 'I'll put them in a vase. Then you two can get on.'

The multi-purpose room had become a studio since breakfast and now the easel, paints and brushes were standing ready and Francesca was itching to start work.

Molly took up her position as soon as she'd removed her coat, standing beside the table in her now custom-ary pose, right in the light with the mermaid plate in her hands. 'OK?' she asked, grinning at Francesca.

Francesca took a long look at her subject and began work without a word, the way she usually did, Molly held her pose, as she usually did, and Agnes clomped about the flat, first arranging the flowers in a vase, then making her bed, and finally producing cups of coffee to sustain them all. She'd just carried the last cup into the studio when the phone rang.

'I'll take it,' she said, setting the cup on the table. It pleased her to be useful while the painting was going on.

It was Henry. 'Can I speak to Francesca?' he said. 'I've fixed a time for tomorrow.'

'She's painting,' Agnes said. 'But you can tell me. I'll pass the message on.'

Disappointment tightened his throat so that he had to swallow before he could answer. 'I'll call for you at eleven. Is that all right?'

'We'll be ready,' she said and hung up.

Henry sat in his comfortable armchair in his comfortable, empty living room with the useless phone still in his hand and felt quite cast down, which was plainly ridiculous. Shamingly ridiculous. If he'd still been a smoker he would have lit a cigarette to comfort himself. As it was, he had to put up with his uncomfortable feelings. I shall see her tomorrow, he thought, trying to be positive. And wondered how long he would be able to spin out the visit to Reggie's.

The next day was cold but clear with a sharp hoarfrost dusting the lawn and a red and gold sunrise blazing above the denuded trees. Henry was heartened by the sight of it and accepted it as a good omen. He took time to choose his outfit, picking his favourite sweater after considerable and unnecessary pondering, and brushing his hair far more carefully than was necessary. Then he sat in front of Candida's dressing table mirror and examined his face. He didn't really look his age, did he? He'd still got his hair and all his teeth except the one he'd lost when that cricket ball hit him in the mouth. Not too many wrinkles and most of *them* were laughter lines. He tried to smile at himself but that looked forced and unnatural. In the end he gave up the unequal struggle for truth of any kind and went downstairs to start his journey. He was better when he wasn't thinking too much but just getting on with things.

Agnes and Francesca were ready and waiting for him, Agnes in a blue skirt and a mottled jersey that looked as if it had faded from some rather more interesting colour, Francesca in jeans and a sea green jumper that reminded him of the mermaid.

'Will we need our coats?' she asked.

'You will when we go out in the garden,' he told her.

'I've got mine.'

So coats, gloves, scarves, and handbags were found and carried out to the car and when Henry had settled Agnes into the back seat explaining that she'd have more leg-room there and ushered Francesca into the passenger seat beside him to his happy satisfaction, they drove back into the country roads, heading for Reggie's.

He and Babs came out onto the front doorstep in their coats and stood between the white columns on either side of it to greet them. Babs was so excited, she said, she couldn't wait to see if their summer-house would suit. 'We've a little light lunch for you later,' she said, 'but maybe we could go out and see the summer-house first? What do you think?'

They went in procession, bundled into coats and scarves, with Reggie leading the way, Babs arm-in-arm with Francesca and a rather disgruntled Henry following behind with Agnes. It was a garden like a park, with long herbaceous borders, a great many shrubs, several imposing trees and no sign of a summer-house anywhere as far as the visitors could see. But they followed a winding path and eventually came upon it nestling in front of beech hedge and, just as Henry had told Francesca, facing a long rose garden and a pretty fishpond full of koi carp.

'What do you think?' Babs asked, waving an arm at it. A sharp wind caught her scarf and blew it before her like a banner and she caught at it and tossed it over her shoulder again. The movement would have made Francesca's mind up for her even if nothing else had done. It was so exactly how she'd visualized this picture.

'Could we get you just to sit inside the house, Reggie?' she asked.

'Of course me dear,' he said, and opened the door at

once. There was a cane armchair covered by an ancient blue and green rug just inside and he sat in it, put his hands on his knees and looked out at her. 'How's that?'

'Do you ever read or write out here?'

'Often,' he told her. 'In the summer of course. It's a bit too chilly in the winter. We shut it up then.'

'And do you have a trug, Babs?'

'I do,' Babs said. 'How did you know?'

'I could see you out here with a trug,' Francesca said. 'A trug and secateurs, cutting roses for the house. Do you do that?'

'Frequently.'

'That's a beech hedge behind you isn't it?'

'It is. Will it do?'

Francesca was taking her sketch-pad out of her handbag. 'I'd like to make a few sketches if that's all right.'

'Do we have to pose?' Reggie asked, holding his head on one side and looking extremely awkward.

She laughed. 'Not yet. I shall just block you in, where I want you to be. This is for background. Could I have the chair out here do you think?'

It was carried out and set reverently in front of her and she took it, pushed it into position, sat in it and started to draw. 'This could take a while,' she said to her hosts. 'You can leave me to it if you like. It's a bit chilly for standing around. I'll come back to the house when I've finished.'

'I'll stay with you,' Henry offered. 'There's a stool in the house I can sit on.'

So it was arranged and when the stool had been carried out and set beside the chair, the other three went chattering off along the path and left them alone together.

It was cold out there in the garden but wonderfully peaceful. Henry watched and didn't talk so as not to interrupt her concentration but after a while a robin started to sing down by the pond and she looked up from her sketch to see where it was.

'It's in that rosebush,' he whispered, pointing. 'Do you see? The third one down?'

She saw and had already turned in her seat and begun to sketch it. 'I love robins,' she whispered as she worked. 'Those sharp beaks opening so wide and the way their breast feathers ruffle under all that effort, like Babs' scarf.'

He knew exactly what she meant. He could see the similarity growing from the end of her pencil, the small quick strokes catching the small fluttery movement to perfection. 'You can talk to me if you like,' she said without looking at him. 'It won't distract me. If I reach the point where I can't concentrate on two things at once, I won't answer but you won't mind that will you?' The sketch of the robin was already done.

'You're so quick,' he said to her.

She smiled at him. 'You have to be to catch a wild bird.'

The words sent ripples through his mind. A wild bird, he thought. It was so exactly what she was like, timid, unobtrusive, quietly beautiful, needing care and protection in a tough world, with a talent as precious and amazing as birdsong. A wild bird. And he wished he knew how to tempt her into his arms. And sighed.

'I think I've just about caught him,' she said and held out the sketch-pad for him to see.

Now that he had the chance to examine it properly he could see that it was a delicate sketch and very touching. It could have been a painting in its own right not just a detail in a double portrait. 'I don't know how you do it,' he said and his admiration was obvious.

'I don't either sometimes,' she admitted, taking the sketch back 'When it comes out well, I mean. It feels easy.'

'I'm sure it's not,' he said. 'I've been watching what a lot of effort you put into it and how you concentrate. It doesn't look easy to me. How are the main sketches getting on?'

'Not quite right yet,' she said, returning to them.

He smiled at that. 'You see what I mean.'

'Um,' she said. But she wasn't listening to him. She was already back to full concentration.

They sat out in the chilly garden for another forty minutes, she hard at work, he beginning to shiver even though he'd wrapped his coat around him as closely as he could and was sitting with his hands in his pockets. Then they heard Babs' voice calling from behind the bushes and presently she came tripping towards them on her high heels, to tell them that lunch was ready.

'Have you nearly finished?' she asked Francesca and Henry noticed that she spoke timidly as if she was in awe of her.

'I've done about as much as I can,' Francesca told her, still looking at the latest sketch. 'It'll do to be getting on with. I might have to come back if it doesn't come out right when I start to paint. To be sure of the colours.'

'Of course,' Babs said. 'But you'll come and have something to eat now, won't you, otherwise you'll freeze to death out here.'

So they carried the furniture back into the summer-house and went up to the house for their 'light lunch.' It turned out to be a full Sunday roast with all the traditional trimmings even down to mustard and horseradish sauce and they enjoyed it very much.

'This is the life, eh?' Reggie said when they'd moved into his long drawing room for coffee and mints. 'Good food, good company. Can't be beat.'

Babs was more interested in discovering when Francesca was going to start the portraits. 'Do you want us to come to yours?' she asked. 'Or will you come here?

Henry explained that all the things Francesca needed were at the flat and told her two models that she was taking a week's sabbatical leave so that she could paint their portrait in time for it to be displayed at the exhibition. They were thrilled to hear about it.

'Imagine that, Reggie,' Babs said, making eyes at him 'We're going to be stars.'

He grinned at her. 'Oh I don't know about that, old thing,' he said. 'I would say the star is going to be our Francesca. More coffee Henry.'

Talk of being the star embarrassed Francesca and Babs saw it and turned the conversation at once asking Agnes when she was going to get 'that awful plaster' off her leg.

'In fifteen days, so I'm promised,' Agnes told her. 'And it feels like fifteen years. Damned thing.'

'It'll soon pass,' Babs said. 'Trust me.'

'What a lot of good things we've got to look forward to,' Reggie said, beaming round at them. 'You getting out of plaster, Agnes, our portrait being painted, Francesca's exhibition, Henry's colour supplement. And when that's all over we shall have Bonfire. How's that going Agnes?'

'Pretty well,' Agnes told him. 'We've got the bonfire organized. It's going to be a Viking ship this year.'

He approved at once. 'Wonderful. Do you need any more volunteers?'

'We can always use more volunteers,' Agnes said. 'You know what it's like.'

He nodded. 'Count me in.'

It's like a club, Francesca thought. I wonder whether they'll let me join it. She felt like a Billy No-mates, sitting there and listening.

And then almost as if he was reading her thoughts Henry answered them. 'We shall have to get you measured for your uniform if you're going to join us this year,' he said to her. 'And you will won't you?'

She was very surprised. 'Uniform?' she asked

'Oh yes,' he said. 'All the societies have their own uniform. Cliffe's is a striped shirt and a pirate cap. You'll look very fetching in it. Agnes'll measure you up for it, won't you Aggie?'

'Course,' Agnes said.

Then they were off on a long conversation about pallets and rockets and brass bands which Francesca couldn't follow. The light was beginning to fade, the shadows in the room deepening and lengthening, but they were all so involved with the preparations for Bonfire that none of them got up to switch on the lights. After what seemed to be a very long time, Francesca managed to catch Henry's eye and look a question at him. He answered it at once.

'We shall have to be getting back pretty soon,' he said to Babs. 'I've got Liam coming over at seven o'clock.'

'We mustn't keep you,' Babs said, standing up. 'You've all got lots to do, I'm sure. Let us know when you want us to come to your flat, Francesca, and what we've got to wear and so forth.'

'Come on Tuesday,' Francesca said, 'and wear the sort of things you'd wear in the summer out in the garden. And if you'll bring your trug and a pair of secateurs and Reggie'll bring a book or a notebook or whatever he writes in when he's working in the summer house, that'll be all we need.'

They promised they would come suitably dressed and equipped. And Babs wanted to know what sort of colours they should wear. 'We've got quite a range,' she said. 'Haven't we Reggie?'

Francesca had thought that out too. Blues, greens, light browns, maybe pinks, or a touch of red, here and there.

'I've got just the thing,' Babs said. 'What about hats?'

'If you usually wear them.'

'This is going to be such fun!' Babs said as they parted. 'I can't believe we're going to be models.'

'I can't believe I've got a whole week with nothing to do but paint,' Francesca said.

'I can't believe I've got to wait fifteen days until I get rid of this,' Agnes growled, glaring at her plaster.

And so they said goodbye. With kisses and laughter.

It was an extraordinarily happy week. Francesca finished the Castle picture on Monday and started work at coffee time on Tuesday on her first double portrait. It took a little while to get her models to relax and be themselves because they both thought they had to strike poses but by dint of making them laugh and keeping them talking she contrived to catch them as they were, he seriously reading his book and she arranging the flowers in her trug and occasionally flirting with him or tossing her chiffon scarf over her shoulder. By the time the light faded on Thursday afternoon, the painting had taken shape and Francesca was almost pleased with it.

'It needs a bit more work yet,' she said, as she turned the easel round so that they could see what she'd done, 'but the essence of it is there.'

They were thrilled with it, especially as she'd painted

pink and yellow roses in the trug 'without seeing them,' as Babs said. 'I don't know how you do it.'

'I painted quite a lot of roses during the summer,' she felt she had to explain. 'While I was staying at Agnes."

'And very good they were,' Agnes said. 'You'll see some of them at the exhibition if I'm any judge.'

'Won't it be wonderful when all your paintings are on display,' Babs said to Francesca. 'I'll bet you're looking forward to it.'

Privately Francesca thought it might be a bit embarrassing but she smiled and agreed with her model.

'What will you do tomorrow me dear?' Reggie wanted to know. 'Have a day off?'

She was just opening her mouth to say she would probably work on some of the other paintings when her phone rang.

'We'll be off then,' Reggie said as she went to answer it and he and Babs walked towards the door, smiling at her as they went.

'You don't have to,' she said as she lifted the phone to her ear but they were already on their way with Agnes hobbling after them to see them out.

It was a voice she didn't know, asking to speak to Miss Jones.

'Speaking,' she said.

'It's Christine from the galleries,' the voice said. 'When would it be convenient for me to come and see the paintings?'

So much for a day off, Francesca thought. 'Tomorrow?' she offered.

'Morning or afternoon?'

'I'd prefer the afternoon.'

'Afternoon it is,' the voice said. 'Half-past two?'

'Yes.'

'Fine,' the voice said. 'I'll see you then. I've got your address.'

'Who was it?' Agnes said, stomping back into the room.

'It was "Christine from the galleries,"' Francesca said feeling stunned at the speed of it. 'Coming to see the paintings tomorrow.'

'I shall make a cake,' Agnes said.

Christine was a business-like young woman wearing a navy blue suit and very high heels, with her dark hair in a bun at the nape of her head and rather severe spectacles on a decidedly Roman nose. At first Francesca was a bit overawed by her but as she examined the paintings and was obviously impressed by them, she relaxed and began to like her.

'I can see why Mr Prendergast speaks so highly of you,' she said, when she'd seen all the big canvases. 'These are very fine.'

'There's another one at my house,' Agnes told her. 'You can have that for display if you like.'

She would like. Very much. 'What have you got in the folders?' she asked looking at them where they stood against the wall.

'They're only small pieces,' Francesca said.

'May I see them?'

'Some are just sketches.'

'I'd like to see them all, if I may.'

They were taken from the folders and examined one after the other.

'They're good,' Christine told her. 'Very commercial. You should display them too. We could get you a good price on them. Especially this one of the chaffinches. That's lovely. We'd frame them of course. The way a painting is displayed makes such a difference. But I don't need to tell you that I'm sure. What do you think?'

Francesca felt rushed. 'I'd like to talk it over with Miss Potts,' she said, nodding towards Agnes. 'And Mr Prendergast. If that's all right.'

'That's fine,' Christine said, adjusting her spectacles. 'There's my card. Just give me a call when you've decided what to do.'

And she smiled at Francesca and Agnes and was gone as briskly as she'd arrived, leaving a rather stunned silence behind her.

'She never had her cake,' Agnes said. 'Silly girl!'

Francesca had been holding on to her self-control so tightly that her neck was aching. Now she saw the ridiculous side of what Agnes had just said and exploded into laughter, control and tension instantly broken and dispelled. Within seconds they were both laughing like hyenas and Francesca had tears streaming from her eyes. Neither of them were in any fit state to answer the door bell.

'Oh – let – them wait,' Francesca gasped between gulps for air. 'Maybe they'll – go – away.'

But whoever they were they had no intention of going away. They rang the bell again, this time longer and louder.

'Oh – oh – dear,' Francesca gasped, struggling to control herself and laughing again. She dabbed her streaming eyes and blundered off to answer it.

It was Henry and he was instantly upset to see her in tears. 'What is it?' he said anxiously, stepping into the flat. 'What's the matter?'

'It's nothing,' Francesca managed. 'Fit – of giggles.' And then she was off again, laughing and choking.

Now that he could see that it was laughter and not

distress he relaxed and smiled. 'Steady on!' he said. But that only made her worse. And Agnes was almost as bad.

'I've got some news for you,' he said, looking from one to the other. 'But I can hardly tell you when you're laughing like drains.'

'Better in – a minute,' Agnes said and made a valiant effort to stop.

'Come out to dinner with me,' he said. 'Maybe a drive'll take it off.'

So they got their coats and dried their eyes and, sure enough, by the time they reached the restaurant they were themselves again.

'So what's this news?' Agnes asked when they were settled at their table. 'You're looking very smug.'

'I think you'll want to buy a copy of *The Times* on Sunday.'

'This Sunday?'

He was grinning like a Cheshire Cat. 'As ever is.'

'That's quick,' Francesca said. 'When did you hear?'

'Late this afternoon,' he told her. 'Good eh? Now we shall see the sales jump.'

'You will,' Agnes grinned. 'Nothing but good can come of it. And all nicely in time for the exhibition. We've got some news for you about that. It's really perfect timing.'

CHAPTER 16

JEFFREY WAS HEARTILY sick of working for a supermarket. He'd been there for over a fortnight now and he hated everything about it, the stupid uniform, the long night hours when he should have been asleep, the repetitive chores, the inanity of his workmates, the way the line leader was forever sneering at him, the harsh lighting, the ghastly smells, every mortal thing. If he'd been paid a decent wage it might have been easier to endure but he earned so little it barely kept him in food and ciggies. And the mortgage demands kept coming in and getting more and more threatening with every post. It was no good them hounding him to settle his account. He couldn't pay them even if he wanted to. He didn't have the money. And the more they hounded him the less he wanted to.

That damned Fran, he thought viciously as he split open yet another package of tinned beans. This is her fault, walking out on me like that. If it wasn't for her I wouldn't be slaving away all night in this hell-hole. She needs a damned good hiding, that's what she needs, and if I ever find her that's what she'll get. That'll teach her to walk out on me. He paused, knife in hand but not in use, and fed his fantasy for a few happy seconds. He'd frighten the living daylights out of her. That'ud show her who was boss. He'd make her beg on her knees for mercy.

'Day-dreaming again,' the line leader said in her snidey voice. Trust her to come creeping up on him.

'Not at all,' he said, putting on his superior expression. 'I was just checking whether one box would be enough.'

'Checking my eye,' his enemy said. 'Don't give me all that tosh. I know a skiver when I see one. Well you can leave that. The Sundays have come in. Go and help Nigel unload. Sharon can do this. She's quicker than you.'

Fucking woman, he thought, as he sloped off to do as he was told. Calling me a skiver. I'm the most hardworking man in the shop. She should be grateful to have me on her team, instead of being on my back all the time. He had half a mind to go and tell her so, but she'd gone off to torment someone else and he couldn't see her. Well she needn't think I'm going to take any nonsense from that stupid Nigel, that's all. If he so much as squeaks at me, I'll beat the fuck out of him.

Nigel was stacking piles of newspapers on a trolley, checking them off on his list and concentrating so hard his long face was creased with the effort he was making.

'Do the *Sunday Times*,' he said, squinting at Jeffrey.

'What's the magic word?' Jeffrey said, deliberately talking down to him.

'What magic word?' Nigel said, scowling at him. 'What you on about?'

'The word you have to say when you want someone to do something for you,' Jeffrey said, massively condescending.

Nigel wasn't impressed. 'If I say jump, matey, you jump,' he said and threw a heavy bale of newspapers straight at Jeffrey's legs. 'Get that lot on the trolley.'

It hit him just below the knee, knocking him off balance so that he had to grab the nearest shelf to stay on his feet and it hurt so much it brought tears to his eyes.

For a few seconds he was too stunned to speak. Then he roared. 'You stinking fucking stinking little toerag!' and lunged towards his opponent, his face contorted with anger.

'Oooh!' Nigel mocked, taking a step backward. 'Naughty, naughty! You wanna watch out our line leader can't see you or you'll be for it big time.'

But Jeffrey had seen something that stopped him in mid roar. Something far more important than a miserable little toerag with dirty teeth. Lying at the top of the pile was the cover page of the *Sunday Times* magazine and bright and clear, just a few feet under his nose, there was that mermaid again and a banner headline. 'Musthaves for Christmas.' That was the answer. Always had been only he'd forgotten about it. New improved clay for a company on the up. He cut the string and pulled the copy from the pile, ripped off the cover and folded it as small as he could get it so that he could tuck it in his trouser pocket. Whatever else he had to do on this hideous shift, he didn't care. He'd get cracking on his real job the minute he got back home. That was where the money was. 'Get out my way,' he said to the toe-rag. 'I've got work to do.'

For the rest of his shift he worked automatically, stacking papers on the stands, filling shelves endlessly, sweeping and clearing and when it was time to scarper he was off out of the building before most of his workmates were aware he'd gone.

Now, he thought, as he drove home at a happily reckless speed. Now I can start making money.

He switched on his computer as soon as he got in and found the company at once. Prendergast Potteries in East Sussex, proprietor Henry Prendergast. Then, growing steadily more excited, he trawled for information about firms that provided 'high quality clay'. I'll have some Coco Pops, he thought, give 'em a chance to get to work, then I'll start ringing round. But as he poured the Coco Pops into one of the new bowls he'd had to buy because Fran had been so foul, he realized that it was Sunday and that everybody would be at home. Never mind, he consoled himself. I'll have a good long sleep, which God knows I deserve, and then I'll get up and shower and go off for a pie and a pint somewhere – I shan't bother going in to Tesco's – I'm done with all that – and then I can be up early on Monday morning and set to work. Oh there'll be no stopping me now.

'There'll be no stopping us now,' Liam said, grinning at his boss. 'That magazine's only been out four days and we've already taken more orders than we've had in the last two months put together. And we've still got another two months to Christmas.' He passed the order book across the desk for Henry's approval. 'Those have been dispatched already.'

'I shall have to order more clay,' Henry said happily. 'I'll go down and check what we need presently. When I've written a notice to spread the good news.'

'It's spreading like wildfire,' Liam said equally happily. 'Molly's been singing since the third order came in.'

She was singing when Henry walked into the workshop and pinned up his notice. 'Is this good or is this good?' she said as he walked towards her.

'Yes,' he told her wearing his serious expression.

'I think we could say it's good.' Then he smiled at her because he couldn't be serious for long, not in these circumstances. 'How are supplies?'

'Clay's running low, I'm glad to say,' she grinned. 'And we shall need more paint in a week or so if this goes on.'

'I'll put the orders in this afternoon,' he promised, looking across the workshop and smiling at Francesca. 'Give me a list if you think of anything else. Cakes for tea?'

'Sounds good. Shall I order them?'

He was already walking towards Francesca. 'Um, yes,' he said, vaguely. 'If you will.' When he'd first come galloping downstairs and walked into the workshop full of his good news, he'd been determined to praise them all and make a fuss of them. Now all he wanted to do was to congratulate his premier artist, to bask in her smile and tell her how wonderful it all was and ask her out for dinner. And the need to do that was so overwhelming he forgot how he ought to be behaving.

Molly watched the speed and eagerness of his walk, and smiled to herself. She been watching him whenever he talked to Francesca for some time and she was beginning to think he was smitten. It would be splendid if he was. He'd been a lovely husband to Candida, nursing her all those years like that, and he was much too nice to go on living alone. She watched as Francesca looked up and smiled at him. That's it, she thought, encourage him. He's a dear man.

But she was giving the wrong answer at that moment. 'Oh yes,' she was saying. 'That would be lovely. Agnes is a bit down today. I'll ring her and tell her. It would do her good.'

No, he thought, I don't want to take Agnes out, fond though I am of her. It's you I want to spend time with.

But he couldn't say so. Now that Agnes had come into the conversation he had to ask how she was. 'What's up?' he said.

'It's the plaster,' Francesca explained. 'She says she's sick of it and I'm sure she is.'

'But she'll be having it taken off soon, won't she?'

'Next week.'

'And then she'll be able to get back to her house again. She must miss it.'

'She does,' she said returning to her painting.

'I must get on,' he said, taking the hint and hoping she would smile at him again. Which she did. Next time I ask her, he thought, I must make it clear that I want a twosome, a proper date, just her and me. The thought of it made him yearn. But there was work to be done, clay and paint to be ordered, orders to be met. The excitement of that caught him up and swept him along, comfortingly away from his disappointment. There would be another chance. He just had to handle it better.

Jeffrey Walmesly had just taken delivery of his 'esteemed order of one sample sack of quality clay'. He was so tantalisingly close to the success and money he wanted that his hands were shaking. He hadn't the faintest idea how to improve the clay but the more he thought about this transaction the less he felt he had to do anything to it. It was perfectly good clay without any alteration or additions. All he had to do was repackage it under his new logo and make sure the Prendergast person believed what he said. Which he would. He was quite sure about that. He was an expert at making people believe things. In his long experience in selling his skills, he'd learned that people believed what they were told if the person doing the telling was an expert. Look how he'd persuaded

Professor Cairns. That had been an absolute piece of cake. No, all he had to do was to make sure this Prendergast person knew how knowledgeable he was and felt he could trust him. That was all. Simples! After all he *was* a geologist even if he hadn't got some stupid degree. He'd had years of experience in the field and that was what counted. And his CV was superb. He might take a copy along with him when he made his preliminary visit just to make sure. Oh he couldn't wait. It was in the bag. He could feel it in his bones. I'll phone him this afternoon, he thought. Lay on the charm, admire the goods, stress my expertise – modestly of course. I've got his number.

Henry had just completed his orders for clay and paint and was feeling pleased with himself when the desk phone rang. He answered it without very much interest but when he recognized the voice he sat up and took notice, his conscience pricking him.

'I hear you've invited me and Francesca to dinner tonight,' Agnes said coming straight to the point. 'She's just rung me.'

'Yes, that's right,' he said. What else could he say? He was pinned to the spot.

'Would it upset you if I said I couldn't come?'

He could hardly answer that truthfully so he took a different tack. 'I'm sorry to hear that,' he said. 'Francesca thought it would cheer you up.'

'Sorry to sound ungrateful but it would take more than a meal to do that,' she said. 'I'm so sick of this stupid plaster. It's like carrying an elephant about. No, no, you two go and leave me be. I just want to sit in a heap and feel sorry for myself.'

He tried to find something to comfort her. 'That's not like you,' he said.

'It's like me today.'

'Well I'm sorry to hear it,' he said and was instantly ashamed of himself because it wasn't really true. He was sorry in one way. Of course he was. He'd have been downright heartless not to have been. But over and above that he was ridiculously, childishly, selfishly glad. He made another attempt to comfort her. 'They'll be removing it soon though, won't they?'

'Next Thursday,' she said miserably, 'and it might as well be next Christmas for all the comfort *that* is.'

Poor old thing, he thought. She *is* low. I ought to try and persuade her to change her mind. Francesca's right. A good meal might be just the thing to pick her up. But he dithered because he wanted his tête-à-tête with Francesca so much. Then he thought he was being selfish and opened his mouth to urge her to change her mind, but she was speaking again.

'I'd be terrible company,' she was saying. 'Much better leave me be. I'll join you next time when I've got my leg back.'

'That's a promise,' he said. 'I shall hold you to it.'

'Sorry to be a moaning Minnie.'

'You're not,' he said. 'You've been very patient for a very long time. I'd have been moaning long before this. I wish there were more I could do to help you.'

'Bring me a bottle of claret,' she said, 'and then I can drown my woes.'

'Your word is my command,' he said and smiled as he hung up. What a day this was turning out to be. Huge orders, Molly singing at her work, the whole place buzzing, and now an uninterrupted evening with Francesca. It was almost too good to be true.

When the phone rang again a few minutes later, he answered it happily, almost sure it would be good news.

It was a strange man's voice asking if he could speak to Mr Henry Prendergast.

'Speaking,' he said. 'How may I help you?'

'Well actually,' the voice said smoothly, 'and if I may say so, it's more how I may help you.'

'Indeed?'

'Allow me to introduce myself,' the voice smoothed on. 'Name of Walmesly, Jeffrey Walmesly. I'm a qualified geologist. My specialities are concrete – you may have heard of my coloured concrete – it's very big in the States – but, more to the point, china clay.' Then it paused waiting for a response.

'I see,' Henry said. Although he wasn't sure he did.

'I've been following the fortunes of your company in the national press,' the voice said. 'Your mermaid dinner service is very impressive, if you don't mind me saying so. I'm lost in admiration. It must be selling like hot cakes.'

Henry murmured vaguely.

'Now the thing is,' the voice continued, silkily smooth, 'it happens that I've just invented a new process that keeps the fluidity and elasticity of natural clay in peak condition for anything up to twenty years. It prevents crazing, retains colour, all that sort of thing. I perfected it last year and it's now fully accredited and ready to market. Then I saw the article about your mermaid dinner service in the *Sunday Times* and I thought, there's a family heirloom if ever I saw one, so naturally I wondered whether you would be interested in testing a sample. One sack perhaps, to give you the feel of it. Of course, with your experience, you would soon be able to judge if it were the sort of thing you could use. It's slightly more expensive than your standard clays, naturally, but you would expect that.'

The businessman began to question. 'How much more expensive?'

Figures were quoted. It *was* more expensive but only marginally and if it really could deliver all those improvements, it might be worth consideration. The sun was shining, the dinner service was selling even better than he'd hoped, he was going to have dinner with Francesca, what could go wrong? 'I'll tell you what,' he said, persuaded despite his grumbling better judgement but feeling that luck was running with him so strongly that he ought to be fair, 'if you can deliver a sack to my workshop within the next forty-eight hours, I will give it a trial.'

'It'll be with you tomorrow morning,' Jeffrey promised, grinning hugely because there was no one around to see him. It was a done deal. He was made.

By the time Henry put the phone back in its cradle he'd forgotten all about clay and Jeffrey Walmesly and even the mermaid dinner service. His mind had instantly slotted itself back into the far more enjoyable business of deciding which restaurant he was going to take Francesca to and what specialities he would order to tempt her appetite. He was so excited about this date he was almost fearful. He spent the next half an hour booking a table at his favourite place and discussing the menu, deciding that lobster thermidor might not suit because he wasn't sure whether she liked shellfish – what a lot he had to learn about her – considering steak or roast duck because they were relatively safe. Then there were flowers to order so as to cheer poor old Aggie up – he still felt uncomfortably guilty about Aggie – and her bottle of claret. Oh it was a delicious afternoon. He felt like a young man again. And he hadn't even begun to consider what they would talk about. There were so many things he wanted to tell her but he knew he mustn't rush it. Oh my dear tender Francesca, he thought, I do so want to make you happy.

His dear tender Francesca had worked extremely hard that day, aware that the demand for her mermaid was growing prodigiously and wanting to meet it as well as she could. From time to time, she sat, paint brush in hand, and wondered what sort of people would use the plate she'd just finished and what they would talk about as they sat round their dining table enjoying their meal. And then she thought how wonderful it was to see Henry so happy and how good it would be to praise him at their own meal that evening and that made her wonder whether Agnes would be coming with them. She'd said she didn't want to when she'd rung her that morning and she'd sounded very determined about it. 'I shall phone Henry and tell him it can't be done,' she'd said. 'He'll understand.' Perhaps I ought to take a bottle of wine home for her, Francesca thought. I don't like the idea of leaving her at home on her own. She's been so patient with this horrible plaster and it's miserable to see her feeling down, especially when I'm so happy. And some chocolates. They're cheering. I'll buy them on my way home.

Which she did and arrived in the flat with her arms full of parcels.

'You're going to be late if you don't look sharp,' Agnes warned her. 'He's coming to pick you up at half past seven.'

'Has he rung?'

'Just this minute. I told him you weren't back.'

'I had a service to finish,' Francesca explained. 'It's

selling so well we're under pressure. I couldn't very well leave it.'

'Go and get showered,' Agnes said, 'and I'll make you a cup of tea. What are you going to wear?'

'I've no idea,' Francesca admitted. 'The autumnal dress maybe.'

'With my necklace and the earrings,' Agnes said. 'Just the thing. I'll look them out. Off you go.'

'Aren't you going to open my presents?' Francesca asked.

'Not till you're dressed. Chop, chop! You don't want to keep him waiting.'

'He wouldn't mind.'

'Possibly not but I would. I want to see you in your finery before he whisks you off.'

She was dressed and ready a good ten minutes before he was due to arrive. Agnes had plenty of time to make tea, open her chocolates, sample them and declare that they were the very thing for a bear with a sore head. Then the phone rang.

'Now what?' Agnes said, making a grimace.

It was Christine-from-the-galleries, asking if she could speak to Francesca. 'Ah!' she said. 'I'm glad I've caught you. Your pictures are framed and ready to hang. When would you like to come in and see them? We need to agree on the prices soon so that the catalogue can be printed. And do you think Mr Prendergast would be prepared to loan us the original of the mermaid?'

She was so quick and business-like that Francesca didn't know which question to answer first so she started with the mermaid. 'I'll ask him this evening,' she said. 'I'm pretty sure he'll let you have it.'

'Good,' Christine-from-the-galleries said and she spoke so briskly that Francesca could see her ticking it off on her list. 'Now when will you visit?'

'Saturday?'

'It'll be cutting it a bit fine but Saturday would do. Say ten o'clock.'

Ten o'clock was said.

'I'll see you then,' Christine-from-the galleries promised and was gone.

'She's so quick,' Francesca said, sitting with the phone still in her hand. 'She takes my breath away.'

'Here's our Henry come,' Agnes said, as the doorbell rang. 'Have you got everything you need?'

'Are you sure you don't want to come with us?' Francesca asked as she picked up her coat and went to open the door.

'Positive,' Agnes said. 'Once I've made my mind up that's the end of it. Hello Henry. You look spruce.'

The word made him laugh. 'That's a new one,' he said, walking into the room. 'You make me sound like a tree.'

Agnes grinned at him and watched as he smiled at Francesca. The expression on his face told her more than he could have imagined. Oh yes, she thought, I've made exactly the right decision. They need an evening on their own together.

'Have fun,' she said to them as they left. 'And don't bring her home after midnight, Henry, or she'll turn into a pumpkin.'

The evening was full of soothing autumnal sounds and enticing smells, a bonfire prickling somewhere on the far bank, the river musty and pungent, making soft licking sounds as it gentled towards the sea, an owl giving its echoing call among the dark trees of Railwayland, distant traffic muffled by a rapidly gathering mist. As they walked out of the close, it seemed perfectly natural

261

for Henry to tuck Francesca's hand into his elbow.

'We'll leave the car here,' he said, 'if that's all right. We're within walking distance.'

She smiled her agreement at him, her eyes shining in the odd mist-haloed light as they walked towards Cliffe High Street. 'I've just had a phone call from Christine-from-the-galleries,' she said. 'She wants you to loan them the mermaid for the exhibition.'

'She'll have to collect it,' he told her. 'I haven't got time to cart it about. Not now. There are too many other things to do. And she'll have to give it star billing. That's essential.'

That made her laugh. 'I'm sure she will,' she said. 'After all that's where all this began.'

'We've come a long way since that day,' he said remembering it.

'We have,' she agreed. 'I have to pinch myself some-times to make sure it's true.'

He squeezed her hand against his side. 'Oh it's true,' he said, 'and it's going to go on getting better and better. Believe me.' Was this the moment to tell her how he felt?

But she deflected him with doubt. 'You're always so sure of things,' she said, her voice full of admiration.

'Not everything,' he confessed and made a joke of it. 'You'd be surprised how often I feel uncertain. Only I keep it to myself.'

She didn't like to argue with him because he was the boss, after all, but she felt quite sure he'd never had any real doubts about anything at all. So she changed the subject. 'She was full of plans,' she said 'She says she's priced everything up and she wants me to come in on Saturday morning and *agree on the prices*.'

'That shouldn't take long. She's got a good eye for business.'

'I don't doubt that,' she said, 'It's just I don't want her to put a price on my pictures at all.'

'Would you like me to come with you? Bit of moral support?'

The thought of having someone to stick up for her was very tempting and he *would* stick up for her, wouldn't he, being the boss and seeing how important the mermaid had been to him? 'Would you?'

'Of course. What time's the meeting?'

'Ten o'clock.'

'I'll be there. Would you like me to pick you up? There's a car park right by the entrance.'

She would and was obviously grateful. Could he speak now? Was it the right time? The trouble was they were very nearly at the restaurant. Maybe he should wait until they were settled at their table.

'Here we are,' he said, standing aside to let her enter the building first. The decision was made. It was better to get settled and comfortable before he said anything. This wasn't something to be rushed. The *maître d'* was already smiling towards them, leading them between the elegant curved screens to their private corner. He noticed in passing what a perfect backdrop the screens provided to Francesca's dress – all that burnt umber and copper – and how well she looked by candlelight. Then the menu was being laid quietly beside their plates and they were left on their own to make their choices and all the talk was of food.

Francesca liked the sound of blue swimming crab and pink grapefruit and asked what he thought of it. So she *does* like seafood. He recommended the roasted breast of duck and suggested that they might have a *tarte tatin* to follow. While she pondered, he gave his mind to the wine list and ordered a Sancerre to compliment the starters. By the time they'd chosen the duck, he'd almost forgotten how he'd planned to open his all-important conversation. But it was a pleasure to see her so happy and looking forward to her blue swimming crab.

'I could get used to this sort of life,' she said as the dish was set before her.

It was the perfect lead. 'I think you should,' he said. 'If anyone deserves it, you do.'

She took it in entirely the wrong direction. 'You think I should ask a lot of money for my paintings. Is that it?'

It was a direct question so it had to be answered. 'No,' he said. 'Not unless it feels right. Wait till you've heard what Christine has to say about it.'

She gave an involuntary shiver so that the candle flames dipped and flickered. 'If I had my own way I'd just go on painting for the fun of it,' she said. 'Putting a price on my work doesn't seem natural. Or right.'

'I put a price on it,' he reminded her.

She grinned at that. 'You did,' she agreed. 'But it worried me, even then. I felt I was cheating you. It was such a lot of money.'

'I hope you don't still think like that. You've earned it several times over.'

'Well no,' she admitted, 'I probably don't. Not now anyway.'

'Only "probably" don't?' he teased.

She ducked her head against his teasing. 'This crab is really good,' she said.

They enjoyed their crab for several minutes without speaking, then he tried another gambit. 'Do you ever wonder what's in the future for you?' he asked.

'Not really,' she said. 'It's all I can do to cope with the present. I mean obviously the mermaid won't go on selling for ever but while it does. . . .'

'How would you feel if I wanted to buy another painting to use on a tea service?'

'Do you?'

'As I happens, yes I do.'

'Which one?'

'The chaffinch feeding her young.'

That surprised her. 'But that was just a sketch.'

The empty plates were being discreetly removed, the wine glasses topped up. They'd be serving the main course soon and he hadn't even started to say the things he wanted to say. 'Have you ever thought about what your life could be if you weren't tied to the factory?' he tried.

'I hope you're not thinking of giving me the sack,' she said and her face was serious. 'I like being tied to the factory.'

'Oh, dear me, no,' he said. 'I wouldn't dream of giving you the sack. You're much too precious.' There, the word was spoken. Now the conversation would change.

But she didn't seem to notice that he'd said something significant. 'I'm very glad to hear it,' she laughed. 'I should hate to have to go back to working in an office. You've no idea how boring *that* was. Oh that duck smells superb.'

He was cast down. It didn't seem to make any difference what leads he gave her or what words he chose. How could he tell her what he was thinking when she didn't pick up any cues? There must be some way of opening this conversation. 'Maybe we've reached the point where we should be making plans for the future,' he tried. And then felt stupid because it didn't sound right.

'My future's going to be helping Agnes through the next few weeks,' she said rather ruefully. 'She's so sure she'll be walking normally as soon as they've taken off the plaster and I've tried to warn her that she might hit difficulties but she won't have it. I mean her muscles will have wasted, won't they.'

'Probably.'

'She'll need physiotherapy and she'll hate that. Being made to do exercises. I mean, imagine it. And she'll probably have to use crutches for a little while. Even a Zimmer frame. Can you imagine her walking with a Zimmer frame? It does worry me.'

'We'll have to take her for outings,' he said. 'Things to keep her mind off it.'

'That sounds like a very good idea,' she said, relieved to be offered practical advice. 'What sort of things?'

'Well your exhibition for a start,' he said. 'And then there's Bonfire. She always enjoys that. Don't worry. We'll cosset her through.'

'Yes,' she agreed, smiling at him. 'We will.'

The smile lifted him a little, despite his disappointment. He might not have said a word he wanted to say but there was still a bond between them. Of sorts.

But as he walked her back to the flat he was cast down. Maybe this was a sign that he shouldn't say anything. Maybe he was too old for her. If only he could be nearer her age things might be different. As it was. . . .

CHAPTER 17

IF THIS DAMNED trolley isn't delivered soon, Jeffrey thought, I shall have words to say. It had been promised at eight-thirty sharp. Eight-thirty sharp and now it was a quarter to nine and there was no sign of the damned thing. It wasn't good enough. Didn't that fool salesman understand how important it was? He'd told him enough times. He glared at the traffic passing by his window and sighed theatrically. People were so unreliable. There'd been enough rubbish in their stupid ads about how trustworthy the company was. It was one of the reasons he'd used them in the first place. And now they couldn't even deliver a simple trolley on time. If it didn't come soon he'd have to go without it and make his entrance to Prendergast Potteries carrying the sack on his back like a coalman. The thought made him squirm. Oh for crying out loud, he thought, where are the fools? What's the matter with them? He'd planned this so carefully and it had cost him a packet. Not that he begrudged the cost. He knew that success lies in getting the details right. Having new sacks printed had cost him an arm and a leg but *they*'d been delivered on time and were well worth it. The original sack of clay was now covered by his company design and his logo, a cunningly entwined JW in red with black edging, wonderfully eye-catching. Just the thing to inspire confidence. But a good strong trolley was essential too so as to make an impression as he wheeled his splendid sample into the workshop. Whatever else he did he meant to be noticed when he arrived. Oh come on, he urged the unseen delivery man, put a jerk on for heaven's sake. My career's at stake.

There was a white van drawing up just along the road. Could this be it? Fat man climbing out of the driver's seat, strolling to the back of the van, bundling a trolley out onto the pavement. Yes. And about fucking time. He picked up his briefcase and bounded down the stairs, arriving on the pavement beside his own car as the fat man blinked towards him.

'Sorry about this, guv,' he said. 'RTA at the junction. Real pile-up. Where d'you want it?'

'In the boot,' Jeffrey said, lifting it, 'and look sharp about it, I'm late enough already.'

'Righto,' the fat man said cheerfully. 'I wouldn't go round the junction if I was you. They're still clearing up. If you wouldn't mind just signing here.'

Stupid fool! Jeffrey thought. What sort of an idiot driver does he think I am? But he signed the delivery note and eased into his car, without saying anything else, eager to start his journey. He'd have to make good speed if he was to get there before eleven. But a promise was a promise and – unlike this fat oaf standing on the pavement grinning – he knew how important time-keeping was.

And after all that angst, it was a fast, easy journey and he reached the potteries comfortably on time. Quick check in the driving mirror, boot opened, trolley unwrapped and stood on the tarmac, sack of clay lifted carefully onto it, logo prominently displayed, and he was ready. It gave him quite a kick to follow the receptionist through the workshop past all those subservient workers in their mop caps and aprons and to know how close he was to success. That's right, he thought, look at me. I'm worth looking at. I'm a cut above any of you. I'm on the up.

Francesca didn't notice him until he was walking past her and then she was so surprised to see him she had to look twice to make sure her eyes weren't playing tricks. Molly was heading her way so she waved her paintbrush at her to call her over.

'Problem?' Molly said when she'd reached the workstation.

Francesca shook her head. 'What's that man doing in here?' she asked, glaring at his retreating back.

'Sales rep, I should think,' Molly said, squinting at him. 'He's got a clay sack on that trolley. Why?'

'I know him.'

Molly was surprised. 'Really?'

'Afraid so.'

'Oh dear,' Molly said. 'That sounds ominous. I gather you don't reckon him much.'

'I don't.'

'Are you saying he's bad news?'

'It wouldn't surprise me.'

'In that case, I'll find out what he's doing here and get back to you,' Molly promised.

Which she did, returning to the workstation ten minutes later with the gossip. 'He's the MD of a new clay company,' she said. 'Something superior by all accounts. *JW Clays*.'

'That's his name. JW. Jeffrey Walmesly,' Francesca told her. 'He's a con artist. I hope our Mr P doesn't get taken in by him.' It was rather worrying.

'No fear of that,' Molly said. 'He's got far too much sense.'

But Francesca worried and went on worrying for the rest of the morning, frowning at the mermaid, who did nothing to reassure her or to solve her dilemma. Henry was the most sensible man she'd ever met and quite the kindest but Jeffrey was the most skilled liar she'd ever met and quite the most unprincipled. He could be telling all sorts of stories up there in that office and Henry might be too honest to suspect them or too trusting to see through them. Just the thought of what might be happening was making her feel so angry she could barely sit still. It was intolerable to think of Jeffrey of all people coming down here to con their lovely Henry. She wanted to storm up to the office and show him up for the dishonest monster he was. But she could hardly go butting in on a meeting. That wouldn't be at all proper, given that Henry was the boss and she was one of his workers. At one point, she tried to phone Agnes because she'd know what to do, but she didn't get an answer and that made everything worse. Damn you Jeffrey, she thought, as her anger and frustration grew. Why couldn't you go and tell your lies to someone else? Why did it have to be our Henry? She kept a very careful watch all morning but there was no sign of Henry or Jeffrey. It wasn't until they broke for lunch and she met up with Molly again that she heard what had gone on while she'd been fretting.

'You won't like this,' Molly said, 'but apparently this is some sort of improved clay. Very high quality. It won't craze and it'll hold its colour for years. Henry's taken one sack on spec and we're to use it and see what we think of it. He's just had me in to tell me.'

'He's been conned,' Francesca said, sadly.

'I don't think so,' Molly said. 'He's too sensible for that. He's being fair.'

'But you won't know if it holds its colour for years, will you?' Francesca said. 'Not till the years are up.'

Molly grimaced. 'Anyway we've got to give it a go,' she said. 'So we shall see.'

Francesca felt horribly depressed. Hadn't she known he'd pull a fast one? And he'd done it and got away with it.

'It might be as good as he says,' Molly tried to reassure her.

And it might not, Francesca thought.

'Oh and some woman's come to collect the mermaid for your exhibition.' Molly said. 'She's making ever such a business of wrapping it up. Brought a blanket for it.'

Francesca had been so angry she'd forgotten all about the exhibition. Maybe I could try to warn him tomorrow, she thought, when we've got all this business of pricing out of the way. She'd have to choose her words very carefully because she wouldn't like him to think she was questioning his judgement, but she couldn't just stand back and let that foul Jeffrey take him for a ride. And she knew that was what he'd done. I'll talk to Agnes about it tonight, she decided. See what she says.

'Up to no good,' Agnes said. 'Plain as the nose on his ugly face. I'm surprised at Henry. I thought he was too street wise to be taken in by a fraudster.'

'He has been though, hasn't he?'

'Looks like it.'

'Do you think I ought to warn him?'

'It's a bit late for that now,' Agnes said, 'if he's taken a sack on spec. I think you'd put his back up. If I were you

I'd keep schtum and wait for him to work things out for himself.'

It was sensible advice but Francesca didn't want to take it. I'll wait and see if an opportunity presents itself, she thought, which it well might and then I'll tell him what I know. It's not fair to leave him in the dark. Besides, I'd like to see Jeffrey get his comeuppance. It's long overdue.

Jeffrey treated himself to a fish supper that night. He reckoned he'd earned it because that Henry Prendergast had turned out to be trickier than he looked and had struck a hard bargain. One sack, trade price, half paid on the spot but the other half to wait until the firm was satisfied with the goods. They would be of course, so the man was nit-picking, but it was annoying to have to wait for payment, especially when he needed the cash so much. Still, never mind, his precious firm wouldn't be able to fault the product and they couldn't disprove any of the claims he'd made for it so it was only a matter of waiting for a week and then he would land a big order and his problems would be solved. Yep, all in all, he'd earned his fish and chips. Maybe he should put in a big order for the clay just to be on the safe side. Tomorrow maybe. Or Monday. Now where's the vinegar? Don't tell me that damned Fran walked off with that too?

He was rooting about in his depleted cupboard when his mobile rang. Calls in the evening were rather rare these days, so he answered it guardedly. 'Yes?'

It was Fran's hideous mother. 'Have you found her yet?' she said.

'I haven't had time for searches,' he told her crossly. 'I've been working twenty-four seven.'

'Oh really!' she said, sounding exasperated. 'You're

not trying hard enough. That's your trouble. Mr Turner says she's got to be found or he can't proceed. I suggest you pull your finger out. If we're not careful we shall lose all our money.'

'I thought it was Fran's money,' he said sourly.

'You know what I mean. She's pretty well bound to share it and I mean that's only fair when it should have come to me in the first place. Anyway, he's getting impatient.'

'Look,' he said. 'It's no good you going on at me. I don't know where your stupid daughter is. I've tried every place I can think of and she isn't in any of them. You know her better than I do. Why don't *you* look?'

Her voice grew sharper. 'We've done everything we can think of too, I'll have you know.'

He was stung and angered. 'Well, so have I. It's no good you going on at me. I'm not a miracle worker.'

'No, you're not,' she said sharply. 'You're a bone-idle useless lump.'

'Now look here,' he said angrily but she'd already hung up.

He was extremely upset. To be called names after such a successful day wasn't just uncalled for, it was hideous. It undid all the good he'd done. I've worked my fingers to the bone on this deal, he thought, right to the bone. I need a bit of appreciation not a load of abuse. Foul woman. It quite put him off his fish and chips. *And* there wasn't any vinegar.

*

Saturday morning was uncomfortably cold. Mist curled from the river in long dank swathes and the sky was metal grey. Francesca decided to wear her boots and her winter coat for her outing to the gallery.

'You need a Cossack hat to go with that outfit,' Agnes

said. 'Don't you think so Henry?'

Henry had only just arrived but he considered it seriously. 'Possibly,' he said. 'But it looks fine to me with or without a hat.'

He's such a gentleman, Francesca thought, admiring him. He's always courteous. He'd never be knowingly unkind to anyone and he certainly wouldn't cheat them. And now that horrid unprincipled hateful man has deliberately tricked him. She was in a passion of protective anger at the thought of it. How dare he do such a thing! And it was all made worse because she hadn't been able to warn him in time. And now, even if she did try to, it might all be too late. She was scowling with anger as Henry eased her into the Merc.

He misinterpreted the scowl. 'Don't worry,' he said, 'I'll see you don't get talked into agreeing to anything you don't approve of. I know Christine will want to price your paintings as high as she can – she's a good business woman – but if you think a price is exorbitant just give me a look and I'll see what can be done.'

She thanked him, feeling worse than ever at the situation he was in.

He smiled at her as he put the car into drive. 'Don't worry,' he said. 'Whatever else, she's on the side of her artists. Always has been.'

She certainly knew how to display her artists' work. That was obvious to Francesca as soon as she walked into the showroom. She was very impressed by what had been done to her paintings, they were all so beautifully framed and grouped so artfully that one picture offset the ones next to it. The picture of the castle was in the centre of the wall that she faced as she walked in with all her preliminary sketches grouped about it so that her eye moved from the originals to the finished work and back again, noticing the nuances and the changes she'd made. The river sketches were set one beside the other to reveal the changing seasons with all her garden sketches grouped about them. By the time she'd walked round the entire display and seen the way the four portraits were featured, she really began to believe that this *was* an exhibition after all and that she really was an artist.

'If there's anything you'd like to have changed,' Christine said, and it was only just a question, 'just let us know. Our aim is to show your work at its very best.'

'No, no,' Francesca said. 'There's nothing at all I'd like to see changed. It's ... well ... it's ... you've taken my breath away.'

Christine smiled. 'That's how we like it,' she said. 'Now when you're ready we'll go to my office and I'll show you the catalogue we've designed.'

It was a handsome cover, very glossy and featuring the mermaid – what else – and lying beside it was a type-written list of all the sketches and paintings arranged, as she was quick to notice, wall by wall. But the prices were much too high. Surely they were. It made her feel grasping and avaricious. She gave Henry a quick look, at once startled and anxious and he smiled at her reassuringly.

'I would like to open the proceedings by buying "Chaffinch and Chick",' he said to Christine.

'That sounds like a good place to start,' she said and grinned at him. 'I trust you've brought your cheque book.'

'Of course.'

Francesca was checking the price of it. £500 seemed far too much for such a little painting. 'It's very small,' she demurred. 'I mean, is it really worth all that?'

'Collectors buy the quality of a painting,' Christine

told her, 'not the size. Isn't that right Henry?'

'It is,' he said, smiling at Francesca. 'And this one is very high quality. Wait till you see what I'm going to do with it. It'll be the star of our spring collection.'

How could she argue with him? He was so happy to be buying her picture it gave her a lift despite her fears of overpricing. 'Well . . .' she said.

Henry was writing his cheque, Christine was fixing a little blue sticker on the frame. 'There you are,' she said to Francesca. 'Your first sale. And it won't be your last, I can tell you that. There's a lot of interest in the castle for a start.'

'At six thousand pounds?' Francesca said her eyes round.

'Oh yes. It's well worth six grand. Trust me. I've got three different sets of people coming to a private view on Monday.'

'Heavens!' Francesca was feeling a bit dizzy. This wasn't the way she'd expected this meeting to go at all.

'There you are,' Henry said to her. 'What did I tell you?' And he turned to Christine and smiled. 'She still doesn't believe how valuable her work is.'

'Come next Friday I guarantee you'll believe it,' Christine said. 'This is going to be a great success. Ah! Here's the coffee.'

By the time Henry drove her back to the flat, Francesca was thoroughly disgruntled and very disappointed in herself. She'd come out that morning full of good intentions and all of them had been turned on their head. She'd agreed to nearly every single price Christine had suggested even though she'd had no intention of doing any such thing. She'd made a stand over her sketch of Tom and talked the price down to £50 because she knew how much Sharon wanted to buy it, but that was all. And worse than all that, she hadn't warned Henry about Jeffrey and she really should have done. But there was no way she could say anything now, not after he'd spent all that money on the chaffinch. And in any case he was busy planning the rest of her week. 'Do you need time off to take our Aggie to the hospital on Thursday?' he asked as he turned into the nearest parking space behind the flats.

She had to admit it would be a great help. 'She's so sure she's going to be skipping about when they take the plaster off,' she said, 'and I know it's not going to be that easy. I'll come in for the morning and cut off at lunchtime, if that's all right. Then I can feed her before we go. It shouldn't take very long, should it? I could be back by mid-afternoon.'

'Take as long as you need,' he said, smiling that lovely easy smile without having the faintest idea that the sight of it was making her feel guilty. 'We can't have our Aggie in a state and with no one to comfort her.'

'I think she's going to need a lot of comfort on Thursday,' Francesca predicted as she got out of the car. Then she remembered her manners. 'Thanks for taking me to the meeting.'

'Pleasure,' he said

*

Thursday began badly, just as Francesca had feared. Agnes stomped about the kitchen on her crutch, frowning and complaining. 'Well I hope they're not going to keep me waiting all afternoon, that's all,' she said, banging the kettle onto its stand. 'I've waited long enough to get rid of this damned plaster, God knows. I shall be furious if they keep me hanging about for hours on top of everything else. Furious.'

Francesca tried to soothe her. 'I'm sure they won't,'

she said. 'Do you want some toast? We could open the plum jam. What d'you think?'

Agnes sat down heavily and shrugged the plum jam away. 'Do what you like,' she said tetchily. 'I can't think about jam when I've got this hanging over my head.'

She's frightened, Francesca thought, watching her anguished face. Poor Agnes. She tried to find something to say to ease her. 'It'll be all right,' she said. 'Really.'

But that only made Agnes more irritable. 'Don't keep saying that,' she shouted. 'You don't know. How can you? It could be awful.'

Francesca made the tea and cut two slices of toast in a vain effort to keep calm. 'Yes,' she said, 'it might, but on the other hand it might be better than you expect. That's a possibility, don't you think. I mean, you're right to say I don't know. That's true. I don't. But then you don't either.'

It was the worst thing she could have said. 'I can't bear this,' Agnes shouted and clomped back to her bedroom, her face set and her spine stiff.

Francesca stood with one hand on the jam jar and the other covering her mouth. This is awful, she thought. I was trying to make things better and now I've upset her. Poor Agnes. It made her feel impotent. I can't say anything to help her, she thought, and I should have done and I couldn't warn Henry, when I'm the one person who ought to have done *that*. She could hear her mother's voice, nagging in her head. '*You're useless. What are you? Useless.*' She felt like a trapped bird, beating against implacable bars, hurting herself and making no progress. She was so tense the clunk of the toaster made her jump but at least the mundane business of buttering toast and opening the jam jar calmed her enough to think of something else she could try. She set Agnes's slice on a tray with the mug of tea she'd left on the table and the marmalade pot – just in case – and carried it to the bedroom door.

'I know you might not feel like it,' she said through the door, 'but I've made you some breakfast. I shall be going to work in a minute. Shall I bring it in for you or leave it here?'

There was a long pause. She was just about to carry the tray back into the kitchen when the door was opened and Agnes held out her hands to receive it. 'Thanks,' she said, gruffly. 'That was kind. It's all a bit difficult, you understand.'

'Yes,' Francesca said. 'I do. Really.'

But Agnes was closing the door and the conversation.

'It was dreadful.' Francesca said to Molly when she got into work. 'She's in such a state and everything I said made it worse. I didn't know what to do.'

Molly round face was wrinkled with concern. 'Poor you,' she commiserated. 'But you'll be going with her this afternoon, won't you. She'll be glad of that. When will you leave?'

'Lunchtime,' Francesca told her.

'Well, wish you luck if I don't see you before,' Molly said and was off on her rounds.

But in fact she made a point of coming back to see her about half an hour before the lunch break. 'I've got something to show you,' she said, her face very serious. 'Finish what you're doing at the moment but don't start anything new.'

Francesca used up the paint on her brush, cleaned it and set it aside, wondering what she was going to be shown. Then she followed Molly's determined back through the workshop and out into the store room. They stopped by Jeffrey's sack of clay, now depleted and lop-sided, with its flamboyant cover torn back.

'Look at that,' Molly said, lifting up the torn flap of the cover. 'See? What do you think of that?'

Francesca stooped, looked and was lifted into such instant and triumphant delight that her worries about Agnes melted away. The torn flap revealed another cover underneath and enough of it was visible for her to read what was printed on it. '*Cornish Clays*' it said. '*High quali. . . .*' 'Didn't I tell you he was no good?' she said. 'He's no more created a new clay than I have. That's someone else's product and someone else's package with his cover put on over the top of it. If he'd worked on the clay he'd have unpacked it the way *you* do and then put it in a new sack when it was ready to sell.'

Molly was looking worried. 'That's illegal, isn't it?'

'Highly,' Francesca said, her pleasure in their discovery growing by the second. 'Or if it isn't it ought to be. Henry would know. See what he says when you show him.'

'Come with me,' Molly said. 'I don't like being the bearer of bad tidings and I shall have to tell him. This JW man is coming back tomorrow, so Liam told me. You could tell Henry all about him, couldn't you, being as you know him.'

Francesca was tempted but when she looked at her watch she knew she couldn't do it. 'I would if I could,' she said, 'but I shall have to go. I want to give Agnes some lunch before I take her to the hospital. Sorry about that.'

'Yes,' Molly said, sighing. 'I'd almost forgotten. Well good luck.'

'And good luck to you too,' Francesca said. But she was thinking maybe I don't need luck now I've got all this to tell poor Agnes. With luck it'll cheer her up and give her something else to think about.

It did even better than that. It gave her something to talk about all through lunch and all the way to the other end of town and the hospital. 'Poetic justice,' she said, as she helped herself to Francesca's tossed salad and a chunk of spicy chicken. 'I always knew he'd come to no good. He had bad lot written all over him, even on a cruise. Well, particularly on that cruise. I haven't forgotten the way he blamed you for getting left behind.'

'No,' Francesca grinned. 'Nor have I. I think my mermaid'll be applauding.'

Agnes' good mood lasted even when they were in the hospital and she was waiting to have her plaster removed. 'Henry'll sort him out,' she said with great gratification. 'I'd love to be a fly on the wall when he does.'

'He's coming back tomorrow,' Francesca told her, 'according to Molly.'

'I'll get my fly kit ready,' Agnes said.

There was a nurse approaching them. 'Miss Potts?' she asked. 'Ready to have this plaster off?'

'Carve away!' Agnes said and followed her out of the waiting room as meek as a lamb.

After her extraordinary see-saw of a morning, Francesca was suddenly struck by how ridiculous life could be and got a fit of the giggles. Carve away! she thought as she struggled to control herself. For heaven's sake! But really it was all too absurd. She'd been worrying herself silly for far too long, sure that she was in for a terrible time of it this afternoon and now this.

She was still giggling and wiping her eyes when Agnes came back, using her crutch but free of the plaster. 'Are you all right?' she asked.

'I'm fine,' Francesca told her. 'I just saw the funny side

of something that's all. More to the point, how are you?'

'Stupid muscles have shrunk,' Agnes said, but she didn't seem to be complaining. She was just stating a fact. 'I've got to go on using this crutch and have physiotherapy which is a bit of a pain but other than that it's fine. Healed up nicely so they said. Shan't be able to get home for a day or two because of the physiotherapy – I've got two sessions booked for next week – but you won't mind putting up with me for a bit longer, will you?'

'Oh I think I could manage it,' Francesca teased. It was such a relief that it had all gone well. 'Have they finished with you for today?'

'They have.'

'Then let's get home and have some tea. It's been a long day.'

'And tomorrow it's your exhibition and that hideous Jeffrey's going to get his comeuppance,' Agnes said with great satisfaction. 'I wish I could book a ringside seat.'

'Me too,' Francesca said.

CHAPTER 18

JEFFREY WORE HIS best suit, his most expensive shoes and his silver-blue silk shirt for his second meeting with Henry Prendergast. He was on a roll now and felt he had to put on some style. By this time tomorrow, he thought as he sped along the motorway, my troubles will be over. I can clear off my debts on that stinking mortgage and stop all those stupid demands they will keep making and then I'll give myself some treats. They're long overdue, God knows. I shall buy myself a pair of swanky boots for a start and a classy overcoat and I'll put a deposit on a new car. Why not? I'm going to make a fortune. The world's my oyster. And I deserve every penny of it, the work I've put in. Oh it was wonderful to know he was going to be appreciated at last. It was a grey, miserable day and the light was fading fast but he was whistling as he drove. By the time he reached the pottery it was completely dark but his mood was still wonderfully upbeat. He followed the receptionist into the workshop with a swagger. That's right, he thought, as heads turned in his direction, take a good look, I'm going to be rich man.

'He's just come in,' Molly said to Francesca. 'Strutting like a turkey-cock.' She'd been standing right next to

Francesca for more than twenty minutes, watching out for him. 'I do wish we knew what Henry's going to do. He could have told us. Just saying '*I see,*' was no help at all.'

'He's a private sort of person,' Francesca said. 'He wouldn't want to worry us with bad news. He'll deal with it, I can tell you that, whatever he's going to do.'

'Mr Taylor's been with him all afternoon,' Molly said, 'so he's got something planned. Just look at the man, will you. I never saw anyone so cocky.'

Francesca turned her seat and looked out into the workshop following Molly's sight line. Which was how Jeffrey found himself staring up at her.

It gave him quite a shock. What's *she* doing here? he thought, stopping in mid stride. Fucking woman. I thought I was rid of her. He felt as though someone was squeezing his throat. I hope she's not going to make trouble for me. I wouldn't put it past her. Fucking woman. Then he realized that people were looking at him quizzically and walked off again. But his spine was stiff with displeasure and the cockiness of his walk was gone.

'Well, well, well,' Molly said, grinning. 'You gave him a turn.'

'Good!' Francesca said and went back to her mermaid.

'Wait here,' the receptionist said, stopping outside the boardroom door. 'Mr Prendergast's secretary will collect you when they're ready for you.'

Jeffrey was a bit put out to be told to wait. But he remembered to be polite and thanked her and sat in the chair she was indicating. It worried him that he wasn't being shown straight in the way he had been last time. It was rude to keep a valuable supplier hanging about. On the other hand, maybe they were finalizing the details of a big order and if that was the case it would be worth waiting for. But as the minutes ticked past he grew more and more uncomfortable and his unease made him want to go to the loo, which set him a problem, firstly because he didn't know where it was and secondly because he didn't want to be somewhere else when they came to collect him.

The door was being opened, a woman in a brown suit was stepping out, turning towards him. 'Mr Walmesly?' she asked and when he stood up, 'they're ready for you now.'

At last, he thought. And not before time. He settled his shoulders so that they looked square and confident and strode into the room. It seemed brighter than he remembered it and rather forbidding. Mr Prendergast was sitting behind his desk and there were two other men positioned one on each side of him. The armchairs had been moved to a corner of the room and there was one, single, straight-backed chair which looked very uncomfortable placed immediately under the central light and facing the desk.

'Take a seat, Mr Walmesly,' Mr Prendergast said, nodding towards the chair.

It was as uncomfortable as it looked and the light above his head felt like a spotlight but he smiled and nodded and tried to look at ease although he felt like a prisoner in the dock.

Mr Prendergast introduced his two companions. 'Mr Spencer, my accountant,' he said, gesturing towards Liam, 'and Mr Taylor my solicitor.'

Jeffrey murmured that he was pleased to meet them and was annoyed to feel his throat being squeezed again. What does he want with a solicitor? he thought. He's only

285

going to put in an order.

'I hope my new improved clay came up to expectations,' he said, trying to thaw the frost in the atmosphere.

The frost congealed, strengthened, became ice.

'I asked my staff to give your clay a thorough testing Mr Walmesly,' Henry said, 'and then to write a report on how they found it.'

'Audience research,' Jeffrey said, nodding to show he understood. 'Very wise.' He was a bit upset because Mr Prendergast gave him a really horrid look. He'd have called it scathing if he'd been in an unkind mood. As it was, he decided to ignore it. 'I hope they were pleased with it.'

'Their opinion of it was unequivocal,' Mr Prendergast said. 'They found it identical to a high quality clay we have used on several occasions. Cornish Clays. You may have heard of them.'

The name made Jeffrey's heart shrink but he decided to bluff it out. 'I believe I have,' he said as insouciantly as he could.

'I believe you have too,' Mr Prendergast said, icily cold. 'That was the company you purchased this clay from in the first place. Am I not right?'

Jeffrey felt the first stirrings of what felt uncomfortably like panic. It was time to offer a confession — of sorts. 'I'll level with you Mr Prendergast,' he said, spreading his hands before him in a placatory gesture. 'I'm still new to this business. I can't fund my own company completely as yet. We all have to start somewhere as I'm sure you'll agree. I did buy clay from Cornish Clays but of course I added to the product and improved it beyond recognition as I'm sure your workers will agree.'

Henry held up his hand like a policeman stopping traffic. 'I'll stop you there, Mr Walmesly,' he said. 'You must understand that we have examined the packaging of your so-called product and the examination has given us very serious cause for concern, hasn't it Mr Taylor.'

'Indeed,' the solicitor said.

'Indeed,' Henry repeated. 'Very well then, Mr Walmesly, explain one thing to me. I will presume you removed the clay from its original packaging in order to add your magic ingredients.' And when Jeffrey nodded – what else could he do? – he continued, 'As we thought. Very well then, tell me this, how did you manage to put your "improved" clay back into its original packaging?'

Jeffrey's heart was beating most uncomfortably but he tried another bluff, comforting himself that he was nothing if not a fighter. 'I have a special hoist, designed for the purpose,' he said. 'I felt a double wrapping would be safer when the clay was in transit.'

Henry slapped the desk with the palm of his hand and laughed out loud. 'I never heard such a load of old codswallop in my life,' he said. 'I've been in this business for years and I've never known any company that double wrapped their clay.'

'Maybe I have higher standards,' Jeffrey said huffily.

Mr Taylor leant across the desk and spoke, gently but clearly. 'You do understand, do you not, Mr Walmesly,' he said, 'that selling another company's goods and profiting by the sale is an offence, answerable in law. It is called selling on and there are legal penalties for it.'

'You are insulting me, Mr Taylor,' Jeffrey said. 'I'm a man of honour. I wouldn't dream of doing such a thing.'

'Then,' Mr Taylor said, 'you will be perfectly agreeable to chemical tests being carried out on the clay you sold to Prendergast Potteries so that we can ascertain whether or not your samples really have been chemically improved.'

Jeffrey was flooded with panic and, as always in such

287

a situation, he responded with roaring anger. 'How dare you doubt my word!' he shouted. 'I'm a man of honour. I've told you. A man of honour. My word is my bond. I've offered you the best clay that's ever been invented. The best. And you turn your idiot noses up at it and call me names. How dare you call me names! It's disgraceful, shameful. Call yourself businessmen! You ought to be ashamed of yourselves.'

Henry was laughing again. 'Methinks,' he said to his two companions, 'the lady doth protest too much.'

The sight of that easy laughter pushed Jeffrey to exploding point. It was intolerable, insufferable. 'How dare you laugh at me!' he shouted. 'I won't stay here and be insulted. God damn it! It's not ethical. You've got no right to insult me. No right at all. I won't stay here. I won't.'

'You may leave whenever you please,' Henry told him. 'We will run the necessary tests on your "improved" clay and then you will be hearing from Mr Taylor. Good afternoon to you.'

'I hope you rot in hell!' Jeffrey shrieked. 'The lot of you!' And he ran from the room, red-faced and weeping and beside himself with anger and frustration, groaning as he ran. Oh God! Oh God! He needed the toilet so badly he was afraid he was going to wet himself. Oh God! How could they be so vile? He had to get out. Now. This minute. Where's the door? There must be a door. Oh for Christ's sake, where's the door? Try that one. A fucking cupboard. Wouldn't you know? That one then. And at last he was out in the car park in the pitch dark and fell towards the nearest bush where he emptied his bladder before the fucking thing burst.

This is all Fran's fault, he thought as he shook off the last drops and yanked up his zip. Fucking awful woman.

She runs off and leaves me with that fucking mortgage, she nicks all my fucking furniture. I didn't even have a glass for my beer that first night. How heartless was that? And now she's told tales on me in this fucking awful pottery and wrecked the best chance I've had in years. God rot her. She needs a good seeing to. I've half a mind to. . . .

There was an eruption of sound somewhere to his left, voices calling and laughing, he could see a sudden beam of light colouring the path. The workers were leaving. It was the end of the afternoon. The sight of them gave him an idea. A very good idea. He'd wait till Fran came out of the damned place, that's what he'd do, and then he'd follow her home and give her a piece of his mind. He was edging round the parked cars, looking for his own and peering into the gloom to see if he could spot her Fiat. Oh it would be a different story then. And she'd got it coming to her, vile woman, the way she'd treated him.

His car was found and unlocked. He sat inside with the heating on and waited, as his eyes grew accustomed to the darkness. More people came wandering out, car doors slammed, feet tramped and scuffled, voices were calling good night. And there she was, swinging towards him. He had to duck right down or she would have seen him. He gave it a minute or two before he sat up to resume watch. And luck was on his side. She was getting into the Fiat. It was no distance away. Right, he thought. Start the engine. Be prepared. Now follow. Not too close. You don't want to warn her. But keep your eyes skinned. You don't want to lose her either.

It was all too easy. Once he knew she was on the Lewes road he tailed her with perfect confidence, feeding his anger as he drove. My God he'd make her pay for this, the bitch. He'd take her apart at the seams.

Francesca was singing as she drove. It had really been quite a good day. She painted more than her usual quota of plates and the thought that Jeffrey was getting his comeuppance up there in Henry's office had warmed her all afternoon. And now it was the opening of her exhibition. She was still a bit apprehensive about it and not at all sure about those high prices but she meant to enjoy it if she could and Agnes and Henry would be with her. She parked neatly and skipped into the flat calling out to Agnes.

'Good day?' Agnes said, walking out of the kitchen into the hall.

'Interesting,' Francesca said. 'Must have a shower then I'll tell you.'

'I've got a meat pie in the oven,' Agnes told her. 'Don't be long.'

'Two shakes of a lamb's tail.'

'Your clothes are on the rail.'

She'd showered, dressed and brushed her hair in six minutes and went back to the kitchen feeling pleased with herself.

'Well you do look nice,' Agnes said. 'That dress suits you. Sit down and I'll dish up.'

But someone was knocking at the door.

'That can't be Henry already surely to goodness,' Agnes grumbled, as Francesca went to answer it. 'Well the pie's ready so he'll have to wait till we've had our supper, that's all. I don't want you going off to an exhibition with nothing in your stomach.'

He won't mind waiting, Francesca was thinking as she walked towards the door. She was warm with pleasure at the thought that she was going to see him so soon and smiling as she opened the door. What happened next was so sudden and so brutal it took away all her power of thought completely. For it wasn't Henry waiting in the porch. It was Jeffrey Walmesly and he was dark in the face and trembling with temper. He pushed her into the hall, glaring and swearing. 'You fucking whore! How dare you tell such lies! You fucking, lying whore!'

The old terror rose in her, paralyzing her, stopping her breath, holding her in a shocked silence. She couldn't speak or think, she could barely listen. 'Why. . . ?' she said, stepping backwards away from him. 'Why. . . ?'

'Why?' he roared. Those terrible black eyebrows were a straight hard line full of hatred. 'You dare to ask me that? That was the best deal I've ever set up. The best. It was absolutely brilliant! Foolproof! And you have to stick your fucking great nose into it. You've ruined it, cut it to shreds.' He was prodding her with every angry word, pushing her backwards, his face distorted with fury.

'Please!' she cried, putting her hands in front of her face to protect herself. 'Please don't. I didn't say anything. . . .'

But he was too far gone in rage to hear her. 'You've had this coming for years,' he shouted, still pushing her backwards with that awful prodding finger. 'You fucking, fucking whore. For years.' They were in the living room – she could feel the carpet under her feet – and he was punching her in the chest and pushing her back, back, back with every punch. Her legs were against the settee and she was bending, falling, off balance and afraid.

'I hate you,' he roared at her. 'Hate you. Hate you. D'you hear me?' His hands were round her throat, squeezing and pushing. She struggled to get away from him, but she could barely breathe and there was no strength in her; she clawed at his hands but he just increased his pressure, his distorted face within inches

291

of hers; she was so frightened she didn't know what to do. And then suddenly she saw Agnes's crutch, raised in the air, silver as a sword, and there was a loud thud and he was lying on the carpet, rolling over onto his back, holding his head and Agnes was standing over him with the crutch jabbed into his crotch and one foot on his chest. 'Phone for the police,' she said to Francesca coolly. 'Dial 999. Your bag's behind you.'

It took Francesca several seconds to pick up her bag and find the phone because she was shaking so much that her hands weren't functioning properly and then it was hard to find the energy to answer the cool voice of the operator. 'Police,' she said, finally, her voice croaky. She was relieved when Agnes held out her hand for the phone and she could sit down and hand over responsibility for all this to someone else. She was still shaking uncontrollably but it comforted her to hear Agnes giving their address and speaking so calmly.

'An assault on a young woman,' she was saying. 'Yes. He tried to strangle her. Yes. I did say strangle. Yes. An intruder. Yes. He's still on the premises. Yes. That would be helpful.' She tossed the phone to Francesca. 'Keep hold of it,' she said. 'They're on their way but we might need it again.'

Jeffrey was rubbing his head and making an effort to sit up.

'Don't even think about it,' Agnes growled at him. 'You just stay where you are or I'll do you a mischief, so help me.'

He was getting his breath back. 'You can't make me stay if I don't want to,' he said truculently. 'I've got my rights.'

It was the wrong tone to take with Agnes Potts. 'You gave up all your rights when you tried to throttle my friend,' she said. 'Now you'll do as you're told and stay where you are till the police get here. Move an inch and I'll lay you out cold. I warn you.'

There was something dripping from his nose and he put up his hand to wipe it away and discovered that it was blood. 'You wicked old witch!' he said, looking at her with horrified disbelief. 'You've made me bleed. It's all over my best shirt. My best silk shirt!'

'Good!' Agnes said. 'Serve you right. Toss him a tissue, Francesca.'

Francesca pulled a handful of tissues from the box on the table and threw them at him. Now that Agnes was so obviously and totally in control, her heart was beginning to steady and she could breathe more easily. She watched as Jeffrey dabbed at his nose and shook his head so that drops of blood spattered his precious shirt. The minutes passed. She could hear her clock ticking. Nothing happened. Jeffrey snorted and shook more blood onto his shirt, almost as if he was doing it deliberately. Then there was the sound of a police siren, the screech of brakes as the car came to a halt and seconds later someone was ringing her doorbell.

'I'll go,' she said to Agnes. And went. Two policemen looking reassuring. 'Miss Potts?' one of them asked. But she was too weary to correct him and simply stood to one side so that they could come in and then led the way into her living room.

'Ah,' Agnes said. 'There you are. That was quick.'

'Are you Miss Potts ma'am?' the older policeman said.

'I am,' Agnes said, 'and this is. . . .'

But before she could say another word Jeffrey interrupted her. 'Jeffrey Walmesly,' he said loudly and firmly. 'I wish to report an assault. This person,' sneering towards Agnes, 'has assaulted me, as you can see.' He laid one hand on his shirt where his bloodstains were drying out but still very visible.

Despite the state she was in, Francesca understood at once that he was going to plead innocence of any attack on her, play the victim himself and put the blame on Agnes. A sudden invigorating anger rose in her. No, she thought, I'm not having this. 'Now look,' she said to the nearest policeman. 'The person who was assaulted was me. Take a look at my neck. That man was trying to choke me. Miss Potts stopped him.'

'I see,' the policeman said, looking at her neck. 'Could I have your name miss?'

'Francesca Jones,' Francesca said, 'and this is my flat and that man has no business being in it.' She was hot with anger.

Jeffrey stood up, straightened his tie, smiled at the policeman in a conspiratorial way and sat himself on the nearest chair like a man who had every right to be there. 'Oh come on Fran,' he said in his persuasive voice. 'I know you're upset about something but you mustn't tell naughty porkies. Tell the constable the truth.' He turned his head to smile at the young policeman again and spoke to him, confidentially, man to man. 'We've been an item for the last five years,' he said. 'I've every right to be here. Fact, I've come here with a message from your mother, Fran. She wants you to ring her. Apparently some distant relative has left you some money. Your father's cousin or some such. I can't remember the exact details. Anyway she wants you to give her a buzz. OK?'

The older policeman took out his notebook and spoke to Jeffrey. 'Can I have your full name and address, sir,' he said.

'Of course,' Jeffrey said. 'You understand that this is just a domestic. She gets a bit hysterical sometimes – you know what women are like – and I was restraining her, the way I usually do.'

'No, no!' Francesca said, her face anguished. 'It wasn't like that at all. He was trying to strangle me. He's making this up. Oh please listen. It wasn't like that.'

Agnes moved into the attack all guns blazing. 'You lying hound,' she roared. 'You pushed your way in here, you screamed abuse, you punched her and then you put your hands round her neck and tried to choke her. You weren't "restraining" her, as you put it. You were beating her up. That's the truth of it. And I stopped you.'

Now that he thought he was in command, Jeffrey was mockingly calm. 'Well she would say that, wouldn't she,' he said to the policeman. 'I'm going to sue her for assault so she has to make up a good story. We don't need to take any notice of *that* do we.'

'Ye Gods! You really are the most objectionable creature I've ever met,' Agnes roared at him. 'Don't tell lies, you vile little worm. You were strangling her and I hit you because she was too shocked to fight you off.'

'Common assault,' Jeffrey said smugly. 'And I'll make you answer for it. Look at the blood. You can't deny blood.' He plucked at his shirt and looked at the policeman for support.

'Name and address, sir, if you please,' the policeman said, massively calm in the uproar. 'Let's take this nice and easy.'

They were all talking at once. Jeffrey easing, 'Of course', Francesca crying 'Oh please. You mustn't listen to him,' Agnes roaring. 'Oh for crying out loud!' And somebody was ringing the doorbell, its sharp call clear even over the racket they were making.

'Are you expecting somebody?' the older policeman asked.

'Yes,' Agnes said, remembering.

'Go and get it Nigel,' the older policeman said and the younger one went to answer the door.

Jeffrey went on talking at the older policeman but Agnes and Francesca held their breath and their peace. And presently their pause was rewarded by the sound of Henry's warm friendly voice greeting the younger policeman. 'Hello, Nigel. What are you doing here?' And Nigel answering equally warmly, 'Hello, Mr Prendergast. It's a domestic.' And then the two of them walked into the living room and Henry's tone changed instantly from warmth to ice.

'What is *that man* doing in this flat?' he asked.

'It's a domestic Mr Prendergast, sir,' the older policeman said.

But Henry wasn't listening to him. He'd seen the state Francesca was in, had crossed the room in one stride and was sitting beside her on the sofa with one arm round her shoulders, massively and furiously protective. 'What's he done to you?' he asked.

'Gave her a mouthful of abuse, punched her in the chest and tried to strangle her,' Agnes said. 'I had to hit him with my crutch to stop him.'

'Good for you,' Henry approved. 'I hope you hurt him.'

'Now look here,' Jeffrey said, looking aggrieved. 'You don't know anything about it and it's none of your business. I suggest you keep out of it and leave it to the police.'

'It's very much my business,' Henry said to him coldly. 'In every sense of the word.' Then he turned his attention to the two policemen. 'This young woman is the premier artist at Prendergast Potteries,' he said, 'and very highly valued. And this *person* is a liar and a

296

fraud, who has been passing off the product of another company as his own, as Prendergast Potteries will prove in court. I think I should tell you he will be hearing from my solicitor at the beginning of next week. And now, as if it weren't enough to be facing a charge of serious fraud, he appears to have added assault and battery to the list of charges he will have to face. I will consult with my solicitor about that in due course.'

'I see,' the older policeman said. 'Can I have your address, sir?'

'Nigel knows where I live,' Henry said. 'Or you can find me at the Potteries if you would prefer. Now I suggest you remove Mr Walmesly from this flat, where he has absolutely no right to be, and give Francesca and Miss Potts a bit of peace so that I can find out whether we need to call a doctor. I can give you his address. It's in my filing system.'

At that, Jeffrey lost his temper and began to rage. 'Why don't you keep your fucking nose out of my business?' he shouted at Henry. 'It's a domestic. That's all. A domestic. Nothing to do with you. Can't you get that into your thick head? Christ Almighty! Have I got to endure this?'

His temper was his undoing. The two policemen looked at one another, plainly changing their opinion of him as he roared. Henry raised his eyebrows at the senior policeman.

It was enough. 'If you'll just come with us, Mr Walmesly,' the policeman said.

And rather to Francesca's surprise, Jeffrey stopped shouting, stood up, shrugged his shoulders, said 'If I must' and went. The relief in the room when he'd gone lifted them like a sunrise. Agnes and Henry beamed at one another and Francesca laid her head against Henry's protective shoulder and closed her eyes.

'I must go and see to that poor pie,' Agnes said. 'It'll have to go in the freezer now. How much time have I got?'

'Take as long as you need,' Henry told her. 'We're late already but I'm sure they'll wait for us.' And when she'd stomped off to the kitchen, he kissed the top of Francesca's head and set about his more immediate enquiries. 'Can I see your neck, my darling?'

She put her hand up to cover her bruises not wanting to make a fuss. 'It's all right.'

He was firm and loving. 'Well, let's hope so but I would like to see it.'

She lifted her chin to give him a clear view and he sat back a little to examine her. 'Nasty,' he said. 'Does it hurt you to swallow?'

'Not now. It did but it's easing off now.'

'Could you face a cup of tea?'

Yes, having thought about it, she could, so Agnes was called upon to provide one, which she did impressively quickly. 'Sip it first,' she said as she handed it over.

It was sipped and enjoyed. 'Oh this is lovely. Nice and warm.' Henry and Agnes exchanged glances.

'What do you think?' Agnes asked her old friend.

He was still anxious. 'Does it hurt you to swallow?' he asked Francesca.

She smiled at him for the first time since his arrival. 'No. It's lovely. I'm all right, really. Are we going to the exhibition?'

'That's entirely up to you.'

'Then we are. I'll just get a scarf and cover this up a bit.'

'I'll get it,' Agnes said. 'I know where your things are.' And went.

'Darling, darling girl,' Henry said. 'You're sure about this?'

She smiled at him again. 'Yes. Quite sure. We can't let them down.'

'All right then,' he agreed, 'but you're to stay by me all the time in case you find the crush a bit difficult.'

'I promise.'

Agnes was stomping back, dangling two scarves in her free hand. 'I've brought you two,' she said. 'They're the best match I could find. What do you think?'

So with the chosen scarf skilfully arranged to hide her bruises and her thick coat buttoned up to her chin to keep her warm, Francesca went to her first exhibition with her most special friends Agnes and Henry. And she hardly felt nervous at all.

CHAPTER 19

HENRY WAS RIGHT about the crush. There were so many people in the showroom that Francesca couldn't see the pictures at all and the pressure of so many bodies all round her made her feel so unsteady on her feet that she had to cling onto Henry's arm for support as they walked into the room. Agnes strode through the crowd using her crutch to insinuate herself into one group after another, greeting people she knew and smiling on everybody who moved aside for her.

'Splendid occasion,' Reggie boomed, striding towards them with a champagne glass in his hand. 'Splendid. Have you seen our portrait yet? It looks top hole.' He was dressed in the clothes he'd worn for his sitting and was twinkling and beaming. 'Have some of this champers. It's deuced good. Evening Henry. Splendid occasion.'

One of Henry's caterers appeared in front of them with a tray full of champagne flutes and Henry took two and gave one to Francesca advising her to sip it when she felt like it. The place was loud with excited voices and in constant and animated movement. People drifted in and out of her field of vision, here Molly in a very pretty dress, waving and blowing kisses, there Tom and Sandra smiling shyly before they were engulfed by another swirl of the crowd. It was like being in the middle of a huge, constantly-shifting kaleidoscope and it made her feel queasy as if she was seasick. Now she was hanging on to Henry's arm to keep her balance. From time to time he patted her hand and told her she was doing wonderfully, which encouraged her, but for most of the time she was confused and unsure of herself. Once, Liam and his wife materialized at her elbow and said how wonderful they thought her pictures were and she smiled and thanked them and said she was glad they were enjoying themselves but after they'd left her she couldn't remember a single thing they'd said; once she heard a voice she thought she recognized, holding forth about how wonderful she was and how she was a *'beacon of light'* to him, *'a true friend, took me in when I'd been thrown out on the street, imagine that. Oh yes, a true friend.'* And while she was still struggling to put a name to the voice Brad came easing through the crowd wearing the green livery of Henry's catering company and bearing a tray full of vol-au-vents.

'Try one,' he urged, beaming at her. 'They're delicious.'

She thought how good it was to see him at work and happy about it. He didn't look so fat and the smile altered the shape of his face. She would have liked to ask him about it but she didn't have the energy. Fortunately Henry seemed to be reading her thoughts and asked for her.

'I gather you're working for Joshua now,' he said.

'Since last month, sir,' Brad said.

'And you enjoy it?' It was only just a question.

'Oh yes,' Brad said happily. 'It's a great job. You meet all sorts of people. Fact I think I can say, I've fallen on my feet in this one.' Then he remembered what he was really supposed to be doing and offered the tray to them. 'Do have one. They're delicious.'

Francesca took one to please him although she knew

she wouldn't be able to eat it and passed it on to Henry as soon as she could. Which was just as well because the next person to edge thorough the crush towards her was Christine, looking very smart in an electric blue trouser suit.

'Are you ready to face the press?' she asked and without waiting for an answer. 'Just follow me. Isn't this a splendid crowd! Your work's really selling. The local paper's come and the TV. They're over there by the mermaid.'

It was a dream of course, a fantasy world peopled by smiling faces and waving hands and excited voices. It wasn't possible that it could have anything to do with her. They reached the mermaid and she was introduced as 'our talented local artist', was aware of cameras and notebooks and a microphone and answered questions as well as she could, with Henry standing protectively beside her. But it was all unreal.

'One more hour,' Henry said, when she was finally allowed to walk away from her questioners, 'and then I'm going to take you home and feed you.'

She felt she ought to confess that she wasn't very hungry.

'Don't worry,' he told her. 'I'm a dab hand with invalid food. I shall tempt whatever's left of your appetite.' He put his arm round her shoulders to steer her through the crowd. 'Now you must take a little look at how well your paintings are selling.'

'Do you really think they are?'

'Oh yes. I know one that went ten minutes after the doors were opened.'

That was a surprise. 'Really?' she said. She couldn't remember anyone coming up to tell him. 'How do you know that?'

But before he could say a word, the answer came rushing through the crush to tell her. Sandra and Tom both beaming all over their faces.

'We got it, Mr Prendergast,' Sandra said. 'We were the first through the door. He sent us three tickets, Francesca, one for each of us and a note warning us to get here early because your painting of our Tom was so moderately priced it'd be snapped up at once, so we got our skates on. It does look lovely all framed and everything. Mr Magnet is over there now buying his portrait too. I'll bet you feel proud of yourself.'

'As she should,' Henry said. 'I'm glad you got here in time.'

They took a gentle stroll all around the exhibition and Henry pointed out every single blue sticker. 'You see,' he said. 'It's a massive success.'

She held his arm and agreed with him. How could she do anything else when as far as she could see three quarters of her paintings had already been sold? Three quarters for heaven's sake and it was only the first night. And while this thought was filling her brain, Molly suddenly appeared at her elbow.

'Do you know what your Henry's done?' she asked, her face glowing. 'He's only gone and bought our portrait and given it to me.'

'With a proviso, don't forget,' Henry said grinning at her. 'She's got to give it back to me whenever I need it for an exhibition or to show at the works.'

He's so generous, Francesca thought, and so kind. And she glad he was going to look after her, even though she knew she'd never be able to eat a meal – not even to please him. But there wasn't time to dwell on that either, because Agnes was heading towards them with Babs and Reggie following in her wake.

'We're cutting off for something to eat,' she said. 'I don't know about you Francesca but I'm starving. How about you two coming with us?'

Francesca looked worried and Henry read her mind again. 'I don't think she's up to facing a restaurant this evening,' he said, 'Are you Francesca? No. Thank you for asking Aggie but we're going to cut off home in a few minutes and I'm going to cook her something easy to eat.'

'Good idea,' Agnes said. 'See you later then.'

The crowd was thinning at last. 'Ready for the off?' Henry said.

He eased her into his car very gently, made sure she was comfortable and fastened the seat belt for her and it was all so solicitously done that she was suddenly overwhelmed and put her head in her hands and began to cry.

'I'm so – sorry,' she wept, struggling to control herself. 'I shouldn't be ... I mean ... I ought to ... Oh, I'm so sorry.'

He turned in the driving seat and put his arms right round her holding her against his chest and stroking her hair. 'Cry all you like, my darling,' he said. 'It's what you need. Tears are healing. You cry all you like.'

And as if he'd given her permission she cried for a very long time and he held her and kissed her hair and called her his darling until she was calm again. Then he produced a clean white handkerchief and wiped her eyes and her cheeks and smiled at her lovingly. 'Better now?' he said. And when she nodded, 'Then we'll go home.'

He drove even more carefully than usual and Francesca closed her eyes and dozed, exhausted by weeping. She was glad when Henry led her upstairs to what he called 'my guest room' as soon as they were both in the house.

'It's nice and comfortable,' he said, patting the huge double bed, 'and it's got an en suite, through that door there and if there's anything you want during the night, I'm just along the corridor. Now I'm going downstairs to cook you supper. Could you fancy a pot of tea with it? Good. I can't provide you with PJ's or a night dress but I'll look out a nice soft shirt for you if you like.'

As that seemed to need an answer, she said, 'Yes, please.' And he went away for a few minutes and returned with a pale blue shirt over his shoulder and laid it on the end of the bed.

'Right,' he said. 'I'll be back presently.'

And was, with a loaded tray on which he'd set out a little pot of tea, with a milk jug and sugar basin to match, two cups and a plate on which he'd set a boiled egg in a matching egg cup and a slice of bread with the crusts removed, carefully cut into long neat slices.

'Oh!' she said, sitting up in bed in his blue shirt. 'Boiled egg and soldiers. I haven't had that since I was a little thing.'

'It's all nice and runny,' he told her happily. 'My egg timer never fails. I've brought two cups so I shall sit on the bed and have a cup of tea and keep you company.'

She ate every last crumb and drank two cups of tea while he talked about the exhibition and how well it had gone.

'Now I'm going to leave you to sleep,' he said when she'd finished. And he picked up the tray, turned out the light and was gone.

I shall never get to sleep after all this, she thought, and fell instantly into a deep and troubled nightmare where frightening creatures loomed towards her one after the other out of a terrible darkness. Faceless men rushed towards her, claws outstretched for her neck as she writhed and twisted to avoid them; her mermaid was dragged away from her, that beautiful tail tied and torn by implacable ropes and her face anguished; Jeffrey stood over her, huge and dark-faced and menacing, shouting 'You've come into money, you stupid bitch. I came to tell you. See? See? You can't blame me for anything.'

She woke with a start, feeling confused and frightened in a dark unfamiliar room, unable to think where she was. She felt she had to do something to find out, so after a while, she got up carefully and walked across to the faint oblong of light that she supposed was a window and stood between the curtains looking out at the darkness. It took quite a long time for her eyes to adjust to it but then, with relief, she saw that it was Henry's spacious garden. Of course, she thought, as the nightmare receded, I'm at Henry's. She could hear his voice speaking quietly to her and realized that there was a gentle light behind her.

'Are you all right little one?'

'A nightmare,' she said, turning to look at him. 'That's all. Just a nightmare. Silly of me.'

He was beside her, turning her gently towards him, his arms around her, warm and comforting. 'Not silly at all after all you've been through.'

She leant her head on his shoulder, glad he was there. 'It's all right,' she said. 'It's going away now.'

He stroked her cheek gently, noticing how cold it was. 'Come back to bed,' he said. 'It's too chilly to be standing around. I won't leave you, I promise.'

She was feeling so much better she smiled at him. 'Then *you*'ll get cold,' she said.

He grinned at that. 'No I won't,' he told her, leading her back to the bed. 'I'm going to stay here and look after you till you're asleep again. That bed's big enough for the both of us.'

Which he did, lying beside her, cuddled together and snug under the duvet in their private darkness as if they'd been sleeping together for years. And somehow it seemed perfectly proper and almost entirely natural.

When she woke for the second time the room was full of muted light, the garden was hidden by a low-lying white mist and Henry was gone. There was a conversation niggling in her mind like a distant echo and she knew it was important and was disturbed because she couldn't remember it. She lay among the pillows and tried to concentrate it into clarity but the harder she tried the more impossible it became.

'Ah!' Henry said from the doorway. 'You're awake.' He was showered, shaved and dressed in his familiar chinos and his favourite jersey. 'What do you fancy for breakfast?'

The memory slotted into her mind at the sight of him, clear and entire, as if he'd triggered it. 'I've come into some money,' she said.

He laughed. 'Was that during the night or while I've been showering?'

'Jeffrey told me. I'd forgotten it. He said "some relation" had left me his money and I was to phone my mother.'

'Last night?' Henry asked. 'Was it true, do you think, or was he making it up?'

'Well,' she said, 'he was using it as a sort of excuse to make the police think he had the right to be in the flat but there might be truth in it. My father had a brother who was supposed to be well off. We hardly ever saw him. I couldn't even tell you what he looked like. My mother was scathing about him. She used to say he was a recluse. But it could be him I suppose. Or it could be one of Jeffrey's lies.'

'Only one way to find out,' Henry said. 'You'll have to ring your mother. But let's have our breakfast first. Could you fancy waffles?'

They breakfasted in the kitchen in a happily leisurely way, she swathed in his dressing gown which was much too big for her and wonderfully warm, he sitting opposite her at the table, admiring her and thinking how good it was to have her there.

'There's a problem with ringing my mother,' she said, holding her third cup of tea in both hands and looking thoughtful.

What a worrier she is, he thought. 'Which is?' he asked.

'I don't want her to know where I am.'

'Then don't tell her.'

'Won't she be able to trace me through my phone?'

'Not unless she's a whizz kid.'

That made Francesca smile but her amusement didn't last long. 'Oh dear,' she said. 'I haven't spoken to her since I left the flat.'

'Do it now. It'll only worry you if you don't.'

'She'll be in the shop,' Francesca said, looking at the clock. 'Maybe I should leave it till this evening. She doesn't like being interrupted in the shop.' Her forehead was wrinkled with worry.

'Drink your tea and do it now,' Henry insisted. 'Where's your phone?'

'In my bag,' Francesca said, 'only I don't know where that is.'

'I do,' Henry told her. He knew he was putting pressure on her, but it was necessary or she'd just go on worrying all day. 'I hung it in the hall last night. Stay there and I'll fetch it for you.'

It was fetched, the phone was found and Francesca made a grimace, took a deep breath and dialled her mother's number, half hoping that she wouldn't answer.

The answer was almost instant. 'Bella's Boutique,' her mother's voice cooed. 'How can I help you?'

'It's Francesca. You wanted to speak to me.'

The voice changed at once. 'And about time too,' it said crossly. 'I suppose you saw the advertisement.'

'What advertisement?'

'Oh, you didn't. I knew it was a waste of money. Don't tell me Jeffrey bestirred himself.'

'He said you wanted to speak to me. Something about a Will.'

'Wonders'll never cease.' her mother said, in her biting tone. 'Well for once in his life, he's got it right. It *is* about a will. Quite a sizeable one. It's that fool Felix, your father's peculiar brother. You remember the one, that stupid recluse. Never came to visit us from one year out to another and now he's died and left you twenty-four thousand, if you ever heard of such a thing. And of course I didn't know where you were, walking off like that, so I couldn't tell you. We've had advertisements in the paper and all sorts.' There was another voice speaking in the background and the tone changed to sugar sweet. 'Dorothy dear, I won't keep you a minute. I've just got to give this person an address.'

So I'm a *person* now, Francesca thought, but she didn't comment.

'Have you got pencil and paper?' her mother said.

'Yes,' Francesca said, miming to Henry that she needed something to write on. A notebook and pencil was quickly on the table before her. 'Skeat and Murchison solicitors,' she repeated, writing quickly. 'Yes

I've got that. 22, Cross Gate, Petersfield. Yes, I've got it.'
But her mother had already hung up.

'Well, well, well,' she said to Henry. 'It *was* the recluse
and he's left me twenty-four thousand pounds.' It made
her giggle to think about it. 'Twenty-four thousand!
Imagine that!'

'If that's the case,' Henry said, in his business-like
voice, 'you'll need a solicitor to act for you. I suggest we
use Mr Taylor. He's a good man. Knows the ropes. I'll get
on to him first thing on Monday morning. I want to see
him anyway to draft a letter to that hideous creature that
tried to throttle you.'

Francesca laughed. 'My mother called me a *person*,
when she was on the phone just then,' she said, 'and now
you've called Jeffrey a *hideous creature*.'

'I could call him a great deal worse,' Henry said, his
face darkening. 'He's the one who needs throttling. But
that's not the point at the moment. The point is, what do
you think about using Mr Taylor?'

It was a serious question and she took it seriously,
impressed by how quickly and easily their conversations could change direction. 'I think it would be a good
idea,' she said. 'I mean, if he handled all the correspond-
ence, I wouldn't have to give that solicitor my address,
would I?'

'Not if you didn't want to,' Henry said. 'Mr Taylor
would know the ins and outs of it. I presume you don't
want your mother to know it and you think it might get
back to her, is that it?'

'The thing is,' Francesca confessed, 'she's not a very
nice person. It know it sounds horrid to say that about
your mother but it's the truth. She put me down so much
when I was little. Calling me a *person* just then was
typical.'

'It hurts you,' he understood, watching the pain on her face.

'Yes. It does. Even after all this time.'

'Then keep out of her way. There's no necessity for you to have anything to do with her if you don't want to. We'll see what Mr Taylor says about the address. And now I think you ought to get dressed.'

That made her laugh again. 'Yes sir, boss,' she said.

'The mist's clearing,' he explained, 'and I'd like to take you out for a walk.'

A walk sounded like a very good idea. 'Trouble is, I haven't got any clean clothes,' she said. 'I'd have to wear my party frock.'

'Not a problem,' he told her. 'Tell me what you need and I'll go to the flat and get it for you. It'll be a chance to check up on our Aggie. See she got back all right last night.'

So Francesca went to wallow in a scented bath in her luxurious bathroom, feeling spoilt and Henry drove through the gentle lanes to Lewes feeling happier than he'd done for a very long time.

Agnes stayed in bed that morning until the mist had cleared and the central heating had warmed the flat. With Francesca away there was nothing to get up for. It was the first time she'd eaten breakfast on her own since she fell out of the tree and it felt dispiritingly lonely, which was ridiculous when she usually ate all her meals on her own when she was at home. But there it was. The flat felt empty without its tenant, the trees were cold and denuded, the river grey and sullen and the square of sky she could see through the window as she ate her breakfast was the colour of dirty dishcloths and enough to depress anyone. Not a good morning, she decided.

I think it's time I went home. I wonder if I could walk without this crutch. I ought to be able to by now. And she decided to try. It lifted her spirits to find that she could walk about unaided. And she was just wondering whether she could manage the stairs at home and feeling pretty sure she could, when the phone rang. Francesca, she thought, picking it up. But it was Babs.

'Good morning,' she said. 'Just a quickie. How would you and Francesca like to come to lunch with us? It was such fun last night we thought it might be nice. Carry on the good work sort of thing.'

'I'd love to come,' Agnes said, 'but I can't speak for Francesca. She isn't here.'

Babs was very surprised. 'Isn't there?'

'She's still with Henry,' Agnes explained.

'Oh!' Babs said. 'Well, well, well.'

'Um,' Agnes said, picking up on the worldly-wise nuance in those three repeated words. 'That's what I've been thinking.'

'Well I hope it won't stop you joining us,' Babs said. 'We could come and pick you up. It's a roast so it'll stretch to three or four. Tell you what, I'll ring you again when I'm going to start the vegetables.'

'There's someone at the door,' Agnes said. 'Better go.'

'Maybe it's her,' Babs said.

'She's got a key,' Agnes said, 'so I shouldn't think it's likely. I'll ring you back if it is.' And she walked to the door without her crutch feeling pleased with herself. It was no surprise to find that it was only Henry who was standing on the step.

'Hello Henry,' she said, standing aside to let him in. 'How's Francesca?'

'She's fine,' he said. 'Much better.' The flat was pleasantly warm after the chill outside and smelt of toast and coffee. 'I've come to get her some clothes. We thought we might go for a walk. No crutch?'

'No,' Agnes said. 'I'm really making progress now.' Then she added slyly, 'Just as well because I'm going to lunch with Babs and Reggie.'

'Oh,' he said vaguely. 'That's nice. We shall probably stop for a pie and a pint somewhere.'

'So she'll need warm clothes,' Agnes said lightly. 'Did she give you a list?'

''Fraid not,' he said, looking slightly abashed. 'She said something about a green jumper and some trousers. I thought you'd know the sort of thing.'

They chose a variety of skirts, shirts and jumpers and Agnes sorted out some underwear and her pyjamas, several pairs of shoes, a raincoat and a pair of boots 'in case it rains' and a selection of toilet things. He watched and was impressed by her speed and she packed as neatly as she could, noticing that he made no demur at the number of clothes that were being packed and wondering just how long Francesca was going to stay with him.

When he'd kissed her goodbye and walked away carrying the suitcase, she dialled Babs' number. 'It'll only be me, I'm afraid,' she said. 'Henry's come to collect her clothes.'

'Well, well, well,' Babs said. 'This is going to be a very interesting lunch.'

And it was.

When Reggie had filled their glasses with wine and carved the leg of lamb and declared it done to perfection and they'd all helped themselves to Babs' splendid variety of vegetables, they settled down to gossip.

'Now then,' Babs said, cutting into her lamb, 'tell all. Is this a romance do you think?'

'It wouldn't surprise me,' Agnes said

'Nor me,' Babs said. 'He was very attentive and she was holding his arm all evening.'

'Ah!' Agnes said, 'but there was a reason for that. She was rather upset yesterday evening. She'd just been half throttled by some foul man.'

Babs' eyebrows disappeared into her hair. 'What!'

So Agnes told her the story at length, starting with the attack and how she'd foiled it, and working backwards to Jeffrey's abominable behaviour while he was on the cruise, all suitably embellished because she could see how much her hosts were enjoying it.

'I never heard anything to equal it,' Babs said. 'Strangling her. I mean to say. I thought we lived in a civilized society. And she'd been living with him you said. Whatever did she see in him?'

'She felt sorry for him.'

'Fatal!' Babs said. 'Don't you think so Reggie?'

'Oh indubitably,' Reggie said. 'More wine anyone?'

'Just as well you and Henry were there to rescue her. No wonder he was so protective. A good man our Henry.'

'A stout feller,' Reggie agreed still pouring wine. 'Good luck to him. He's been alone in that great house quite long enough.'

'I wonder what will happen next,' Babs said. 'Do you think they'll get married? That would be fun.'

'We shall have to wait and see,' Agnes said. 'I can't imagine our Henry rushing anything. But I can tell you what I'm going to do next.'

'Tell on,' Babs urged.

'I'm going back home to see if I can climb those stairs. It's about time I stood on my own two feet again, if you see what I mean.'

'Very sensible,' Babs said. 'We'll take you there later. Won't we Reggie? How would that be?'

'That would be handsome,' Agnes said.

CHAPTER 20

HENRY AND FRANCESCA were driving through the wintry countryside, heading south towards the sea. It was warm and comfortable in the car with one of his gentle CDs playing and the cold fields securely outside the windows and Francesca snuggled into the luxury of it and was happy to be there. The horrors and puzzles of the previous evening were behind her now. She was with Henry and perfectly safe.

'Nearly there,' Henry said, turning his head to smile at her.

'Where's there?' she asked, smiling back at him dreamily. She really didn't mind where they were going.

'Rye,' he said. 'It's a very pretty place. Used to be one of the Cinque Ports until the river changed direction.'

'Do rivers change direction?' she said. 'I never knew that.'

'Anything can change direction,' he told her. 'Even dyed-in-the-wool oldies like me.'

She laughed at that. 'I wouldn't call you an oldie,' she said. 'Dyed-in-the-wool, maybe, but not an oldie.'

He was ridiculously and understandably pleased to hear it. 'Well thank you ma'am,' he said. But then he thought he'd better confess his age as the subject had come up. 'I *am* an oldie though. I shall be forty-five next birthday.'

'That's not old,' she said. 'Wait till you're eighty.'

He wanted to kiss her so much that he didn't know what to say. Patience, he told himself. Don't rush this. He had such hopes of this outing and he didn't want to spoil things by speaking too soon. Fortunately they were passing a road sign and he could divert the conversation to safer ground. 'There you are,' he said. 'Rye.'

'Is this where we're going to have our walk?'

'Among other things.'

Now she was intrigued. 'What other things?'

His face was mischievous. 'You'll see,' he said. 'We'll take a leisurely stroll round the town and then I'll show you.'

They strolled arm in arm through the cobbled streets, uphill and down, past a history of houses, Georgian and half-timbered Tudor, past tea shops and antiques stores and quaint inns and potteries. 'Not a patch on yours,' Francesca said. They saw an ancient town wall and a tower called Ypres and a sleepy river. It was like walking through a film set or spending time in another century and she was highly taken with it. Eventually they came to a halt in front of a large half-timbered building, covered with ivy.

'We're here,' Henry said, watching her face to see what she would make of it.

She was impressed. 'Very grand,' she said.

He was wearing his Cheshire cat grin. 'Ah, but look at the name,' he said.

It was *The Mermaid Inn*.

'Oh,' she said. 'What a perfect choice.'

'That's what I thought,' he said. 'Come on. I've booked us a table.'

'When did you do that?' she asked, following him.

'While you were wallowing in the bath,' he teased, holding the door open for her. It had come to him like an inspiration and he'd acted on it at once. 'There you are. What do you think of it?'

She was surrounded by golden light and the warmest of rich colours, bronze and burnt umber, ochre and cadmium yellow. There was a scarlet carpet under her feet, a yellowing panel on the wall and the beams across the low ceiling were a rich Vandyke brown. 'It's like something in a fairy story,' she said. 'All this gorgeous colour. It makes me think of unicorns and huntsmen in scarlet with hunting horns or Cinderella seeing the royal palace for the first time or Beauty asleep for a hundred years and surrounded by luxury.'

'I knew you'd like it,' he said. 'Wait till you see the fire.' And he led her through into the lounge bar where rows of golden bottles stood on long glass shelves backed by mirrors all artfully set to reflect and glimmer in the soft light.

It was the biggest log fire she'd ever seen, spreading across the entire width of the wall with a huge oak beam above it supported on two formidable stone piers. 'I see what you mean,' she said. 'It's magnificent. I'll bet it's old.'

'Built in 1156,' Henry told her, grinning at her delight. 'Rebuilt in 1420. So yes, it's a good age. Can I get you a drink?'

She was removing her coat and scarf and saying 'I must hang these up first,' when a young man appeared at her elbow and took charge of them, waiting patiently until Henry had removed his overcoat too. Then they settled before the amazing fire and drank aperitifs while they waited to be shown to their table.

'You've been here before,' Francesca said impressed by how well he knew his way around.

'Many times,' he said. 'It was a favourite of ours.'

'Yours and Candida's?'

'She liked the food,' he said. 'I thought you might too. It's French. I can recommend the steak.'

She would have liked to ask him if he still missed his Candida and to commiserate with him if he did, but he'd turned the conversation so neatly that she felt she ought to follow it. 'You're making my mouth water,' she said.

'I'm glad to hear it. You didn't eat anywhere near enough yesterday.'

'Yesterday was rather different,' she said, making a grimace.

'But you're feeling better today.'

'I'm feeling spoilt.'

'Quite right,' he said, 'so you should be.' Was this the moment?

But no, it wasn't. There was a waiter smiling towards them to escort them to their table.

The restaurant was a soothing, welcoming place, all crisp white tablecloths and sparkling glasses and golden light. She chose the steak, as he'd recommended it, and so did he and they talked about how beautiful the inn was until they were served. The meal was as good as Henry had led her to expect and she ate every mouthful with relish, while he watched her with admiration. The desserts were chosen, more wine ordered and served and the meal and the conversation went smoothly on but he still hadn't found the right moment to speak as he wanted to and he was beginning to feel a bit despondent.

And then, just when he'd almost given up hope the moment arrived, perfect, open, ready and waiting for him.

She'd put down her spoon when she'd eaten the last mouthful, and smiled at him across their sparkling table. 'This is the lap of luxury,' she said. 'My mother would be so cross if she could see me.'

'Cross?' he said, sounding as surprised as he felt.

'Oh yes,' she said, dabbing her mouth. 'It wasn't part of her plan for me to be successful.'

'That sounds peculiar to me,' he said, drinking the last of his wine. 'Most parents are mad keen for their children to succeed. Not that I'm an expert, never having had any.'

'She *is* peculiar,' Francesca said. 'I had to face that years ago. Everything has to fit her view of the world, you see, otherwise there are temper tantrums. So if she says you're never going to amount to a row of beans, that's what's got to happen to you and she gets annoyed if it doesn't.'

'Just as well you don't see much of her then,' Henry said.

'Yes,' Francesca said and added, after a few seconds' quiet thought, 'She wasn't very good at loving, that's the truth of it. I don't think she's ever loved anybody, not really, sad though that is. I've never seen any signs of it. But a good thing came out of it, despite her. Or at least *I* think it's a good thing.'

'Which is?' he prompted.

'I made up my mind that if I ever had children I would love them properly.'

That intrigued him. Until that moment he'd always assumed that loving children was something you did naturally. 'Properly?' he asked.

'Unconditionally,' Francesca explained. 'As they are, no matter what that's like. Not trying to change them. I had a long conversation with Agnes about it when she first moved into the flat. She said it was an old debate. Nature versus nurture, she said, and her money was on nurture being the most important. *Her* mother was tricky too. She bullied her to make her tidy, which isn't in her nature at all. In fact Agnes said she thought her mother being so ruthless about tidiness had turned her into the sort of person she is, someone who can't throw anything away. I think that's likely, don't you. She said: if your parents love you as you are and allow you to *be* as you are, you grow up happy in your skin. And I thought that's the sort of love I'd like to give my children.' She smiled at him, wondering whether she'd been talking too freely. 'If that makes sense.'

It was the chance he'd been waiting for. Given to him like something magical, here in this magical place, just as he'd hoped. 'It makes perfect sense to me,' he said and plunged into the truth. 'It's the way I love you.'

She looked at him steadily, caught up in the spell of the place and the moment, almost afraid to breathe. 'Do you?' she said. But it was a rhetorical question. She knew he did. He'd been calling her darling ever since he rescued her from Jeffrey. Darling and *my* darling and little one. She should have known it then or perhaps she had and she just hadn't recognized it.

He leant across the table, took her hand and kissed it gently. He felt as if the air was singing. 'Yes,' he said. 'I do. Very much. I think I've loved you ever since that morning when I first saw the mermaid. And always as you are. I would never want to change you.'

She didn't know how to answer him. She felt she ought to say 'I love you too' the way they did in the soaps but she wasn't sure what she was feeling. She was very fond of him – who wouldn't be? – very, very fond and he'd looked after her so well and been so kind to her, but was that love? The affection on his face was so moving she was afraid she was going to cry. 'Oh Henry!' she said. 'I think the Unicorn just walked in.'

'Or Sleeping Beauty just woke up,' he said, in his half-teasing way. 'I would kiss her to make sure if we weren't in such a public place.'

How easily he can shift into a lighter tone, she thought, wondering what to say to him this time, and what it would be like to be kissed by him, but before she could think of answer she caught a glimpse of a waiter hovering. 'I think we're being looked at to see if we want coffee.'

They drank their coffee in a daze of deferred attraction and left the Mermaid with their arms round each other but he didn't kiss her until they were back in the privacy of their car and curtained by the darkness of approaching evening. Then he kissed her so passionately that they were both shaken. 'My darling, darling, darling,' he said. 'Stay with me.'

She was caught up in sensation, drunk with it. 'Yes,' she said, her mouth close to his. 'Yes, of course.' And was kissed again. If this is love, she thought, it's wonderful. None of the men she'd taken pity on had ever kissed her like this. 'Yes.'

Neither of them knew how long they kissed one another, they were enjoying it so much but eventually he paused for breath and said, 'We should be in bed.'

'Yes,' she agreed. 'We should.'

'Home James, in that case,' he said, beaming at her and he chose a suitable CD, switched it on and put the car in forward.

Hours later, when they were still lying sleepy and satisfied in her luxurious bed, Francesca's phone rang. She switched on her bedside light, pulled on her borrowed nightshirt and wandered off to find it in the tangle of clothes they'd left scattered on the floor, scampering back to the warmth of the bed and his arms as she answered it. It was Agnes.

'Hello,' she said. 'Thought I'd better tell you. I'm back home.'

'Heavens!' Francesca said, mouthing 'Agnes' at Henry.

'Babs and Reggie brought me here after dinner,' Agnes explained. 'I wanted to see if I could manage the stairs and I could so I'm staying here. Will it be all right for me to collect my things tomorrow?'

'Yes, of course,' Francesca said, feeling guilty. 'Would you like us to pick you up?'

'No, no. I can drive. I took the old banger out for a spin this afternoon. I'm right back to normal. I can get to the hospital to see the physiotherapist and everything.'

'Heavens!' Francesca said again, raising her eyebrows at Henry. 'OK then. What time will you be there?'

'Ten?' Agnes asked.

'Ten it is,' Francesca said. 'See you then.'

'Evening or morning?' Henry asked.

'There's no rush,' Francesca said. 'We were talking about tomorrow morning.' And told him the news.

'Good old Aggie,' he said. 'She's a feisty lady.'

They lay comfortably side by side in the crumpled bed. 'It's quite dark,' Francesca said idly, looking around at the shadowy room. 'What's the time?

'Half-past six,' he told her looking at his watch.

'It'll soon be supper time.'

'After all you ate at lunch!' he teased. 'Shame on you Francesca Jones. You're getting greedy.'

'That's your fault,' she teased back. 'You shouldn't feed me so well.'

'Does your greed extend to other things?' he said, propping himself on one elbow and turning to face her.

'Oh that too,' she said. 'I'm quite spoilt now.'

'Good,' he said and kissed her.

They had an extremely leisurely breakfast the next morning. They were still languid with love and in no mood to hurry anything so it was two minutes to ten by the time they got to her flat and Agnes was sitting outside in her car waiting for them.

'Hello me dears,' she said. 'Lovely morning.' She was in a very jolly mood, beaming at them both as she swung her legs out of the car. And it *was* a lovely morning with a weak sun doing its best to shine and the sky bright.

Henry kissed her as Francesca opened the door. 'Breakfast or coffee?' she said.

Agnes chose coffee, saying she'd only just had breakfast, so coffee was made and they sat in the kitchen and drank it and told her about Rye and what a pretty place it was, while the sun dappled the wall with swirling patterns from the river below them.

'Now I must get on,' Agnes said when her mug was empty, 'or I shall have Bonfire rushing down on me and nothing organized.'

'I can't believe that,' Henry teased, laughing at her. 'I thought it was all under perfect control.'

'There are always volunteers to gee up,' Agnes said. 'They need telling what time to arrive. And the pallets haven't arrived nor the shirts so they'll need chasing.'

'It's all got to be perfect,' Henry said to Francesca, 'or the sky might fall.'

'You'd be the first to complain if it wasn't,' Agnes told him, standing up and wearing her stern face. 'Come on. We've got work to do.'

She had so few belongings it didn't take them long to gather them together and carry them out to her car. She gave Francesca a hug saying, 'Thanks for having me. You've been a brick,' kissed Henry on both cheeks, got into the car in the most sprightly way and drove away, waving at them as she left.

'She's a girl!' Henry said, waving back. 'Now what? Home?'

'Have you got a mixing bowl?'

'I don't think so. Why?'

'I'd like to make cakes.'

'Homemade cakes!' he said. 'Now you're making *my* mouth water. I can't remember the last time I had a homemade cake.'

'In that case,' she said, 'I shall go and get all the things I need.'

Which she did and was touched when he sat in his luxurious kitchen and watched her as she made pastry and cut it out with her fancy cutters and whipped the ingredients for the filling. 'Do they have a name, these tarts of yours?' he wanted to know as she put the baking tin into the oven.

'Maids of honour,' she told him. 'Speciality of the house.'

'Now what will you make?'

'A Victoria sponge or chocolate cake. Your pick.'

'This is luxury,' he said, which made her smile. She was rosy with the warmth of cooking and transparently happy.

'Domestic bliss,' she teased.

'Maids of honour and chocolate cake,' he said. 'We could have them at lunchtime. Can I lick the bowl?'

'You can do whatever you like,' she said, happily.

'Good,' he said. 'Then we'll do that too. When we've

had our tea and cakes. Which reminds me. Should I nip out to the chemist?' And when she gave him a quizzical look, 'Or are you on the pill? I should have asked before this I know that. It's a bit remiss to have left it this late. But we ought to think about it.'

She was beating butter and sugar together but she paused and gave it thought. 'Yes,' she said, 'we ought. And no, I'm not on the pill. But. . . .' Then she stopped because she wasn't at all sure what he would say if she told him what she was thinking.

He looked at her steadily, smiling his nice warm smile. 'You can't stop there,' he said. 'But what?'

'Well . . .' she said. 'What I mean to say is. . . . The thing is . . .' and then because he was still smiling encouragement at her, she told him in a rush of words. 'It might be a nice idea to let nature take its course, the way people did in the old days, when babies sort of just came. But not if you don't want to, naturally. We'd have to both want it.'

He laughed at her and caught her hands, fork and all, 'Are you referring to our baby as it?'

Our baby, she thought. 'Then you wouldn't mind.'

'I think it's a lovely idea,' he said kissing her sticky fingers. 'It means we can be *old-fashioned* whenever we want.'

It was quite a jar to both of them when they woke on Monday morning and had to stop being old-fashioned and put on their working clothes and face the twenty-first century.

'I shall phone Mr Taylor first thing,' Henry said, as he drove them both through the quiet lanes. 'If you're going to sue that odious creature for assault, he can attend to both cases at the same time.'

Francesca was feeling sleepy and forgiving. 'Do you

think I should?' she said. 'Maybe it would be better to forgive and forget.'

'It's up to you, of course,' Henry said, although his face was giving her a different answer. 'If it were me he'd be in court before his feet could hit the ground. He needs pulling up short.'

Francesca looked out of her window at the leafless trees and wintry fields and thought how stern they looked. 'Maybe I should then,' she dithered.

'I tell you what,' Henry said, finding a compromise. 'Let him deal with your mother's will first. You don't have to make up your mind yet awhile.' He was turning in to the grounds of his pottery. 'Back to our mermaid.'

'I feel as if I've been away for months,' Francesca said and she wondered what her workmates would say if they knew what she'd been doing over the weekend. But she needn't have worried because what set them off into shrieks of horror were the bruises in her neck. Molly noticed them at once.

'What *have* you done to your neck?' she said. 'You look as if someone's been strangling you.'

'Someone tried,' Francesca said and told her what had happened. And while she was telling her story her fellow artists arrived at their workstations and listened too.

'The vile man,' Toby said. 'I hope you'll sue him.'

'I probably will,' Francesca said. 'Henry thinks I should.'

'He's quite right,' Molly said. 'Now are you going to be all right to work?'

'Yes, yes, I'm fine. Really. It looks worse than it is.'

'Well, give me a call if you need a rest,' Molly said. 'Don't struggle on feeling grotty. Mr P wouldn't approve of that.'

The story spread and caused a stir all morning and

her workmates came over one by one to commiserate with her and tell her what they thought of her assailant. Susan said he was a nasty pig and she hoped Francesca would 'throw the book at him and make him jump about a bit'.

'Mr Taylor's here,' Molly said joining them. 'The sparks'll fly now. You mark my words. Were those packing cases all right Susan?'

Half an hour later she was back at Francesca's station beaming all over her face to say that Henry had sent for her. And she seemed to have told everybody else on her way across because the workshop erupted into a chorus of well-wishes as Francesca walked through it. I shall have to sue him now, she thought wryly. I'll be letting the side down if I don't. I wonder what Mr Taylor's like. I hope he's understanding.

Tall with greying hair and a very serious face, lots of laughter lines and a warm smile. 'Mr Prendergast tells me you would like me to act for you in the matter of your mother's Will,' he said.

She nodded at him.

'And that you don't want members of your family to be given your address.'

'No. I don't. That's right.'

'That can be arranged,' he assured. 'All business can be done through my office. Perhaps you would like me to phone your Mr Skeat and arrange a meeting. I could do it now if you were agreeable.'

She was agreeable and it was done, very smoothly and easily. A time was suggested, checked with her and agreed. 'There you are,' Mr Taylor said as he put down the phone. 'Eleven o'clock on Thursday.'

'And we'll come with you,' Henry said. 'To see fair play.'

That surprised her. 'Both of you?'

'Of course,' he said.

She felt she ought to thank them both. 'That's very kind.'

'It's what we're for,' Mr Taylor said. 'Isn't that right Henry?'

The office of Skeat and Murchison solicitors was in a quiet street just off the centre of town and easy to find despite its discreet fascia. The reception desk was 'manned' by two friendly middle-aged woman and lined by comfortable armchairs where Francesca and her two companions sat and waited; and the office to which they were finally ushered was quietly elegant, with an impressive desk and three more easy chairs set ready for them in a semi-circle before it. It was all very soothing.

Mr Skeat was vaguely middle aged and peculiarly hairless, pinkly bald and so clean-shaven that his rounded chin made Francesca think of a baby's bottom. But he was courteous and friendly, introducing himself, thanking them for coming and shaking hands with all three of them as warmly as if they were being introduced at a party, indicating with a nod of his bald head that they should make themselves comfortable in the armchairs.

They made party-style small talk for a few minutes before settling to the matter in hand. Henry confirmed that he *was* indeed the owner of Prendergast Potteries and Mr Skeat told him that his fame had preceded him. Mr Taylor established that all business should be conducted through his firm and gave Mr Skeat the address.

'We've had quite a job to run you to earth Miss Jones,' Mr Skeat said but it was an opening gambit rather than a rebuke.

'So I believe,' Francesca said.

'Your mother will have told you what this is about.'

'She said my father's brother had left me some money in his will.'

Mr Skeat noticed that she didn't call her benefactor 'my uncle' and seemed remarkably unmoved at the prospect of inheriting his fortune. 'Did she tell you how big this bequest was likely to be?' he prompted.

'She seemed to think it would be around £24,000.'

'That is the amount of capital the gentleman left,' Mr Skeat told her. 'However there is also the matter of the house and its contents both of which are currently being offered as an executor's sale. You would like to see a copy of the will, perhaps.'

'Indeed,' Mr Taylor said.

The will was produced from Mr Skeat's folder and he and Francesca read it together. 'All perfectly straightforward,' Mr Taylor approved.

'The price put upon the house by the estate agent is somewhere in the region of a hundred and twenty-five thousand, 'Mr Skeat said. 'Of course, given the uncertainty of the current market it might not realize such a figure but I would be surprised if it didn't make a hundred thousand. All in all, this is quite a sizeable bequest.'

'Yes,' Francesca said calmly. 'I see.'

'That being so,' Mr Skeat continued, 'perhaps this would be a suitable point at which to consider some possible options. It is, for example, possible that you might wish to share your bequest with your mother and sister. Your mother felt this would be a likely step you would wish to take.'

Francesca was still completely calm. 'Oh did she?' she said. 'Why was that?'

'I believe she felt that your uncle was rather a – shall

we say – *distant* relation,' Mr Skeat said. 'Is that not the case?'

'I suppose you could say that. We very rarely saw him.'

'Quite. That is what your mother led me to understand. She told me that, since your father died, he had become something of a recluse and that he had no blood relations except her and your sister and you. She felt that, given that there are three of you and that he knew so little about you, his original intention might well have been to divide the bequest between you.'

'Oh did she?' Francesca said again and this time her tone was so icy that Henry was alerted by it and nodded to show Mr Taylor that he should intervene.

'However, this would be an entirely voluntary arrangement, would it not,' Mr Taylor said, leaning forward. 'Miss Jones would be under no obligation to agree to it.'

'Oh no, of course not,' Mr Skeat hastened to assure. 'No obligation whatever. It was simply her mother's suggestion.'

'Then if that's the case,' Francesca told him, 'we will let the Will stand and I will be the sole beneficiary of it, which will be altogether simpler and more straightforward. Now, if there's nothing else that needs discussing. . . ?' The words were so coldly spoken that Mr Skeat was quite awed by them and inclined his head to signify that no more discussion was necessary. 'Good,' she said, standing up and making it clear that she was leaving. 'You've got Mr Taylor's address and telephone number haven't you? Thank you for the information. I've no doubt we shall be hearing from you in due course.' And she shook his hand firmly and led the way out of the room.

'I'm sorry to be so angry,' she said to Henry and Mr Taylor when they were out in the street, 'but I can't believe my mother. She spent my entire childhood putting me down, telling me I'd never amount to a row of beans, that I was useless, a waste of space, all that sort of thing. And now she seriously thinks I would hand over two thirds of my inheritance to her and my sister. It beggars belief.'

Henry was impressed to see she had so much fire. 'Be as angry as you like,' he said. 'You've every reason. Don't you think so, Mr Taylor? How about a spot of lunch?'

Mr Taylor smiled courteously but declined Henry's invitation to lunch. 'I'm afraid I shall have to be cutting off in a few minutes,' he said. 'I've got an appointment in Barcombe at two.'

'Then we mustn't keep you,' Henry said. 'Thank you for all your good work. It's been a most successful morning.'

'Yes,' Francesca said, when Mr Taylor had walked off to his car. 'It has, hasn't it. I'm going to be a rich woman. Imagine that!'

'And quite right too,' Henry said. 'What do you fancy for lunch?'

CHAPTER 21

JEFFREY WALMESLY WAS so angry he didn't know what to do with himself. His face was puce with fury and he was spluttering and spitting and kicking the furniture as he paced the kitchen. How dare they send him threatening letters! Who did they think they were? It was despicable, disgraceful, disgusting. They should be ashamed of themselves. He'd never done them any harm. Never. He was a good law-abiding citizen. Always had been. And then they write to him like this. And not just one letter but two. Two! It was enough to try the patience of a saint. God damn it! Who do they think they are?

The two offending letters lay on the worktop where he'd flung them, neat, straight-edged and implacable. He couldn't believe the cruelty of them. For that horrible potter to accuse him of fraudulent activity was foul enough but for the bank to write and tell him they were going to foreclose on his mortgage unless he paid off all his arrears was too terrifying to be faced. He'd be turned out of his home. And then what would he do? It was no good them coming after him for money, especially when it had run into thousands. He didn't *have* any money. It didn't grow on trees. He'd have to go back to shelf filling if he wanted to eat. Oh dear God! What was he going to do? They were going to throw him out of his home.

He sat down at the table, his hands shaking and his brain in turmoil. Why was everything so fucking unfair? He turned himself inside out to give people a good service, inside out, he couldn't work harder if he tried, and God knows he tried, and this is how they repaid him. With threats and solicitors' letters. First his God-awful wife and her God-awful daughters being so unkind to him and then Fran walking out on him and taking all his furniture and wrecking his chances with that stupid potter. And now this. It was more than he could bear.

Well if that's the way they're going to behave, he thought, glaring at the letters, I shall leave the country. I'm not staying here to be bullied and abused. There *are* limits. But where would he go? And how would he raise the fare? The problems seemed insurmountable. Think! He urged himself. Think hard. If only that stupid Professor Cairns had taken me on the way he should have done none of this would have happened. Fucking man. And after all the good work I did for him. But the name gave him the germ of an idea. I wonder where he is, he thought. If it's somewhere accessible I could say I was going to work with him. That would get me through Customs and all their stupid questions and I could sell the furniture for my fare. I can't take it with me and I'm damned if I'm going to leave it here for someone else to make a profit on it. I shall take my laptop. Laptops impress people. A plan was forming.

'All set?' Henry said, putting on his Bonfire cap. He glanced in the hall mirror to check that he was correctly dressed and decided that he looked quite racy in his striped jersey and his white trousers and that Francesca looked absolutely delectable, like a flower in full bloom.

'Will I do?' she asked, checking her appearance too.

'I'd show you if we had the time,' he said, making eyes at her, 'but it wouldn't do to be late. Aggie would skin us alive.' The sky had been peppered with fireworks ever since it grew dark and Bonfire was loudly and obviously under way.

She took his arm and they stepped out together into the prickling air. 'Is it always like this?' she asked, sniffing the unfamiliar scents.

He smiled at her. 'Has been for as long as I can remember,' he said. 'Wait till you see the tar barrels.'

'Tar barrels?' she asked. 'What tar barrels?'

'You'll see,' he said, grinning quite devilishly as he opened the car door for her. 'Hop in.'

They parked in her space behind the flats because it was nearer the start of the action and strolled off to the local pub where the Cliffe Association was gathering. The place was packed with stripy shirts and beer-warmed faces and Agnes was in the midst drinking from a pint mug which she waved at them happily.

'Sup up,' she said. 'The band's arrived.'

And so it had, a big brass band, big bass drums and all, to play them on their way. And standing by the door to make sure they were all fully equipped were Reggie and Babs with a pile of metal torches, which they lit and handed across as soon as they were burning brightly. They marched to Cliffe High Street in a state of happy excitement holding their now flaming torches aloft.

'This is amazing,' Francesca said. 'I wish I'd brought a sketch-pad.'

'Would a camera do instead?' Henry offered. 'Just point me in the right direction and tell me what you want recorded.'

'There's so much,' she said. 'The way these flames are moved by the wind, for a start. Look at them. They're all streaming in the same direction and yet they're all different shapes. And the banner. I must use that.'

'At your service,' he said and pulled his mobile from his pocket.

From then on he took photographs at every point along the first part of their route, whenever she called 'Ah! Look at that!' or he could see from the expression on her face that she was intrigued by what she was seeing: the long column of marchers, the streets packed with sightseers, their eyes dark and their faces whitened by firelight, a banner bent sideways by a gust of wind, the bearers struggling to right it again, fireworks exploding in cascades of impossibly bright stars in the black sky. After years of simply taking part and hardly noticing it, he was seeing it through her wide eyes and enjoying every minute of it.

'Where are we going?' she asked, as the band led them into a narrow twitten.

'To the tar barrel race, eventually,' he said. 'We have to beat the bounds first.'

'You and your tar barrels,' she teased. 'They'd better be good.'

'You'll love them,' he told her. He was confident of it.

As she did, waving her torch with delight as the two-man teams pulled their blazing burdens towards the bridge, wanting to know all about them. 'They're not barrels are they? They look like oil-drums cut in half.'

'They are,' he said, snapping happily.

'Just look at the flames,' she said, entranced. 'They're twice as high as the cart. How wonderfully dangerous. And all these people watching. I didn't expect anything like this. It's pagan.'

He hugged her as well as he could for the torches. Pagan was exactly the right word. That, he thought, admiring her, is because she's an artist. She sees things more clearly than other people. And there was still a lot more for her to see.

They took another band-led detour round the town and arrived in front of the War Memorial at their allotted time. She picked up the atmosphere of the ceremony even before it began, watching wide-eyed as the stewards took their places and the crowd grew hushed, as their wreath was laid and The Last Post was played, standing totally still during the silence, absorbing it all. And then they were off again and heading for the start of the Grand Parade.

If what she'd seen of Bonfire was thrilling, the Grand Parade was so overwhelming it took her breath away. The stunning images crowded in upon her so fast she could barely take them all in, the torches and the great burning crosses carried before them blazing white fire, the mixed sounds of bands, songs and cheers that rolled up and down the hills of the High Street like great sea waves, the extraordinary costumes, Tudor ladies in full rig, a Zulu warrior as black as boot polish could make him, with a headdress of ostrich feathers more than a foot high, Red Indians cavorting, pirates with cutlasses, clowns clowning, St Trinian's schoolgirls, sexily dishevelled, Roundheads in helmets and armour, and, carried head high among the marchers, effigies of all kinds, from a Pope in his triple crown sitting solemnly on his papal throne, to a huge puppet of Rupert Murdoch looking villainous dangling his own smaller puppets, which were Blair and Brown – weren't they? – and a seemingly endless variety of Guy Fawkes puppets being borne in triumph to their individual incinerations. And on either side of the road an absolutely enormous crowd, blurred by their passing into a scarfed, hatted, round-faced, dark-eyed, open-mouthed cheering multitude, standing like a vast human backdrop to the passion, humour and determination that surged through the street.

'Good?' Henry shouted, when she turned her shining face to look at him.

'I've never seen anything like it,' she shouted back. 'I can hardly believe it.'

'And there's still the bonfire to come,' he said.

The Cliffe bonfire was huge, as she expected, and it burned with a roar like a furnace but even so it was marginally quieter there in the outer reaches of the town and once the bonfire speeches were over, conversation was possible.

'You'll be painting for weeks after this,' Agnes predicted.

'If I can find out how to paint heat and noise and excitement,' Francesca told her. 'I've been standing here wondering how to do it. My head's full of it.'

'If anyone can find a way, you will,' Henry said. 'And I've got the perfect room for you to work in.'

That surprised her. 'Have you? I mean I can't use any of your lovely living rooms. You do know that, don't you? I'd ruin the carpet.'

He grinned at that. 'Make no decisions until you've seen what I've got planned.'

She was intrigued. 'What have you got planned?'

'I'll show you tomorrow when it's light,' he promised.

In the red light from the fire, Agnes was looking dev-ilish. 'You know what it is don't you?' Francesca said.

'I think so,' Agnes said, 'but don't worry Henry. I won't spoil your surprise.'

There was a sudden roar which pulled their attention

back to the bonfire. The guy had caught fire and was spraying spectacular fountains of white sparks from the top of his head and all his limbs. And Henry, seeing the instant delight on Francesca's face took yet another picture.

Saturday morning brought more surprises than Francesca expected. They slept late so it was light before they woke and by then Francesca was so full of curiosity that she insisted on being shown the surprise room before they had breakfast. And although Henry teased her and complained that she was a terrible bully he happily did as he was told, leading her along the corridor, past his old bedroom and his office until they reached a rather smaller door right at the end.

'We're going into the oast house,' he said and teased 'Be prepared to be amazed.'

'This had better be good,' she teased back, 'the fuss you're making about it.'

They were inside the round tower of the oast house in an empty room that had picture windows all the way round. The light would be absolutely right for painting whatever time of day she chose.

'Well,' he said, beaming at her, 'what do you think?'

'It's perfect,' she told him, still gazing at it. 'Absolutely perfect. Has it always been like this?'

'No,' he said. 'This was where they dried the hops. It was open to the chimney because they needed a draught to draw the fire and when we came it had a plain brick wall and one very small window. I had these windows put in. I gather you like it.'

'I shall go and get my paints as soon as we've had breakfast,' she said. 'I can't wait to start.'

'I'll take you,' he said, 'providing you let me have my

339

waffles first. And then I must put the pictures on my laptop if you're going to start straight way.'

They talked about the paintings she was planning all the way to the flat and she ran in to her old living room to gather her things as soon as she'd opened the door. Henry picked up her mail before he followed her.

'Most of it's junk,' he said, when she glanced at it. 'But this one's a letter.'

'I don't get letters,' she said, folding up her easel.

'You've got one now,' he said and handed it to her. 'Take a look.'

She opened and read it perfunctorily, then realized what it was and gave it her full attention while he waited. 'It's a reminder about this flat,' she said. 'I took it for three months and the time's nearly up. This is to tell me next month's rent is due on Wednesday. I'd forgotten all about it.'

'So what will you do?' he asked, sitting down on her sofa. 'Take it for another month or let it go?'

'Let it go, I think,' she said. 'I could move all the things I want into the oast house room, couldn't I? I mean, there isn't very much of it. Books and videos and things like that. And that sofa. I rather like that sofa. And my clothes, of course. I'll have to write and tell them what I've decided and then I suppose I'd better sort things out and hire a van. I shall sell anything that's left over.'

'We'll do it between us,' he said. 'And we'll hire a proper firm to move you. I'm not having you lugging furniture about.'

'You do look after me,' she said, smiling at him.

'And quite right too,' he said.

It took them the best part of the weekend to sort out her things and write the necessary letter, make the necessary phone calls and organize a removal van for Tuesday. It was rather a nuisance when she wanted to get on with her painting but it had to be done.

'I shall have to take Tuesday off,' she said when all the arrangements had been made, 'but I'll paint as many mermaids as I can on Monday, I promise.'

'I'm not going to rush you' he said.

'I know,' she told him. 'That's why I'm going to do it.'

They went back to work on Monday morning feeling they'd lived a lifetime since they were last there. And the world seemed to have moved on while they'd been away. Henry was met outside his door by Liam who'd obviously been lurking for him and was full of the good news that 'a sheaf of orders' had come in by email and then Yvette rang in not long after he'd sat down at his desk to say she'd got Mr Taylor on the phone and should she put him through.

'Thought you ought to know there's been no answer from Mr Walmesly,' Mr Taylor said, 'and it's a week now since we sent our letter. Do you want us to send him a reminder?'

'Yes, of course,' Henry said. 'If we don't keep him on his toes he'll think he's only got to lie low and we'll go away.'

'How about Miss Jones?' Mr Taylor asked. 'Does she want us to proceed against him, do you know?'

Henry explained that she was moving house but promised he would test her opinion.

'I hear Bonfire went well,' Mr Taylor said. 'Our neighbours were there and they said it was the best yet.'

'Yes,' Henry said. 'I think it was.' And he thought of Francesca's shining face and had to control the urge to find some pretext to go down to the workshop and see her. Fortunately Yvette came in with her notebook ready to do the letters, so he had to be sensible and get on with the usual events of his day. But it didn't stop him wondering how she was getting on.

In fact she was doing exactly what she'd promised to do, sitting at her workstation painting doggedly. From time to time her workmates came over to ask her what she'd thought of Bonfire and she told them how wonderful it had been but she didn't stop working, partly because she'd given Henry her word and partly because Molly had told her a new lot of orders had come in and the thought that she'd be taking a day off at just the wrong time was making her feel guilty. But over and above everything else, her mind was full of happy images, Red Indians dancing among the flames, rockets erupting into cascades of stars in a pitch black sky, the stillness and peace at the War memorial with the watchers humbled by the sacrifices they were honouring and the torches flickering, that long complicated, noisy parade filling the High Street. You'd have needed to have been in a helicopter to take it all in, she thought. And even before the thought was fully in her mind she could see her first painting in all its complicated detail, living and growing. Oh if only it wasn't November and she could start on it the minute she got home. The weekend was such a long way away.

The move went as well as moves usually do and by the end of the day she'd arranged her furniture in her lovely new studio and set up her easel and even made a rough outline of the first painting she wanted to do. Then it was a long wait till Saturday. But the day finally arrived and was given over to painting while Henry cooked their meals and wandered in and out of the studio while she was working to watch and admire. And the painting grew very satisfactorily. By the time the light faded on Sunday it was shaped.

'How are our love birds?' Babs asked. She and Reggie had asked Agnes over to Sunday lunch and were agog for news.

'Settling in as far as I know,' Agnes said. 'I phoned them yesterday evening and Henry said she'd been painting all day. He sounded very happy.'

'He's a good chap,' Reggie observed. 'Haven't I always said so? Deserves a bit of happiness.'

'Wedding bells then?' Babs asked.

'I wouldn't be surprised,' Agnes said. 'If he can peel her away from her easel. She works all hours when the spirit moves her.'

'I hope they buck up,' Reggie said. 'I love wedding cake.' And was surprised when both women laughed at him.

But in the event it wasn't Reggie's love of wedding cake or Henry's ability to peel his beloved away from her easel that was the deciding factor.

Francesca worked on her bird's-eye picture of the parade for the next three weekends even though the declining light gave her less and less time for it. But by the end of November she'd done enough to know that it was going to be good.

'It'll soon be Christmas,' Henry said as they lay in bed one Sunday evening.

'I suppose it will,' Francesca said. How the time had rushed them along.

'Four week's time,' Henry said 'Let's have a party on Boxing Day. What do you think?'

But the fact that Christmas was only four weeks away

was making Francesca think of something else. She hadn't had a period for ages. She couldn't be pregnant, could she? She'd have to find her pocket diary and check the date of the last one. She was warm and comfortable for the moment, cuddled up in their great bed, and she didn't want to go on a diary hunt but she would find it in the morning.

She discovered it after breakfast, hidden away in one of her summer handbags and did the maths when she was sitting at her station and preparing to start work on yet another mermaid. It was nearly seven weeks. Then I must be, she thought. How great is that? She was tremulous with excitement at the mere thought. *Our* baby, she thought, remembering the way he'd spoken about it. *Our* baby. I'll drive into Lewes after work and get a testing kit. What a good job I've got my car. Henry had meetings that went on long after work on Mondays so they'd got into the habit of using both cars on that day. I shall get the kit and do the test and if it's what I think I'll make something special for our dinner and tell him while we're eating it.

But once she'd used the kit, she was too excited to wait as much as a minute and rushed at him as soon as she heard his key in the door.

'Guess what!' she said.

'What?' he said, laughing at her.

'You know we said we'd let nature take its course. Well it has. I've got pheasant for dinner and a charlotte rousse. I thought you might like to celebrate.'

He was so delighted he knew he was grinning like an idiot. 'My dear, dear darling,' he said. 'When will it be?'

She'd done that maths too. 'June.'

He was full of practical concern. 'Have you seen a doctor?' he asked, hugging her.

'I haven't got a doctor.'

'Then you must see mine. She's excellent. And when that's settled I suppose I'd better make an honest women of you.'

'There's no rush,' she told him. 'We've got months yet. And weddings take a bit of arranging.'

'I'm an expert at arranging things,' he said. 'You can leave it all to me. It'll be a doddle.'

'Let's dish the pheasant up first,' she said laughing at him.

After they'd eaten their charlotte rousse, they made the first of their plans. They would hold a very special Boxing Day party and invite all their friends to the wedding by putting invitation cards on their plates at supper. Henry was bubbling with the delight of it. 'We won't say what it's for,' he said. 'We'll just ask them to keep the date free and tease them a bit.'

So the party was planned and they set about choosing the date and the place. Neither of them wanted a church wedding and, once they gathered a selection of brochures, Francesca said of all the possible places they could be married in she would much prefer the castle. By the time the cards were printed, the arrangements had been made. When they walked in to supper, their friends found a Boxing Day card beside their plates asking them to mark Easter Saturday in next year's calendar and to keep it free for a special party in the Castle.

One or two were mystified and looked across at their hosts for an explanation but Agnes and Babs were onto it at once.

'You're getting married!' Babs squealed. 'You absolute darlings!' And rushed round the table to kiss them both.

And Agnes followed her, saying, 'Me dears. Best news I've had in a long time. Every happiness and all that.'

And then had to blow her nose quite fiercely because her eyes were full of happy tears.

'Ah well!' Henry said pretending to be disappointed that they'd worked it out, 'then I suppose I'd better tell you the rest of our news. We're expecting our first baby in June.'

And at that they weren't just kissed but cheered. And Henry had his back slapped until it was sore and it took quite a long time before they could all settle to supper and champagne.

It was, as he and Francesca told one another when they finally got to bed in the early hours, one of the best parties ever.

CHAPTER 22

IT WAS EASTER Saturday and the wedding guests were gathering in the castle keep, the spring sun warm on their carefully arranged hair, their feathery fascinators and their extravagant hats. The bridegroom was waiting quietly in the first chair to the right of the carpeted aisle, his hands on his knees and his face serious. From time to time he turned his head to smile at his old friend Agnes Potts, who was sitting on the other side of the aisle, resplendent in a huge straw hat smothered in bright and impossible flowers. The musicians sat, tuned and waiting, under their white canopy, the registrar stood, smiling and waiting, centre stage and elegant in a long dress the colour of bluebells. There was a chirrup of greetings and happy talk, a flutter of multi-coloured movement as the last of the guests scampered to their seats across the gentle green of the lawn. It would soon be time for the service to begin.

He's nervous, Agnes thought, watching Henry as the wait went on. It seemed out of character in a man so sure of himself but rather touching. Come along Francesca, she thought. Don't keep the poor man waiting. The car must have collected you by now.

It had arrived at the house at exactly the set time, its

white ribbons a-flutter, the chauffeur smart in his grey uniform. And the bride had been ready for it and had smiled as the chauffeur held her bouquet while she took her seat. It had all gone according to plan. And now she was on her own, the way she'd wanted to be, climbing the winding path that she'd painted in that long ago summer, remembering and savouring, enjoying the sight of the white and gold ribbons that decorated the guide ropes and thinking how well they matched her white and gold bouquet, the sun warm on her head, her sea-green gown soft against her skin and draped prettily over her bump, the baby kicking its feet as steadily as a heartbeat. She climbed in a happy dream, each careful step taking her away from her old, timid life, up and up towards another and better one. Even now when she was minutes away from making her vows, it was still hard to believe that she'd come so far and changed so much, even though the facts were singing in her head like birds. The mermaid was still selling well and so were the chaffinches. She was an established portrait painter. She had more money than she could ever have dreamed possible. She had friends. She was loved.

Somewhere above her an orchestra began to play and she listened to it happily. It was several seconds before she realized that they were playing the Wedding March and that it was being played for her and then she was in the Keep and all her new friends were turning in their seats to smile at her and Henry was standing at the end of the aisle waiting for her. Oh such a joy to walk towards him and to stand beside him with her hand in his. Dear, dear Henry.

'Good morning ladies and gentlemen,' the registrar greeted them in her quiet clear voice. 'Good morning and welcome to you all. We are gathered here this morning to witness the marriage of Henry Arthur Prendergast and Francesca Jones. . . .' Their new lives were beginning.

The ceremony passed in a happy haze, they signed the register in a dizziness of triumph and delight and then they were walking together down the long carpet as their friends threw confetti and kisses at them. And Francesca looked ahead and saw, with a sudden shock of surprise that there was a photographer waiting for them at the end of their walk. She was instantly alert and anxious, wondering if he'd been invited and who had done it and how Henry would cope with seeing him there. Would it be possible to warn him before he. . . ?

'Bride and groom, Mr Prendergast,' the photographer called, 'with all your friends around you. How would that be for a first shot?'

And Henry was actually smiling at him and saying 'Why not?' as if he didn't mind at all.

Francesca was so surprised she didn't know what to say. 'Are we. . . ? Are you. . . ?'

'Yes,' he said, smiling at her. 'We are. Don't look so worried. It's all right. We're going to begin as we mean to go on. This is a red letter day and I want a record of it.'

The guests were grouping themselves on either side of them, the photographer was giving instructions, the musicians were still playing, the sun was warm as summer. 'Dear, dear Henry,' she said.

From then on cameras seemed to be clicking at them from every side and on every occasion, as they got into Henry's Merc, as they drove away, as they toasted one another in champagne when they arrived back at the house, as they greeted their guests, as they cut the cake.

And what a cake it was, carried in shoulder high by two of their green-clad caterers and set before them with a flourish and to prolonged applause. Somehow or other the chef had reproduced their mermaid in full colour just as she'd been painted, swimming in her blue-green sea across the snow white icing, like a creature from a fairy tale, her bronze hair flowing and her golden eyes smiling and intelligent.

Francesca was so surprised she put up a hand to cover her mouth and Henry beamed at her. 'What do you think?' he asked.

'It's amazing,' she said. 'How on earth did they do it?'

'Trade secret,' he said, smiling at her.

'It's beautiful. Much too good to eat.'

One of the caterers presented them with the ceremonial silver knife which was the grandest she'd ever seen and Henry took it, laughing with delight at the success of his long-planned surprise, and positioned it on the cake ready for the first cut.

'Don't worry, my darling,' he said to Francesca. 'Our mermaid is eternal, like all works of art. Even if we eat every scrap of her image on this cake she'll still be in our lives. She'll be in our lives for ever.'

Francesca was so moved and so overwhelmingly happy she hardly knew how to answer him. 'Oh Henry,' she said. 'I do love you.' And she put her hands on either side of his face and kissed him tenderly, as their guests cheered and cameras whirred and clicked. It was a perfect moment in a perfect day.